FROM LA TO LONDON, WITH LOVE

ELIZABETH LULY

In loving memory of Harvey
(also known as Hoovey, Hoove, Hubert, King Hoofrey,
Hibbleton, Sir Hoovalot and Lord Hoovington)
the inspiration for Alfie

Copyright © 2022, Elizabeth Luly

Cover design © 2022, Elizabeth Luly

Cover design and illustration by Melody Jeffries

The moral rights of the author have been asserted. All rights reserved. No part of this book may be reproduced, stored in a retrieval system, stored in a database and/or transmitted or published in any form or by any means, electronic, mechanical, photocopying, recording or otherwise (other than brief quotations embodied in critical articles or reviews) without the prior written permission of the author.

This book is a work of fiction. All characters and events in this book are fictitious or are used fictitiously. Any similarity to real persons, living or dead, is purely coincidental and not intended by the author.

All brand names and product names used in this book are trademarks, registered trademarks or trade names of their respective holders. The author is not associated with any product or vendor in this book.

ISBN 9780645580808 (paperback)

ISBN 9780645580815 (ebook)

CONTENT WARNING

This book contains swearing, open-door sex scenes, and situations involving—and references to—homophobia, racism, non-consensual sharing of intimate images, home-lessness, and difficult family relationships.

CHAPTER ONE

CHRIS

DON'T THINK *about the photos.*

I scrolled mindlessly on my phone, trying to muster enough energy to do something. Something, anything, to take my mind off recent events. Work out in the gym? My muscles, which had been at their peak when I finished filming the latest *Muscle Man* movie just months ago, had started to atrophy. Swim in the infinity pool? Perhaps the view over the hazy urban sprawl of LA would put my problems in perspective. Or take Alfie, who was wrestling with his favorite toy alpaca on the rug, to the yard to burn off steam? Some fresh air might do me good.

After this morning's stomach-churning realization that the milk I'd been pouring into my coffee on autopilot—and, apparently, drinking on autopilot—for the last two weeks was well past its expiration date, I'd sworn things would change. That is, after I'd finished spitting out the coffee and dry retching.

But here I was, back on the couch, like every other morning.

As if he'd read my mind, Alfie abandoned the alpaca,

bounded up to me, and started tugging at my sock with his teeth. He looked up with his best puppy dog eyes, and a pang of guilt vibrated through me.

I should give the little guy some attention.

I was leaning down to grab my shoes, much to Alfie's joy, when my phone buzzed. I sat up and groaned when I saw who it was—Serena, my agent.

"Sorry, buddy. I just have to take this first."

Alfie whined and slumped down into a furry golden puddle by my feet, unimpressed.

Bracing myself, I answered the phone. I needed to rip the band-aid off. The curdled milk incident was a wake-up call. I couldn't hide from her forever.

"Chris? I'm so glad I finally got ahold of you. I've been trying to reach you for *ages*." Serena sounded surprisingly upbeat for an agent whose star client's reputation had been torn to shreds. "Did you get my messages?"

I winced. I'd been ignoring Serena's calls, voice mails, emails and texts for days. "Err, sorry, Serena. I've been a bit distracted recently," I said after an awkward pause.

"Of course, that's totally understandable." Her voice softened. "How are you holding up?"

"I'm okay."

Alfie raised his head off the ground. I could have sworn he lifted a skeptical eyebrow.

"Hmm. Have you been getting out and about? It's not good for your mental health to be cooped up by yourself."

"Yeah," I said noncommittally.

Alfie shook his head in despair. Or maybe he was just scratching himself. Whatever Alfie was doing, he knew the truth. I hadn't left this monstrosity of a mansion for almost two months.

"Anyway, you've been to my house. I'm not exactly cooped up here."

While there were a lot of things I now hated about this house, you couldn't accuse it of being cramped. With twelve bedrooms, fifteen bathrooms, a gym, a pool, a home cinema, and an expansive open-plan living area, there was more than enough space for me and Alfie. Too much space. More than once, Alfie had gotten lost in it and had to bark for help. Hell, even I'd gotten lost in the damn house. Cold and sterile, it felt more like an airport terminal than a home, with its soaring ceilings, blank white walls, and polished concrete floors Alfie constantly slipped on. I'd bought the house because Vanessa loved it, but we'd never gotten around to decorating it.

"Ha! That's true." Serena paused. "Have you spoken to Vanessa?"

"No," I said firmly, staring at the letter sitting unopened on the coffee table in front of me.

It had arrived from Vanessa this morning, but I couldn't bring myself to read it. There was nothing she could say that could make things better. While our relationship had been rocky, I never expected it to end like this. Vanessa might have been stubborn and impulsive, with questionable taste in houses, but I'd loved her. And trusted her.

"I haven't spoken to her since the photos came out, and I'm not going to. Look, I don't want to talk about her. So what were you calling about?"

"Ah, yes!" Serena's tone brightened. "Well, I have just the thing to cheer you up! Matt Brandon pulled out of the lead role in a period drama due to start filming in London in a few weeks. Clare Caldewald is co-starring, Melanie Chester is directing, and the film already has Oscar buzz... and they want you to take Matt's role! I emailed you the script the other day, but I'll send it to you again. I've read it, and I think you'll love it! You'd play a troubled duke who has to overcome his demons to keep his title and find love."

Serena was bursting with excitement. I imagined her pacing up and down in her shiny glass office in Beverly Hills, yelling into her headset, her black curly hair bouncing as she walked.

I sat up, the most interested I'd been in anything for months. Serena's enthusiasm was contagious.

"That's not a terrible idea. It would certainly be a refreshing change from Muscle Man." After five *Muscle Man* films, the novelty of playing a superhero was wearing thin, and the risk of being typecast was growing exponentially. "And it would be nice to get out of LA for a while." And this goddamn house, with its constant reminders of Vanessa. "And if it really was Oscar worthy...Well, being connected to an Oscar-winning film, or even being nominated, might help redeem my reputation."

It wasn't just that. For the sake of my mental health, I needed to start working again. Acting kept me sane. While I'd lost some of my passion for it recently, I loved the challenge of becoming someone else, of losing myself in a character and experiencing everything through another person's eyes. It allowed me to forget my problems, escape the everyday reality of my life.

And I currently had a lot of problems that needed forgetting, and reality that needed escaping.

"Chris, I've told you so many times, but I'll say it again. Your reputation doesn't need redeeming. I know it's been an awful few months for you, but you didn't do anything wrong. You were the victim here. And if anything, the photos made you more popular. Your Instagram followers increased by half a million after they were made public."

My chest tightened as I began to spiral thinking about the photos, but Serena's words pulled me back.

"Chris, are you still there?"

"Yes, sorry. Sure, send it to me again and I'll take a look. When do I need to decide?"

"Officially, it was yesterday. But if we come back to them today, it'll be fine. I've just sent it. It should be in your inbox now."

Alfie, who had remained at my feet the entire call, bounced into action as soon as I hung up. He grabbed one of my shoes in his mouth and dragged it toward my foot.

"Very subtle, little man," I said, tussling his golden head.

Energized by the phone call, I got off the couch, pulled my shoes on, and made my way to the yard, grabbing one of Alfie's tennis balls on the way. He bounded after me, barking with joy. As much as I was itching to read the script, Alfie clearly needed to burn off some steam first.

———

A FEW HOURS LATER, I called Serena back.

"I'm in! It's great. My only concern is the accent. I've never had a great ear for them. The last thing I need right now is to be ridiculed for that as well."

She let out a squeal and clapped her hands.

"Fantastic! Don't worry about the accent—we'll get you a dialect coach, and you'll be speaking flawless Queen's English in no time. You're going to be fabulous, Chris!"

I really hoped she was right. After the last few months, I couldn't afford to be anything less than fabulous.

CHAPTER TWO

SOPHIE

"JOSH, I'm almost at the mothers' group. I need to hang up," I groaned.

I stopped the pram outside Cynthia's house, located on prime real estate overlooking the sprawling woodland and meadows of Hampstead Heath. Josh's call had been a welcome, unexpected interruption from the monotony of Monday, and I was disappointed I had to cut it short, even if it had primarily consisted of me giving Josh a pep talk about his client meeting this afternoon.

"I don't know why you keep torturing yourself with the mothers' group," he said. "They sound dreadful—a whole lot of white, wealthy, unhappily married women going on about designer baby clothes, posh schools, and bilingual nannies."

I sighed. Josh was right. The group was meant to offer new mums support and bonding. But as reassuring as it was to hear that their babies also snored like freight trains and had disturbingly hairy backs, I'd struggled to bond with any of the women. As far as I could tell, all I had in common with them was that we lived in Hampstead, gave birth to our first child around the same time, and had signed up for the local mothers' group.

"It's good for Elliot to interact with other babies, even if all they're doing is trying to steal each other's toys. And it's not just that. Everyone else—you, my parents, the rest of the gang—all have full-time jobs. As much as I love Elliot, he can't exactly hold a conversation or do...much at all, really. Except for poop and pee with abandon, guzzle milk, and fight sleep." I looked down at Elliot in the pram with affection. "No offense, little man, but I miss adult company. As much as I hate to admit it, sometimes being around people, even if they're not my preferred company, is better than nothing." Besides, I was used to feeling like I didn't belong.

"Hmmm, fair enough. Maybe I should take a day off soon, and we can take Elliot to the zoo. That seems like the sort of thing a godfather should do."

I smiled. Josh was a good egg.

"That would be lovely. Now, I really have to go. We're running super late. Good luck with your meeting. You're going to nail it!"

I hung up, took a deep breath, and then pressed the buzzer at the front gate. The lock clicked, and I pushed the pram through, parking it next to seven other monstrous prams in Cynthia's garden.

The front door opened just as I'd unbuckled Elliot.

"Sophie! We didn't think you were coming," Cynthia exclaimed, her signature lipstick-covered lips forming a smile that didn't reach her eyes.

My heart sank. *It might just be her botox. Don't take it personally.*

"Sorry about that. We had an emergency nappy change just as we were leaving. But we're here now!"

Cynthia ushered us inside.

"Thanks so much for having us over."

"It's my pleasure." The unconvincing smile reappeared.

I followed Cynthia down the long hallway, wracking my brains for something to say. I was usually a decent conversationalist, but every time I hung out with the mothers' group, I struggled. *Babies, Sophie, just talk about babies —that's what we all have in common.*

"How's Harriet?" I smiled at Cynthia.

"She's good, although I think she likes Marine more than me." Cynthia rolled her eyes.

I'd really taken to Marine, Cynthia's French nanny, the few times I'd met her. Marine seemed genuinely fond of Harriet, and the feeling was mutual. In fact, it was a shame Marine wasn't part of the mothers' group.

Cynthia's voice lowered. "You know, I've actually been thinking of getting rid of her and getting another one that Harriet's less attached to."

My heart plummeted. Poor Marine. And poor Harriet. Now, I really had no idea what to say. Relief washed over me when I realized Cynthia was ushering us into her living room, and so no response was necessary.

Bec, one of the other mothers, was gesturing wildly as we walked in, clearly part way through a dramatic retelling. I smiled at her captivated audience and waved hello, but they didn't seem to notice me. Heat crept into my cheeks. I plonked Elliot and his rattle next to the gaggle of babies on the rug and helped myself to some tea. On the plus side, at least I didn't need to make any more awkward small talk while Bec was holding court.

"And then, he put the nappy on backwards and dressed her in green trousers that clashed with the red top she was wearing. The poor thing looked horrific!" It was clear from Bec's intonation that the subpar fashion choice was a much more serious crime than the incorrect nappy application.

We all shook our heads in sympathy.

I took a seat on an overstuffed floral armchair, shifting my weight around, trying to get comfortable. The floral furniture, combined with the lace curtains, rose-colored walls, and pink rug—currently covered in babies—created a "girly meets grandma" vibe. It was most definitely *not* my cup of tea, I thought, as I sipped Earl Grey out of a delicate porcelain cup.

It quickly became apparent the mums were taking turns regaling each other with tales of their husbands' various failings. These failings seemed to fall into two main categories —either not helping enough with the baby, or trying to help and messing things up. This was one of their favorite topics of conversation, and not one I could contribute to, thanks to my lack of a key ingredient—a husband.

In contrast to the women sitting sedately around the edge of the room, there was chaos on the pink rug in the center. The babies were sucking on toys, grabbing at each other, or trying to eat their feet—in some cases, all of the above. Elliot, hurling his rattle around with great determination, stood out in his plain Marks & Spencer's onesie. The other babies were dressed in designer baby wear—the girls in dresses, sporting headbands with enormous flowers, the boys in various stiff-looking trousers, paired with braces, shirts and/or shoes. All very cute, but not exactly practical or comfortable.

A whimper broke my thoughts.

Daphne's headband with the fake pink rose had fallen over her eyes, blinding her. She writhed around on the floor, crying, and nearly took Elliot out with a kick. Her mother, Bec, who only moments ago had been complaining about her husband not properly supervising Daphne, was oblivious to Daphne's plight. I leaned over, pulled the headband up, and was rewarded with a relieved gummy smile. Daphne returned to sucking her thumb.

"Sophie." Cynthia turned to me, looking curious, and my heart sank. "I hope you don't mind me asking... "

Oh boy. I braced myself. In my experience, people only said that before asking questions I *did* mind them asking.

"You look so exotic. What's your background?"

I fought back a sigh. I'd been asked this question so many times, but it never stopped being irritating. It was amazing how many people found my appearance—brown hair, eyes, and skin, and features they couldn't immediately attribute to a particular race—deeply confusing and felt the need to clarify my heritage so they could work out how I fit into the world.

At least she didn't ask where I was from, and then when I responded "London," ask where I was *really* from. Or *what* are you? That really pissed me off.

"My dad is Indian, and my mum is white." I gave a forced smile.

Cynthia's features softened. "Ah, that explains it. Mixed-race people are always so beautiful."

Again, nothing I hadn't heard before, but it still made me shift uncomfortably. For the first time since I'd joined the mothers' group, I wished the conversation would turn back to hopeless husbands. I knew she meant it as a compliment, but it never felt like a compliment. It just made me feel self-conscious and othered.

"And what about Elliot? He has such a lovely skin color. What race is his dad? I always thought it would be so cute to have a mixed-race baby." Cynthia peered approvingly at

Elliot, who was now sucking on Daphne's fake rose. "His skin looks a little lighter than yours? And his hair as well?"

Heat rushed to my face. I was used to people questioning me about my heritage, but I wasn't prepared for them to start on Elliot. He was only six months old, for god's sake. I'd always found the Western obsession with mixed-race babies disturbing, but having my own child being subjected to scrutiny over his heritage really brought home how screwed up it was.

Cynthia, seemingly oblivious to my reaction, continued. "If I'd done IVF by myself, I would have probably picked out a Black sperm donor. Or maybe a Vietnamese one. Ohhh, or a South Korean one could be nice."

Oh. My. God. She sounded like she was trying to decide what to order for dinner on Uber Eats. What the hell?

This was not the first time something like this had happened. Their surprised faces when I told them I didn't have a husband, telling me in patronizing voices I was "so brave" for doing it alone. Their assumptions I was straight and just hadn't found the right man or was too "picky." Intrusive questions about why I hadn't waited until I was older or frozen my eggs. Sure, I was more aware of other people's potential sensitivities than the average Brit, but these women were completely oblivious. They thought BLM was a sandwich.

I drew in a deep breath, hoping it would have a calming effect. It didn't.

"As you know Cynthia, Elliot doesn't have a dad. He has a sperm donor." I struggled to keep my voice steady.

"You know what I mean—dad, sperm donor, whatever." She shrugged. "So, what race is he?" She squinted at Elliot, as if trying to assess his exact racial mix, down to at least two decimal places.

"The race of the donor is none of your business," I said, unable to hide the frustration—or anger—in my voice.

Cynthia's eyes widened. Her eyebrows looked like they were attempting a frown against all botoxed odds. "I'm sorry if you're offended. I was just asking." She shook her head slightly in disbelief, looking around the room as if seeking reassurance I was being unreasonable by refusing to satisfy her curiosity.

Anger welled in my body. I didn't need to divulge Elliot's personal information to placate her. In fact, I didn't need to spend another moment in this environment. Screw mothers' group. Screw Cynthia. I'd finally gotten to a really good place in my life and didn't need to put up with this. I'd just need to find Elliot and myself some new friends to hang out with while I was on maternity leave.

"We'll be heading off now. Thanks for the tea," I said, my lips pressing into a line.

I stood abruptly from the hideous armchair, picked up Elliot and his rattle, said goodbye to Daphne, and walked with purpose toward the door.

CHAPTER THREE

SOPHIE

I WAS STILL FUMING as I strode back down the hill toward my parents' house, gripping the pram so tightly my hand cramped as it bumped over the uneven pavement. I was *done* with the mothers' group.

It was hot for London, even in the middle of summer, and sweat pricked my skin. I'd usually be enjoying the deep, verdant green of the tall lime trees which lined the street, the smell of freshly mowed lawn, and the gorgeous red brick houses. But today, I was too distracted by Cynthia's comments to appreciate them, the surroundings a blur of green and red.

I was focusing on deep breathing exercises and relaxing my jaw, which I realized I'd been clenching for the last half hour, when...*wham*!

I rammed the pram right into a man standing on the footpath, typing a code into a security gate. *Shit*.

"Ouch!" He flung his hands up in surprise and dropped the drink he was holding.

All over Elliot.

Who started screaming hysterically.

"Fuck, fuck! I'm so sorry," he said in an American accent.

My heart jumped. I sprang to the front of the pram, panicking that Elliot had been doused with scalding liquid. It looked like coffee but, judging by the ice blocks melting on Elliot's lap, it was an iced coffee.

Relieved, I started throwing the ice on the pavement with one hand, searching in Elliot's nappy bag with the other to find something to dry him, and trying to distract him by pulling silly faces. Motherhood had definitely upped my multitasking skills.

Out of the corner of my eye, I saw the American glance across the road and make a strange hand gesture. That was weird, but I didn't have time to dwell on it with Elliot in his current state. The American then started searching through his pockets, presumably looking for a tissue or something to help clean Elliot up. He came up short and stood there staring helplessly at Elliot, who was still screaming. I unbuckled the seatbelt so I could try to calm him in my arms.

Elliot's screams amplified.

The American flinched. "Shit. Let me go grab a towel from my house...or you're welcome to come inside, if that's easier?"

It suddenly dawned on me where I was. I was standing outside of *the* house. The Castle. The house I'd been obsessed with since I was a kid. I used to walk past it on walks to the Heath with my parents. I'd called it the Castle, not very originally, because of the red brick turret on one side of the three-story house, the curtain of ivy draped across it, and its imposing, Medieval-looking front door. It had a fairytale quality which had captured my overactive, only-child imagination.

It had been advertised for rent recently. Thrilled to finally get a glimpse inside, I'd inspected the listing closely. The photos gave a tantalizing peek, but they'd been a bit too "arty" to give me a real feel for the place. A close up of an ornate ceiling light, a photo of half of a heritage fireplace, a reflection of the long hallway in the hall mirror. I wanted more.

I regretted not snooping around the Castle during the open house. I'd convinced Josh to come with me and pose as my husband, but then chickened out once I saw the asking price. I knew it would be expensive but...wow. One month's rent of the Castle was almost as much as I had been paying *per year* for my apartment before I moved back in with my parents. The estate agent would take one glance at us and know we weren't earning that kind of money.

Unexpectedly, I now had a second chance. But it didn't seem like a great idea to go into a stranger's house alone. I took a closer look at the man in front of me, trying to size him up while jiggling Elliot in my arms.

The guy looked slightly shady. With a baseball cap pulled low over his eyes, sunglasses, and a closely cropped beard obscuring most of his lower face, he could be a criminal on the run. He was also jacked. My rusty Jujitsu skills would struggle if anything bad did happen.

Should I accept his invitation? He must be loaded if he could afford the Castle, but that didn't mean he wasn't a massive creep. In fact, I'd found rich guys were often worse. Self-entitled pricks who thought their wealth meant they could get away with anything.

Just then, Elliot upped his screaming to a new decibel level I didn't think possible. The American took off his sunglasses, revealing a genuinely concerned expression on his face. That wasn't the look of a creep. And Elliot really needed a change of clothes ASAP. And I *really* wanted to see inside the Castle.

My curiosity and my desire to preserve what was left of my hearing got the better of me.

"That would be great, thanks, so I can quickly change him. He won't make it home in this state."

Elliot's face was as red as a double-decker bus from screaming, and he showed no signs of calming down.

"No problem. Let me take this." He opened the gate so I could walk through and then lifted the pram effortlessly, as if it were a pack of baby wipes, rather than a very sturdy all-terrain vehicle with its under basket stuffed to the brim.

Holding Elliot, still howling, with one arm as I followed the man up the stone stairs, I pulled my phone out of my back pocket and one-handedly shot off a message to Josh. I struggled to type, so I kept it brief.

Sophie: *Going inside the Castle. If you don't hear from me in 30 mins send cops.*

The American ushered Elliot and me through the impressive door into the entrance hall, where he left the pram, and then into a living room.

"I'll grab something to dry him off." He rushed out, returning moments later with a pile of thick, blue towels. "Let me know if there is anything else I can get you."

"Can you grab the nappy—I mean diaper—bag from under the pram? Thanks," I said briskly. I didn't have time for pleasantries with Elliot in his current state. I lay Elliot, still screaming and thrashing about, down on a towel and stripped him off.

An ice block, half melted, fell out of his top as I removed it. No wonder he'd been distressed. It must have slithered down his front and been pressing against his round potbelly. Poor little fellow.

I gave Elliot a vigorous rub down with the towels, which were remarkably absorbent, and he started to settle. He was back to his usual self by the time I'd wrangled him into dry clothes, and looking around, wide-eyed. I breathed a sigh of relief.

I finally had a chance to take in our surroundings as well. The living room had a beautiful wooden floor covered in a rug, two comfortable looking sofas, and a gorgeous period fireplace. A large antique vase was in one corner of the room. Another corner must have been the bottom of the turret, because it had an unusual circular shape. It was warm, inviting, and felt like a home I could relax in. Just how I'd imagined the Castle would be. And a world away from Cynthia's ghastly house.

I suddenly remembered the American, who was sitting on a sofa, watching me look around his living room with interest.

"It's nice, isn't it?" he said, smiling.

"It's lovely. I've always wondered what this place was like inside. I was obsessed with the turret as a kid. I used to make up stories about the house—I called it the Castle—having secret passageways and Narnia-like wardrobes that were portals to a magical world. I don't suppose you've come across any?" I asked, only half joking. This place really did look like it might have a hidden room behind a bookcase, or a trapdoor under an old rug.

He chuckled. "I haven't, I'm afraid. But I've only recently moved in, so it's possible I just haven't discovered them yet."

Still on the floor with Elliot, I unashamedly leaned back to look through a partially open door. If I remembered correctly from the floor plan on the real estate listing, it led to the kitchen. I didn't care if I was being obviously nosy.

This was my last chance to see my dream home in the flesh.
I wouldn't let embarrassment stop me this time.

I caught a flash of a gleaming stainless steel oven before
I lost balance. *Shit.* I put my hand on the sofa to steady
myself. *Could you be any more obvious, Sophie, or more
uncoordinated?*

The American's mouth twitched. "Would you like a
tour? That way, you can check for yourself—for magic
portals, I mean. I assume that's what you were just doing, or
at least trying to do."

He grinned, and heat rose up my cheeks. So much for
being unashamed.

"And I'm Chris, by the way."

His smile was playful, almost teasing, and it put me at
ease. That wasn't the smile of a creep. It was, however, the
smile of a *very* attractive man. Chris had to be well over six-
foot, with those impressive pram-carrying muscles, and
while he was still wearing that ridiculous cap pulled low
over his face—perhaps he was trying to hide a terrible haircut, or a receding hairline—I could make out warm brown
eyes, strong cheekbones, and a rugged jaw. And he had that
killer smile...

Urgh. My heart sank. I'd sworn off relationships when I
got pregnant with Elliot, and well before that, I'd sworn off
dating men. Just my luck, the first spark of attraction I'd felt
toward anyone in a long time was some rich white guy,
exactly the sort of person I'd vowed never to date again.
Some of the worst memories started flooding back.

Nope. I was not—well, at least I didn't want to be—
attracted to this man.

I realized those warm brown eyes were staring at me
expectantly, waiting for me to respond to his question. I
forced myself to focus on the present. And the fact we'd just

been offered a personal tour of the Castle. After seeing the living room and a tantalizing glimpse of the kitchen before I lost balance, I was dying to see more.

"Sorry. I'm Sophie, and this is Elliot. We'd love a tour. Since you've just moved here, we really should check, for your own safety, that there aren't any hidden portals to another world. It would be the neighborly thing to do, not at all motivated by wanting to satisfy over thirty years of curiosity about this house...You don't want to be woken in the middle of the night by a centaur galloping through your house, especially not with all these breakable objects." I gestured at the antique vase.

"How very thoughtful of you." Chris grinned. "Do you provide this service to all new residents of Hampstead?"

"Not yet, but perhaps I should." I stroked my chin, as if seriously considering the issue. "I wonder...Do you think I could monetize it? Everyone else seems to have a side hustle these days. Maybe it could be mine."

Chris looked thoughtful. "I'm afraid I can't comment until I see how you perform today. I'll be more than happy to provide a glowing reference if you protect this gorgeous vase from destruction by other-worldly creatures."

"It's a deal! And for you, my first client, I will generously provide this service for free." I felt the need to pinch myself. Was this actually happening? Having a ridiculous conversation about magic portals with a smoking hot guy inside my dream home was not how I expected my Monday to turn out.

"Too kind." He flashed me another one of his smiles, his eyes twinkling, and then swung open the door to the kitchen.

I picked Elliot up and followed him.

"First stop on the tour, the kitchen."

Chris led us into the large kitchen, which immediately filled me with envy. It had recently been renovated and had two stainless steel fridges, two ovens, an industrial steel range hood, a walk-in pantry, and a huge kitchen island. My parents' modest kitchen paled in comparison.

"Wow! This is amazing. It also smells incredible. What are you cooking?" Something was in the smaller oven, filling the room with a rich, savory aroma.

"It is great, isn't it? The kitchen actually inspired me to cook again. I'd got very lazy back home. I'm trying a stuffed eggplant recipe. It'll probably be disastrous because I'm very out of practice, but at least I enjoyed making it."

"If it tastes even half as good as it smells, it'll be delicious." God, the smell was making my stomach rumble. I regretted not eating any of the cakes on offer at Cynthia's before I stormed out. I should have grabbed some to go. "And you'll be surprised how quickly it'll come back to you —at least it did for me. I moved back in with my parents just before this little guy made an appearance and rediscovered my love of cooking."

I immediately regretted mentioning my parents. I didn't usually open up to strangers like this. When I finally got pregnant, they'd encouraged me to move back home so they could help with Elliot. Living with my parents in my mid-thirties wasn't exactly part of my life plan, and while it made sense for now, I still felt slightly embarrassed.

I wondered if Chris had someone to cook for. I hadn't seen any signs of anyone else living in the house yet. There were definitely no parents hovering around.

I kept speaking, keen to move the conversation away from my living situation. "Although, having said that, cooking under the influence of a baby is dangerous. I'm having way more mishaps as a result of sleep deprivation—

burning pots, forgetting to turn the oven on, putting salt instead of sugar into a cake. I don't know who came up with the phrase "sleep like a baby," but it wasn't someone who knew anything about babies. Thank god for Uber Eats as a trusty back-up option."

Chris chuckled. "Uber Eats is great, but definitely only as a backup option. Not as a three-times-a-day option, which is the hole I fell down before I moved here." He looked at his stomach, which looked flat as a washboard to me, pinched a bit of flesh through his top, and shook his head.

Unsure what to say in response to this Adonis's apparent body image issues, I poked my head into the huge larder.

"Now, let me just check your larder for centaurs."

The larder was massive but disappointingly empty. The man needed to go shopping, that's for sure. What was the point of having a larder the size of a walk-in wardrobe if you didn't fill it to the brim with all the staples and other goodies?

"Lah-dah," Chris said thoughtfully, perfectly copying my pronunciation.

I'd forgotten Americans called it a pantry, but the way he'd repeated the word was odd, like he was tasting it, focusing on the sensation in his mouth as it rolled off his tongue.

Was he making fun of me? He didn't look like he was joking, though. His expression was serious. A hint of pink touched his cheeks as he caught me staring at him.

I considered asking him what he did for a living but decided against it. He'd almost certainly be an investment banker or something else boring and corporate-y to afford these digs, and I wasn't in the mood to hear about it. Even thinking about his potential job reminded me of the mothers' group. Some of the mums, and almost all of their husbands, worked in the financial sector.

I realized that I'd been staring at him for more than a beat too long. Worried I'd made him feel uncomfortable, I started babbling about the first thing that came into my head.

"You know, the smell and these ingredients you have out reminds me of an Ottolenghi aubergine recipe I used to love. I gave up making it because I instituted a fifteen ingredients max rule, and this one went way over." As soon as it was out of my mouth, I realized he probably didn't know who Ottolenghi was. *God, Sophie, you need to work on your small talk game.* "Sorry, Ottolenghi is a well-known chef in London, famous for his complicated but delicious recipes. I'm not sure his fame's spread to the States."

He laughed again, looking at me with surprise. "It is actually an Ottolenghi recipe. You must have an amazing sense of smell. Have you ever considered a career as a perfumer?"

Wow, that was...I was impressed with myself too. "Magic portal inspector, perfumer...have *you* ever considered a career as a career advisor? Or maybe a chef—that recipe is hard."

Chris grinned, and I couldn't help grinning back. He really did have an amazing smile.

"I have been thinking about a career change lately..." He looked thoughtful. "I'll need to see how this dish turns out before I make my final decision. I have a sneaking suspicion I overextended myself. Two pages of ingredients should have raised alarm bells. But I powered ahead anyway because I've got plenty of free time at the moment, and I find cooking relaxing. All the rhythmic chopping and grating, it's like a mindfulness exercise. So, even if it doesn't turn out, at least I enjoyed the process, right? And, as you know, there's always Uber Eats."

Into cooking and mindfulness? Has plenty of time on his hands? This guy wasn't what I was expecting. I didn't know any investment bankers who shared these interests. They were more into cocaine or expensive cars. I was having to rethink my first impressions...Maybe he was a trust fund baby? Or the American heir to a fracking or pharmaceutical fortune, or something similarly unfortunate.

We compared notes on our favorite Ottolenghi recipes as Chris showed me around the rest of the floor. The back of the house was open plan, with the kitchen, another living area, and the dining room all in one big space. Behind the living area and dining room, there were large French doors which opened to a deck and then a small green garden. It had been renovated to meet modern tastes, but thankfully, they'd kept many of the heritage features.

I sighed. It was perfect.

He stopped at the staircase, gesturing down the stairs. "The basement is hazardous at the moment—I'm in the middle of turning it into a gym, and I can guarantee you, there's nothing magical down there, just half-unpacked boxes—but I'll show you guys the upstairs rooms."

That sounded suspicious. Was it really just an unfinished gym, or something else he didn't want us to see? My imagination started to go into overdrive. A meth lab, hydroponics for growing weed, or even fully furnished sex dungeon. *Really, Sophie?*

Despite telling myself I wasn't attracted to this guy, my mind had jumped into the gutter very quickly. I gave myself a mental shake. Given how ripped he was, perhaps it wasn't so unbelievable he was converting a quarter of his house into a gym...I could definitely imagine him bench-pressing hundreds of pounds shirtless, sweat dripping from his brow furrowed in concentration. Oh no. *Sophie, get a grip.* I hoisted Elliot onto my hip and followed Chris up the wooden staircase.

"Now, if there's an enchanted wardrobe anywhere in this house, it'll be here." Chris grinned as he gestured to a massive ornately carved wooden wardrobe in an empty room overlooking the street. "Taa daa!" He made a big show of opening it, but it only had a few old coat hangers clanking around and smelled of moth balls. Disappointing.

We peered into the other rooms. The bathroom had one of those cool, clawfoot tubs. I imagined myself soaking in it while reading a fast-paced thriller, but that immediately morphed into an image of my buff tour guide squeezing himself into it to have a bubble bath. I suppressed an urge to giggle. He'd be much more at home soaping himself down in the large, modern shower, his biceps rippling...

I hurriedly walked out of the bathroom and went into the next room, a large bedroom overlooking the back garden. Half-unpacked suitcases and piles of clothes were sprawled on the floor. The bedroom gave the impression its inhabitant was only staying for a fleeting visit, one that didn't warrant going to the trouble of folding clothes into drawers and putting shirts onto hangers. Chris looked slightly embarrassed.

"Sorry about the mess. I'm still putting everything away." Now it was his turn to hurriedly leave a room. "And that brings us to the end of our tour."

We walked back down to the front living room.

"While I'm disappointed by the lack of secret passages or portals—perhaps I should rethink my career as a magical house inspector—it's otherwise just as I imagined it. Absolutely gorgeous." I could easily picture myself living in this house, sipping coffee on the deck in summer and in front of a burning log fire in winter, filling the larder with delicious jams, chutneys and all the staples, and playing with Elliot in the garden.

Unfortunately, with London property prices the way they were, I could never afford a place like this—unless I won the lottery, or my business plans with Rose and Mia really took off in an unexpected way. My parents were lucky they'd bought their house in Hampstead back in the 1980s, when it was still affordable, before it became one of the most expensive areas in London. Most of their old friends in the neighborhood had cashed in and moved elsewhere, but Mum and Dad loved their old, slightly dilapidated house and its proximity to the Heath too much to do the same.

"I love it too." He paused and then frowned. "I'm sorry. I totally forgot my manners. Would you or Elliot like something to eat or drink? I'm afraid the eggplant dish won't be ready for another hour, so that's off the menu—unless you'd like to stay for dinner? But I think I have some cookies, I mean biscuits, and tea or coffee, if you're interested. And Uber Eats is just a click away if you're craving something else." To my surprise, he sounded genuinely keen for us to stay.

"Don't apologize. I was the one who nearly bowled you over and made you drop your iced coffee everywhere. But water would be amazing, thanks. And I wouldn't say no to a cookie-slash-biscuit either, if you do have some." I was thirsty after working up a sweat storming down the street. I was also happy to have an excuse to spend more time in the house of my dreams and, to my surprise, with Chris. Our friendly banter was a welcome distraction from dwelling on

Cynthia's comments. And while my attraction to him was a less welcome distraction, I was ignoring it as best I could.

We were brainstorming other ludicrous career options when my phone rang. I apologized as I pulled it out of my pocket. It was Josh. Shit.

"Soph! Oh my god! Are you okay? I just walked out of a meeting and saw your message, which you sent like an hour ago!" Josh spoke quickly, with an uneven pitch that suggested he'd been freaking out. "I thought I'd better try you first before I called the police. What the hell is going on? Are you safe? Can you talk freely, or is someone with you? If you're not okay, say "Yes"."

Crap. I'd totally forgotten about the cryptic message I'd sent Josh. No wonder he was worried about me. He'd probably been imagining me tied up in that mysterious basement, and not in a consensual I'm-having-fun-in-a-sex-dungeon kind of way.

"Sorry about that. Everything's fine. I'll explain later. Bye!" I hung up before Josh could further cross-question or yell at me, feeling guilty I didn't ask how his meeting went.

I looked at Chris. "I'm sorry. I didn't realize how late it was. Unfortunately, we should head home—got to get this little guy ready for bed."

Did a look of disappointment flit across his face, or was that just my overactive imagination again?

Right on cue, Elliot yawned and let out a grumpy screech, so I hurriedly threw everything under the pram. Chris carried it down the front steps. He waited until Elliot, who wasn't taking kindly to being restrained in the damp seat, was firmly buckled in and then held the front gate open.

Chris took a breath and opened his mouth as if he was

about to say something, then promptly closed it. Intrigued, I wondered what I'd just missed out on.

"Well, thanks again for the tour. And apologies again for ramming you! Enjoy your dinner. Hopefully you won't need Uber Eats tonight!" I said, feeling slightly awkward. If Chris had been a woman, I would have definitely suggested exchanging numbers. But with him, I hesitated.

"No problem. Maybe I'll see you guys around. Bye, buddy!" he said, waving at Elliot, who wriggled about uncomfortably.

I set off quickly toward my parents' house, keen to make it home before Elliot started screaming again. My ears had had enough for one day.

CHAPTER FOUR

CHRIS

THE AFTERNOON SUN streamed into the living room, filling the room and my body with warmth. God, I loved this house. When I first arrived in London, I'd stayed in a serviced apartment while I looked for a more permanent place to live. I wanted somewhere that felt like a home after spending so much time in my sterile LA mansion. This house was one of the first places I'd viewed, and I'd fallen for it immediately. Cozy and comfortable, with an old-world charm, there was enough space for a gym in the basement and a yard big enough for Alfie to burn off steam, but the house wasn't so large that either of us would get lost in it. It was the complete opposite of my LA mansion. Thankfully, it was also ready to move in immediately.

"My dah-ling Eliza, you ah the..." Shit, that sounded bad. I sat on the couch, practicing my lines in a British accent. It was still terrible, despite almost two weeks of coaching, and I was struggling to focus.

The glorious weather wasn't helping, but Sophie was primarily to blame. I hadn't stopped thinking about her since she'd left yesterday afternoon, striding off down the street, pushing the stroller. Sophie had quite literally bowled me off my feet. While I had a bruise on my leg from Elliot's stroller smashing into me, she'd left an even stronger impression on my mind.

It took me a few seconds after impact to realize she wasn't a disturbed fan trying to mow me down and, in fact, was just a very attractive woman pushing a baby down the street with significant force. A baby covered in my iced coffee and screaming. Luckily, I signaled to the security guard I had stationed across the street that everything was fine before he crash-tackled Sophie, thinking she was out to get me.

On an impulse, I invited her inside—that's the last thing I'd usually do on meeting a stranger, especially in my current   *I-never-want-to-interact-with-anyone-ever-again* state. But I didn't make a habit of dousing babies with freezing cold drinks and had panicked at Elliot's ear-shattering screams. I'm sure the fact she was gorgeous, had an air of confidence I found very attractive, and appeared to have no idea who I was also influenced the split-second decision.

Once Elliot had calmed down, I'd really enjoyed showing her around the house, seeing it all through her beautiful brown eyes while we bantered back and forth. It felt so...natural. So relaxed. I hadn't smiled that much for months.

It was probably for the best that I'd chickened out of asking for her number when she rushed off, given my "no relationships" policy, but I couldn't help feeling bummed I might never see her again. At least, if she wanted to find me, she knew where I lived. Although, I wasn't holding my breath that she'd seek me out. Even though it sounded like she was single—she'd mentioned living with her parents—I hadn't picked up any signs she was attracted to me. While that was also refreshing—I was used to getting a lot of attention from women—it was also slightly disappointing.

My phone started ringing. It was my assistant, Jenny.

"Hi, how are you settling in?" Jenny was still in LA, looking after Alfie while we got all the paperwork ready to fly him over.

Jenny was another doubtful Vanessa acquisition. She was friendly, vivacious, and a dog lover, but she didn't have any qualifications making her suitable to be my PA. Vanessa had met Jenny at a party, they'd hit it off, and Vanessa, knowing I was looking for an assistant, offered her the job without consulting me. So far, Jenny had failed to do anything I'd asked her to do properly, except for those tasks relating to Alfie. Recent failures included forgetting which dry cleaners she'd left one of my Armani suits at—she'd rung about twenty before she tracked it down—and, before I went into hiding, reserving me a table at La Chouette in Paris, rather than the restaurant in LA of the same name. We didn't realize the mistake until we were downtown, insisting we had a reservation. I had considered firing her, but despite her incompetence, I was fond of her and so was Alfie, and with all the other recent changes in our lives, I couldn't bring myself to do it.

"Good, thanks. Fully unpacked now. What's up?"

Jenny cleared her throat nervously. "So, um, I called because...Vanessa called again. She really wants to talk to you about what happened and—"

Nausea flooded over me at the mention of Vanessa.

I cut her off. "Jenny, I've told you. I don't want to talk to her. I don't want to even hear her name again, okay?"

"But—"

"Seriously, Jenny, please don't mention her again. I've gotta go." I hung up, trying to push the thoughts of Vanessa out of my head. God damnit, there was no way I could concentrate on my accent after that conversation. And now I was feeling guilty that I'd been short with Jenny as well. Being caught between me and Vanessa couldn't be easy.

I stared out the front window, where birds were chirping in the trees. It felt like they were taunting me to go outside and enjoy the good weather.

Screw it. I grabbed my cap and sunglasses. Fresh air might clear my head. And maybe I'd run into Sophie, since it sounded like she lived nearby. My spirits lifted at the thought. If I ran into her, we could have a friendly, platonic chat. My dialect coach recommended I spend time with Brits to help my accent, so it would really just be more voice practice. If I ran into her, I wouldn't even need to feel guilty about quitting my voice exercises to go for this walk. It would be just an accent-improving chat. Yes, purely platonic and educational.

Satisfied my motivations had nothing to do with my attraction toward her, I set off.

The warm breeze hit my face as I walked out of the house. I headed down the street in the direction Sophie had gone yesterday. I kept going until I almost reached the main street, which was bustling with pedestrians and cars. It felt too risky to be amongst so many people—I didn't want to be recognized—so I turned back. I wandered up and down the relatively quiet side streets of Hampstead, keeping an eye out for Sophie and trying not to think about Vanessa. Or the photos.

The fact that Hampstead felt worlds away from LA helped keep my mind off my troubles. Instead of iconic LA palms, the old trees lining the streets were lush and leafy. And the place felt steeped in history. I passed houses with blue plaques noting famous, long-dead painters, poets, and writers who'd been former inhabitants and an ancient well with a stone engraving stating that it had been given to benefit the "poor of Hampstead" in 1698. Very different from my neighborhood back home, Hollywood Hills, where the "old" houses only dated back to the 1920's, and more white, gleaming mega-mansions seemed to be popping up every day.

However, despite the welcome change of scene, I still hadn't shaken off my fear of being spotted. Each time I saw a figure in the distance, I'd tense. After checking it wasn't Sophie, I'd take a deep breath, duck my head, and pretend to look at my phone until I walked past the person, only relaxing once it became clear they hadn't recognized me.

After over an hour of aimless wandering, I gave up and headed home. I'd avoided having my cover blown, but I didn't want to push my luck.

When I reached my front gate, I looked both ways—yesterday's collision had made me more cautious about checking what might be hurtling toward me—and saw a figure with a stroller walking up the hill.

I paused. Could that be Sophie?

As the figure came closer, my heart jumped. It *was* her, striding up the street. I loved the way she walked. Confident, brisk, with an energetic bounce.

She waved and greeted me with a big smile as she got closer. "Hello! I was actually coming to see you. I realized this morning that I'd stolen one of your towels. I must have thrown it under the pram when I was rushing out. Sorry about that." Sophie bent under the stroller, her shiny brown hair falling like a curtain around her face. She retrieved the towel and handed it to me.

Damn. She was just as beautiful as I remembered. Intelligent brown eyes, brown skin and hair, long dark eyelashes, and a stunning smile.

"Thanks for that! No problem at all." My palms suddenly felt clammy. My social skills were rusty after months of hiding, but I really didn't want her to leave. I panicked and lied. "I was just heading out for a walk. I don't suppose you'd like to come along as well?"

Shit. I really hoped she hadn't seen me already walking up the street to my gate. I smiled at Elliot, who eyed me with deep suspicion. Did he remember I was responsible for his impromptu ice bath yesterday? Or did he have a special skill for detecting liars? Whatever it was, he'd clearly decided I was not to be trusted.

"Sure. We were heading to the Heath to enjoy the weather. I thought we might go up Parliament Hill. Are you happy to head that way? I can keep the towel in the pram for now."

"Sounds good. It would be great to have a local show me around." Relieved she hadn't shrugged me off, my chest relaxed as we set off toward the Heath.

"After your tour of the house yesterday, it's only fair that I return the favor." Sophie turned to me, smiling.

God damn, she had a gorgeous smile. It was the eyes that really did me in. When she smiled, they crinkled and sparkled, sending a blast of warmth right to my chest and making it almost impossible for me not to smile back.

She continued, seemingly oblivious to the effect her smile had on me. "So, how was dinner? Is a career change still on the table?"

I chuckled. "It turned out surprisingly well. But I think I'll keep cooking for relaxation. In my experience, turning hobbies into careers can make you lose your passion for them. I don't want to ruin cooking." As soon as I said that, I kicked myself. I hoped my comment wouldn't pique Sophie's interest in what my actual career was.

Thankfully, she didn't ask. "Fair enough! I'm glad it turned out well. Chris: One, Uber Eats: Zero." She paused for a moment. "So, how long have you been in London?"

"I flew in just over two weeks ago. I'll be fil—" *Shit*. I caught the words as they started coming out and turned them into a not-very-convincing cough. "Sorry, I was saying that I'll be staying here for around four months. So far, I'm really enjoying the change of scenery. I don't know why people always complain about London's weather. It's been gorgeous, much nicer than LA when I left." My body tensed, worried Sophie had picked up on my stumble, or would ask why I moved.

To my relief, she focused on the weather.

Sophie shook her head. "This won't last for long, believe me. Based on a lifetime of experience, it'll probably be freezing and torrential rain tomorrow, and you'll be longing for the LA sunshine. Although, I don't really know much about LA's climate. In my head, it's *Baywatch* weather— sunny and warm all year round, and everyone just lounges about in T-shirts and shorts or bikinis, sipping green smoothies. Is that right?"

I smiled. "Pretty much, although green smoothies are *so passé* these days. Perhaps a matcha iced tea or turmeric latte." To be honest, I had no idea what was popular right now, but Jenny loved both those drinks, and she always seemed to be on the cutting edge of cool. I hadn't been to a cafe in LA for a long time. Sunday brunch wasn't so relaxing when you were being swarmed by fans.

A middle-aged woman, weeding her front yard, looked up as she heard our voices, and I quickly turned my head away from her, pretending a cat across the street had caught my interest. My fear of being recognized had increased exponentially now I was with Sophie. I wanted to hang on to my anonymity around her for as long as possible.

"Ah yes, you Americans and your delicious flavored lattes!" Sophie chuckled. "I lived in New York for a few years and developed a taste for pumpkin spice. I know they're considered basic, but I unashamedly love them. Unfortunately, they are hard to find here, unless it's Christmas."

"Damn, that's not what I want to hear, especially with fall coming soon." I actually hated pumpkin spice lattes with a passion, but she clearly adored them, and I didn't want to say anything that might dim the sparkle in her eyes.

We'd reached the Heath now and were walking on a dirt path surrounded by trees forming a canopy, letting dappled sunlight through. Invisible birds chirped overhead. I glanced at Sophie, wondering if she needed help pushing the stroller on the bumpy path, but the change in terrain hadn't affected her pace at all. Without thinking, my eyes dropped to her chest. She wore a figure-hugging T-shirt that flattered her curves. Sophie started turning her head toward me.

Crap. I didn't want to come across as some gross, lascivious guy checking her out. I quickly looked up at the trees, pretending to admire the verdant canopy.

"I think that's a great tit," Sophie said casually.

My stomach flipped, and heat spread across my cheeks. "I'm...I'm sorry?" *Oh god.* Had she noticed my eyes wander, and this was her way of calling me out? It was certainly a strange way of going about it, but maybe it was a British thing. I'd heard they had a dry sense of humor. Based on my brief glance, they *were* great...but "tit" singular made less sense. There were definitely two of them, and they *both* looked great to me. Two very nice, firm...

"The birds," Sophie cut into my thoughts, pointing to the trees. "The Heath has heaps of amazing birds. Woodpeckers, tawny owls, kingfishers, falcons, blue tits, great tits, and so many more. My mum's a bit bird-obsessed, but I can only recognize a few of them."

"Oh, right." I let out a deep breath. *Thank god.* "They sound lovely. I'll have to keep an eye out for them." I quickly changed the subject. "You mentioned you used to live in New York. How long did you live there for?"

"Five years. It feels like a lifetime ago now. So much has changed. I wanted to visit LA but never had enough, as you Americans call it, *vacation.* It's just a bit far to fly for a weekend, and I always used up my vacation days coming back to London. And now, of course, traveling isn't so easy." Sophie looked down at Elliot. "I got him a passport pretty much as soon as he was born. I'd planned to be one of those cool parents who sling their baby in a carrier and head off to exotic locations on a whim. But the reality of traveling with a baby has sunk in, and it all seems overwhelming, especially as a single mum. For someone so small, he requires a *lot* of stuff—mountains of nappies and baby wipes, multiple changes of clothes, a pram and a cot, and now he's on solids, food as well. So, I'm resigned to staying in London for now. LA, and all the other amazing destinations on my list, will just have to wait." Sophie let out a sigh. "What about you? Are you planning to do any traveling while you're here?"

So, she was single. My heart jumped. I'd suspected as

much from our earlier conversation but was pleased, self-ishly, to have confirmation there wasn't a partner in the picture. Not that it mattered, I reminded myself. It's not like I was looking for a relationship or anything. I was also impressed. Being a single parent was a big deal.

After I swore off relationships, I'd spent time slumped on the white couch, considering whether I would adopt one day. I'd always wanted kids. But my filming schedule wasn't exactly baby-friendly, especially as a single parent. If I was going to be a father, I wanted to do it properly. I didn't want to be like my biological dad.

Don't start thinking about him now. That's the last thing you need. I forced myself to focus back on our conversation, remembering she'd asked me a question.

"Because my—" I cut myself off. Not thinking, I'd almost told her that my filming schedule wouldn't leave much time for traveling. Speaking to Sophie, I realized how much of my life was caught up with acting. Not mentioning it was a lot harder than I expected. I really needed to get some other interests outside of acting, working out, and cooking.

"I'm hoping to do a few weekend trips away," I said, before focusing the conversation back on her. "I totally get how traveling by yourself with a baby would be daunting. I mean, I think most people find traveling solo a bit daunting —not having someone to share the experience with, good or bad. Adding a baby to the mix would definitely make it more stressful. It's not like Elliot's old enough to appreciate a stunning sunset or the best pizza you've ever had in your life, or help decipher the map if you get lost."

Sophie laughed, looking at Elliot, who had fallen asleep on the bumpy path, with affection. "Yeah, he'd probably eat or vomit on the map, and then I'd be totally screwed!"

I couldn't help sneaking glances at her as we walked through the Heath. She wasn't tall, blond, and stick-thin, like many of the women I'd dated in the past, but that didn't matter. I struggled to keep my eyes off her. And it wasn't just her appearance drawing me in. She was confident, smart, and funny.

A gangly teenager walking an overweight black Labrador came toward us, staring at me for a moment too long. His eyes widened in recognition, and my chest tensed, thinking he was going to say something or pull out his camera. But to my relief, he gave me a knowing smile, which I returned, and kept walking. And Sophie, who was admiring the Labrador, missed our interaction completely.

Conversation flowed easily as we chatted about our wish lists of places to visit and funny travel stories. I kept almost blowing my cover, itching to tell her about the time I was chased down the Champs Elysees by a horde of American tourists when I visited Paris for the premiere of *Muscle Man* 3. Or, when I was in Berlin two summers ago for another publicity tour, getting stuck in a hotel elevator with two wealthy German women in their seventies who turned out to be die hard Muscle Man fans. They kept vigorously insisting I take off my shirt so I didn't overheat.

Despite the stories I was holding back, I was envious of Sophie's tales of backpacking around Europe and living in Madrid for six months. Until I'd landed the Muscle Man role, I hadn't had enough cash to travel. Once I'd landed it, I was too famous to go backpacking and have the adventures she'd experienced. I needed to stay in hotels with security, not youth hostels with cheap alcohol and fellow travelers looking for a good time. And I'd thrown myself into acting with such intensity I didn't have time for much else. Most of my travel consisted of brief publicity trips and going home to Chicago. It dawned on me I'd spent so much of my life pretending to be other people, I hadn't properly lived my own. I filed that thought away for later, when I was back at the Castle alone. Now was not the time to have an existential crisis.

As we got closer to the top of Parliament Hill, Sophie's pace slowed, and she started to tire, so I took over stroller-pushing duties. While I was sure Elliot would not have approved, he was still fast asleep and none the wiser.

At the top, beyond the grassy slope of Parliament Hill, stunning views of the London skyline greeted us.

"Wow!" I took a deep breath in and released it, feeling my whole body relax. It was so good to be out of LA. Nothing in London reminded me of Vanessa. I could start making new memories here, without being weighed down by old ones.

"That shining building with the dark top that looks like a...um...stretched egg is The Gherkin." Sophie pointed to a phallic-looking building. "The pointy one over there is The Shard. And if you're more into buildings of historic note, you can make out the dome of St Paul's Cathedral over there." The view was breathtaking, but so was Sophie's face in profile. I struggled to draw my gaze away from her to focus on the buildings she was describing.

Elliot started to murmur, interrupting Sophie, who glanced down at him. "Damn. We should probably head home now he's waking up. He's only happy sitting buckled into the pram for so long."

Disappointment washed over me. For the second time in months—the first being that hour with Sophie yesterday —I'd forgotten my public humiliation and the breakup and felt like...myself again. I'd been so present in the moment, enjoying our conversation and the views of the Heath, the

London skyline...and Sophie, there was no room for my worries to consume me.

As we headed back home, Sophie muttered "Oh shit" under her breath and furrowed her brows. I followed her gaze down the path. A woman was walking toward us with a stroller, waving. My heart sank.

Please don't recognize me.

I knew if I kept spending time with Sophie, she'd eventually find out who I was. She'd inevitably ask me what I did for a living—I was surprised she hadn't already—and despite my panicked white lie earlier in the day, I wasn't in the habit of lying to people. But I'd been hoping to put that moment off for as long as possible.

The woman, petite, tanned, and blonde, looked overdressed for a walk in the park, wearing a floaty floral dress, strappy shoes, a big floppy hat, and heavy make-up. I wondered how she knew Sophie. Based on appearances alone, they seemed like very different people. I tugged my cap lower, putting my face into neutral.

"Sophie, I'm so glad I ran into you! Look, I just want to apologize again for yesterday. I really didn't mean to offend you. I didn't realize you were so sensitive about it." The woman's tone implied she thought Sophie had completely overreacted to whatever had happened.

My curiosity was well and truly piqued. What on earth had this woman said to offend Sophie?

Sophie gave a forced smile and turned to me, ignoring the woman's halfhearted apology. "Chris, this is Cynthia and baby Harriet. We're in the same mothers' group. Cynthia, this is Chris. He's just moved into the neighborhood."

She looked at me.

I held my breath.

Please, please don't recognize me.

For a second, I thought that the cap, beard, and sunglasses combination had done the trick, but then that all too familiar look of recognition flashed across her face.

Fuck.

CHAPTER FIVE

SOPHIE

MY HEART SANK when I saw Cynthia walking toward us. She'd given me another feeble apology, and now she was staring at Chris with a strange expression on her face.

"Oh my god!" Her voice sounded odd, her eyes wide. Was that surprise or terror on her face?

My heart started beating double time, an uneasy feeling growing in my stomach.

What the hell was going on? Did Chris have a spider on his head? I looked at him. No spider. A shiver went through me. *Oh god, I hope he's not a criminal on the run.* Perhaps my initial concern that he was a creep was well-founded. It would be just my luck that the first person I'd met for ages who I actually clicked with would be shady.

While a hot, rich white American man seemed like an unlikely choice for a new friend, I'd really been enjoying his company. Conversation with him was easy, he didn't ask me intrusive questions, we shared a similar sense of humor, and he was...well, he was very easy on the eyes as well. Not that his looks were relevant, given I wasn't inter- ested in dating. Definitely not. And unlike my existing friends, he actually seemed to be available during the week. I'd sensed he was holding something back, though. A few times, he'd started to say something and then stopped abruptly before changing the topic. Could that relate to whatever was causing Cynthia to behave so strangely?

"Sophie, you never mentioned you two were friends!" She looked at me, astonished, her eyes flashing with excitement.

Okay, excitement at least meant he wasn't a serial killer. But what—who—was he, then? Why was Cynthia smiling, pink-cheeked, and smoothing her hair with a shaky hand? I didn't like the feeling Cynthia knew something about Chris that I didn't, especially given it was clearly something important.

"It's so lovely to meet you. I'm a huge fan. Would... would you mind if we took a selfie? No one is going to believe I just ran into you on a walk unless I have some proof." Cynthia's voice was shaky with nerves.

I let out a breath. He must be famous. Hampstead had its fair share of celebrity residents, but I hadn't seriously considered the possibility he might be one of them. He was obviously rich and good-looking, but he just seemed so... normal. I guess that also explained the cap and sunglasses combo. He wasn't hiding from the cops—he was hiding from the public eye.

While relieved he wasn't a criminal, disappointment washed over me. A hot, rich, *famous* white guy seemed an even more unlikely candidate for a new friend. I thought we'd hit it off, but how much could I really have in common with this man? And why would someone like him want to hang out with me?

"Sure. But, um, I'd appreciate if you didn't mention you

ran into me here. I'm hoping to lay low for as long as possible." Chris sounded friendly, if slightly forced.

"Actually, Sophie, can you take the photo?" Cynthia handed me her phone without waiting for a response, barely looking at me. She ditched Harriet in the pram, bounded over to Chris, and struck an artificial pose that would be more at home on the red carpet than a dirt path on Hampstead Heath. Lips pouting, one leg in front of the other, one hand on her hip, and the other around Chris.

"Just a sec." He removed his cap and sunglasses, revealing a thick, well-groomed head of brown hair. That cap certainly wasn't hiding a receding hairline or a bad haircut.

I stared at him, wracking my brain as to who he could be, but came up blank. I'd been so busy in the last few years, with moving back to London, starting a new job, IVF, and now Elliot, I hadn't kept up with pop culture. Given Chris's good looks and Cynthia's reaction, he was presumably an actor, musician, or reality TV star, but that was as far as I got.

I snapped a few photos of them and handed the phone back to Cynthia.

"We should head home," I said abruptly. Elliot had started to fuss, and my stomach was still queasy not knowing *who* Chris was.

"Well, it was amazing to meet you. I'm so sorry about the breakup and the photos, but if it's any consolation, you looked super hot in them," Cynthia said, her eyes locked on Chris. She let out a nervous giggle and twisted her hair flirtatiously.

Breakup? Photos? My mind started to race.

Chris gave a smile that looked more like a grimace. "No problem. Enjoy your walk," he said, his voice flat.

Cynthia turned to me. "Sophie, we should catch up again soon."

I gave her a tight smile but didn't say anything. After yesterday, I wasn't keen on spending any more time with her, especially not one on one.

As soon as Cynthia walked out of earshot, we turned to each other.

"Okay, so you're clearly someone famous I should know. Who are you?" I asked, unable to keep a slightly accusing tone from my voice.

Chris looked at me, an eyebrow raised. "I have my own questions. What on earth did Cynthia say or do to you yesterday? I have a feeling it will be a shocker."

"Hey! Nice try. You can't distract me that easily. You first." I didn't feel like reliving yesterday's events and was itching to find out who Chris really was.

We started walking back toward home.

Chris rubbed the back of his neck. "So, I'm Chris Trent." He swallowed, watching my face for a reaction.

I stared blankly at him. That name didn't ring any bells. "I'm sorry. I'm going to need more than that."

"Muscle Man?" he asked, still looking nervous.

That sounded vaguely familiar. Had Josh tried to drag me to the cinema to see a *Muscle Man* movie when I was pregnant? In fact, I was pretty sure Josh had a thing for Muscle Man.

"Okay, I have heard of that. So, you're an actor. Sorry, I haven't been to the cinema for ages. I'm clearly out of the loop. And what were those photos Cynthia mentioned?"

Chris went bright red and bit his lip. "Some...umm... private photos I sent to my ex were posted online a few months ago, just after we broke up."

Crap. I hadn't thought it would be something so serious.

I'd been expecting photos of a minor wardrobe malfunction exposing his six pack, or him making out with a gorgeous supermodel in public. But based on his expression, the photos were a lot more revealing than that. My mind went into the gutter, speculating about the subject matter of the photos, but I quickly shut it down.

"I'm sorry. That's really awful." I looked at him sympathetically.

"Yeah, thanks. It's been a tough couple of months. I moved over here partly to get some distance from it all, but unfortunately, it's hard to escape the internet. Anyway, enough about me. How did Cynthia offend you?"

He was clearly uncomfortable talking about the photos. My heart went out to him. Chris seemed so confident, but now I was seeing a more vulnerable side of him.

I maneuvered the pram around a hole in the path before telling him what happened at the mothers' group. It was his turn to look sympathetic. I suspected that, like me with the photos, he'd thought it would be something more light-hearted.

"That's terrible. I'm sorry you have to deal with people making comments like that." He seemed genuinely upset, his big brown eyes looking at me with concern.

"It is shitty. You'd be surprised how often it happens too. And having Elliot subjected to it as well makes me sick. I know it's no excuse, but that's why I wasn't looking where I was going when we smashed into you. I was coming back from Cynthia's and still furious."

"That's totally understandable. And look, don't feel bad about the collision. It's no wonder you were distracted. I'm actually glad you guys rammed me. It's been nice to meet some locals. Well, you and Elliot, not Cynthia." He grimaced again before continuing. "I don't really know anyone over here, only a few celebrity acquaintances who I wouldn't exactly call friends."

I smiled at him. For a hot, rich, famous white guy, he seemed surprisingly friendly, open, down-to-earth, and... inoffensive. There was no mansplaining, no sleazy comments, no self-entitled statements. Maybe we could be friends after all.

Not in the mood to talk about yesterday's events, or entrenched racism, more generally, I changed the subject. "So, are you here for work, or an extended vacation?"

"Work. I'm filming a period drama in a few weeks' time and came early to work on my British accent and escape LA. *What do yow thoynk of eet?*" he asked, in a terrible British accent that sounded like some bizarre combination of a Texan and a Brummie.

My expression must have betrayed my concern. Chris laughed.

"Okay, I purposely made that bad. But I'm not sure my accent when I'm actually trying is much better, to be honest. I've got a dialect coach coming over every morning, so hopefully by the time filming starts it will have improved markedly." He rubbed his forehead, not looking optimistic.

"I feel your pain. When I first moved to New York, I received so many blank stares because of my accent, it was almost like we were speaking different languages. I had to learn to 'speak American' to get by."

Chris's eyes lit up slightly. "Oh yeah? And how did you do that?"

I paused, thinking. "So, putting what I learnt in reverse, some of my key tips are—don't be *stoopid,* be *stewpid,* make sure you put the *arh* in *arse,* rather than *ass,* and make sure you drink lots of *worter,* rather than *waadder.* But I'm probably not the best person to be giving you advice. Even after five years living there, I often had to rely on my friends or my ex, who was American, to translate for me."

His face dropped. "Oh god, five years? That's not what I want to hear!"

"But I'm not a professional actor," I responded hastily, trying to sound reassuring. "I'm sure you'll catch on much faster. I may have a good sense of smell, but my ear for accents is very weak. Do you like acting?"

We passed a young couple with a pram, who both looked at Chris and then at each other, whispering with excitement. Had people been doing that the entire walk, and I'd been completely oblivious to it? God, I could be hopeless sometimes.

"I love the acting part of being an actor. Immersing myself in a character, trying to understand their perspective, and seeing the world through their eyes." His eyes, which had been sparkling, dulled slightly as he continued. "I'm not so keen on the by-products. The paparazzi, the speculation over my personal life, constantly being recognized." Chris gestured back at the couple. He must have noticed their reaction as well. "And it's been worse since those photos were published. Now, when I see that familiar jolt of recognition cross people's faces, I don't know if they're thinking, 'Oh cool, that's Chris Trent, Muscle Man!' or 'That's the dude who Vanessa Milan cheated on and whose dick is plastered all over the internet.'"

My eyes widened. Shit, the photos were *very* revealing then.

"But I shouldn't complain. I know I'm very lucky that I can do this for a living."

"That must be really tough. I can't imagine being recognized all the time by strangers." It reminded me of the times men I didn't know stared at me, unashamedly checking me out, their stares sometimes accompanied by wolf whistles or unwelcome comments about my body.

"Yeah, on balance, it's usually worth it, although the last few months have made me question everything." He turned to me. "So, what do you do for work? I avoided asking you in case it prompted you to ask me the same question. It was kinda nice to spend time with someone who didn't have a clue who I was!"

We crossed the road, leaving the Heath behind us, and started to walk down the pavement toward the Castle.

I laughed. "I intentionally avoided asking you as well. I'd got it into my head you either had a really boring invest-ment banking job or were a trust fund baby. Not that you're boring or come across as an entitled brat!" I said hurriedly, wishing I hadn't mentioned my working hypothesis about his employment, or lack of. "Well, at the moment, I'm on maternity leave, but I head up the diversity and inclusion team at a big law firm here. We do a lot of different things, but in a nutshell, my team is trying to encourage diversity in an environment traditionally dominated by privileged old white guys. For example, developing policies to encourage diverse hiring and trying to improve the culture so that our diverse staff feel safe and included and don't leave—which isn't as easy as it sounds, unfortunately."

Chris looked at me with genuine interest. "That sounds fascinating but also pretty challenging. Do you enjoy it?"

"It can be very rewarding, although sometimes it feels like I'm fighting an uphill battle. There are a lot of men who don't know how to respond to a brown woman telling them that their policies and hiring practices are sexist, racist, and transphobic. Just before I went on maternity leave, I got all the law firm partners to do unconscious bias tests, and the results horrified them, so I'm hoping that will spring them into action. But while I've been off work, I've been talking with my friends, Rose and Mia, who have similar jobs, about setting up a diversity, equity, and inclusion consulting firm. It might give me a bit more flexibility with Elliot, and it would also be nice to have some more...diverse work." I smiled at him. "So, you know, instead of just trying to change old white men in law firms, I could also try to change old white men in accounting firms or banks."

I was really excited about our business plans. While I wasn't under any illusion that starting a new business would be easy, with Rose and Mia onboard I was confident we could make it work. This conversation reminded me that I needed to finish researching potential clients and email Rose and Mia my thoughts. Before we quit our jobs to go out on our own, we wanted to make sure there was actually a market for our services.

Chris laughed. "Setting up a consulting firm sounds like a great idea. The film industry could definitely use your services as well. There are a lot of old white men in the studios."

I rolled my eyes. "Unfortunately, they're everywhere! No offense." I grinned at him.

"Hey! Are you calling me old?" Chris asked in mock outrage.

"Well, you will be one day," I replied, smiling. I suspected he was around my age—mid-thirties—not exactly elderly.

We reached Chris's front gate. I was surprised how much I'd enjoyed the walk—apart from Cynthia's guest appearance, of course. Chris wasn't how I imagined a celebrity would be. He didn't come across as narcissistic or out of touch with reality. He just seemed like a warm, funny guy. Despite all that, I couldn't help feeling skeptical that I could have much in common with this rich, handsome man, whose world was so different from mine, or that he'd want to spend time with a single mum who lived with her parents.

But in my day job, I was always trying to get people to look beyond race, gender, sexual preference, and class, to stop stereotyping and to be open-minded and tolerant. Shouldn't I practice what I preach? Sure, he wasn't the sort of person I'd usually hang out with. But that shouldn't stop me exploring this potential friendship. And he'd said he was glad he'd met me, so why was I second-guessing myself?

Feeling down about my social life after the mothers' group yesterday, I'd unsuccessfully searched for activities Elliot and I could do to meet other babies and parents, so I wasn't exactly overwhelmed with options right now. I'd signed me and Josh up to volunteer at a local LGBTQ+ youth center on Wednesday nights, but that was unlikely to be a good source of friends around my, or Elliot's, age.

Fuck it, I might as well see if he wants to hang out again. It's not like I have much to lose.

I swallowed, suddenly nervous. "This has been really nice. I'm glad you were there to distract Cynthia, even if she blew your cover. If you'd like to hang out again, let me know. Elliot and I don't have a lot going on at the moment, especially now that I've cancelled mothers' group."

Chris gave me another one of those smiles and my heart fluttered. "That sounds great. How about another walk Thursday afternoon?"

Surprised he seemed so keen and wanted to meet up again so soon, I smiled back. I'd been half expecting he'd say something non-committal and never see him again.

"Perfect. We can meet you here at four p.m., if that works for you? And if you need to contact me in the meantime, my personal number is on my business card." I opened my phone case and handed him one of the cards I kept there. Heat crept up my face. Was I being too forward? Would he think I was coming on to him now I knew he was famous?

It's too late now, you turkey.

Unlikely friendship or not, I was already looking forward to Thursday afternoon way more than any mothers' group meeting.

CHAPTER SIX

SOPHIE

"JUST SO I have this clear, you've been hanging out with CHRIS TRENT, and you're only telling me now? And you nearly gave me a frigging heart attack on Monday because CHRIS TRENT was giving you a personal tour of his house?" Josh exclaimed as we walked to the LGBTQ+ youth center in Kilburn for our first volunteering session. Josh's curly reddish-brown hair took on a life of its own when he was worked up, bouncing in every direction. It was currently out of control.

We'd reached West Hampstead and were strolling down the main street, which was bustling with people taking advantage of the warm summer evening.

"Is something going on between you two? OMG, is he as well-endowed in real life as those photos suggest? You know what, you should invite him to karaoke on Saturday so we can all meet him!"

I already regretted telling Josh about Chris. I knew he'd be interested, but I didn't expect him to be quite so intense. His usually pale white face was flushed pink with excitement.

"Calm down! And don't yell his name like that. He's trying to keep a low profile." I looked around, but no one was paying us any attention. "Nothing is going on between us. There's no way he'd be interested in me. And anyway, I know he's hot, but I'm just not attracted to him like that." I'd been telling myself that was true, that I was an exhausted single mother and sex was the last thing on my mind, but... I'd been thinking about him a lot since we'd first met. When pushing Elliot in the pram, a slow-motion video of Chris lifting it up the stairs to the Castle, his biceps bulging, would appear uninvited in my mind. Or I'd get into the shower, and suddenly, an image of Chris in the shower at the Castle, soaping his washboard abs down, would materialize. I was ashamed to admit I'd even thought for a second about looking at those leaked photos, a thought I'd quickly dismissed.

"I don't know how that's humanly possible. He's *literally* the sexiest man alive, Soph, at least according to *People* magazine...and me." Josh winked.

I winced. Josh was still speaking way too loudly for comfort.

"I know. I Googled him when I got home yesterday. And no, I didn't look at *those* photos. I want to respect his privacy." I glared at Josh, who clearly hadn't shared my qualms. "I'm not sure if it's because of the hormones and sleep deprivation, or if all those bad dating experiences have turned me off men for good, but I'm just not into him like that."

While I might not have been telling Josh the complete truth about my feelings for Chris, I wasn't lying about the bad dating experiences and the effect they'd had on me. A few years ago, when I was ready to dip my feet back into the dating pool after an emotional breakup, I'd naively filled out my online dating profile honestly. Bisexual—yes. Mixed race—yes. Serious relationship—yes. And then been bombarded with messages from men which ranged from mildly to downright offensive.

My face flushed as the memories came flooding back. There were those standard gross messages that, unfortunately, most women receive. Unsolicited dick pics, requests for photos of my boobs, general lewd comments. And then there were messages that were clearly prompted by my appearance or the words "bisexual" and "mixed race". Despite the fact I'd said I only wanted a serious relationship, men saw those three words and assumed they'd hit the jackpot—obviously, I must be promiscuous and up for three-somes and casual sex. I received countless comments about my skin color, comparing me to honey, caramel, or milk chocolate—effectively reducing me to a delicious treat—as well as an onslaught of sleazy invitations for threesomes or one-night stands.

Unfortunately, a number of the dating candidates who passed the first, admittedly low, bar—not sending sleazy and/or racist messages or propositioning me for threesomes —fell down at the second—the first date. On multiple occasions, I'd turned up to a first date under the impression I was meeting a single man, to discover he'd brought along his significant other in the hope all three of us would hit it off. Or, more commonly, it quickly became clear my date was after one thing, and it wasn't a serious relationship. Thankfully, I'd never felt physically in danger, but I had felt extremely uncomfortable.

Eventually, I gave up, blocked men, changed my sexuality on the apps to "queer," and my dating life improved markedly—usually queer women actually read my profile and didn't send me gross messages. Unfortunately, not markedly enough that I found the love of my life before my biological clock got so close to midnight that I decided to go down the IVF route by myself.

While I'd turned many of the failed dates into funny stories to entertain my friends, they'd had a long-lasting impact on how I felt about dating men.

"Well, I'd bang him in a heartbeat. It's a shame he's not gay." Josh's words pulled me out of my thoughts.

I smiled. "You never know. He could be bi. You shouldn't make assumptions!" People assuming someone's sexuality based solely on their dating history was a pet peeve of mine.

"I can only hope." Josh clasped his hands together dramatically, as if he was praying.

"To be honest, I've been really surprised how well we're getting along. At first glance, this guy is everything I don't usually like, but we have a lot in common. I'd much rather hang out with him than anyone in the mothers' group. Anyway, that's enough about him for now. We're here."

We stood out in front of a red-bricked, slightly dilapidated two-story building, which must have been well over a hundred years old. Over the doorway, "Pride House" was written in rainbow letters, with Pride flags flying on either side. We walked through the open front door and into a large room filled with people, mostly teenagers, chatting animatedly. Some were standing, others sitting on bean bags or around tables. The colorful posters on the walls didn't conceal all of the cracks in the plaster, and the carpet was worn. Despite being slightly shabby, the room was warm and inviting.

A person wearing an outfit almost identical to mine—black jeans and a gray T-shirt, but sporting a cool mullet which I definitely could *not* pull off—approached, wearing a label that said "Alex, They/Them."

"Hello, I'm Alex. Are you our new mentors?" Alex grinned at us welcomingly.

"Yes. I'm Sophie, and this is Josh," I said, gesturing at Josh, who smiled.

"Awesome! Great to meet you both. So, hopefully you had a chance to read the induction materials I sent through this morning and do the online training course, but in a nutshell, every Wednesday evening, we have a social mentoring night, where young LGBTQ+ people spend time with LGBTQ+ mentors in a social setting. We have activities—card and board games, sometimes a drag queen comes in to host bingo, and we do movie nights too. Your role is to spend time with the young people and try to make sure no one is left out. Just be yourself—play games, chat—whatever you feel like." Alex handed us some white sticky labels. "Here, write your names and pronouns on these labels, and then I'll show you around and introduce you to everyone."

The room was full of the teenagers and volunteers chatting, laughing, and playing games. Both the young people and the volunteers were a diverse mix of ages, genders, and races. I sighed happily. I loved queer spaces like this, where people could be themselves without fear of judgement.

I spent the next hour playing board games with three girls in their mid-teens who, despite their constant bickering, seemed to be best friends. I glanced over at Josh a few times, deep in an animated discussion with two boys of a similar age.

I let out a deep breath. I was really glad I'd signed up to do this. Tonight was the first time I'd been out in the evening since Elliot was born, and it felt good to not be sitting at home, quietly reading or watching TV with my parents. The evening went quickly, and I was disappointed when Alex said it was time to finish up.

"Will you come back next week, Sophie?" one of the teenagers, Erin, who had brown hair, a smattering of freckles covering her white skin, and a big friendly grin, asked as we packed away the board game.

I thought I detected a hopeful note in her voice, and warmth filled my chest.

"Definitely! I need to reclaim my dignity after all my losses tonight!"

Erin walked with me to the shelves where the games were stored and cleared her throat. "Do you mind if I ask you something?"

"Of course not," I said, noticing Erin was fidgeting nervously with her hands.

"So...I'm thinking about coming out to my parents. They're pretty conservative, but recently, one of my brother's friends came out, and they were totally chill about it, so I'm thinking I'm just gonna go for it. Are you out to your family?" Erin let out a shaky breath.

I put the boardgame on the shelf and turned to Erin, pleased she felt comfortable confiding in me but also concerned I'd say the wrong thing. I couldn't remember reading anything in the induction materials about how to handle this type of situation.

"That's a big step. I came out to my parents when I was about nineteen, when I had my first girlfriend. I was so nervous about telling them, even though I thought they'd be fine with it because they are both pretty liberal. And I was right—they were very accepting. I was really lucky. But it was still hard to tell them. It must be way more scary if you're not sure how they are going to react."

Erin's brows furrowed. "Yeah, I'm pretty worried about

it. But I don't want to keep hiding this huge part of my life from them. I don't want to lie to them all the time. And when I get a girlfriend, I want to be able to bring her home." Her eyes welled with tears. "Do you think I'm doing the right thing telling them?"

My chest tightened seeing Erin's obvious distress. Oh god. I wished I could say something to make everything better. But I knew that wasn't possible. How her family responded was out of my control.

"Hmmm. I don't think there's any right or wrong way to go about it. Some people wait until they're dating someone, others want to share the news as soon as they've worked it out themselves, and some people don't want to come out at all. All of those approaches are totally valid, and unfortunately you won't know how your parents will take the news until you tell them. I'm sorry I can't be more helpful, but it's such a personal decision." I looked at Erin, grimacing sympathetically.

Erin sighed. "Yeah, I know you're right. I just wish I knew how they were going to react."

I remembered the induction materials had mentioned that a counselor was available one night a week at Pride House. "If you think it'd be helpful to speak to a counselor about it, we could ask Alex to set something up?"

"Yeah, maybe."

Erin didn't look too excited by the idea, so I left it alone.

"If you'd like to practice telling them with me, or if there is anything else I can do to help, just let me know." I gave her my best reassuring smile.

"Thanks." Erin sighed again. "We should finish packing up."

I took the hint and didn't mention it again.

Packing up done, Josh and I said goodbye to the young

people and Alex, and started to walk back toward my parents' house as the sun set. Josh lived in Camden, but he insisted on walking me home safely, before heading back down to Hampstead Station to catch the train back to his apartment.

I sighed happily. "That was so nice. I wish I'd had Pride House when I was a teenager."

"Tell me about it. Although my parents would never have let me go to something like that, even if it had existed back then." Josh blinked. While it was years since he'd spoken to his family, he was still hurting.

"That reminds me, one of the teens asked me for advice about whether she should come out to her parents, and I didn't really know what to say. She's worried they'll react badly. I almost told her your story but thought better of it, in case it scared her off. I didn't want to influence her one way or the other. I hope I did the right thing." I bit my lip.

Josh waited until we'd crossed the road before responding. "That's tricky, but it sounds like you handled it pretty well. I'm still glad I came out to my parents, even though it went worse than I could've imagined. And she might be pleasantly surprised. I mean, you were surprised how well your grandparents took the news."

"That's true. I forgot to tell her about that." I smiled, remembering just how well my Church of England and Hindu grandparents had reacted when I told them I was bisexual and, a few years later, pregnant—intentionally, by myself, using an anonymous sperm donor. I'd been worried how they'd take the news. While they'd been taken aback, after gathering their thoughts, both sets of grandparents had said that as long as I was happy, that was all they cared about. "But I'm still not telling my relatives back in India about me being bi or Elliot. Sometimes, it's just not worth it."

Josh raised his eyebrow at me. "Weren't you just raving last week about how you couldn't wait to visit India with Elliot when he's older? How are you going to explain suddenly appearing with a school-aged child no one's heard of?"

I grimaced. "Yeah, I'll have to rethink the whole thing when he's older, but for now, it's not worthwhile causing Dada and Dadi heartache. They already had to deal with their relatives being scandalized when Dad married Mum, and the gossip mill in their hometown would go into overdrive if they found out that not only did I date women, but I'd had a child by myself. They're in their eighties, that's the last thing they need."

Dadi and Dada had been supportive of my parents' marriage, but the family they left behind when they moved to England in their early twenties had not. While attitudes toward marriage and sexuality were slowly changing, there was still a fair way to go—and not just in India. I was pretty sure my white grandparents hadn't been exactly shouting from the rooftops of their conservative English village that I was bi.

I smiled. "To be honest, I'm convinced they're going to blow my cover at some point. You know how much they adore Elliot, and I can tell they're itching to show off photos of him. I have to keep reminding them that Elliot's cute photos would quickly get buried by questions about who his father was and why I wasn't married."

"Well, if you need me to pose as Elliot's dad, I'm happy to accompany you guys to India one day—all expenses paid by you, of course!" Josh grinned. "Changing the subject, when am I going to meet Muscle Man? Seriously, invite him to karaoke on Saturday. We've booked a private room, so he doesn't need to worry about being recognized or swarmed by fans. Pleeease!" Josh looked at me hopefully.

"The private room won't protect Chris from you, though!" I said, only half joking.

I considered Josh's invitation. While my initial reaction was that it was a terrible idea, Chris might appreciate meeting some other people, since he'd said he didn't know many people here. And I was fairly confident my friends would hit it off with Chris once they got to know him.

"Look, I'll see how tomorrow goes. And if I do invite him, you have to play it cool, okay? Don't start fanboying all over him." I took my phone out to check the time and saw I had a message from an unfamiliar number. It was Chris.

Chris: *How do you feel about having a picnic lunch tomorrow instead, maybe around 1? If it doesn't work, I'm happy to stick with our 4pm walk plan.*

I paused, thinking. A picnic could be nice. Elliot could play on the picnic blanket instead of being stuck in the pram the entire time.

Josh peered over my shoulder. "Oooh, you just got a message from him, didn't you?"

"Yep. He suggested changing tomorrow's walk to a picnic."

Josh's eyes narrowed. "A picnic sounds verrrry date-like. Are you sure there's nothing going on between you two?"

"Completely and utterly sure," I said firmly, hoping to shut Josh's speculation, which was starting to get annoying, down.

CHAPTER SEVEN

CHRIS

"SO, HOW'S LONDON?"

It was good to see Mitch's smiling face, framed by his short brown hair, even if it was only on my phone. Mitch was an early riser and had called me just as I'd returned home from a stressful visit to the local Italian deli to source picnic supplies. It was the first time I'd been into a shop for months—I'd been getting food delivered and, when I felt brave, picking up takeout coffee from a hole-in-the-wall cafe —and I'd been paranoid the entire time I'd be spotted. I was now lying on a deck chair in the backyard, recovering from the ordeal and chatting with Mitch.

"It's great! My British accent still sucks, but leaving LA has done wonders for my mood. And I found this beautiful old house to rent. It's such a nice change from my life in LA."

Mitch was one of my oldest and closest friends. As a young boy, in the space of a few years my dad vanished, my mom remarried, and we moved to Chicago. Unsurprisingly, it had been a difficult time for me, and my friendship with Mitch had helped me through it. On my first day at my new school in Chicago, he'd come up to me and invited me to play ninja turtles with his friends. Since then, Mitch had always looked out for me. He'd been checking in on me regularly since the breakup and dick pic fiasco to make sure I was coping okay. He was one of the few people outside my immediate family I really trusted.

"That's great! You're certainly looking and sounding way better than you have been. I was worried you might find it lonely over there, especially before filming started." Mitch grinned at me, looking genuinely relieved. He was sitting on his couch, and behind him, I could just make out the painting of Lake Michigan on the wall in his living room. I felt a pang of homesickness, thinking of all the times we'd watched football together in that room.

I almost told Mitch about Sophie but stopped myself. He knew I'd sworn off dating and would just give me shit if I told him I'd made a new female friend...a female friend I couldn't stop thinking about in a very non-platonic way.

"Oh shit. You've met someone, haven't you?" *Damn it.* Mitch had always been good at reading my facial expressions.

"It's not like that. I just met a single mom who lives nearby. We've hung out a few times, but only as friends. She's on maternity leave, and I think she's lonely as well."

A bird with a blue chest flew down to perch on the deck railing, and I wondered if it was a blue tit, smiling as I remembered my horror on Tuesday when I thought Sophie had caught me checking her out.

"Uh huh." Mitch didn't look or sound convinced. "I saw your face when you were thinking about her, and that smile just then as well. Come on, Chris, you can't hide from me. Spill." He leaned toward the screen, staring at me sternly.

I sighed. "Okay, so I'm attracted to her. She's smart,

funny, and confident. Initially, she had no idea who I was, which was nice. I didn't need to worry that she was just hanging out with me because I'm famous, or surreptitiously glancing at my groin all the time, thinking about the photos." I wondered if she'd gone straight home and Googled them. The idea of Sophie looking at the photos made my stomach churn. "I haven't felt this comfortable around someone new for a long time. You know most of my 'friends' in LA are just people I make small talk with at parties and premieres, not like you and the rest of our gang. But there's something about her that put me immediately at ease. If I'm being honest, she's got me questioning my decision to never date again. But she's a single mom with a six-month-old baby—who isn't at all keen on me, by the way—so I'm sure dating is the last thing on her mind right now. She also seems to have her shit together. She has an interesting corporate job, and she's even planning to set up her own business. I can't imagine her wanting to get involved with someone like me." I nearly said a "mess like me" but knew Mitch would pull me up immediately if I did.

The strength of my attraction to Sophie had taken me by surprise. The whole fiasco with Vanessa had shaken my confidence in my judge of character and exacerbated my already existing trust issues. I'd decided I was done with relationships. It just wasn't worth it. I'd been feeling good about my no-relationships rule, but that was easy when the only people I interacted with were Jenny, who was in her early twenties, my housekeeper, who was sixty-five with four grandchildren, and my jovial gardener, also in his sixties. None of them were exactly my type, or appropriate to date, for that matter, given they were all employees.

"She sounds awesome. And since you're awesome, too, I don't see why she wouldn't be interested in you." Mitch cleared his throat. "Look, I don't want to be a buzzkill, but have you checked she's legit? I know you've been burned before."

I inwardly sighed. Mitch could be overprotective, but I knew he had my best interests at heart.

"Yep. She gave me her business card the other day. I Googled her, and everything I found was consistent with what she'd told me. She works at a law firm in their diversity and inclusion team, and no alarming news articles popped up about her being a celebrity stalker or anything like that."

Some light sleuthing had uncovered her bio on her law firm's website, with a photo of her looking very professional in a suit, and her Facebook profile. While her Facebook page was private, she had a cute profile picture of her laughing, with her head tilted back, that I'd looked at a couple of times since I'd found it. Okay, more than a couple. It was a *very* cute photo.

"What's her name? Let me look her up, too, just to make sure." Mitch gave me a cheeky grin.

"You just want to see what she looks like, don't you?" I laughed. "Her name is Sophie Shah. Look at the Facebook photo."

"Am I that obvious?" There were a few seconds of silence, and I could see him focus on typing her name into his phone. "Oh, she has a really warm, open smile. She doesn't look like any of your exes. For a start, she actually looks like she'd be fun to hang out with." Mitch hadn't taken to Vanessa or any of the other women I'd dated since moving to LA.

I glanced at my watch casually. "Shit, I have to go. We're going on a picnic, and I have to finish getting ready."

Sophie was coming around in ten minutes, and I still hadn't packed the food into my backpack.

"A picnic sounds...romantic. You've got it bad, don't you?" He laughed. "Well, good luck! Talk to you soon."

As I hung up and made my way inside to the kitchen my stomach fluttered nervously. When I'd texted Sophie yesterday, I thought a picnic would be a nice change from walking. It was lovely weather, we could avoid the crowds, Elliot could hang out on the picnic rug, and I could look at her directly instead of sneaking surreptitious glances as we walked. But was a picnic too much? Did it scream "I'm into you"?

My intercom buzzed.

Sophie.

Well, it was too late now.

***

"DO you know what you're doing right now is a criminal offence?" Sophie asked.

We were walking through Hampstead Heath toward The Hill Garden and Pergola, which Sophie had suggested as a picnic location. I'd been trying to distract Elliot, who was getting antsy in his stroller, by singing "If You're Happy and You Know It (Clap Your Hands)". Elliot wasn't impressed.

I looked at Sophie and raised an eyebrow. "Hey! I know I'm not the greatest singer, but I didn't think I was *that* bad!"

Sophie laughed. "It's got nothing to do with your singing skills, although now you mention it..." She grinned. "No, in all seriousness, Hampstead Heath has a number of bizarre "byelaws" which ban things like singing, playing games, tree climbing, training dogs, and mending chairs. They're all written in old-school Edwardian language. I've never heard the no-singing rule being enforced, but you can't be too careful," she said conspiratorially, looking around as if a cop might jump out of the bushes at any moment.

I chuckled. "That's just what I need. After a few rough months in the press, I get arrested for singing! I can see the headlines now, 'Jailhouse Rock: Chris Trent sings his way to prison.'"

Sophie laughed. "So, how's the accent coming along? Have my tips been helpful?"

"I think it's improved a little, but to be honest, I'm pretty worried about it. If I screw up, I'll embarrass myself in front of millions of people. After the last few months, the idea of being publicly humiliated again makes me sick. On the plus side, it's great motivation to get it right." I wouldn't usually be so open with someone I'd just met, but it felt natural with Sophie. But was it really a good idea to let my defenses down, especially with someone I didn't know that well? The last time I'd dropped my guard with Vanessa, it had gone terribly wrong.

"That does sound stressful." Sophie's eyes were soft with sympathy. "If you ever want to practice with me, I'm more than happy to. I promise I won't laugh."

"Thanks. When it's a bit better, I might take you up on the offer. And you are helping, anyway. My dialect coach said just listening to Brits speak would improve my accent."

"I'm glad I could be of service!" Sophie said in an over-the-top posh accent. "On a related note, how are you doing understanding us Brits? Have you had awkward moments when you've been stared at blankly or completely misunderstood someone?"

Given my hermit lifestyle, there hadn't been much opportunity for cultural or language-based misunderstandings. But I didn't want Sophie to know that, apart from my walks with her, I'd barely left the house. Relief, mixed with embarrassment, hit me as I remembered I had, in fact, had one such misunderstanding on my first day in London.

"Actually, yes," I said, wincing.

Now it was Sophie's turn to raise an eyebrow. "I saw that wince! Come on, tell me!"

I took a deep breath. "So, in my defense, I'd just landed in London. I hadn't slept at all and was feeling pretty rough. I'd booked a serviced apartment while looking for a house to rent, and it was on the first floor. I couldn't wait to dump my bags, have a shower, and crash. But when I got there, the key just wouldn't work. I started vigorously rattling it and shaking the door, thinking it was jammed. I was so desperate to get in, I was...Well, let's just say, more ener-getic than I'd usually be. I'd almost taken the door off its hinges when I heard a woman's voice inside yelling that she'd call the police if I didn't stop." I rubbed my forehead, remembering how embarrassed I'd felt. "So, it turns out, what we Americans call the first floor, you Brits call the ground floor. I'd tried to get into an apartment on the wrong floor and scared the shit out of the poor woman living there. I still feel terrible about it. She must have thought I was trying to break in. I was too embarrassed to face her, but I slipped a note under her door the next day, apologizing for the whole thing. Luckily, that's been it so far."

Sophie covered her mouth with her hand, trying not to laugh. "Oh no! That poor woman."

"I know. So, what was your funniest misunderstanding when you were in the States?"

"Hmm." Sophie furrowed her brow, looking completely adorable in the process, before her face broke into a smile. "Okay, this one is maybe not the funniest, but will be an important lesson for you. So, once, my American boss sent around an email saying that the dress code for the office holiday party included pants for women. In the UK, *pants* means *underwear*, not trousers, so I was pretty concerned that they needed to tell staff to wear underwear and started wondering how wild that holiday party was going to get! I was disappointed when it turned out to be a rather staid affair." Sophie pulled a face. "Just something to keep in mind if you're talking with the costume department about your pants, or things could get awkward!"

I chuckled but kept note. I didn't want to be in the news for a sexual harassment claim, especially with everything else that had been going on.

"We're here!"

Caught up in our conversation, I hadn't been paying any attention to our surroundings. But now, I looked around. Sophie's warning that London's streak of gorgeous weather wouldn't last hadn't yet come to fruition. It was another beautiful day, the grass was bright green, and lush vines hung from the stone pillars and arches of the Pergola. Sophie had mentioned this was a popular wedding spot, and I could see why. The Hill Garden was overgrown, the Pergola and stone terraces were crumbling, and the overall atmosphere was one of faded grandeur.

Mitch was right—this was kind of romantic.

Was this a date after all? I looked at Sophie, who was busy unstrapping Elliot from the stroller. I sighed. I wasn't picking up any signs she was interested in me like that.

We chose a grassy spot next to an ornamental pond full of reeds and water lilies. I spread out the picnic rug I'd bought this morning and started unpacking the food from my backpack.

"So, I got a bit carried away at the deli and bought

enough stuff to feed a family of eight, but I couldn't help myself. It all looked so good." Fresh sourdough, a selection of cheeses, a duck terrine that looked amazing, a few salads, and a fruit platter I'd put together myself. A flush of red heat spread across my face. Had I gone to too much trouble?

"Yum! This looks incredible. Thanks so much. What a treat!" Sophie lifted Elliot out of the stroller, plonked him on the rug next to her, and gave him some toys to play with.

Elliot seemed to be warming to me—we made eye contact, and he graced me with a gummy grin.

We tucked into the food with gusto.

"Mmmm, this terrine is so good."

Sophie let out a moan that immediately made me imagine her naked in bed with me, kissing her soft lips, then making my way slowly down her body...*Get a grip, Chris.*

"And this rhubarb fizzy drink goes down so easily." Her choice of words sent my mind further into the gutter.

Mitch was right. I *did* have it bad.

A cute dog resembling Alfie walked past and provided me with a welcome distraction.

"My dog, Alfie, is arriving soon. He'll have an absolute ball here. I've been surprised how much I've missed him, even though he's a little terror of a puppy." I couldn't wait to take Alfie on walks through the Heath, hopefully with Sophie and Elliot by my side.

"You didn't mention you had a dog!" Sophie said, glaring at me in mock outrage. "I love dogs. I've been so tempted to get one but thought a baby and a dog might be too much. Do you have any photos?"

I showed Sophie my phone lock screen, which displayed a photo of Alfie looking particularly goofy, a shoe in his month.

"Aww! What a cutie!"

"Don't be taken in by his good looks. He's an absolute menace. That shoe has bite marks all over it," I said fondly.

We kept snacking on the food and chatting. I loved the way Sophie's eyes lit up every time she talked about something she was passionate about, whether it was cooking, hiking, or her new business. I wanted to know everything about her.

She leaned over to cut some more triple cream brie, and a lock of her hair fell over her face. I had the sudden urge to tuck it back behind her ear, cradle her face in my hands, and kiss her.

I inwardly groaned. *Pull it together, Chris.*

Trying to throw cold water on my feelings for Sophie, which were getting stronger by the minute, I raised the least sexy topic I could think of.

"So, have you had any more run-ins with our good friend Cynthia?" I winked.

Sophie rolled her eyes. "It's funny you should ask. I got a text this morning, saying she was having some 'girlfriends and their hubbies' over for dinner. She wanted to know if I'd like to come and bring you as well. I'm sure she only asked because she wants some more photos with you and to show you off to her friends. I hope you're not too disappointed, but I declined."

"I'm devastated." I pretended to wipe tears from my eyes. Part of me liked that Cynthia had invited us as if we were a couple. Had she picked up on some chemistry between us? Perhaps I was just so used to women being into me because of my money and fame that I wasn't able to detect genuine interest.

My heart fluttered with hope.

If Sophie was interested in me, maybe I would make an exception to my no-dating rule. I had qualms about jeopardizing my only friendship in London, but my attraction toward her was showing no signs of dying down. In fact, thinking about the possibility of Sophie and I actually getting together was fueling the flames.

Just as I was getting more hot and bothered at the prospect that maybe something was going on between us, Sophie's words cut into my thoughts.

"Cynthia always rubs me the wrong way. Even in her text, I couldn't stand the way she referred to her 'girl-friends'. Why not just call them friends? If she had any male friends, which I doubt, she'd never call them her 'boyfriends'. Using 'girlfriend' in that way means that if I use it to describe a woman I'm actually dating, I get confused stares. People assume I'm just referring to a friend." Sophie gave a frustrated sigh, completely oblivious to the impact her words had on me.

Damn.

She's gay.

It hit me like a tidal wave, washing away those feelings of desire, and leaving me disappointed and embarrassed. My face flushed with heat.

Of course, the first woman I've been attracted to in ages was unavailable.

CHAPTER EIGHT

CHRIS

"THIS CALLS for Muscle Man's arms. Mine are about to fall off." Sophie handed me the pestle and mortar, which she'd been using to grind six different spices together. "I still don't agree with your argument that because there are two of us cooking, the recipe can have up to thirty ingredients."

She pouted petulantly, and I had the urge to bend down and plant a kiss on her lips. Needless to say, my attempts to get over my crush on Sophie were *not* going well.

The summer rain Sophie forecast had finally arrived yesterday after the picnic and hadn't stopped since, so I'd invited her and Elliot over to the house for lunch. I worried I was being too full on suggesting we see each other again so soon, especially since I'd only met her on Monday and we'd hung out almost every day this week, but I enjoyed her company so much, I'd pushed my worries aside. And Sophie seemed quite happy to accept my invitation.

Elliot lay on the floor in the living/dining area, watching us with interest while he chewed on a stuffed cow. I was enjoying our easy-going banter as we prepped the meal, washing and cutting vegetables, grinding the spices and making the lemon tahini dressing. We were a good team in the kitchen, although I kept getting distracted by my proximity to Sophie. She turned her head to smile at me, and my heart jumped. We bumped into each other reaching for the same knife, and a tingle shot up my arm.

Get a grip, Chris. She's not available.

Since the picnic, I'd been trying to convince myself it was for the best she was gay. This way, there was no risk of me ruining our new friendship because of my feelings toward her, or having my heart broken again. All I needed now was for these damn feelings to disappear.

Unfortunately, it wasn't that easy. Sophie began telling me about her volunteering at the local youth LGBTQ+ center with her friend, Josh, her eyes flashing as she spoke enthusiastically about the young people she'd met. My chest fluttered. Damn, she was cute when she was excited.

Sophie stopped chopping and looked at me. "That reminds me, I've been meaning to ask...Would you have any interest in coming to karaoke with me and a few of my friends tomorrow night? We're all terrible singers and have a tendency to get carried away, but it's usually a lot of fun. No pressure at all if you're not feeling it, but we've hired a private room at our favorite spot in Soho, so there'll be a reasonable amount of privacy. We're planning to meet at ten p.m."

While pleased Sophie had invited me, the idea of going out in a crowded area like Soho and spending time with people I didn't know, even if they were Sophie's friends, sent my stomach into turmoil. I wondered if they'd seen the photos. I wondered if Sophie had seen the photos. I gave myself a mental shake.

Stop thinking about the photos.

But I loved karaoke. And I really needed to get used to

being around people, especially strangers, given filming would start in a few weeks. And if Sophie's friends were anything like her, I was bound to have a good time.

"That sounds fun. I've got a call with my family at nine p.m., so I'll be a bit late, but I'll be there." My parents were having my half-sisters over for lunch, and I'd promised to Skype them all mid-afternoon Chicago time.

"Great! I'll text you the details." Sophie looked pleased. "Now, what do we need to do next?" She bent over the cookbook, studying it intently.

God, I loved the way she furrowed her brow and bit her lip when she focused on something. *Snap out of it, Chris. She's not interested in you, and she never will be.*

A terrible odor, like rotting cabbage, hit me.

"What's that smell? Something must have expired." I started picking ingredients off the counter and sniffing them, trying to work out where it was coming from.

Sophie laughed. "Sorry, it's Elliot. He's been super gassy today. I gave him some beans last night for the first time, and his baby digestive tract is struggling. I'll just check it's not an actual poop."

"I don't know how something that small and cute can make a smell that bad." I stared at Elliot, who looked back at me with wide, innocent eyes.

Sophie's phone started vibrating.

"Tell me about it! Sorry, I'll just get this."

I returned to cutting carrots but looked up almost immediately when Sophie gasped. "Oh my god! Is he okay?" She paced around the open plan area, listening intently. "I'll be there as soon as I can. Thanks for calling me."

She put down her phone. "Shit!" Sophie looked at me while rubbing her forehead, concern splashed across her face.

"Is everything okay?"

"Josh was hit by an idiot on an electric scooter and is in hospital. It sounds like he's concussed. They're still doing scans to find out how bad it is. I'm sorry, I need to go to the hospital. His family cut him off when he came out, so I'm his emergency contact and the closest thing he has to family."

"Of course. I'm so sorry. Can I do anything to help?"

Tears welled in Sophie's eyes, and I fought the urge to throw my arms around her and comfort her.

She started packing up. "Crap. I wish my parents weren't at work right now. I don't know what to do about Elliot. It'll take ages to get to the hospital on public transport, especially given how bad the weather is at the moment. It always slows things down."

"How can I help? Can I call you an Uber?" I picked up my phone.

"I'm not sure I'll be able to get a taxi or an Uber with a child seat for him. And if I need to stay for a while, he's going to get so cranky...If Josh has a head injury, the last thing he'll want is to be greeted by a screaming baby."

"Well, why don't you leave him here with me? We can hang out together, can't we, buddy?" I shot Elliot a tentative smile.

Elliot didn't look at all convinced it was a good idea. To be honest, neither was I. While I'd spent some time with my half-sisters' kids when they were babies, I'd never been left alone unsupervised with one. At least Elliot seemed more comfortable with me since we'd played on the picnic rug yesterday.

"Are you sure?" Sophie looked at me as if she was sizing me up, trying to decide whether she could trust me to keep Elliot alive and well.

I nodded.

"Okay, well...that would be amazing, thank you. He's just had a feed, so he shouldn't be due another one for about three hours. If I'm not back by then, I have an emergency formula sachet and baby bottle in the nappy bag, along with nappies—diapers—of course. Just call me if there are any issues."

I hoped Elliot wouldn't need formula or a diaper change because I didn't have a clue how to do either, but I thought it best not to mention that to Sophie. I was fairly confident that, with the help of Google and YouTube, I could work it out, and if not, I could call one of my sisters. It would be morning in Chicago, so they'd be up.

"That's totally fine. We'll have a great time, won't we, mister?" I said, giving Elliot's head an affectionate ruffle. He shot me a look of derision.

We waved Sophie off as she jumped into a cab. As soon as she'd left, I realized that foul smell had followed us out to the doorstep, and that Sophie had never got around to checking Elliot's diaper. I sniffed his butt.

"Shit," I muttered under my breath. This wasn't a promising start to my first babysitting attempt.

Elliot smiled angelically at me and then proceeded to vomit down my shirt. God damn.

"Oh dear, buddy. Let's go inside and get both of us cleaned up."

Holding Elliot in my arms, I was struck by the realization that this tiny, vulnerable human was depending on me to keep him alive for the next few hours. I was simultaneously stressed by the responsibility I'd taken on and pleased Sophie trusted me enough to leave him in my care.

I sat him next to me on the rug in the living room and peered inside the diaper bag. It was overflowing with stuff.

The diapers helpfully had the word "back" written on one side, so at least I knew which way around they went, but that was as much as I could work out.

Elliot grabbed the diaper rash cream jar out of the bag and started gnawing on it with delight. With difficulty, I pried it out of his hands, worried he'd pull the lid off and eat the cream. I was shocked at how strong his little hands were. How the hell could such a tiny creature have such a powerful grip?

I pulled up YouTube on my phone and searched for "How to change a diaper." The ads took forever to play, and the smell was getting worse every second, but once the instructional video started it didn't seem too hard. I laid down the change mat on the rug, carefully placed Elliot onto it, took off his pants and the foul-smelling diaper, and wiped him down. Oh god. Just my luck that Elliot's first experience with beans exited his body while I was in charge. Trying not to breathe through my nose, I crammed everything into a small plastic bag. The bag would be going in the trash can outside at the first opportunity. I looked at my phone to check what the next step was.

Elliot, sensing an opportunity while my head was turned, suddenly rolled at speed across the living room floor toward a large antique vase, half naked. *Crap!*

I leaped up and raced after him. Not only was this kid strong, but he could roll as well. I grabbed him just before he smashed into the vase.

As I breathed out in relief, I looked around the living room with fresh eyes. This place was *not* baby proof. There were hazards everywhere. Power outlets and cords, sharp edges, and breakable objects within Elliot's reach. I'd need to do something about this if Elliot was going to keep hanging out here.

I placed him back on the change mat. This time, I kept my hand on his tummy to stop him from commando rolling while I re-watched the YouTube video.

I was turning back to maneuver him into the diaper when my face and chest were suddenly hit with warm liquid. I flinched.

What the hell was that?

I looked down at Elliot, who was giving me what I could only describe as an evil grin, and realized there was now a small puddle on the change mat around his butt.

Oh. Oh gross. It was pee. At least it didn't seem to smell too bad, especially not compared with that poop, but still...

After wiping myself and Elliot off with a towel from the diaper bag, I got the diaper fastened on him and breathed a sigh of relief. That was a lot more challenging than I'd expected. It was up there with some of Muscle Man's most difficult stunts. While I hadn't been paying a lot of attention, I was pretty sure when Sophie changed Elliot in my presence she'd done it in under a minute, without imperiling any vases or being soaked in pee.

"Good work, buddy. We got through that all right in the end, didn't we?"

I packed the diaper bag away, washed my hands, and put Elliot back down next to his toys, but he didn't seem keen on any of them. His bottom lip trembled, and he made some plaintive whimpers that were like daggers in my heart. Poor little fellow. He probably missed Sophie.

I tried playing peekaboo. Not impressed.

I blew a raspberry. His lip trembled even more.

I started singing "Twinkle, Twinkle, Little Star." The whimpers amplified. I'm not the best singer, but I didn't think I was *that* bad. His reaction didn't bode well for my performance at karaoke tomorrow night.

My phone rang. I grabbed it, thinking it might be Sophie. My heart sank when I saw it was Jenny. She was calling to confirm arrangements for Alfie's flight, so I put her on speakerphone while I pulled silly faces at Elliot, hoping that would cheer him up.

"Awesome, thanks, Jenny. I can't wait to see Alfie. How's he doing?"

"He's great."

Just then, Elliot started to wail.

"Is that a baby in the background? Where are you?" I could hear the curiosity in Jenny's voice.

I paused. I didn't want to tell Jenny about Sophie. If I did, I was sure Jenny would work out in a flash that I was interested in Sophie and then bombard me with awkward questions.

"Yep. I'm at home. Just looking after a friend's baby for a couple of hours. I don't suppose you have any ideas for how to entertain a six-month-old? He's getting upset and doesn't want to play with his toys."

"A friend? What friend? I didn't think you knew anyone in London." She sounded suspicious but thankfully seemed to treat her questions as rhetorical. "Hmmm, I don't know much about babies. My nephew used to love chewing on my fingers when he was around that age. You could try that?"

I offered Elliot a finger. He snatched it enthusiastically and dragged it to his mouth.

"Ouch!" A sharp pain shot through my finger, and I pulled it away. "He must have teeth, very sharp teeth. That hurt. I think he drew blood."

"Oh yeah, as soon as my nephew got teeth, we stopped that game right quick. Their teeth are like little piranha's. Sorry, I should have mentioned that."

I ended the call with Jenny and examined my finger. Elliot's front bottom tooth, which I hadn't noticed before, had punctured the skin, and some blood had dripped onto my shirt.

My phone pinged. It was a message from Sophie.

Sophie: *How are things? Josh is doing much better than expected, thank goodness. I'll be home soon.*

I sat Elliot on my lap and posed for a selfie with him with my thumb up, making sure I positioned him so the pee, vomit, and bloodstains on my shirt weren't visible. The finger biting incident seemed to have perked him up, although I wasn't keen on sacrificing another one any time soon.

Chris: *All well here! Glad to hear he's on the mend. See you soon.*

I turned my attention back to Elliot.

"Okay, buddy. We've got to get tidied up before your mom gets home."

When Sophie walked through the door about forty minutes later, I was wearing a clean shirt, serenading Elliot with "I Want It That Way" by the Backstreet Boys, and he was waving his arms about in delight. It turned out, it wasn't my voice after all. He just wasn't keen on nursery rhymes. Nineties boy bands were more his jam. We were having a great time.

"Your son has excellent taste in music. I decided to kill two birds with one stone and entertain Elliot while I practiced for karaoke."

Sophie laughed, looking around the room. "Wow! What happened here?"

I'd moved all the breakable objects out of Elliot's reach, rearranged the furniture so it acted as a barrier between

Elliot and the power cords, and tied a necktie around the handles on the TV cabinet so Elliot couldn't open it.

"Just a bit of baby proofing to make sure this place is safe for Elliot if he comes over again," I said, smiling, hoping that he would.

Despite the rough start, the last few hours had been surprisingly fun.

CHAPTER NINE

SOPHIE

"I'M SO EXCITED! This is the first time I've been out—not including volunteering, which doesn't really count—since Elliot was born. And last night he slept through the entire night, and I'm just feeling amazing! I'd forgotten how nice it is to have a proper night's sleep."

The Uber I was sharing with Josh whizzed by the neon lights and the lines of people waiting to get into the clubs. I hadn't been to Soho since I'd met Mia and Rose for cocktails —well, a mocktail for me—a few months before Elliot's birth, for a "business planning session" which involved very little business planning. I'd made Mia and Rose promise there would be no business talk tonight. As excited as I was about it, this evening I just wanted to relax and have fun.

I turned to Josh, and my spirits dropped slightly at the state of his face. "But are you sure you're up to this?"

Josh was sporting some bad bruising around his right temple and eye, as well as some stitches above his right eyebrow. While he claimed he'd made a full recovery, I was pretty sure he was only saying that because he wanted to meet Chris.

"That's awesome, Soph! And yes, I'm fine. It's not like I was hit by a truck, just a scooter."

Staring at him skeptically, I vowed to keep a close eye on him and send him home if he showed any signs of being unwell. I still hadn't recovered from seeing him lying in the hospital bed, pale with bandages around his head, and I didn't want this karaoke night to jeopardize his recovery.

I also hadn't recovered from walking in on Chris serenading Elliot with the Backstreet Boys. It was a cuteness overload. I'd been distraught at the news of Josh's accident and overwhelmed at the prospect of lugging Elliot to and from the hospital when I made the split-second decision to leave Elliot with Chris. But the entire time I was away, I'd worried whether I'd done the right thing. While I'd thought I could trust Chris, I really hadn't known him for very long at all. It was a huge relief to get back to the Castle and see them having such a great time. I did notice Chris was wearing a new top and wondered what had happened but thought it better not to ask. Knowing Elliot, it could have been any number of bodily fluids.

"So, is Muscle Man still coming tonight?" Josh couldn't hide his excitement. A wide grin filled his face.

"Yes. He's got a call, so he'll be late, but he said he'd come. Please don't be too over the top, Josh, and definitely do not mention the photos."

I felt a little apprehensive about Chris coming. He should get on well with everyone...as long as they weren't too starstruck in his presence. Josh was my main concern.

"I will be super chill, babe," Josh said, looking anything but chill, his eyes flashing with anticipation.

Soho was buzzing as we got out of the Uber. I bounced up the stairs to the karaoke lounge, unable to contain my excitement. When we arrived, performances were in full swing. Sharon and Tina, who'd been together since university and had booked a babysitter for their twin daughters for the night, were belting out Miley Cyrus's "Wrecking Ball", while Amir, Khanh, Mia, and Rose cheered them on, already tipsy. They gave an even bigger cheer when they saw Josh and me walk into the dark room. Warmth filled my chest. This was my crew.

I grabbed a drink at the bar and selected a few songs. You had to get in early with this lot—there were a number of attention hogs in the group. I took a seat in between Josh and Rose on the long couch and watched Sharon and Tina's grand ending.

It felt so amazing to be hanging out with everyone, just like old times. While they'd been checking in with me regularly since Elliot's appearance and I'd caught up with them all individually, we hadn't gotten together as a group post-Elliot.

Looking around the room, it dawned on me that, possibly for the first time in his life, Chris might feel like a minority among my friends. I wondered if I should have given him a heads-up. Then, I remembered all the times I'd been the only queer person or person of color in the room. No one had ever warned me in advance. And it would be kind of weird to say, "Oh, by the way, you might feel a bit out of place tonight as the only white, probably straight cis man." It wouldn't do him any harm to experience that for once. In fact, it could probably do him some good.

A familiar tune started playing.

I'm not an amazing singer, but I've done enough karaoke to know that energy is significantly more important than voice quality. I downed my drink, channeled my inner Whitney, and grabbed the microphone.

I was pouring my heart and soul into singing "I Wanna

Dance with Somebody," when out of the corner of my eye, I noticed the door open and somebody walk into the room.

Chris.

He looked straight at me and smiled.

A million-dollar smile. A smile that lit up his eyes and sent an electric shock reverberating through my body.

It felt like that smile had summoned Cupid to this karaoke room in Soho, sending an arrow directly into my heart.

Yes, as much as I'd been denying it, I was already attracted to him. But this was different. A bolt of intense attraction that made me freeze in place and stumble over my lines.

My stomach flipped.

I struggled to keep singing. Everything around me except Chris seemed to fade away.

We stared at each other. I couldn't break eye contact; a magnetic force was pulling us toward each other. With some effort, I turned to the screen and used all my energy to concentrate on the lyrics. I knew the song by heart, but I needed something to focus on, something to draw my gaze away from Chris.

Panic rose in my chest, and the warm fuzzy sensation I'd been enjoying being surrounded by my friends was replaced with blood pounding through my body and sweaty hands. What the hell was going on? I'd never been this attracted to anyone with such intensity before. How had I gone from platonic—well, mostly—friend vibes to intense romantic feelings with one look? I was sure Chris and everyone else in the room must have witnessed my reaction, it felt so extreme. But if they had, they didn't show it.

Please, please, please let me not have fallen for him.

That would be really annoying on so many levels. He

was already an unlikely friend. He was an even more unlikely object of my affections. I had flashbacks to high school, when I had a huge crush on my best friend. My straight, female, best friend. It had made things so awkward between us that we'd grown apart. In Chris, I'd finally found someone I enjoyed spending time with while everyone else was at work, and I didn't want our new friend-ship to be similarly jeopardized. I could only hope that I'd wake up tomorrow morning and all my feelings toward Chris would have reverted to purely platonic. Or even how I was feeling before tonight. I could handle—well, ignore—a few sparks of attraction, but not this.

I struggled through the rest of the song, took some deep breaths, and walked over to introduce Chris to everyone. My mind and body were whirring, but I focused all my attention on trying to behave normally.

While I was completely thrown by the intensity of my feelings for Chris, as I'd expected, Chris hit it off with everyone. Before I could blink, Chris and Josh were up on stage, doing a duet of "A Whole New World" and tipsily trying to recreate a carpet ride. Josh got so into it, his curls bouncing at double time, I was concerned he might incur another head injury. Just as that thought popped into my mind, Josh tripped over the microphone stand. Chris caught him, earning Chris a round of applause and cheering from the group. Josh looked absolutely stoked to be in Chris's arms and took a bit too long to stand back up, milking the moment for as long as he could. I chuckled, shaking my head at Josh's antics.

While I tried to concentrate on the music and enjoying the evening with my friends, I couldn't stop thinking about Chris. When he wasn't performing or buying rounds of drinks, he sat next to me on the couch. I was acutely aware of his presence. Each time our legs touched, an electric shock traveled up my thigh. Each time Chris leaned over to speak to me, my heart picked up pace, conscious of his face close to mine.

Shit.

About two hours in, Chris put his hand on my back and asked if I wanted another drink, sending an intense euphoric sensation washing over me. I had to excuse myself to go to the bathroom. I needed a cold shower, but since that wasn't possible, cold water from the sink would have to do.

I bumped into Josh on the way back.

"Chris is awesome, Soph!" he exclaimed. "And even hotter in real life, if that's possible. I don't know how you aren't head over heels for him." Josh's hair was flopping all over the place with excitement. "Arrrgh! I can't believe I just did a duet with *Chris Trent.* Did you see how he caught me when I fell?"

"Shhh! Please don't scream his name like that, Josh. We don't want people to know he's in there." I glared at him. "Are you sure you should be drinking with a head injury?"

Josh looked at me, and despite his head injury and alcohol consumption, he knew something was wrong. I'd never been good at hiding my emotions from him.

"What's wrong?" Josh narrowed his eyes and stared at me.

"Nothing. I'm fine. I just got hot in there. It's pretty stuffy," I said, hoping he'd buy it.

He didn't.

"Is it about Chris?"

I swallowed and nodded. Even though Josh was in no condition to provide any useful advice, I needed to confide in someone.

"I seriously don't know what just happened. So, maybe

I wasn't telling you the complete truth the other day when I said I wasn't into him. I was a bit attracted to him. But tonight, when he walked in and smiled at me, things went from mild attraction to..." I shook my head. "Is love at fifth sight a thing? Because it feels like that's just what happened to me."

"That's awesome, Soph!" Josh looked inexplicably happy.

"No, it's not! For so many reasons. Firstly, there's no way he'd be interested in me."

Josh raised an eyebrow but let me continue.

"Come on, Josh. He's a famous, very good-looking, movie star. As you keep reminding me, the sexiest man alive. He dates famous singers and supermodels, not single mums who live with their parents. We're from completely different worlds. Can you see me hanging off his arm at fancy parties and film premieres?"

"Soph, you're a catch. You're gorgeous, smart, and a genuinely nice person. I don't know why you would think he wouldn't be interested in you. If I was straight, I would bang you in a heartbeat!"

I rolled my eyes.

"And haven't you guys seen each other almost every day this week? That's just-started-dating-and-head-over-heels frequency, not new-platonic-friends frequency."

Hmmm. We *had* been spending a lot of time together since meeting on Monday, but that was because we were both lonely and liked each other's company as *friends*...wasn't it?

"Also, I don't want a relationship right now. Especially not with a guy. My priority is Elliot and starting the business with Mia and Rose. I don't have time for dating. It's one thing to be friends with him, another thing entirely to date him."

"I still don't understand why you've sworn off dating men. I know you've had some bad experiences, but we aren't all assholes." Josh looked at me petulantly.

Rationally, I knew Josh was right—not all men were shit —but the bad dating experiences made me reluctant to go down that path again. I was still scarred by them. If I caught a guy checking me out, I'd immediately think back to those messages and disastrous dates, sending a shudder down my spine.

"Those experiences definitely put me off. But it's not only that. I usually connect better emotionally with women, and the sex is *way* better. I also think women are more likely to be accepting of Elliot than men. If they're dating other women and want kids, they're used to the idea that children can only be biologically related to one parent. Straight men are more likely to want their children to be biologically theirs. If I did ever date again, Elliot's best interests would be my top priority."

"Straight men often have stepchildren or are open to adopting, Soph, so I don't think it would necessarily be a deal breaker. And you can train men to be better in bed. God knows, I've done it a few times!" Josh said, with a cheeky grin on his face.

"I don't have the time for that! In any event, he's only here for four months, so not exactly a long term dating option, or much time for sex education, for that matter. These stupid feelings are just going to make things super awkward, which sucks because I was really enjoying spending time together as *friends*." I sighed.

Just then, Mia poked her head out, her usually pale face flushed pink. "What are you two doing, gossiping out here?

Amir and Khanh are very keen for you to come back in to witness their...errr...performance." She giggled.

I let out a deep breath, relieved I had an excuse to escape Josh. I regretted saying anything to him now, especially since he didn't seem sufficiently sympathetic to my plight. We returned to the room, where Amir and Khanh were getting carried away singing Ginuwine's "Pony", replete with a lot of suggestive dance moves. Chris, who had been vigorously cheering them on, looked up when I entered and gave me a smile. My heart bounced.

Damn my body and its involuntary reactions.

I threw myself into singing the chorus with everyone else, hoping that these feelings would dissipate by the morning.

CHAPTER TEN

CHRIS

"HEY MAN, are you free for a chat?" I was sitting in bed in my boxers. I'd been trying to fall asleep but couldn't stop thinking about Sophie. One benefit of having friends in different time zones is that you could FaceTime them at two a.m.

"Sure. We've just finished dinner. It must be late at your end. Is everything okay?" His voice reverberated with worry.

"Yeah, sorry. I just got home from karaoke with Sophie and her friends."

Mitch's face relaxed into a smile. "Ohhhh, you met her friends? That sounds promising. How was it? And how are things going with her?"

"Her friends were great. But things with her are... complicated." I sighed. "I *really* like her, and it turns out she is gay. Seriously, I have the worst luck with women."

Mitch's face twitched. He was clearly trying to hold back laughter.

"Oh no, I'm sorry. That is bad luck."

"To be honest, it's driving me crazy. I really enjoy

spending time with Sophie, so I don't want to stop seeing her, but the more time I spend with her, the more I'm attracted to her. I've even resorted to Googling 'How to stop being attracted to someone.'"

It had been particularly bad tonight. When I'd walked in, she had been singing "I Wanna Dance with Somebody" with such passion, my heart skipped a beat. When she saw me and we locked eyes, I could have sworn it stopped beating completely for a few seconds. My reaction was so intense, it seemed impossible that everyone in the room, including Sophie, hadn't noticed it.

"That sucks. What did Google recommend?" I couldn't hear suppressed laughter in Mitch's voice anymore, just sympathy.

"Nothing I actually wanted to do. I don't want to cut off all contact with her. She's my only friend here, and I'm enjoying her company too much. It also suggested focusing on her negative qualities, but I haven't noticed any. Dating other people—I'm not interested in anyone else. Or telling her how I feel, which would almost certainly make things really awkward and likely screw up our friendship. So, I'm just trying to ignore my feelings and focus on enjoying her company as a friend, but it's not working too well."

"Maybe it will get easier with time. I'm glad to hear you've been getting out at least. How are you feeling about everything else?"

Even though Mitch didn't have any answers, it was still good to talk to someone about my feelings.

"Definitely better than I have been. I've been keeping busy with working out, the dialect coaching, and spending time with Sophie." I'd come a long way from lying on a white couch in a white room, surrounded by dog pee and obsessing about my public humiliation. It wasn't like I'd completely forgotten about the photos—I still had moments when I was overwhelmed with shame—but at least they weren't constantly at the forefront of my mind. "I'd been nervous about going out tonight, but it was totally fine. Even though I'm sure some of Sophie's friends would have seen the photos, no one said anything to me about them, or stared at my groin with a weird look on their face. It certainly made me feel less worried about starting filming."

"Well, that's great progress! I'm proud of you. And how's the accent?"

I cleared my throat and put on my accent. "The accent, kind sir, is extremely questionable, but my dialect coach has faith that I'll get there by the time filming starts."

Mitch laughed. I changed back to my normal voice.

"But enough about me. How are things going with you?"

"So, that's actually one of the reasons I called you last week...We have some exciting news. We're having a baby! He's due in February."

Warmth filled my chest at Mitch's news. "That's awesome! I'm so happy for you guys. How's Liz feeling?"

"Good now. She was pretty sick for the first ten weeks, but that's gone away thank goodness."

A twinge of envy muddied my excitement for Mitch and Liz. They had a great relationship. Not only were they best friends, but they still couldn't keep their hands off each other, even nine years after first meeting at law school. They'd got married last year and bought a house not far from my childhood home.

When I'd chosen this career, I hadn't thought about how it would affect my chances of meeting someone and having a family. I found it almost impossible to meet people who weren't famous. If I went to a bar, I'd be swarmed by fans wanting selfies. If I tried online dating, I'd be met with the online equivalent—or kicked off the app for "impersonating" Chris Trent, which had happened to me twice. Meeting Sophie in the street had been a complete anomaly.

That left me with dating people I met on set or at Hollywood parties, who, if they weren't celebrities, were at least celebrity-adjacent. As my relationship with Vanessa had demonstrated, dating another celebrity was fraught with difficulties. It amplified the media attention at least twofold. The constant media speculation about our relationship had put enormous pressure on us. If we so much as looked at each other in public without a loving smile plastered on our faces, the internet would be flooded with articles that "Chranessa", as they called us, was on the rocks. Those articles would trigger niggling doubts in the back of my mind. Were we on the rocks? Was Vanessa looking at me with disgust?

It wasn't just the media coverage. Schedules as hectic as ours would have tested even the strongest relationship. In the last year, Vanessa had been on tour the entire time, and I'd been busy filming. As a result, we'd only spent a few months physically together. I'd felt us growing apart but didn't know how to fix it. Perhaps Vanessa had felt the same —Alfie had been a present to keep me company in her absence.

And then she'd cheated on me and shared those photos with the world.

I started to spiral again thinking about it, nausea flooding over me.

Get a grip, Chris. Mitch just shared huge news with you, you should be focused on celebrating with him. Stop being so fucking self-absorbed.

I focused my attention back on our conversation.

"That's such good news, I can't wait to see you guys when I come home for Thanksgiving and celebrate in person! I also have some tips about changing diapers and baby proofing, which I'll need to share. Now, do you have any names picked out yet?"

CHAPTER ELEVEN

SOPHIE

CHRIS and I were cooking in his kitchen. He came up behind me, put his arms around my waist, and kissed my neck, sending shivers down my spine. He'd just turned me around to kiss my lips when Elliot's cries woke me from my dream.

God damn it. I wasn't sure if I was more disappointed about missing out on my dream kiss with Chris, or about the fact I was dreaming about him in the first place. Crap. Those feelings were still there. And they were decidedly *not* platonic.

Bleary-eyed and groggy, I pulled myself out of bed and opened the curtains, letting the morning sun stream into my room. I was back in my childhood bedroom, but the posters of Buffy and school art projects were long gone. Mum had been using it as a study before I moved back in, and now the walls were bare and white. I wasn't planning to stay long enough to bother redecorating. Once I went back to work, I'd look for an apartment nearby. I loved my parents, and they'd been a huge help with Elliot, but I missed having my own space, and I suspected they missed their studies.

I'd forgotten what it was like to wake up after drinking too much and staying up too late. Unfortunately, the days of being able to sleep in after a big night were over. Elliot woke like clockwork at seven every morning.

I walked to the small bedroom next to mine, which used to be my dad's study, got Elliot up, gave him a feed, and took him down the wooden stairs into the dining room, hoping one of my parents was up so they could entertain him while I had a shower. A shower might make me feel more human and help clear my head of thoughts of Chris.

Dad was sitting at the table, coffee and cereal in front of him, reading the morning news on his iPad. Mum was sitting next to him, looking concerned. Dad stood when he saw me.

"Sophie, there's something you should see. I'll swap you." He handed me his iPad and took Elliot, careful to keep him away from his hot mug of coffee.

I had to blink a few times to work out what I was looking at. It was photos of Chris, me, and Elliot while we were picnicking at the Pergola the other day. Chris and I eating on the picnic rug, Chris playing airplanes with Elliot, Chris pushing Elliot's pram as we walked home. The photos were on one of the tabloid websites with the headline: *Is Chris Trent a baby daddy?*

I read on, my mouth open.

Chris Trent, in London to film a period drama, has been spotted with an attractive mystery brunette and a baby, having a romantic picnic at the Pergola on Hampstead Heath. Fresh out of his messy breakup with the singer Vanessa Milan, Chris seems to have bounced back quickly...

Taken aback, I shook my head. I'd seen no sign of the paparazzi at the Pergola. My stomach felt uneasy at the thought of Elliot's paternity being speculated about by a trashy tabloid, although I got a slight kick out of being described as an "attractive brunette." For my grandparents' sake, I hoped my relatives back in India didn't read the British tabloids, or they would have a *lot* of questions.

"Is this true, Sophie? Well, not the bit about the baby daddy—*humph!*—but the bit about you two dating? I thought you were just friends?" Dad asked, watching my face closely.

Mum jumped in before I could answer. "Are you sure it's really wise to be spending time with this man? The paparazzi are terrible. You know what they did to Princess Di and now poor Meghan. I don't want anything to happen to you or Elliot."

My parents had mixed feelings when I told them about Chris. While happy I was getting out more, Mum had made it clear she would have preferred it wasn't with a world-famous celebrity. When she'd voiced some concerns about whether the paparazzi might hassle us, I'd rolled my eyes, but now I wondered if I'd been too hasty in brushing off her worries. On the other hand, it turned out Dad had seen all the *Muscle Man* movies, and he kept suggesting I invite Chris around, presumably so he could grill him about them. I had no intention of doing so.

"We *are* just friends, Dad. You know you can't trust anything in the tabloids. And Mum, it's fine. Chris isn't British royalty, and I'm definitely no Princess Di or Meghan Markle. We won't be chased down in cars or out of the country. We didn't even notice these photos being taken."

I studied the photos carefully. I had to admit, it did look like we were having a very romantic picnic. The photographer had captured us looking at each other and laughing. The way Chris stared at me did appear very...loving.

Was it possible he was interested in me? Josh and the

tabloids seemed to think so. Maybe I hadn't imagined the chemistry between us last night.

But, even if he was into me, would I really be interested in actually dating him? Deep down, I knew Josh was right. It wasn't reasonable to dismiss all men just because of my past bad experiences. Not all men sucked. And while I was telling myself I didn't have time for dating with Elliot and the new business, I had managed to see Chris almost every day last week without any issues.

But even if I ignored my no dating, no men rule, would Chris fit into my world? Sure, we got on well together, and he'd made a good impression on my friends last night. But he was so different from us. Rich, famous, probably straight —Josh had reported with disappointment last night that his gaydar wasn't picking up any bi vibes from Chris—and, not to mention, the sexiest man alive.

And would Elliot and I fit into his world?

I mentally gave myself a shake. I was getting ahead of myself. He dated singers and supermodels, not single mums who live in T-shirts and jeans covered in baby vomit.

It's all in your head.

My phone buzzed. I pulled it out, and my heart leaped. Chris. God, now I was nervous, my stomach flipping over and over. This whole crush thing was *not* pleasant. I walked into the living room to have some privacy from my parents, staring at the painting above the mantelpiece in the hope it would calm me down.

"Hi Sophie, thanks again for inviting me last night. I had a lot of fun. I hope you're not too dusty this morning?" Chris's voice was warm and friendly.

I couldn't help wondering where he was. Was he sitting up in his bed, bleary-eyed, or had he been up for hours, already worked out and sipping his second cup of coffee in the living room?

"I've felt better, to be honest, but it was so much fun. Definitely worth it!"

"So...um, listen, Sophie..." Chris sounded nervous. I tensed, wondering what was coming next. "I was ringing because some tabloids got hold of photos of us having that picnic last week and wrote some articles about us."

I breathed out. Oh, right. "Yeah, I saw. My Dad just showed me."

"I'm so sorry. It's so frustrating that I can't spend any time with a woman without everyone assuming it's romantic. How ridiculous! I'll speak to my publicist about the best way to handle this." I could hear the annoyance in his voice.

A hot flush rushed over my face. Of course, the idea of Chris and I together was ridiculous. I was stupid for thinking there might be something between us.

"It's fine. At least they were flattering photos, and they didn't name us. Don't worry about it," I said, trying to ignore the wave of disappointment washing over me.

"Still, it's really shitty and not fair on you guys at all. I'm so sorry. I'd just let my full-time security detail go because it didn't seem necessary over here. Now I'm having second thoughts." He paused, and then his voice lightened. "Hey, in other news, Alfie will be arriving on Thursday. Would you and Elliot like to come on his first walk to the Heath? And I was also thinking of exploring Kenwood House on Tuesday afternoon, if you and Elliot fancy an excursion."

Kenwood House was a gorgeous stately home on the edge of Hampstead Heath.

"I haven't been to Kenwood House for years. That sounds fun. And we're also in for Alfie's first walk on the Heath. That would be lovely. I can't wait to meet him."

Once we'd made arrangements, I hung up, unsettled. There were so many good reasons why I wouldn't want to date Chris, so why was I so bummed that he'd brushed off the idea as ridiculous?

I sighed. I needed to focus on quashing these feelings for him before they got out of control.

CHAPTER TWELVE

CHRIS

I WAS SIPPING my morning coffee on the couch in the now baby-proofed living room, practicing my accent. I hadn't been as diligent with my voice training over the past few days because I'd been pissed off about the tabloid articles. While Sophie had told me not to worry, it killed me that Sophie and Elliot had been dragged into my mess. I knew how protective Sophie was of Elliot. And I felt protective of them both.

A phone call from Jenny interrupted my thoughts. I answered it with a sense of foreboding. It was around midnight in LA, late for her to be calling me. Alfie was arriving this morning. In fact, he should have just been picked up by my driver and on his way over now. My heart sank.

"Hi, Chris, um, so, you know how Alfie was flying into London this morning?" Jenny asked, her voice wavering.

"Yes." My heart sank even further. I hoped he hadn't been injured during the flight or stopped at the border because his immunization papers weren't correct. An image of that little furball sitting on a metal chair, being interrogated by border control, popped into my head. If he could talk, he'd definitely incriminate himself—or at least pee on the chair and piss off border control.

"Well, he accidentally got on a flight to Barcelona instead."

My heart had now well and truly bottomed out. If I hadn't been so concerned about Alfie's wellbeing, I would have laughed at the way Jenny had made it sound like it was Alfie's fault. While Alfie had a lot of accidents, getting on the wrong plane wasn't an accident of his own making.

"What! How did that even happen? Is he okay? Where is he now?"

"Apparently, someone picked him up from Barcelona airport."

Nausea washed over me.

"What the hell? Does the airline know who it was? Surely they don't just hand over puppies without seeing some identification or proof of ownership."

"No. The person who picked him up signed for him, but they can't read the signature. The airline sent it to me, and I can't make it out either. I'll send it to you. I'm so sorry, Chris."

My heart softened slightly. I knew how fond Jenny was of Alfie, and she sounded genuinely upset.

"That's outrageous. Who would have picked him up? How could the airline let this happen? What the hell are we supposed to do?"

I didn't know where to start. How do you track down a missing dog, especially in a foreign country? I couldn't imagine the police would be interested, so I'd probably have to hire a private investigator, or maybe a pet detective, if they existed outside of the movies. I started looking up flights to Barcelona. I wanted to be there when Alfie was found, to comfort him and bring him safely back to London.

I'd felt badly enough about the little guy being alone in the plane for the trip from LA to London. And now he'd been picked up by a stranger, in a new country, with a different language. Although, to be honest, since he'd never learned any commands, he probably wouldn't notice the language change.

After hanging up on Jenny, I went to call Sophie to cancel our plans when an idea dawned on me. On our first walk together, Sophie said she missed traveling and spontaneity...

Could Sophie and Elliot come with me and make an adventure of it? Besides making the whole trip a lot more fun, Sophie spoke Spanish, which would be extremely helpful. And the rest of the time, she'd speak in English, which would be good for my accent.

If I planned everything carefully, I might have a chance of convincing her to come with me. Maybe going on a trip with a gorgeous, unavailable woman I was pining after wasn't the best idea, but...*screw it*.

I picked up the phone.

CHAPTER THIRTEEN

SOPHIE

"HEY SOPH, what's up? Is everything okay?" Josh sounded surprised.

"Sorry—yes, everything is fine, but do you have time to speak? I know you're at work." I'd just gotten off the phone with Chris and was agonizing over what to do. Josh was the only person I'd confided in about my feelings for Chris, so I hoped he could help. I paced the living room, fizzing with nervous energy.

"Yep, I'm on my lunch break."

"Okay, great. So, Chris just invited me and Elliot to go to Barcelona with him...this afternoon."

Elliot, vigorously sucking a blue pear-shaped teething toy on my parents' living room floor, was completely unaware he might be jetting off on his first overseas trip in a few hours.

"What! Why? That sounds...amazing!" Josh's voice bubbled with excitement.

"His dog was sent there by mistake, and he's going to find him. He wants me to come because I speak Spanish, and so I can help with his British accent so he doesn't get too far behind. And for company too. He's planned it all meticulously. Business class tickets and two rooms, one with a cot for Elliot, at a five-star hotel, which looks incredible." I'd Googled it as soon as I got off the phone with Chris. It looked more luxurious than anywhere I'd ever stayed. "He also arranged for a chauffeured car with a baby seat to pick us up from the airport and drive us around. He's booked for three days because he's not sure how long it'll take to find his dog. If we go, I'll need to pack right now. What do you think, should we go?"

Chris had made it clear there was absolutely no pressure on us to come. He said everything he'd booked was refundable, but I suspected he was just saying that to make me feel better if I decided not to go.

"That all sounds great. But you're not convinced. Why not?" I could hear Josh chewing on his lunch.

"I'm so torn. On one hand, spending three days alone with a man I've suddenly developed strong feelings for doesn't sound like a great idea, especially when he's not interested in me—and I'm not sure I'd want to date him even if he was. I'm also not sure how Elliot will take to traveling. He might hate it and make the entire trip really stressful. But then, I've always wanted to go to Barcelona. And while I've been too anxious to travel with Elliot so far, with Chris planning everything and being there too, it seems more manageable."

More than manageable, in fact. Appealing. The private car meant I didn't need to worry about maneuvering Elliot and the pram on and off public transport. Having Chris there to lug bags around and help with everything else would make it so much easier.

"And despite my feelings for Chris, I do enjoy his company. A lot. It might be good for Elliot to be exposed to a different environment. And did I mention the hotel looks incredible..."

Josh snorted. "I think you've just convinced yourself. But if you don't want to go, please tell Chris I'm more than happy to accompany him. I'll gladly throw all my energy into pet detecting if it means I can holiday with him in Spain. Just let him know separate rooms aren't necessary."

I laughed, rolling my eyes. "You're right, I've convinced myself. I'm gonna do it. I'd better call Chris then. Thanks for picking up. I knew I could count on you to help!"

I sprang into action and started packing, calling Chris on speakerphone to let him know Elliot and I were both in.

"EXCUSE ME, could I please have some more wah-tah?"

I choked on my own water, trying to suppress my laughter. To make up for missing his voice coaching lessons while we were away, Chris had decided to speak in his British accent for our entire trip. Despite his concerns, he was doing a great job. However, the shock of hearing him speak in perfect Queen's English when I was used to his relaxed, American drawl kept threatening to send me into hysterics.

We were on the plane, flying over Spain. Chris had been updating me on his progress canine sleuthing.

"So, don't laugh. My lawyer hired a private investigator specializing in missing pets–apparently pet detectives are actually a thing–and he'll start looking for Alfie tomorrow morning. He'll come to our hotel first thing so we can give him a briefing." Chris had been propping Elliot up against the inside of the plane so he could see the clouds out the window. Now, Chris was sipping his water while Elliot, sitting on his lap, tried to bite one of Chris's fingers. It killed me how cute Elliot and Chris were together. Ever since Josh's accident, they'd been getting along like a house on fire. And if I kept going with the fire analogy, seeing them together really poured oil on the flames of my feelings for Chris. I was glad he'd booked three seats, even though we only needed two, because Elliot had to be on our lap most of the flight. The plane ride would have been excruciating if we'd been pressed up close together. It was bad enough as it was.

"When we get off the plane, why don't we make a few enquiries at the airport, just in case we can fast-track the search? My Spanish skills were one of the reasons you invited me, so we might as well put them to good use and see if we can get anywhere this afternoon."

I wanted to do as much as I could to help find Alfie. Chris didn't seem his usual cheerful self, and it was clear he was worrying about his dog. I desperately wanted to see the sadness in his deep brown eyes replaced with their normal sparkle.

"Sure, that would be great, if you're up for it. Ouch!" Chris's smile turned into a grimace as Elliot chomped hard on his thumb with his three teeth.

The plane landed smoothly. Just like at Heathrow, a few travelers did a double-take when they saw Chris, nudging their companions and staring, but to my relief we weren't swarmed by fans like Chris had warned me might happen. He'd had his bodyguard accompany us through Heathrow, just in case, but hadn't made arrangements for Barcelona airport.

Once we got our bags and popped Elliot into the pram, we headed toward the service desk where a friendly airline employee greeted us. In Spanish, I explained our rather unusual predicament to the man who, according to his name badge, was called Carlos. I sensed Chris looking at me, impressed as the words rolled off my tongue, and couldn't help feeling pleased with his reaction. Spanish was coming back to me more quickly than I expected.

Carlos, a dog lover, was very sympathetic to Alfie's plight, shaking his head and apologizing on behalf of the airline. He showed us a picture of his own dog, a slightly manic-looking Chihuahua called Gloria Estefan.

"Awwww," Chris and I said at the same time.

"Please wait a minute. Let me see what I can do," he said, before disappearing through a door behind him.

"Did he just say that terrifying Chihuahua was called Gloria Estefan?" Chris whispered in his British accent, sounding like a befuddled Oxbridge professor, as soon as Carlos left.

I couldn't help laughing. "Wow, you are really committing to this whole British accent thing. And yes, that's exactly what he said."

"You should be lucky I'm not going full method actor on you and behaving like an arrogant duke circa 1815," he whispered, close to my ear. His breath gently tickled my cheek and sent a tingle down my body. More than one tingle. A lot of tingles... *Oh god.*

Was he being flirtatious, or was it all in my head? And why was the idea of him being a self-entitled duke turning me on? Gross, Sophie. Self-entitled men were usually everything I hated.

Carlos reemerged, smiling. He ushered us through the door and into a small, dark room filled with screens. A man hunched over them, studying them intently. He looked up and briefly acknowledged us before turning back to the images.

"Francisco will look for the recording of your dog being

picked up. You said it was this morning, around seven a.m.?"

I nodded.

Francisco fast-forwarded through CCTV footage of the cargo area, where pets and other packages that weren't accompanied by passengers were sent. Large suitcases, strangely shaped packages, and some smaller crates appeared. He paused when a larger crate arrived and zoomed in.

Chris and I peered over his shoulder, our bodies touching as we strained to see the screen. God, he smelled good—a woody cedar smell with a hint of musk. Warm and masculine. It took all my effort to focus on the screen instead of daydreaming about us on a romantic horse ride in Regency attire, his body pressed against mine as we galloped through a cedar forest.

"Does that look like him?" Francisco asked, pointing at the crate and, thankfully, breaking my thoughts.

We could just make out a small golden fluff ball looking frightened in the crate. Even though Chris didn't speak Spanish, he understood the question.

"That has to be him!" Chris exclaimed, returning to an American drawl in his excitement.

Francisco hit play, and we watched people pick up the various packages until only the crate and possibly one or two other packages behind a bin remained. A woman walked up, peered into the crate, looked at the label on the lid a few times, glanced around, and then picked it up. She carried it over to the counter to sign something and then walked away.

"Okay, that's who you are looking for," Francisco said. He rewound and zoomed in on the woman's face.

She looked confused and not at all like a dog-napper.

Chris and I leaned in further. I took a deep breath of cedar and forced myself to focus on the woman. While it was hard to make out her features, she had brown hair, and based on her outfit, I suspected she was in her twenties.

I had an idea. "She's looking around like she isn't sure this is the right parcel. Did any other packages arrive at the same time that weren't picked up? It looks like there may be at least one behind the bin there, which she might not have spotted." I said to Francisco, pointing to the screen.

"I'm sorry, I don't know. I just do security," Francisco replied, sounding apologetic. "But Carlos might be able to help you with that."

We thanked him and returned to Carlos, who called the cargo area. Two packages hadn't been picked up after this morning's flight from LA.

"I can't give you their details for privacy reasons, but both parcels are still sitting there. So, if you just happen to see them yourself, there's nothing I can do about it," Carlos said with a wink.

He gave us directions to the cargo area and wished us all the best, and we set off. When we arrived, another flight must have just landed, because the airline employees were offloading more packages and pets in crates. We searched through the packages sitting there for stickers indicating that they had come from LAX this morning. There seemed to be a lot of musical instruments and sporting equipment, with a smattering of pets, but they'd all recently arrived from Paris. Elliot was fascinated by a tabby cat in a crate near the pram, who kept hissing at him.

"Found one!" Chris said at the same time I found another. We sorted through the rest of the packages but didn't find any others from the LAX flight.

Both packages we'd found were addressed to women—Laura Suárez and Isabel Torres.

"Here's the signature of the person who signed for Alfie," Chris said.

We huddled over his phone, comparing it to the two women's names. The signature was such an unintelligible scrawl that it was impossible to tell whether it was Laura's or Isabel's. But at least now we had two names and addresses to work with. Chris typed the addresses into Google maps. I peered at his phone, our shoulders touching. God, he really smelled good. I inhaled deeply.

"It looks like we're in luck," he said, slipping back into his posh accent yet again. "They both live near downtown Barcelona. We still have a couple of hours before Elliot's bedtime, right? Why don't we take the parcels, deliver them to their owners, and see if either of them has Alfie?"

"They won't just let us take the parcels, Chris," I said with mild frustration. Ah, the confidence of the privileged white male.

He didn't seem fazed. "Given they let someone else take Alfie, they obviously don't pay that much attention to ensuring only authorized people pick up the packages. I'm at least going to try."

Chris, channeling the arrogant duke, strode up to the counter and signed for both packages. I held my breath, convinced he'd be stopped. I didn't fancy having to use my Spanish-speaking skills to defend Chris against charges of stealing packages. I had *not* signed up for a trip to the Barcelona police station. My heart beat faster as the attendant handed him some papers to sign. Surely she would notice Chris signing for two different people, both of whom were women. But she didn't bat an eyelid. I breathed out a sigh of relief as Chris walked back to me, holding the two packages and smiling.

Manuel, the driver Chris had hired for the trip, was waiting for us at the pick-up location. He greeted us with a big smile. His English was excellent, but when Chris started telling him why we were visiting Barcelona, the look of confusion on his face indicated he thought he'd misunderstood something. I confirmed in Spanish that no, his English wasn't failing, and yes, we were here on a mission to find a dog. I guessed it wasn't every day he got to help reunite a celebrity with his lost puppy.

Isabel Torres was the first stop along the way.

CHAPTER FOURTEEN

SOPHIE

THE EXCITEMENT really hit me as Manuel drove the car toward El Poble Sec, a neighborhood nestled between the foothills of Montjuic and the port. There was a distinct Mediterranean feel to the place. Old buildings with cast iron balconies painted in warm orange, peach, and yellow tones, the roll-up doors of the closed shops at the base of the buildings covered in colorful street art. A smattering of palm trees. People sitting out on the pavement or in leafy green squares, enjoying after work drinks. We most definitely weren't in London anymore.

The streets narrowed as we got closer to our destination.

"Here we are," Manuel said, pulling up outside Isabel's elegant old apartment building.

Manuel couldn't park on her street, so he dropped us outside the front door. I could smell the sea in the breeze. We must have been even closer to the port than I realized. We walked up the stone steps, and Chris pushed the buzzer in front of an imposing wooden door.

"Hola," a woman said.

My stomach fluttered with nerves. Just this morning, I'd

been hanging out at my parents' house with Elliot. Now we were in Spain, trying to track down a lost dog and delivering packages to strangers. What the hell were we doing?

"Hello, is this Isabel Torres?" I asked in Spanish.

"Sí," she replied.

"We have a package for you."

Chris and I looked at each other in anticipation.

We both exhaled as she buzzed us in. There was no elevator in the building, but thankfully, she only lived two floors up. Her package was heavy—I guessed books—so Chris carried it up the stairs while I held Elliot.

I knocked on the door, and an elderly woman answered. My heart sank. It was definitely not the woman we'd seen pick up Alfie's crate. But perhaps a friend or relative had picked it up for her? I peered over her shoulder, trying to inconspicuously look for signs of a dog, but all I could make out was a blue couch and a rug. No dog toys, water bowl, or half-chewed shoes.

Chris handed her the package.

"Oh, thank you! I meant to pick this up from the airport today, but my leg was playing up. I didn't realize the airline did home delivery." She looked Chris up and down with approval, completely oblivious to the fact he was a movie star, and then looked at me and Elliot with confusion.

Presumably it wasn't common for delivery men to be accompanied by women and babies in Spain.

I had to come clean. "We actually aren't from the airline. We're looking for our dog who we think was accidentally picked up from the airport this morning. We saw your package hadn't been collected and thought we'd drop it off to you and check that you hadn't picked up our dog by mistake."

She looked taken aback. "I'm sorry, I don't have your

dog. But I hope you find him soon." With that, she closed the door.

———————

MY STOMACH FLUTTERED AGAIN as we drove to Laura Suárez's apartment in the Gothic Quarter. Had I sent us on a wild goose chase? We could be relaxing at the hotel right now and letting the private investigator do his job, instead of being a parcel delivery service.

Manuel weaved his way through the narrow cobble-stone streets until we arrived at Laura's apartment block. She buzzed us into the dark, musty foyer dominated by a dilapidated staircase. I looked at it with some trepidation. Laura lived on the sixth floor, and there wasn't an elevator. At least her package, while bulky, wasn't as heavy as Isabel's —or Elliot for that matter—so Chris carried Elliot up the stairs, which creaked ominously under the weight of all his muscles, and I carried her package. I was panting by the time we reached her floor. Chris, who offered multiple times to carry both the package and Elliot, didn't break a sweat, patiently waiting for me to catch up at each landing. I thought I was in pretty good shape due to my regular walks on the Heath, but they hadn't prepared me for this.

We heard noises coming from the apartment as we approached–sneezes, crashes, and yelps that sounded like a dog. Chris and I exchanged excited looks, raising our eyebrows. This was promising, if slightly concerning.

A woman in her twenties, with long brown hair and red, watering eyes, opened the door, looking stressed and holding a tissue. My heart jumped. She looked like the woman from the CCTV footage.

A chaotic scene lay behind her. Ripped up paper and

socks were scattered on the floor. A bowl was upturned in a puddle of water. There were a few other puddles around the apartment which may or may not have been water. Chris had mentioned Alfie struggled with toilet training.

The woman started speaking quickly in Spanish, which I struggled to follow.

"I'm so sorry. My boyfriend just gave me a puppy, and he is out of control. My boyfriend moved to LA for six months and told me he'd sent me a package to cheer me up. I went to the airport this morning, and this poor dog was waiting for me. My boyfriend must have thought I needed company. I don't know what he was thinking! I can't even keep a houseplant alive, let alone a dog. And apparently, I'm allergic to dogs too." She stopped suddenly, as if remembering she was speaking to two complete strangers. Well, three if you counted Elliot, who seemed to be experiencing a sensory overload, his eyes so wide it looked like his eyeballs might drop out of his head. "Sorry, you mentioned you had a package for me?" She sneezed furiously, as if to prove a point. Elliot jumped in Chris's arms at the sound.

At that moment, a golden streak shot out the door and tried to climb Chris's leg.

"Alfie!" he exclaimed, bending down to pat him with his free hand.

"You know this dog?" Laura asked, her eyebrows furrowing with confusion. A shock of recognition flashed across her face as she looked more closely at Chris. "And... are you Chris Trent?"

"Hola," Chris said, smiling while he continued to pat Alfie. He looked at me expectantly, waiting for me to explain in Spanish.

"Yes, this is Alfie, Chris's dog. He was put on the wrong

flight. We think you may have accidentally picked him up instead of this," I said, handing her the parcel.

Laura looked horrified. "I'm so sorry. I couldn't read the label properly because it was torn. I just assumed it must have been my parcel since it was the only one left." She shook her head. "I can't believe I stole Chris Trent's dog. But I have to say, I'm very relieved he isn't mine."

I translated Laura's words to Chris.

"Please tell her not to worry. I'm just glad Alfie is okay," he said to me.

I passed on his message to Laura.

"Thank you so much for bringing this to me." She opened the package, looked inside, and then blushed and slammed the lid down. "I'll just put this away and get his leash and crate," she said hurriedly.

"Can you let her know that if Alfie destroyed anything, I'm happy to pay for it?" Chris asked, looking at the mess in her apartment with some trepidation.

I'd taken Elliot from Chris, and Chris was now giving Alfie, who seemed intent on licking Chris's face off, an enormous cuddle. Damn, they were so cute together. Chris's broad, buff, six-foot something frame a stark contrast to the small, goofy golden puppy in his arms. This was just painfully adorable. And I thought Chris couldn't get any more attractive.

Laura came back with Alfie's belongings, still sneezing. I translated Chris's request to her, but she refused to take any money. "It was completely my fault. And I'm sure in a few days, I'll be laughing about this and telling everyone about the time I stole Chris Trent's dog! Thank you for being so nice about everything."

"What do you think was in the box?" I asked, giggling, as we made our way down the stairs. Thankfully, going down was much easier than up. "Did you see her face? She looked mortified."

Chris laughed. "She most definitely didn't want us to see whatever it was. Maybe something else to keep her company?" He winked at me with a wicked grin on his face, setting off a throb between my legs. *God damn.* "But I'm quite happy remaining in blissful ignorance. Well, I guess I should cancel the private investigator, then. Now, back on the topic of careers. Have you ever considered a career as a pet detective?"

CHAPTER FIFTEEN

CHRIS

"WOULD you like a complimentary upgrade to our penthouse suite, Mr. Trent? It has two bedrooms," the receptionist asked, smiling over the marble desk in the hotel's foyer, completely oblivious that Alfie had just destroyed someone else's apartment.

Thankfully, all the excitement seemed to have caught up with him, and he was now sitting obediently next to me, looking as if butter wouldn't melt in his mouth. Perhaps he'd exhausted himself wreaking havoc in Laura's apartment.

I looked at Sophie. God, she was hot when she spoke Spanish. And I loved the way she'd thrown herself into finding Alfie. Her quick thinking had saved poor Laura from being further terrorized by Alfie and reunited us in record time. I was also having so much fun making her laugh with my stupid accent, although I might have gone a bit too far with my arrogant duke comment. I hadn't meant it to sound flirtatious, but I'd just got carried away in the moment.

The sensation of whispering into her ear, breathing in her scent, my body itching to be closer to hers, kept coming back to me. Damn it. This trip was not helping with my crush on her. I was more into her than ever.

With my attraction to Sophie growing even stronger, I wasn't sure sharing a suite together was a great idea. But Sophie's eyes widened at the mention of the penthouse, reminding me that most people weren't as jaded by luxury hotels as I was. And it's not like we'd be sharing a single room.

"Would you be happy to share the penthouse suite? I'm happy either way. If you'd prefer two separate suites, that's fine with me. I don't want Alfie to disturb you and Elliot." I looked at her, trying to keep my voice as neutral as I could in my British accent.

"The penthouse sounds amazing to me!" Sophie said, her eyes sparkling with excitement. "If you're okay with sharing with Elliot and me, that is..." Her voice trailed off.

"Of course." I smiled, happy and apprehensive that we were all going to be suitemates for the next few days.

When we opened the door to the penthouse, Sophie let out a gasp.

Okay, this was nice, even by my standards. The suite was massive. Two rooftop terraces with sweeping views over the Barcelona skyline. In the distance, I could make out the iconic church, La Sagrada Familia. Two living areas, with comfortable but stylish cream sofas and rugs. Each bedroom had its own bathroom decked out in marble with gold fittings. They had set a cot up in one bedroom. I was pleased it was the larger of the two rooms, so Sophie couldn't protest when I insisted she take it. There was even a water bowl and a dog bed for Alfie.

"Wow! This is incredible, Chris. The view, the furniture, the bathrooms, everything! I can't wait to enjoy it properly, but first, I should give Elliot a feed and put him to bed.

It's pretty late for him, and he's had a big day." Sophie disappeared into their room, holding Elliot who was rubbing his eyes vigorously.

I stood on the terrace, watching the sunset and waiting for Sophie to finish with Elliot. Seeing the hotel room through her eyes was a welcome reminder of just how lucky I was. I felt a twinge of guilt that I'd been so miserable the past few months when I was so privileged. Not many people could decide, at the drop of a hat, to fly to Barcelona and stay at a hotel that cost more per night than most people's monthly rent.

Sophie walked over to me and leaned against the railing. "He went out like a light. He must have been exhausted. How are you? Everything okay? You look very serious."

"Yeah, I was just feeling embarrassed about how sorry I felt for myself before moving to London. I have so much to be thankful for. I don't need to worry about money, I've got a job millions of people would kill for, I'm healthy and so are my family and friends, but despite all that, I've spent the last few months wallowing in self-pity." I was surprised at how easy it was to confide in Sophie.

Sophie looked at me, her brown eyes soft with concern. "You're being too hard on yourself. Breakups are difficult no matter how much money you have, or how successful you are. And most people can at least deal with their breakups privately. I can't begin to imagine how hard it must be having it plastered all over the news and social media. And those photos being made public must have made the whole thing even more difficult. You're allowed to wallow, even if you are rich and famous."

"Thanks for saying that." I paused. I'd wanted to ask her if she'd seen the photos since Cynthia had blown my cover, but it always felt too awkward to raise. Now was my chance.

I wasn't sure why it was so important to me, but I wanted to know. I swallowed. "Have...have you seen the photos?"

Sophie shook her head. "No."

My chest released some of its tension. "Well, it seems like you're in the minority. Most people I know who have seen them have told me not to worry, that I look good. But even if they are flattering, I just feel so...exposed having them out there. They were private photos that I never expected anyone but Vanessa to see."

Sophie nodded, looking sympathetic.

"And then there are those people—some people I know, but mainly people online who I've never met—who say I should have been more careful, that it was my fault for taking them and sending them to Vanessa. But I trusted her. She was on tour, we hadn't seen each other in person for over a month, so she asked me to send her some pics, and I did. I never thought for a minute that she'd share them with the world. I also thought she had enough integrity that she would have at least broken up with me before hooking up with someone else. And that obviously didn't happen either." I blinked tears away, hoping Sophie hadn't noticed.

Get it together, Chris, and just enjoy this lovely evening with Sophie by your side and Alfie safe and sound.

"It's not your fault. You were the victim here." Sophie rubbed my back with her hand.

Mitch was the only other person I'd confided in, but I knew I could trust him. Could I trust Sophie? That familiar sensation of paranoia crept through my body, setting me on edge. As I'd just been telling her, I was clearly a terrible judge of character. Just because I felt confident Sophie was trustworthy didn't mean she actually was. I shook off my thoughts.

Sophie has done nothing to make you doubt her, Chris. You need to snap out of this before you spiral.

"Right, that's enough wallowing for now!" I said with forced cheer. "I'm going to see if there is any champagne in the mini bar to accompany this sunset, and should we order room service for dinner?"

"Umm, yes please! All that detecting, and walking up those stairs to Laura's apartment, has really made me build up an appetite!" Sophie said.

I realized I was starving as well, which might in part explain why I'd gotten all emotional. Low blood sugar did that to me.

After we'd ordered room service, we opened the champagne and a packet of crisps from the mini bar. I cleared my throat.

"I would like to propose a toast. To your exceptional detective work and to Laura for keeping Alfie—and herself —alive long enough for us to find him. Cheers!" With two handfuls of crisps in me, I already felt a little better.

Sophie smiled at me as we raised our glasses and clinked them together. "Cheers! It was definitely a team effort. I couldn't have carried those parcels and Elliot up all those stairs myself!"

We watched the sunset on the balcony, sipping champagne and waiting for room service to arrive. This felt...very romantic. And Sophie was looking particularly beautiful, her face lit up by the fading pink sunset. I had to fight the urge to put my arm around her and draw her close. I inwardly groaned. Why did I keep putting myself in these romantic situations when there was no hope of any actual romance happening?

"So, is there anything you'd like to see or do while we're here? Apart from getting tickets to La Sagrada

Familia, I didn't plan anything because I wasn't sure how busy we'd be looking for Alfie, but thanks to you, our calendar is wide open." I was so caught up talking to Sophie about the photos that I'd forgotten to speak in my British accent, but I remembered halfway through the sentence and abruptly made the change from Chris to arrogant duke.

Sophie snorted with laughter so forcefully she spat champagne over the balcony.

"Oh my god. I hope I didn't spray any unsuspecting passersby. I think some champagne came out of my nose as well. You can't do that to me when I'm eating or drinking!" She gave me a teasing shove.

I straightened my back, put on my best incredulous expression, and dialed my accent up to the highest levels of pomposity. "Are you saying that you have a problem with *the duke?*"

Sophie dissolved into giggles. She looked at me, still laughing, and our eyes locked. Electricity zapped through me. Oh god. I wanted to walk over to her, place her champagne glass on the table, wrap my arms around her waist, pull her to me, and kiss her so badly it hurt.

A knock on the door interrupted my fantasy.

"That must be room service," I said with relief.

Not only had those crisps barely made a dent in my hunger, but I needed to stop thinking about Sophie in that decidedly non-platonic way.

"AND ANYTHING FOR YOUR SON? We can do a babycino?" the waiter asked me in English after taking our food order.

I looked at Sophie and winked. "Would *our son* like a babycino?"

"That sounds great, thank you." Sophie smiled, her eyes crinkling.

We were sitting at a cafe in a square full of tall palms which surrounded a decorative bronze fountain. We'd discovered this cafe, a short walk from the hotel, on our first morning here and had returned for our last lunch in Spain. Alfie stretched out at my feet in a warm patch of sun. It was probably the tenth time since we'd arrived in Spain that someone had assumed Sophie and I were a couple and Elliot was our son. We'd initially tried correcting them but had eventually given up.

It did almost feel like we were a family unit. We'd been spending all day together sightseeing, and in the evenings after Elliot had gone to bed, we would sit on the terrace chatting, looking out over the rooftops as the sky turned pink and then darkened. After the sun set completely, we would retreat to the couch, where Alfie would snuggle against Sophie. I was more than a little jealous of him. And also slightly offended that he seemed to prefer Sophie over me.

Since we'd been reunited, Alfie had been having the time of his life in Barcelona. I hadn't wanted him to feel abandoned again after what he'd been through, so we'd spent most of our time doing dog-friendly activities. We'd picnicked in historic Park Guell, with its striking colorful mosaics, got ice creams and walked along the beach, had coffee and pastries at dog-friendly cafes, and eaten tapas at restaurants with outdoor seating. Manuel had dog-sat Alfie while we visited La Sagrada Familia and did a private cooking class with a top Spanish chef, which I'd arranged as a surprise for Sophie.

We'd had a great time at the class. Well, at least Sophie and I had. Elliot hadn't been impressed initially but lightened up once we gave him a spatula to suck on and bash things with.

As our drinks arrived, a smiling woman in ripped jeans and an ironic band T-shirt approached our table. I braced, thinking she'd recognized me. *Damn it.*

But instead of making excited eye contact with me, she looked at my feet.

"He's so cute. Can I pat him?" She smiled at Alfie, and I breathed out.

To her, I was clearly just the owner of a very cute puppy.

Alfie looked thrilled at the prospect of more pats, and I relaxed. On this trip, Alfie and Elliot had been getting a lot more attention than me, and I wasn't complaining. At all. This wasn't the first time I'd thought someone was going to ask for a selfie, only for them to either pat Alfie or tell us that "our son" was very cute. I'd found people were less likely to recognize me outside of LA and New York, where they were primed to be on the lookout for celebrities, and Barcelona was no exception.

Another person, a man, slowed down and looked at us. Again, I tensed, and again, I quickly realized he wasn't looking at me at all. This time, he was focused on Sophie. The hairs pricked up on the back of my neck. I didn't like the way he stared at her. At all. Lascivious? Lecherous? Whatever it was, it was not okay.

He said something loudly in Spanish to Sophie and kept walking. Sophie glared at him. While I didn't understand Spanish, it was clear he'd said something insulting.

"What did he say?" I asked, a heavy feeling in my stomach.

"Don't worry about it," Sophie said. "Nothing I haven't heard before."

Shit. I was almost certain he'd said something racist or sexist or, even worse, both. Here I was, complaining about attention from paparazzi and fans—the by-product of a successful film career—while Sophie was dealing with actual prejudice and harassment. Blood drained from my face.

I should do something. Run after the man and give him a piece of my mind? Or say something to Sophie...I just had no idea what.

"Are you okay?" Sophie looked at me with concern.

"Sorry," I stumbled. "I just...I think I got the gist of what he said to you, and I...I don't know what to do. I can't believe people go around saying things like that. I mean, I guess I knew it happened but...I'm so sorry, Sophie." The thing is, I did know it happened. I'd even witnessed it before, but I'd never seen it happen to someone I knew and cared about. But seeing it happen to Sophie really affected me.

Sophie reached her hand over to mine and gave it a squeeze. "It can be shocking to witness racism. It's totally understandable that you're feeling thrown."

Heat rushed to my cheeks. I was such a fucking idiot. How did I manage to make this all about me? "I'm so sorry. You've just been verbally abused, and now you're comforting me. I should be helping you. Is there anything I can do?"

"Thank you, but I'm okay. You know, as part of our new business, we'll actually provide training to people—especially white people—on how to handle these types of situations because they can be so difficult. It's called bystander awareness training. People want to be good allies, to speak up against racism, but often don't know what to say. And in some cases, it may not be safe or beneficial to speak out. We want to give people the tools to help better navigate these situations. However, in this case, there wasn't much you could have done, especially since you can't speak or understand Spanish! I obviously could have said something, but to be honest, I just didn't have the energy. I want to relax and enjoy the rest of our time here, rather than spend time engaging with idiots."

I knew Sophie was right. I wouldn't have been able to effectively give that dickhead a piece of my mind given my lack of Spanish language skills. I'd probably just have made a scene which, knowing my luck, would have been caught on camera and shared around the globe. But I wished I could have done something. I vowed to read up on the subject when I got home so that, if it ever happened again, I could be a better support to Sophie.

"So, what's been the highlight of the trip for you?" Sophie asked, changing the subject.

"Hmmm, that's a tricky one. Probably all of the times you've spat your drink everywhere, snorting with laughter at my accent, even if it hasn't exactly instilled a lot of confidence in my abilities." The memories eased some of the heaviness in my stomach. God, I loved making Sophie laugh, even if it was unintentional. "What about you?"

"As amazing as the trip has been, I think it's got to be meeting this little guy." Sophie leaned down and gave Alfie a pat.

I smiled down at him, watching him melt under her hand.

While I'd been critical about Jenny's skills as a personal assistant, her skills as a dog trainer were stronger. She'd actually had some success toilet training Alfie—he'd had very few accidents since we had been reunited, and luckily none at all in the hotel.

Ah, Jenny. Thinking about her made my stomach more unsettled again. I turned to Sophie.

"Can I ask for your advice on something? I'm not sure what to do about Jenny. I don't know if she was to blame for the mix-up with Alfie—it might have been the airline—but even if she wasn't, she's dropped the ball so many other times I've lost count. I'm at the point where I don't want to ask her to do anything because it's faster and I'll get a better result if I do it myself. I like her as a person, but I think I'm going to have to fire her." I sighed. "But I really hate conflict, and the thought of firing her makes me sick too. I don't know what to do."

Sophie looked thoughtful. "I guess for most jobs you study beforehand or get on-the-job training, or both. And then if you screw up, you're performance managed. It sounds like she hasn't had any of that. From what you said, Vanessa just found her at a party and appointed her as your assistant, without any experience or training. Could you find a personal assistant course she could do and try giving her some constructive feedback? It wouldn't really be fair to fire her without giving her an opportunity to improve first. But, pro tip, definitely don't do it in your British accent, or she won't take it seriously." Her eyes twinkled.

I knew Sophie would have a sensible suggestion. "That's a good idea. Apart from working in cafes when I was younger, I've only ever known acting. And acting didn't really prepare me for the responsibility of managing employees. I guess I've been too conflict-averse to say anything to her, but you're right, I need to give her a chance first." I paused and smiled at her. "Speaking of my British accent...So, you've now spent almost three days with me speaking my best Queen's English. What's the verdict?" While I'd kept my tone light, I felt surprisingly nervous, waiting for Sophie's opinion of my accent.

"Absolutely magnificent! I couldn't distinguish your dulcet tones from that of the most noble of dukes," Sophie said, putting on a posh British accent before falling back into her normal voice. "In all seriousness, despite the fact it's sent me into hysterical giggles on multiple occasions, I think it's really, really good. It's come a long way in the last two weeks."

Relieved to have Sophie's stamp of approval, I breathed out, relaxed into my chair, and took another bite of the delicious seafood paella in front of me.

As we sat in the sun, enjoying our last lunch together in Spain, a rush of sadness that this would all be over soon washed over me. Back to the real world meant I wouldn't wake up to the sound of Sophie and Elliot playing in the living room each morning. Back to the real world meant I wouldn't get to spend every waking moment together with them. Not only would we be back to living in separate homes, but I'd be starting my grueling filming schedule next week.

With my accent endorsed by Sophie and feeling more comfortable being around other people after spending time out and about with her, I wasn't as nervous about starting filming as I had been. But I also wasn't as excited as usual. Filming would leave little time for hanging out with Sophie, Elliot, and Alfie. I'd miss our make-pretend family of four.

CHAPTER SIXTEEN

SOPHIE

"THE HOTEL WAS AMAZING! We had *two* rooftop terraces with incredible views over Barcelona! And we did lots of sightseeing. I'd been nervous about how things would go with Elliot, but having Chris and his driver there made it so easy. And, oh god, the tapas we had were just mind blowing! I bought a recipe book so I can try to recreate them for you sometime." I couldn't stop raving to Josh about it. The trip really had exceeded all my expectations.

"Yes, please! I'm getting hungry again just thinking about it."

We'd stopped in at our local cheap and cheerful Mexican restaurant for a quick dinner before volunteering at Pride House. Josh had scoffed down an enormous burrito with tortilla chips and a vat of guacamole. There was no way he could possibly be hungry. I was halfway through my giant burrito and was already eyeing it with defeat.

"And how did things go, you know, with Chris?"

I sighed. "Well, it certainly didn't help my crush on him. Elliot spewed on him one morning, and the image of him pulling his T-shirt over his head, his abs rippling and biceps flexing, is just playing on repeat in my head." It was *very* distracting.

"I would watch that movie," Josh said, licking his lips and discovering a stray bit of guacamole in the process, which he quickly devoured.

"I kept feeling chemistry between us. We'd touch, or look at each other, and it was like a taser hitting me in the chest." I groaned. "And, you know, it's not just physical. We get on so well. We spent three whole days together and never ran out of conversation. Not only that, everyone around us assumed we were a couple." It had given me a kick each time someone thought we were a little family—me, Chris, Elliot, and Alfie.

"But nothing happened?" Josh had gotten his phone out and put it on selfie mode to check he didn't have any other burrito remnants on his face.

"No." I shook my head. "And if he was interested, he had plenty of opportunity to say something. I mean, he's Chris Trent. He'd be so used to getting any girl he wanted, he wouldn't exactly be lacking confidence in that department." I took another mouthful of burrito and regretted it immediately. I pushed my plate away from me so I'd stop eating it.

"Well, you're not just any girl. And also, *you're* interested—even if you have some reservations—and *you're* not saying anything to him. Perhaps he feels the same way?"

"Mmmm," I said, not convinced. "Anyway, he started filming on Monday. Having some time apart might help me shake off these feelings, or at least put them in perspective. Should we make a move? I'm so full, and we'll be late if we don't head off in the next few minutes."

We stood up, tucking the red wooden chairs back under the rickety table, and went to pay.

Chris's filming schedule was punishing, with early morning starts and twelve-plus hour days. While we'd been exchanging regular text messages, I hadn't seen him since Monday night. So far, the time apart hadn't helped my feelings, but it was still early days. I was already missing his company. At least Alfie was providing Elliot and me with some companionship. One minute, he was aggressively wrestling with his stuffed white alpaca or zooming around my parents' house, much to Elliot's delight, and the next he was exhausted and snuggling up on the couch with me or, in the evenings when my parents were home from work, my dad. Chris had intended to have Alfie on set with him, but on their first day Alfie had barked at some horses, causing a mini stampede. Luckily, no one was hurt, but the event hadn't endeared Alfie to the director. After Chris told me what happened, I'd offered to look after Alfie during the week while Chris was filming.

"That reminds me. Chris invited me, Elliot, and Alfie to visit him on set next week, which should be fun. Dad is basically dying of envy and keeps on making up reasons why he should come with us."

We exited the restaurant and started walking toward Pride House, my stomach aching from burrito overload. Hopefully, the walk would help with digestion.

Josh laughed. "Ah, Mr. S. I can just imagine him cornering the director and peppering her with questions while she's trying to direct a critical scene." Josh had spent a lot of time with my parents. Because he was estranged from his family, he'd often spend Christmas holidays with us, and he was very close to them both. He knew how excited my dad could get about these things. "And how's your mum coping with your friendship, or whatever it is, with Chris now?"

I grimaced. "Mum wasn't at all thrilled with Elliot and I jetting off to Barcelona on a moment's notice, especially with a man I'd only known for a couple of weeks, or the paparazzi photos for that matter. I get it. She's just very protective of us, but it's a little irritating."

Mum's concerns were partially annoying me because I knew she had a point. I was a pretty private person and had a strict no-photos-of-Elliot-on-social-media rule because of privacy concerns, so I wasn't exactly thrilled about photos of us being in the news. And yes, it was a little strange to go traveling with someone I'd only known for a week and a half, but Mum didn't understand how quickly Chris and I had become close.

ALEX SMILED at us as we walked into Pride House. This was our third time volunteering, and it had already become one of the highlights of my week. I'd just said hi to Erin and her friends and sat down with another group of teenagers to have a chat when Alex cleared their throat to make an announcement.

"Hi everyone! Great to see so many people here tonight. As you all know, this place has gotten pretty run down. It wasn't in the best shape when it was gifted to us, and after the storm the other week, things have gotten even worse. There's been a lot of water damage to the back rooms, so we've had to cordon them off. Unfortunately, it's going to be expensive to fix it up, so we're hoping to do a fundraiser to raise money for repairs." Alex looked around the room and smiled. "We were thinking of doing a talent show and an auction. You're all a talented bunch, and we'd love everyone who's interested to take part, whether it's singing, dancing, comedy, or something completely out of the box! And if you know any businesses who could donate any items for the auction, please let me know."

A buzz filled the room as soon as Alex stopped talking, the teens clearly excited at the prospect of performing on stage.

I'd just finished brainstorming with two teens about potential talent show ideas when Erin walked up to me.

"Sophie, can I talk to you about something...in private?" Erin's eyes were watery, and her voice shaky.

Shit. My heart plummeted.

"Of course, why don't we grab those beanbags in the corner?" We walked over and plonked ourselves down on the bean bags. I winced. My stomach didn't appreciate the sudden movement. I shifted, trying to get comfortable. Why did bean bags always look so much more comfy than they actually are?

"What's going on?" I looked at Erin with concern.

"I came out to my parents on the weekend, and they took it really bad. Like, way worse than I'd expected. Apparently, while it's okay for other people's kids to be gay, it's not okay for their own daughter to be." Erin's voice broke, and a tear rolled down her face. "Dad gave me an ultimatum— 'stay straight' and stay at home, or live a life of sin and leave. I chose sin." Erin managed a weak smile.

I put my arm around her, furious at her parents. How could they kick a sixteen-year-old out on the streets?

"Oh my gosh, I'm so sorry, Erin. Where are you staying now?"

"I've been sleeping on the sofa at one of my friends' houses, but I can't stay there. Their sofa is really uncomfortable, and I can tell her parents aren't keen on me staying for too long. I spoke to Alex, and they're gonna call a charity that has housing for teens like me, to arrange something more long term." Erin took a deep, shuddering breath. "You said your parents were okay when you came out, so I guess you didn't go through anything like this?" She looked at me, wiping her tears away.

"I was very lucky that I didn't. But Josh did. Do you think it would be helpful chatting to him about it?"

I glanced over at Josh, who was miming pulling down his pants to a group of teenagers. While Josh had a silly side to him—which I loved, but also sometimes drove me up the wall—he was also a thoughtful, kind person, who could be serious when the situation called for it. Despite his current antics, he'd know exactly what to say to Erin. I just hoped the fact that Josh still hadn't reconciled with his parents, over a decade later, wouldn't be too much of a downer for her.

Erin gave me another weak smile. "Yes, that would be good, thanks."

"Just give me a sec." I awkwardly struggled out of the beanbag and walked over to Josh who, it turns out, was entertaining a group of teens with a story about the time his shorts fell down during a high school play.

"Sorry to interrupt. Josh, can I steal you away?"

Josh must have picked up something in my voice, or perhaps seen Erin and I speaking, because he immediately excused himself. I filled him in quickly as we walked back to the beanbags. Josh lowered himself onto a beanbag with significantly more grace than me, and spent the rest of the evening deep in conversation with Erin. As Erin was leaving, I went over to say goodbye and see if her chat with Josh was helpful. To my relief, while still understandably upset, she seemed slightly more positive about her future.

I found Josh stacking chairs after I'd waved Erin off.

"Urgh, poor Erin. My heart breaks for her. Thanks for talking to her, it sounds like it really helped."

"I'm glad. I think just hearing about how I still managed to go to university and found my own 'chosen family' gave her some comfort that her life wasn't over. I hope her parents will come around, but if they don't, at least she has the Pride House community to lean on for support." Josh paused as he lifted a chair high into the air, dropping it on top of a tall stack. "Thank god Alex is going to sort out accommodation for her. Having somewhere safe to stay will make a huge difference. I spent my first two years out of home couch surfing, sometimes sleeping on the streets, and it was really tough."

My chest contracted. Josh had never told me he'd had to sleep on the streets before. The idea of him or Erin being forced to do so made me sick to the pit of my stomach. "Once we've finished packing up, let's ask Alex if we can help out with this fundraiser. This whole thing with Erin has really drummed home how incredible Pride House is," I said.

The last chair stacked, Josh and I walked up to Alex, who was staring at a water stain on the carpet, frowning.

"I didn't see this before, but I think the flooding affected the carpet in here as well."

Josh groaned. "Urgh, that sucks. I'm so sorry about all the damage. I'll have a chat with my boss at work about whether we have any spare merchandise we can donate for the auction."

"That would be amazing. Thanks, Josh." Alex lowered their voice. "I didn't want to say anything in front of the kids, but it's actually quite serious. If we can't raise at least £20,000 by the end of the year, maybe more given the state of this carpet, we'll have to close the center. There are pretty serious plumbing and damp issues, and we can't let it get to the point where it's a health and safety hazard."

My heart sank. The thought of this fantastic space closing made the burrito sit even heavier in my stomach. What would happen to teens like Erin if Pride House closed down? "Oh no! That's terrible. Let us know if you need help organizing the event, or if there is anything else we can do."

"If you could help getting the word out, that would be great. I can MC the talent show, but if either of you, or both of you together, could be the auctioneers, that would be amazing!"

Josh looked at me, raising an eyebrow, and I nodded.

"Sure, we can do that. As long as we can bring two huge gavels to dramatically slam down whenever there's a sale," Josh said, vigorously miming smashing down a gavel in an attempt to cheer up Alex, who was rubbing their forehead and looking generally downcast.

Alex managed a weak smile. "Sounds perfect."

CHAPTER SEVENTEEN

SOPHIE

"WHAT THE HELL is going on there?" Rose asked as I fended off Alfie, who kept trying to lick my face or leap over me to lick Elliot's face, bumping my phone in the process.

"Sorry, when I suggested having this meeting via Zoom, I didn't take into account the fact that I'd be squashed in the backseat of a car between Elliot and Alfie, on our way to a film set, and that Alfie would be quite so...enthusiastic about everything." I pulled an apologetic grimace at Rose and Mia, who were both in their offices, pretending to do actual work for their companies rather than planning their escape.

"Ha! Don't worry, I think we've covered pretty much everything I wanted to talk about anyway—timing, potential clients, starting on a draft marketing plan. Mia, Soph, was there anything else you wanted to discuss?"

"Nope, all good here!" Mia said, smiling.

I straightened my phone and shook my head. "I'm good too. Next time, let's meet in person, and I'll leave Alfie at home!" I hung up, my chest filled with warmth. I was so excited about going into business with two of my closest friends.

Sitting in the middle car seat, trying to keep Elliot and Alfie away from each other while I spoke business with Rose and Mia, I hadn't been paying much attention to the scenery. The car initially crept through Hampstead, before picking up pace as it got onto the A406 and then the A40. Houses, shops, and trees whizzed by in a blur. But as the car slowed and the grand old manor came into view, a buzz of anticipation washed over me. Was the buzz caused by excitement at getting a behind-the-scenes look at a movie set, or the prospect of seeing Chris again? Probably both. We'd spent most of Sunday, his only day off last week, together, and I'd seen him when he'd finished early on Monday, but I already missed him. God, I was pathetic.

The car drove us to the security checkpoint where the security guards, after checking my identity, called someone on the radio to pick us up. Before long, a young woman with wavy blond hair falling a few inches below her shoulders, dressed in jeans and a T-shirt that said "Strong Female Protagonist," bounced toward us, smiling.

"Hi, I'm Jenny, Chris's assistant. You must be Sophie and Elliot. It's great to finally meet you. And I already know Alfie!"

Alfie bounded up to Jenny and started jumping all over her, looking thrilled to be reunited. Jenny bent down to give him a vigorous pat.

"Now Alfie, are you going to behave this time? Chris had to beg to have you back for a visit after last week's antics." She looked up at me. "I was so relieved you guys found him so quickly in Barcelona. Poor little guy. I hear you're primarily to thank for that, so thank you! Now, please come with me, and I'll take you to Chris's trailer." She started heading back the way she'd come, holding

Alfie's leash, making sure she kept him well away from the horses.

Alfie haphazardly leaped around, overwhelmed by all the exciting smells and the hive of activity.

So, this was Jenny. On first impressions, she seemed friendly and outgoing, and she clearly loved Alfie, which immediately put her in my good books. I could see why Chris hadn't wanted to fire her, even if she hadn't been doing the best job. Chris had mentioned that he'd chatted with Jenny about some areas for improvement, which she'd taken surprisingly well. He'd also found an intensive week-long executive assistant course starting next week in London. While aimed more at executive assistants for CEOs and other senior corporate roles, they'd both thought it would still be useful.

As we walked, I felt almost as overwhelmed as Alfie. The place bustled with activity. I had to focus hard on not ramming Elliot's pram into the crew members, actors in period outfits, and shining horses that strode purposefully around us. Jenny led us to an area where there were several large trailers and knocked on the largest. It was bigger than a school bus and painted a shiny silver and white.

"Chris? Sophie and Elliot are here," Jenny yelled.

After a pause, the door opened.

Oh god. I swallowed. I wasn't prepared for this.

Chris appeared in full period costume—white pants with knee-high boots, a dark fitted tailcoat that went to his knees, with a waistcoat and white shirt that ruffled around his neck underneath.

It was the arrogant duke in the flesh.

And he was *hot*.

My heart started pounding in my ears. I'd always had a

thing for period romance, and seeing Chris dressed like Mr. Darcy was just too much.

I stood there, my mouth open.

The world seemed to shift beneath my feet, my legs almost buckling under me. Holy crap. I wanted Chris to sweep me off my feet. I wanted him to carry me up the trailer stairs and throw me onto something—a couch, a bed, even a table would do. I wanted *him*.

"Hello! Welcome to nineteenth century England." Chris smiled as he strode down the trailer steps and gave Elliot and Alfie both a pat on the head. Thankfully, he seemed completely oblivious to my reaction.

"The timing has worked perfectly. I just finished shooting my first scene and don't have another one for a couple of hours, so we have plenty of time to hang out. Since we're in between scenes at the moment, I can show you around." He looked at Jenny. "Jenny, are you okay to mind Alfie while I give Sophie and Elliot the tour? I don't want him to pee on a period lamppost or scratch anything in the manor after last week's shenanigans."

Jenny nodded happily.

"Great, thanks!" Chris turned to me. "Well, if you're ready, let's go to the London set first."

He strode off, and I followed meekly—out of character for me—struggling with the pram as we walked over slightly muddy ground. Was I imagining things, or had his usual walk been replaced with a confident swagger befitting an arrogant duke?

But suddenly, he stopped and turned. "Sorry, here I am, racing ahead. I got caught up in the excitement of getting to show you two around. Why don't I push the stroller? This mud isn't great, and there'll be some cobblestones to navigate soon."

I relaxed slightly. That was the Chris I knew. I happily let him take over the pushing. Rose would probably bristle at what she called "benevolent sexism"—like guys holding doors open for women. But since Chris, with his Muscle Man muscles and height, could handle the pram a lot better than me over this terrain, I wasn't going to object.

Chris led the way to two replica London streets in a field next to the manor. When we reached the first one, my jaw dropped. To my eyes at least, it seemed incredibly realistic. One cobblestone street was lined with an assortment of shops—Jones the Draper, the Fashionable Clothes Warehouse, Grose's Milliner, Arpthorpe's Furier, to name a few. There were also street carts piled with fruit, coaches waiting for their horses, and old lamp posts. The details were astonishing, from the black bowler hats, ladies' bonnets and gloves displayed in the windows of Lillington's Hat, Hosiery, and Glove Warehouse, to the aged sign for Bromstead's Perfumery hanging over its entrance door.

"Wow! This is so realistic. It's like I've been transported back two hundred years. But it also looks so strange, sitting out here in this muddy field, like it's fallen from the sky." I felt out of place walking around in nineteenth century London in jeans and a T-shirt, next to this handsome man decked out in Regency garb, even if he was pushing a very modern-looking pram.

"They've done a great job, haven't they? They've made a huge effort to make sure everything is accurate for the period, down to the smallest detail, and it really shows." Chris looked proudly around.

I kept sneaking glances at Chris, trying to not too obviously check him out. He'd taken off his tailcoat while we walked, and his butt looked incredible in his trousers...or were they called breeches? They appeared to have been perfectly tailored to his body. An image of him pushing me up against Jones the Draper's facade and reenacting one of his steamier romance scenes, thrusting with that taut, firm butt, flashed into my mind, sending my heart racing. Trying to collect myself, I took a deep breath.

After I'd peered into all the shop windows, admiring the displays, Chris took us to the other "street," which contained a row of grand townhouses. "This is where the duke lives when visiting London," Chris said, pointing to a particularly large townhouse. While impressive, they weren't as interesting as the street of shops.

"So, that's London—now for my country house!" Chris led the way up a gravel driveway lined with manicured trees to the manor, an imposing three-story limestone building, with a gray lead roof and grand staircase leading up to a large wooden door. Twenty times the size of my parents' house, it looked like it had come straight out of a Jane Austen novel.

We carried the pram up the front steps to the entrance, Elliot shrieking with glee as it bounced up and down.

"Please, come in. Welcome to my humble abode," Chris said in his British accent, flinging the front door open.

"Humble?" I snorted as I stepped through the door and looked around the great hall, with marble floors, a grand staircase, chandeliers, and gloomy portraits of people long dead festooning the walls. A faint musty scent made my nostrils twitch. "Now *this* looks like it'd have a secret passage or two."

"Ah, the magic portal inspector is back!" Chris said, his mouth twitching.

He paused beneath a drab painting of a dour old woman. "My beloved grandmother, may she rest in peace." He clasped his hands and wiped a fake tear from his eye.

I laughed. "I'm so sorry for your loss, your grace."

Chris ushered me into a large room, decorated with ornate green wallpaper, red curtains and drapes, a wooden sideboard and chairs, an uncomfortable-looking chaise lounge, a grand piano, and a harp.

"Please, make yourself at home in my drawing room," he said, still in his pompous British accent, before switching back to his normal voice. "This is where most of the action takes place in the house. We even get up to a bit of hanky panky on that chaise lounge." He grinned and gave me a wink.

"Ha! I was just thinking how uncomfortable and rickety it looked. Are you sure it's strong enough to withstand your...hanky panky?" A flush of warmth spread across my cheeks.

"There's only one way to find out!" Chris grabbed my hand, dragging me toward the chaise lounge.

Oh. My. God.

My heart pounded with adrenaline. Did he want to make out with me on the chaise lounge? Despite my misgivings, if he made a move right now, I wouldn't hesitate. Who could say no to hanky panky with Mr. Darcy crossed with an arrogant duke?

Chris pulled me onto the chaise lounge and looked into my eyes, his hand still holding mine. He had such deep, warm, brown eyes. I'd never looked at them this closely before. Were those flecks of gold?

Oh God. Was he learning forward slightly? Should I lean forward too? My heart almost jumped out of my chest. Was he going to kiss me? Surely, surely, I wasn't imagining this chemistry. I bit my lower lip, moistening it in the process, and tentatively started to form my lips into a pout, ready for him.

And then he dropped my hand.

And proceeded to bounce comically on the chaise lounge, as if he were exercising on a fitness ball, a goofy expression on his face. My heart, stomach, everything, plummeted.

Yep, I'd imagined it. I was such an idiot.

"Yeah, we should be fine! I pronounce this chaise lounge hanky panky proof," Chris said, bouncing energetically while it creaked ominously.

Chris was being so over the top that I couldn't help but laugh, but inwardly I groaned. My feelings for him right now were excruciating.

"On a more serious note," Chris said, bringing his face only inches from mine. What was he going to say now? He had a strange expression on his face. He opened his mouth and then paused for a moment. "Are you hungry?" he asked abruptly, his tone changing. "They're serving lunch now, so we can grab food if you are. It's usually pretty good."

"Sounds great!" I sprang off the chaise lounge, desperate to put some distance between me and Chris and breathe in some fresh air, which I hoped would help clear my head. We retraced our steps down the stairs and the driveway, picked Alfie up from Jenny so Chris could introduce him to some of the cast and crew who'd missed him last Monday, and walked toward a tented area near the trailers.

The tents sheltered long tables covered in large bowls of salads, plates of meat, sandwiches, and fruit platters. Crew members and actors piled their plates high and took their seats at tables nearby. After we helped ourselves, Chris led us to a table, gently touching my back to direct me. As usual, Chris's touch sent a shock through my body. I sighed. These physical reactions were really starting to get to me.

We sat at the end of a long table, Elliot in his pram and Alfie at Chris's feet, searching for dropped food. Focused on ensuring Elliot was comfortable, I didn't register who was sitting across from us. I'd just taken an enormous bite into a baguette overflowing with brie, tomato and prosciutto, when Chris introduced us.

"Sophie, I'd like you to meet Clare. Clare, this is my friend, Sophie, who I was telling you about, and her son Elliot. And the infamous Alfie is somewhere under the table. Alfie!" Chris bent his head to look for him, leaving me staring at Clare Caldewell across the table. *The* Clare Caldewell. The Oscar and multi-BAFTA-winning Clare Caldewell.

Starstruck, I desperately tried to chew the baguette down without looking like a complete idiot. I may not have known who Chris was when I first met him, but I knew who Clare Caldewell was. Every Thursday night for three years, she'd transfixed British audiences by playing a tortured young detective tracking down a serial killer. She skyrocketed to fame locally before embarking on a successful international film career that had garnered her two BAFTAs and one Oscar.

Clare was an incredibly versatile actor. She'd won her Oscar for a devastating portrayal of an American midwestern woman who lost her family tragically in a fire and had to rebuild her life, but she'd also starred in one of my favorite enemies-to-lovers rom coms set in New York. In both films, she had an impeccable American accent. I knew Clare was co-starring with Chris, and I'd been excited at the prospect of potentially getting a glimpse of her, but I hadn't thought I'd actually get to *meet* her. And now here she was, sitting directly in front of me while I hastily chowed down the baguette. She wore a dressing gown over a period dress with ornate beading and looked absolutely stunning.

Clare gave me a dazzling smile, revealing a perfect set of gleaming white teeth. "So nice to meet you. I hear you're to thank for Chris's British accent being so good!" Clare said warmly.

I swallowed the last piece of baguette in one big gulp, the lump traveling down my throat uncomfortably. "I think all the credit needs to go to his voice coach. I just taught him how to say water, arse, and stupid." I laughed nervously and winced. Now that was a *stoopid* thing to say.

She laughed, tossing her flowing brown hair back. "Three very handy words."

Wow, she was lovely and beautiful. How had I even thought for a minute Chris was interested in me? Why would he be when he was around women like this all the time?

Come to think of it, I was pretty sure Clare was single. And, from what I'd gathered from tabloid headlines, it was common for co-stars to hook up in real life. I wondered if that would happen to Chris and Clare...

You don't even want to date him, Sophie. Stop being so dramatic.

After Chris retrieved Alfie from under the table to introduce him to Clare, who'd missed both Alfie and the horse stampede last week, Clare and Chris started talking about their holiday plans. They had a break over Thanksgiving. Chris was flying home to Chicago, and Clare was planning to hire a private jet to fly her family to the south of France. That sparked a discussion about private jets, a topic that, unsurprisingly, I could not contribute to.

My stomach was queasy, and I didn't think it was indigestion from forcing down that gigantic bite of baguette too quickly. Private jets seemed like a complete waste of money. It pained me that people spent money on extravagances like that, when Pride House might have to close because of lack of funding. How could anyone justify spending tens of thousands of dollars on a few hours in the air, when so many people in the world were in need? I bet a one-way trip on a jet to the south of France would cost more than what Pride House needed to stay afloat.

And were Clare and Chris flirting with each other? Clare was touching her hair a lot, and Chris seemed to be smiling more than was necessary. A knot rose in my throat. Private jets weren't *that* funny. In fact, they weren't funny at all.

I looked around, trying to distract myself. Wow, they hadn't taken a leaf out of Shondaland's *Bridgerton* and done color-blind casting, or hiring more generally, for that matter. All of the actors, and most of the crew, were white. And there were a *lot* of men. Chris was right—the film industry could do with help from a diversity and inclusion perspective. But with his star power, couldn't he help? I remembered stories of male stars insisting their female co-stars got equal pay. He could do something similar.

I forced down the rest of my baguette, smiling and nodding along with Chris and Clare's conversation and trying to hide the mixed bag of emotions threatening to overpower me. There was discomfort over the current conversation and lack of diversity, admiration for Clare who —despite her predilection for private jets—did seem, I had to admit, quite lovely, and jealousy, though I hated to admit it. I let out a breath in relief when Elliot started to get restless and I realized he was due for a feed. An excuse to escape.

"Chris, Elliot needs a feed. Is there somewhere quiet we

could go?" Now it was my turn to sound abrupt, but I'd had enough.

"Of course, let's go back to my trailer. I should start getting ready anyway." Chris shoveled a few last mouthfuls of food down. Did a look of concern flit across his face, or was I imagining it?

We said goodbye to Clare, cleared our plates, and walked back to Chris's trailer.

I parked the pram next to the trailer steps and carried Elliot, who was really starting to fuss, up the stairs. I did a double-take when we entered. For some reason, I'd been expecting the interior of the trailer to look like the caravan my parents had rented one summer holiday—cheap linoleum floors, laminate cabinets and dusty curtains. Instead, it had polished hardwood floors, a sparkling kitchen with marble worktops, a wooden bar cabinet presumably stocked with booze, and a living space almost as big as my parents' living room, lined with plush couches.

Again, I took the extravagance of it all as a slap in the face. This trailer probably cost as much as a real house. *Sophie, you're clearly in a terrible mood. You weren't complaining the other week about the luxurious penthouse in Barcelona and flying first class.* I had an inkling that my disappointment on the chaise lounge and jealousy over Chris and Clare were more to thank for my bad mood than anything else. I gingerly took a seat on the couch and fed Elliot while Chris got ready for his scene.

Elliot stopped feeding, milk drunk and pink-cheeked, and gave an impressive yawn.

"Well, we should head off now," I said with forced cheer. "The little man is due for a nap. He's not used to this much excitement!"

That look flashed across Chris's face again. A twinge of guilt about how I was behaving prodded me in the chest.

Chris followed me down the stairs. Elliot's yawns became even more dramatic, and by the time I had exited the trailer and put him back in the pram, his eyes were firmly shut.

"Since he's sleeping now, do you want to hang around and see part of our scene being filmed?" Chris asked.

I glanced down at Elliot, who was sound asleep and emitting adorable little snores. God, he was cute. He'd most likely wake up if I put him in the car, so I was probably better off staying at the set until he woke. Plus, I *was* interested to see filming in action. And I really needed to stop being such a grump after Chris had gone out of his way to show us around.

"That sounds good. He'll probably wake in about forty minutes, so we'll come for the first half hour and scurry away before he starts screaming and ruins your take!"

"Sounds like a plan! After last week's incident with Alfie, I think the director would be less than thrilled if that happened."

The scene was set in the formal gardens at the back of the manor. Chris hadn't told me anything about what they were filming, but it became apparent as soon as I heard the words "Lights, camera, action" that it was a romantic scene between Chris and Clare's characters. They were standing facing each other and holding hands. My heart sank.

Of course, just what I need.

"Eliza, I cannot go on any longer with this charade. From the moment I saw you, I have been transfixed by your wit, your good heart, your headstrong nature. My heart is yours. Do you feel the same?" Chris gave Clare a look of desire and longing, and a pain shot into my chest.

"I do, but—"

Before Clare had finished her sentence, Chris had drawn her to him and was passionately kissing her. He grabbed her hair, and she clutched his back, hungrily devouring each other. The chemistry between them was undeniable. A lump formed in my throat. I'd seen enough.

So, it appeared, had Alfie, who had been sitting happily in Jenny's arms next to me, watching the scene being filmed. As their lips locked, he jumped out of her grasp and raced toward the intertwined couple. Chris and Clare were too caught up in their kiss to notice the bundle of fur hurtling at them. Alfie leaped into the air. I could have sworn he was trying to break them up, like a teacher at a school dance when the students' PDA got out of hand, but he misjudged his leap and got tangled under Clare's voluminous dress. Trapped in fabric, Alfie panicked, jumping and yelping, almost toppling Clare over.

Everyone had frozen, watching Alfie's mad dash in horror, but once Clare started teetering precariously, the set leaped into action. Jenny, looking aghast, and three other crew members raced toward Clare and Chris. Chris got down on his knees, trying to untangle Alfie from Clare's dress. I stood there helplessly—with Elliot in the pram, there wasn't a lot I could do, since I wasn't going to leave him unattended. As Chris got further into Clare's dress, the dark cloud that had been hanging over me for most of the set visit lifted slightly. Despite my discomfort at their kiss, I had to fight the urge to giggle at the sight of Chris burrowing around under layers of fabric, his perfect tight butt high in the air, his upper body hidden under Clare's dress, and poor Clare's shocked face.

The director, a serious-looking woman with short brown hair and thick black glasses, had a pained expression on her face as she watched it all unfold. "That dog just ruined the entire take, and they were nailing it too! He better not have damaged her dress, or it'll throw out the whole schedule. Not to mention the cost...I'm going to kill Chris. He promised me he'd control the dog this time," she muttered to the assistant director standing next to her.

All of the yelling and barking woke Elliot up, who started screaming at the top of his lungs. I unbuckled him quickly and bounced him in my arms, trying to calm him down. I gave the director an apologetic grimace as she glared at us.

Chris, Jenny, and some other crew members finally untangled Alfie, Chris emerging from under Clare's petti-coats looking disheveled. He'd definitely need hair and makeup before filming proceeded. Much to everyone's relief, Clare's gorgeous gown wasn't damaged—Alfie had only got caught up in the petticoat underneath, although he had put a run in her stockings.

Alfie retrieved and Elliot awake and happy back in his pram, I decided it really was time to head off. I didn't want to watch them re-film that kiss, and I was fairly confident the director had just banned Alfie, and possibly Elliot, for life.

CHAPTER EIGHTEEN

SOPHIE

I GROANED. "I'm usually a pretty level-headed person, but I was all over the place. It was a complete emotional rollercoaster. One minute, I was ready to jump Chris, and then the next, I was really irritated that he could actually hold a conversation about private jets. And then I was filled with intense jealousy seeing him and Clare making out."

Josh and I were in my parents' living room, sitting on the floor playing with Elliot. Josh had dropped around ostensibly to visit Elliot and say hello to my parents, but mostly to drill me about what it was like on set.

He started singing Beyonce's "Crazy in Love" at Elliot, who giggled with glee, waving his hands about. While pleased Elliot was a Beyonce fan, I was less impressed with the implications of Josh's song choice.

"Josh! I'm not in love with him. Okay, I might have a small—a *very* small—crush on him, but that's not love." Describing it as small might have been an undersell. To be honest, I hadn't been able to stop thinking about Chris. Each time my phone pinged, I'd jump up to check it immediately in case it was him. I constantly wondered what he was doing and had to resist the urge to message him silly updates about Elliot and Alfie all the time.

In fact, I'd been missing his company so much, I'd resorted to watching all his movies with Dad in the evenings, even though Dad drove me up the wall with his constant questions and comments. "Are his muscles that big in real life, Sophie, or do they CGI them?", "He is such a good actor, see the way he looks at her right there...Let me pause it so I can show you..."

But just because I missed Chris didn't mean I was in *love* with him...right?

Josh had stopped singing but was still humming the tune as I continued.

"It's a small crush, which I just need to get over so I can enjoy hanging out with him without these distracting thoughts. Anyway, I'm sure there's something going on between him and Clare. You can't fake that kind of chemistry."

"You're overreacting. You said you felt real chemistry between you two on the chaise lounge as well, right? So why do you assume the chemistry in the scene with Clare was real and not his chemistry with you? Perhaps you're underestimating his acting skills." Josh, bouncing Elliot on his knee, was getting so riled up that poor Elliot looked like he was a jockey in the Royal Ascot Races.

"Elliot's going to vomit if you keep that up! You didn't see them together. I mean, even Alfie picked up on it. I'm pretty sure that's why he ruined their take."

A lump in my throat, I looked up at the painting above the mantelpiece. The vibrant still life of gerbera daisies in a decorative red vase, striking blue and green wallpaper behind it, had always had a calming effect on me—although recently, not so much. Trying to relax, I focused on the thick brush strokes of paint.

"Earth to Sophie! Hello? Are you okay?" Josh's voice sounded soft with concern.

"Yeah, sorry. This whole Chris thing is just messing with my head. And lately, I can't stop staring at the painting and wondering if I'll ever have something as special as what my parents have."

I didn't need to explain it to Josh. My mum had told him the story of the painting many times before.

Mum, a twenty-year-old art history student, had been walking down Queen Street in Oxford when a sudden downpour forced her to take shelter in an art gallery. The painting —a warm, colorful, welcoming contrast to the wet, cold, and dreary weather outside—was the first thing she'd seen on entering. She'd wandered around the gallery multiple times, waiting for the rain to stop, but kept being drawn back to the painting of the gerberas. The price was well beyond what she could afford, but after the rain subsided and she left the gallery, she couldn't stop thinking about it—or talking about it, according to Dad—who usually piped up at this point, patting her affectionately as he rolled his eyes.

Dad had saved up to buy it as a surprise first anniversary present, sacrificing his weekly cinema habit for months and taking on extra tutoring jobs. According to Mum, it had made her fall even more in love with Dad. Dad jokingly claimed he regretted setting the bar so high for their first anniversary present and that nothing he had given her since had been so well received.

To their surprise, the artist's career skyrocketed a few years later—their works now hung on the walls of The National Gallery and the National Portrait Gallery. While the painting was worth a lot these days, Mum had no interest in selling it. It had too much sentimental value. I'd always loved the painting, but recently it had been a bitter-sweet reminder of what I was potentially missing out on. As much as I told myself I was happily single, it would be amazing to have the sort of relationship my parents had.

"Well, I hate to break it to you, but if you continue with your 'no dating' policy, then you definitely won't have a relationship as special as your parents. Or any relationship, for that matter."

"I know, I know." I sighed. "I can't handle having any more emotional rollercoaster rides at the moment. I need to stamp out this crush. That Sophie at the set isn't me, or, at least, isn't who I want to be."

"Uh huh. And how are you planning to do that?"

"Well, I've done some research..."

Josh raised an eyebrow.

"Fine, by research I mean just Googled 'How to stop being attracted to someone.'"

"Okay, and what did Doctor Google say?"

"I didn't like most of the suggestions. But...you'll be happy to hear that they did say dating other people might help...So, I was thinking of putting my no dating policy aside for a while and dipping my toes back into the dating pool again, women only. I'll test out if I can date while still keeping Elliot and the new business as my priority. Maybe it won't be as hard as I think. I mean, I saw Chris all the time before he started filming, and it didn't interfere with that other stuff, so it might be doable. And you're right—if I want a happily ever after like my parents, I need to actually put myself out there."

"Dating other people, hey? Well, while I still think you and Chris would be super cute together, if you're not willing to pursue it, then I may have a potential suitor for you." Josh looked thrilled. Was he just desperate for me to couple up? "Do you remember my friend Pete?"

I looked at him, surprised. "Um, yeah. Isn't he married?"

Yikes. Josh must be *super* desperate if he's trying to set me up with a married man.

"Yes, but I met his sister, Nicole, at his birthday party on the weekend, and she was saying she found it hard to meet women. She's a doctor around our age. She loves kids and seems really nice. If you're considering jumping back into the dating pool, she would be perfect for you! I'd been thinking about setting her up with Rose, but I'll give you first dibs."

"You're too kind," I said sarcastically.

Josh, ignoring my comment, unlocked his phone. "Let me see if I can find a photo." Thirty seconds later, he shoved a photo of a smiling brunette in hiking gear in my face. "So, what do you think? Should I set you guys up on a date?"

I paused. A date with a cute doctor might be just what I needed to move on from Chris.

"Sure, I'm in."

THAT WAS how I found myself sitting at my favorite local wine bar a week later, waiting for Nicole to arrive. In winter, I loved sitting in the wooden booths near the cozy fireplace, but it didn't hold the same attraction in summer, so I'd secured a spot on bar stools by the front window, looking out over the busy main street in Hampstead. It was a perfect place for people-watching if we ran out of conversation. I hadn't been to the bar since I'd gotten pregnant. It was strange to be back here again, even stranger to be back here for a date. I kept nervously checking my phone in case Nicole had texted me to cancel at the last minute. To be honest, I was sort of hoping she would cancel so I could go back home and hang out with my parents, as sad as that sounded. This suddenly seemed like a really stupid idea.

I'd casually mentioned to Chris I was going on a date when we'd been hanging out over the weekend, not giving any details. I'd studied his face, trying to work out how he felt about me dating, but I couldn't tell. Maybe he'd seemed surprised but not, to my disappointment, devastated. At least on the weekend, I'd been more like my usual self with him again—back to lusting after him, but without the jealousy and disapproval. While relieved those feelings had vanished, I was still desperately waiting for the lust bit to vanish as well.

As I checked my messages for the fifteenth time, Nicole walked through the front door of the bar. I hurriedly put my phone back in my handbag and stood up to greet her. She was dressed in tight black jeans, ankle boots, and a cute leather jacket that perfectly fitted her petite frame. Her brown hair fell in waves around her face. She was gorgeous. My stomach fluttered.

Nicole gave me a warm smile that immediately put me at ease. "You must be Sophie. It's so lovely to meet you. Josh has told me so much about you."

Nicole was even more appealing than Josh had made her sound—smart, vivacious, and clearly kind-hearted. Over the next two hours, she told me about her time working with Médecins Sans Frontières at a refugee camp in South Sudan, quite a contrast to Chris's privileged lifestyle. We bonded over the latest season of RuPaul's Drag Race and our love of travel. She asked about Elliot and was suitably impressed by the photos of him. She ticked all the boxes and yet...I couldn't get Chris out of my mind.

All night, I bit back starting sentences with, "When Chris and I..." or "My friend, Chris, thinks..." I was like one of those annoying people in relationships who couldn't stop talking about their significant other, except I wasn't in a relationship. Was this a bad idea? I'd convinced myself I was genuinely open to dating Nicole, that I wasn't just using her to move on from Chris, but I suddenly felt uncomfortable. Dating someone, especially someone as nice as Nicole, just to get over a crush was a shitty thing to do.

At the end of the night, we stood outside the bar.

"This was lovely. I'm keen to do it again if you are," Nicole said, smiling.

I paused. She was exactly what I was looking for in a partner. We had a lot in common. She was gorgeous, funny, smart, and it was clear she'd be supportive when it came to Elliot and work. So why couldn't I stop thinking about Chris? I told myself it wasn't likely that just one date would suddenly make my feelings for Chris disappear, and I should give her a chance. But was I really giving her a chance, or unfairly leading her on?

While I agonized, Nicole's smile started to falter. I couldn't leave her hanging any longer. I panicked.

"Yes, I'd like that."

We looked at each other. *Oh shit.* I'd forgotten about this part—the whole "should we kiss, hug, or run away and never see each other again" moment that often made the end of first dates so awkward. The kiss option didn't feel right, considering my feelings for Chris. Hopefully, in a few more dates, we wouldn't be able to keep our hands off each other, and Chris would be the last thing on my mind.

Give her a friendly hug and then make a quick getaway before it all gets too awkward.

I leaned in, arms open so she knew what to expect, and gave her a brief squeeze. As I pulled away, there was a sharp yank on my hair.

Ouch. What the...? Oh no. My hair was caught on the zip of her jacket.

My face was stuck an inch away from her cheek, and I couldn't move further away without pain shooting through my scalp. She was wearing Miss Dior, one of my favorites. But it didn't have the same effect on me as Chris's cedar scent.

Stop comparing their smells and get it together.

Nicole shuffled her feet, and I realized I'd been standing there in an awkward embrace in silence for way too long. So much for making a quick getaway.

"I'm so sorry. I've caught my hair on your jacket," I said sheepishly.

"Oh shit! I was wondering what was going on! I thought you were just intoxicated by my scent or something." Nicole laughed, and I winced, glad she couldn't see my facial expression. "Let me see if I can untangle it."

She moved about, her breast grazing mine. While this felt very intimate, I wasn't experiencing any of the tingles contact with Chris gave me.

"I'm sorry. The angle is really awkward. I'll have to take off my jacket." Nicole gently maneuvered herself out of her jacket, trying not to pull my hair. Unfortunately, she wasn't completely successful. Once Nicole had it off, I bent down on the footpath, and she set to work extricating my hair from the metal zip.

"If it's too hard, we can just cut it off," I said. I had a flashback to when I was six and put chewing gum behind my ear, inspired by Violet Beauregarde from *Charlie & the Chocolate Factory*, and Dad had to cut a large chunk of hair off after it turned into a sticky, knotty mess. I felt as embarrassed now as I did back then.

"I don't want to do that to your beautiful hair." I could hear the concentration in Nicole's voice.

People were walking around us, giving us a wide berth. We were standing on one of the main streets in Hampstead, and I was eager to stop being a spectacle for the cars and passersby as soon as possible.

"I've done it!" Nicole finally pulled her jacket up.

I stood and nearly fell over, dizzy from bending for so long. Hot and flustered, I blurted out, "Thank you! Let's do this again soon, without the hair drama, that is!"

She laughed. "Yes. There are better ways to get me to take off my clothes than that!"

I blushed, giggled nervously, and hastily made my getaway.

CHAPTER NINETEEN

CHRIS

CAMERAS FLASHED, blinding me. Fans yelled my name. Reporters stood near the red carpet, waiting to ask me questions. The lights, the sounds, the smell of my sweat was overwhelming. Pain stabbed my chest and I struggled to breathe.

It's just a mild panic attack, you'll be okay. Slow breaths. The last thing you need is to break down in front of all these people and have it captured on camera.

I'd negotiated a few days off from filming in London to attend the LA premiere of the latest *Muscle Man* movie and do an intensive round of media interviews to promote the film, and I wasn't coping well. That might have been an understatement.

Being back in LA, back in the mansion, had brought back a lot of bad memories.

And now, standing on the red carpet by myself, I felt exposed and alone. The humiliation of the leaked photos had come flooding back as soon I stepped out of the car and into the media glare.

Just keep moving, Chris. The cinema door isn't far away now.

As tempting as it was to make a run for the door, I wanted to do right by my fans. I approached the crowd, plastered a smile on my face, and prepared myself for the dozens of selfies they would inevitably request. I'd made it partway through when an excited woman, in her early twenties with long platinum blonde hair and a short strapless dress, shoved a large piece of paper in front of me, asking me to sign it.

I was reaching forward with my pen when I realized what it was. A photo of my dick, blown up twice its actual size, every vein and wrinkle shown in detail.

I stepped back, reeling in shock. The chest pain intensified. My throat constricted. *Fuck.* This wasn't a mild panic attack anymore. I looked around the crowd. Were people laughing at me? Had they all seen the photos?

Dizzy, I took another step back, muttering excuses and trying to keep it together. I gave the crowd a wave, put a forced smile back on my face, and then made my way to one of the film publicists, feeling off balance. Everything had an air of unreality to it.

"I'm sorry. I'm not feeling well. I have to sit down," I said, trying to stop my voice from shaking.

She looked concerned—more for the film's publicity, I suspected, than my wellbeing—and ushered me into the cinema. "Can I get you some water? Will you still be able to give some opening remarks?"

I nodded. I sat staring at my phone blankly while I focused on breathing, trying to calm my body and break the cycle of negative thoughts about the photos and Vanessa threatening to overpower me. The next hour was a blur, but

I managed to stand up on stage with the director and my co-stars and crack a few jokes, before taking my seat to watch the film. Just before it ended, I snuck out of the darkened cinema to avoid having to interact with anyone.

My heart began to return to its usual pace as soon as I got into the car. My driver, a pleasant middle-aged man of few words, greeted me and then focused on the road. Relieved to be heading home, even if it was to the white mansion, I slumped back in my seat and let out a long breath. Part of the way home, my heart rate started up again as I remembered the London premiere. It was on Saturday. I couldn't go through that again by myself.

Would it be a bad idea to invite Sophie? Since the set visit, things had felt a little off between us. I'd freaked myself out by nearly kissing her on the chaise lounge in the manor. I got carried away in the moment. For a second, I'd thought there really was chemistry between us, but I knew that had to be all in my head. For the rest of the set visit, it seemed like something was wrong with Sophie, but that might've been all in my head as well.

Since then, we'd still spent most of my free time together, but something...didn't feel quite right. Had she worked out I had feelings for her and was withdrawing as a result?

And then last week, Sophie had casually mentioned she was going on a date. I knew I should be happy for her, but all I felt was jealousy.

But, on the other hand, having Sophie by my side would make the whole ordeal a lot more bearable. I couldn't imagine doing that all over again without someone there for moral support.

I'd also been missing her. Before filming started, I'd got

used to seeing her and Elliot nearly every day. It had been a shock to go from that to only seeing them once or twice a week, thanks to my punishing filming schedule.

Screw it. I glanced at my watch. It would be mid-morning in London. I dialed Sophie's number.

"Hello! How's LA?" Sophie sounded upbeat.

In the background, I could hear Elliot laughing at something. And was that Alfie yelping? A stab of homesickness hit me. While I'd only been living in London now for a few months, it felt more like a home than LA ever did. Right now, I'd do anything to be hanging out with them, rather than heading home to my deserted mansion.

"Okay." I tried to keep it together, although part of me wanted to tell Sophie in detail about my emotional last few hours and just how much I missed her. "These publicity trips are always draining. I was asked twenty times today about my workout and diet regime to get in shape for Muscle Man and had to answer each time as if it was an excellent question I'd never heard before. How are Elliot and Alfie?" I didn't want to ask her how the date had gone in my current state of mind.

"They're both good! Elliot started commando crawling, which Alfie isn't too thrilled about. His tail has been yanked a few times."

"Poor Alfie! Just wait until Elliot starts walking. He'll be in real trouble then."

"I think we all will! Apart from that, I've been pretty busy talking business strategy with Rose and Mia and helping out with the fundraiser event for Pride House. I don't think I mentioned it to you, but they desperately need cash for repairs, so the kids are putting on a talent show, and Josh and I are going to host an auction."

"Oh no, I'm sorry to hear that. Good on you and Josh for coming to the rescue," I said, slightly absentmindedly as I gathered up my courage to ask Sophie to the premiere. "So… I was wondering if you'd be interested in coming to the London *Muscle Man* premiere with me on Saturday night? I'd love some company. I just went to the LA one alone, and it wasn't fun. It was the first time I've been out in public at an event since the breakup. I was already feeling pretty overwhelmed with all the attention, and then a woman shoved a massive photo of my"—I swallowed—"my dick in my face and wanted me to sign it. Who signs photos of their own dick? I guess maybe pornstars? Needless to say, I didn't sign it. But it kinda sent me into a tailspin." While I'd tried to keep my voice light-hearted, I could hear it tremble slightly. *Damn.* I should have stuck to my initial plan to not tell Sophie what happened.

"Oh my gosh, Chris. I'm so sorry. That sounds terrible," Sophie said sympathetically, but without responding to my invitation.

Trying to anticipate her concerns, I jumped in. "I'll make it clear to all the press that we're just friends—that will hopefully throw water on any more tabloid articles about us."

"That's fine. Look, assuming Mum or Dad are free to babysit, I'm happy to. Although I'm not sure I have anything to wear to a film premiere. What's the dress code?" Sophie asked, apprehension in her voice.

Relief flooded over me. I wouldn't need to go through it alone again afterall. "Why don't I get Jenny to take you shopping? She knows the drill and is flying back tomorrow. Plus, she has a credit card for expenses that she can use." As soon as the words were out of my mouth, I had misgivings. While I knew Jenny would leap at the opportunity to take

Sophie shopping, I had some concerns about her and Sophie spending a lot of time together. Jenny seemed quite bemused by my relationship with Sophie, and I was pretty confident she suspected the feelings were more than platonic on my side.

Apart from accidentally letting Alfie loose on set—which, to be honest, was my fault for insisting he visit after the horse stampede incident—Jenny had been doing a much better job recently. I didn't know if it was thanks to my efforts to be a better boss, the personal assistant course she'd done the other week, or if she'd just adjusted to the role. Whatever the cause, I was relieved that things were working out, and I didn't need to fire her.

"That would be great if Jenny could help pick something out, but I can pay for it myself."

I smiled to myself. I loved Sophie's independence, but there was no way I'd let her pay for the dress. I doubted she realized just how much a red-carpet-ready dress would cost.

"Come on, I insist on paying for it. I'm the one inviting you to an event where an overpriced, will-probably-never-wear-again dress is called for."

Sophie put up a fight about me paying for the dress, but I eventually convinced her. I hung up feeling much better. Hearing Sophie's voice and Alfie and Elliot in the background had a calming effect on me.

I dragged myself to bed, exhausted, but as I was about to turn off the bedside lamp, my phone lit up. It was a news alert I'd set on my name—probably not the best idea for my mental health, but I wanted to know what other people were reading about me.

"Chris and Clare Caught Getting Cozy On Set."

I groaned and clicked on the link. The article had photos of Clare and I kissing and holding hands, taken when we were filming. There was even one of me under Clare's dress while I tried to disentangle Alfie. According to the article, "sources close" to me claimed Clare and I were having a whirlwind romance after hitting it off on set. Just what I needed. The media circus was never-ending.

CHAPTER TWENTY

SOPHIE

"SO, THE "T-REX" is a popular one. You bend your arms like a T-Rex—pretend you're holding a tiny clutch—but don't be too rigid. This way, you have something to do with your hands, and you can show off your bracelets or rings." Jenny stopped suddenly on the sidewalk, much to the annoyance of a man walking behind her, and struck a pose, her elbows pointing out and her hands touching like a T-Rex just under her belly button.

People slowed down, staring at her and giving her a wide berth, but she continued to pose, unfazed.

Oh god. What had I gotten myself into? Rings? Bracelets? I was not into jewelry. I might have a bracelet somewhere...but I couldn't pose like a dinosaur without being laughed off the red carpet. I hadn't thought about having to pose for photos, until Jenny started giving me lessons on busy Oxford Street on our way to find a dress. Now I worried I'd wake up on Sunday morning to more tabloid articles about me and Chris—not what I needed when I was trying to get over him—and they would prob-ably all be about his date's strange poses.

Jenny must have sensed prehistoric posing wasn't my thing.

I winced as she stopped walking again, and a group of teenagers almost crashed into her.

"The 'look back' is a classic." She turned her body and then shot me a coquettish look over her shoulder.

"I don't have the confidence to pull that one off either," I said, shaking my head and laughing at the same time.

"Well, how about the good old 'hand on hip' pose. Shoulders back, elbow bent, hand on hip, like so." Jenny slapped a hand on her hip, stuck her elbow out—nearly taking out a young woman walking by in the process—and pouted. "Simple, elegant, timeless."

"Okay, *that* I can do."

"Great! I'm glad we got that sorted because we're here. Ready to find your perfect dress?"

A doorman dressed in a suit opened a gold door, and we stepped into a palatial-looking designer clothing store, McKinnon. Jenny assured me this was *the* place to find a red-carpet-ready dress. Sparkling chandeliers hung from the ceiling, gold wall panels gleamed, and marble tiles added to the luxurious feel. A poised shop assistant, wearing a black suit and dark brown hair pulled tightly back into a ponytail, approached. She looked us up and down and gave us a stiff smile. I immediately regretted wearing my second best pair of jeans and scuffed flats on this shopping expedition. McKinnon was a world away from H&M or GAP, which is where I got most of my clothes.

"Can I help you?"

Jenny, unperturbed by the shop assistant's disapproval, smiled. "We're looking for a dress for my friend to wear to the film premiere of *Muscle Man 4* tomorrow night. She'll be in lots of photos, so we want her to look smoking hot."

Lots of photos? My chest tightened at the thought.

The shop assistant's forced smile disappeared and was replaced with a genuine one. Perhaps Jenny's comment about the premiere made her realize we hadn't walked into a high-end boutique by mistake on our way to Primark.

"We can certainly help with that! Now, would you ladies like some champagne?"

"Yes, please," Jenny said, looking at me with a raised eyebrow.

I shook my head. I didn't want to make a fool of myself in front of this shop assistant by getting tipsy.

While the assistant poured Jenny's champagne, I browsed through a nearby clothing rack. A plain white silk shirt caught my eye. It didn't look bad—I could picture myself wearing it when I returned to work. I flicked the tag over to see the price, and my heart skipped a beat. £875. I stepped back and bumped into the pram. Was that a typo? Maybe it was £87.50. I surreptitiously checked the price tag of some other shirts. Nope, they were all between £500 to £1,000. *Shit*. If a plain shirt cost that much, how much were the dresses?

Chris sounded so miserable on the phone that I agreed to attend the premiere without thinking it through. Now I was having serious second thoughts. Spending thousands of dollars on a dress, even if it wasn't my money, made me feel uncomfortable. Even being in this store made me feel uncomfortable. And I hated to think how uncomfortable I'd feel tomorrow night on the red carpet. I did *not* like being the center of attention.

I'd hoped Chris might retract his invitation now that it was all over the news that he was dating Clare, but he hadn't. That would have been one good thing to come out of the news. The fact I'd been right about Chris and Clare wasn't making it any easier to deal with. Maybe they were still trying to keep a low profile. I took a deep, fortifying breath. As much as I was dreading the whole thing, I'd told Chris I'd come so I couldn't pull out now. Resigned to my fate, I walked over to Jenny, who was pulling dresses off racks with enthusiasm.

She turned to smile at me. "This place has some beautiful stuff. I've already found a couple of dresses that I think will look amazing on you. Leave Elliot with me and try these ones on."

Jenny casually tossed the pile of dresses at me, untroubled by the fact they were probably worth tens of thousands of pounds. I flinched as I caught them, handling them as if they were explosive devices, and gingerly carried them to a large changing room covered in mirrors, where I hung them on hooks. I didn't want to look at the price tags.

I delicately took a gorgeous long sequined dress off its hanger. The rich purple bust gradually melted into gold at the waist. I unzipped the back and carefully stepped into it. It wouldn't go over my hips. I'd need to try over my head.

"How is everything going in there? Do you need help with anything?" The shop assistant was clearly having a slow day because I'd been in the changing room for literally one minute.

"I'm fine, thanks." I didn't want her help right now. I'd slept badly last night—ever since I'd heard the news that Chris and Clare were dating, I'd been having trouble falling asleep—and then Elliot had woken up early this morning. In my brain fog, I'd pulled on some worn beige underpants with holes near the saggy waist band and one of my least attractive maternity bras. I now regretted this decision. This wasn't the underwear of a woman who belonged in this store. It was even a step down from my second best jeans and flats. One glimpse of my sad-looking lingerie and the shop assistant would usher us out of the shop with her stiff smile.

I pulled the dress over my head and, with some squirming, maneuvered it over my curves. I looked in the mirror. Wow, this would look incredible...if I were six foot tall and stick-thin. At least a foot of gold sequined material trailed on the floor, and the dress was unflatteringly tight around my belly.

I bet Clare would look amazing in this.

I quickly pushed the thought out of my mind. I was generally pretty relaxed about my post-pregnancy curves and stretch marks—it had all been worth it to get Elliot—and I didn't like the way comparing myself to Clare made me feel. I put on the ridiculously high heels the shop assistant had provided, but even they couldn't elevate me to the height required to do the dress justice. Tucking my bra into the dress so it didn't show, I opened the door and teetered out. I was glad I'd refused the champagne. There was no way I'd be able to walk in these heels if I was tipsy.

Jenny, halfway through her glass of champagne, and the shop assistant were standing outside, waiting for me.

"This one is lovely, but it doesn't fit quite right, and it's way too long."

They nodded in unison.

"We've got two more dresses in there, and they are both shorter," Jenny said encouragingly.

I inched back into the changing room, shut the door, undid the zip, and started to wriggle my way out of the dress, holding my breath. The sequins felt like they'd been hand sewn using the most delicate threads and might fall off if so much as a light breeze wafted over them. I'd made good progress and had just pulled the bottom of the dress over my head, my arms straight in the air, when it suddenly stalled. *Shit.* The dress was stuck over my boobs, my face covered, and it wasn't moving any further. I tried pulling it back down again, but my arms were trapped in the fabric.

Panic rose in my chest. I wasn't good in small, enclosed spaces, and having my head and arms trapped in fabric was about as enclosed as you could get. Sweat pricked my skin. *Fuck, I also forgot to put on deodorant this morning. I hope I don't stink out this gown. Could it even be washed?* Irrational anger, directed at the dress for being so impractical, flooded through my body. At least most of the stuff at H&M and GAP were washing machine and dryer friendly.

I really wasn't having any luck with clothes at the moment. This was bringing back memories of my date with Nicole last week. My one and only date with Nicole. As amazing as she was, by the next morning, I'd decided that even if dating was a good way to get over someone else, it didn't feel right to pursue a relationship with Nicole while I was still hung up on Chris. I had, however, suggested we be friends and really meant it. I also intended to introduce Nicole to Rose. Josh's initial matchmaker instinct was right—I was confident they would hit it off.

Distracted thinking about Nicole and Chris, I almost lost my balance.

Bloody hell, Sophie. Why didn't you take the heels off before you started undressing?

I took a few deep breaths to steady myself. "What goes up must come down, so surely what goes on must come off?" I muttered a few times as a mantra, trying to remain calm as I attempted to inch the fabric over my head. I wasn't getting anywhere. Had my boobs and shoulders somehow expanded while I was in this damn dress?

"How are you going in there, Sophie?" This time it was Jenny checking in.

"Not great," I mumbled, hoping the shop assistant couldn't hear. "I'm a little stuck." The dress muffled my voice.

"Did you say you're stuck?" Jenny asked loudly.

I winced.

"Yes," I hissed.

"Okay, well, let me in and I'll sort you out." Jenny was sounding remarkably cheerful, given the circumstances.

She reminded me so much of Josh—that was exactly the sort of reaction I'd expect from him on hearing news I was stuck in a hideously expensive designer dress. I made a mental note that Josh and Jenny should never meet. I had a feeling they'd get along like a house on fire and get up to way too much mischief.

"No, I don't need help," I said stubbornly.

Another minute of careful wriggling passed in silence, except for the sounds of sequins rubbing together.

"Sophie, seriously, if you're still stuck, just let me in." Jenny's tone had lost some of its playfulness. "The change room is big enough to fit the two of us and the stroller."

Crap. I knew I needed help. I steeled myself. I'd been enjoying hanging out with Jenny, but this was the second time I'd met her, and we weren't at the "I'm comfortable with you seeing me in my underwear" stage of friendship yet, especially not *this* underwear.

"Fine, just as long as you promise not to laugh at my underwear." I gritted my teeth.

Because my arms were stuck above my head, to open the door, I had to bend my whole body and then feel around for the latch on the door and turn it.

Elliot gave a delighted squawk as they entered.

"Oh wow, I see what you mean," Jenny said, her voice shaky. Was she trying to suppress giggles?

I wasn't sure if she was talking about my underwear or being stuck, and I didn't want to know. A surge of heat shot up my neck and across my face. I hoped my underwear wasn't as bad as I remembered and that Jenny had shut the door behind her so I wasn't exposed to the entire snooty staff and clientele of McKinnon.

Jenny tried to pull the dress over my head. She used a lot more force than I had, but it still wasn't budging. My arms were aching, and my non-deodorized armpits were right near Jenny's face. How humiliating.

After a few minutes of yanking, Jenny stopped and started giggling. "I'm sorry, Sophie. The champagne's gone right to my head. I can't get it off. I'll need to get the shop assistant."

My heart sank. Jenny left, coming back a minute later.

"So, the shop assistant is busy with a super intimidating, posh-looking woman. I actually think she might be royalty because I'm pretty sure the shop assistant called her 'Lady' something or other. I started to approach, but she gave me the death stare, so I panicked and walked back here. Will you be okay if we wait a few minutes before I try again?"

If Jenny, who generally seemed to give zero fucks about anything, was intimated by this woman, then she must be really something.

"Okay, thanks," I said through the fabric and sequins. I shuffled uncomfortably on the seat, the sequins rustling next to my ears. Sharp pains were shooting through my arms. How much did this dress cost? Were they going to have to cut me out of it?

There was silence for a minute, and then Jenny started talking.

"I'm really glad you and Chris met. He's been doing so much better since he moved to London, and I think you're to thank for a lot of that. His eyes always light up when he talks about you and Elliot."

That was nice. Calm washed over me momentarily, imagining Chris's face lighting up. It quickly dissipated. Of course, now he had Clare. I'd been tempted to ask Jenny about what was going on with Chris and Clare all afternoon but hadn't mustered up the confidence. Now, with my face covered, it seemed less nerve-wracking. One benefit of having a dress stuck over my head was that my facial expressions couldn't betray me. I was just about to ask Jenny, when she spoke again.

"I was worried about Chris before he moved over. The whole thing with Vanessa and the photos really fucked him up. Vanessa once told me he had trust issues because of his dad leaving him as a kid. Well, she certainly didn't help with that."

I made some sympathetic noises through the dress. It felt strange having such a serious conversation while effectively blindfolded and exposed in my underwear. I'd gathered Chris's biological father wasn't in the picture but hadn't realized his departure had been so traumatic for him. I wondered what had happened, but I didn't want to ask Jenny. It was up to Chris to decide if he wanted to share something so personal with me.

"It's also had a big impact on me," Jenny continued. "I was feeling really out of depth in this role. I'd never done something like this before, I didn't have any qualifications, and I felt anxious, made a few stupid mistakes and found myself in a spiral of being so anxious I kept screwing up. But since we've been in London, Chris has been really supportive—taking the time to give me feedback, sending me on that course—and I've been feeling heaps more confident and screwing up less. If you had anything to do with that, thank you." Jenny squeezed my hand.

"Oh, I'm so glad to hear that you're feeling better about work. That's great Jenny," I said, feeling touched. The discussion with Jenny had taken my mind off my current situation, but then another pain shot through my arm, making it impossible to ignore.

After a few moments of silence, I said, "Is it worthwhile checking if the shop assistant is free yet? I won't be able to hold my arms like this for much longer."

Jenny went to check. I didn't hear the door click and really hoped she'd closed the door behind her.

"How are you doing, Elliot?" I said into the sequins, no idea where Jenny had put his pram. He giggled and made some babbling sounds, which suggested he was having a great time. I guess it wasn't everyday he got to see Mum in a strange new outfit. He probably thought I was playing a long game of peekaboo.

I was considering lying on the floor, just to give my arms a rest, when a voice I didn't recognize said, "Oh my!"

Please let that be the shop assistant and not a random person, or the posh lady. And please let her be referring to my predicament with the dress rather than the state of my underwear or smell.

"Dearie me, that does not look comfortable," said another, posher-sounding voice.

Bollocks. Well, at least I knew she wasn't talking about my underwear—they might have been ugly, but they were *very* comfortable.

"Let me just..." Someone's hands brushed against mine and fiddled with the back of the dress.

Suddenly, the fabric released, and it came over my head

with a swoosh. I blinked, drawing in a deep breath of fresh air and letting my aching arms fall to my side. The initial relief of being freed was immediately replaced with a rush of embarrassment as I registered my surroundings. I was staring at a beaming Jenny, the shop assistant, a middle-aged lady dressed as if she was about to meet the Queen—pink dress and jacket, pearl necklace and earrings, and a large pink hat—who were all staring back at me through the open door. The wide open door. *Bloody hell.* The store was busier than when we first arrived, and in the distance, I could see some other customers watching me sitting there, in my worst underwear. The mirrors in the change room reflected my underwear from every unflattering angle, over and over into infinity. Heat flooded my face. *Oh god.*

"You just hadn't done the zip all the way down," the shop assistant said with a judgmental purse of the lips.

Seriously, what is it with me and zips recently?

"Whoops! Thanks so much. I guess I should try on the other two dresses," I said hurriedly, grabbing the red dress and holding it in front of me to hide my shame.

As soon as they left, I shut the change room door, let out a breath, and I looked at my sad-looking underpants and bra more closely, sighing. They were even worse than I remembered—I spotted another hole near the elastic and noticed the nursing bra was stained with Elliot spew from this morning's feed. My ears burned with embarrassment.

I eyed the remaining two dresses hanging on the hook as though they were gladiators with whom I was about to go into battle.

Much to my relief, I readily stepped into the red dress and pulled it up. It was made of much sturdier material. Now *this* would withstand a few Sophie-induced mishaps. I looked at myself in the mirror. It didn't look half bad either.

I walked out of the change room.

Jenny gasped. "You look stunning, Sophie! What do you think?"

"Let's get it and get out of here."

It looked good, it was robust, and I didn't need to pull it over my head to get in and out of it. I was sold. I'd had more than enough shopping for the day.

CHAPTER TWENTY-ONE

CHRIS

I STOOD OUTSIDE SOPHIE'S PARENTS' place, a charming old red-brick house covered in ivy, with a black limo waiting in the street.

I smoothed my jacket with my slightly sweaty hands, even though it was perfectly ironed. It was like I was back at high school, picking up my prom date. I'd invited Sophie because I thought her company would calm me and help stave off another panic attack. So why was the thought of seeing her having the opposite effect?

I shook off my nerves, took a deep breath, and knocked.

Thirty seconds later, the door opened and Sophie appeared. *Shit.* My heart skipped a beat. She looked incredible. The long crimson dress with matching lipstick was striking against her brown skin. Her hair fell in long shiny waves, framing her face. Spending an evening with my unrequited crush looking this stunning might cause some heartache, but at least it would take my mind off the media circus.

She smiled at me, and all my prom night nerves dissolved. I let out a breath.

"You look lovely," I said, smiling back at her.

"You scrub up pretty well yourself."

Her parents hovered in the hallway, and the prom night vibes came rushing back. Flashbacks of meeting the parents of my actual prom date, Kim Bowes, in a similarly awkward fashion raced through my mind. At least Sophie's dad wouldn't pull me aside to give me a cringeworthy safe sex talk like Mr. Bowes did. Well, at least I really hoped he wouldn't.

I waved at them. "Hello! I'm Chris. It's nice to meet you both."

They walked to the door. "Lovely to meet you. I'm Marie, and this is Anil." I could see Sophie in her mom's smile and in her dad's deep brown eyes. "We've heard a lot about you. We'd love to have you over for dinner sometime, although Sophie tells us your schedule is pretty hectic at the moment."

"That sounds lovely. Sophie's told me great things about your cooking," I said, smiling at her father.

He smiled proudly. "Ah, she's a good girl." He opened his mouth, a question forming on his lips, but Sophie hurriedly cut him off.

"Well, we'd better be off. We don't want to make the leading man late to his own premiere," Sophie said briskly. She'd warned me her father was a massive film buff, and I suspected she was keen to leave before he started cross-questioning me.

We spent the limo ride to the premiere catching up on the events of the last week. Sophie had me in stitches telling me about getting stuck in a dress yesterday.

"Last week was a big week for Elliot and Alfie too. I already told you that Elliot learned how to commando crawl. Well, in other news, on Thursday morning, I did an intensive training session with Alfie to teach him 'roll over' and 'sit.' Elliot, who as you know is already a master roller," —I knew too well, after the babysitting incident—"was watching closely, but I didn't think anything of it since he's fascinated with Alfie. But then, a few hours later, Elliot suddenly sat up by himself for the first time! I don't know if it was a huge coincidence or if Elliot was taking notes in Alfie's training session, but I'm thinking I should do joint training sessions from now on. 'Catch' is next on our list!"

I couldn't help laughing at Sophie's story, despite the pang of regret that I'd missed Alfie and Elliot reaching these milestones.

"I wish I'd been here to see that, instead of moping around in LA. All the media attention and the 'dick in my face' incident brought back a lot of bad memories."

Sophie squeezed my hand sympathetically, looking at me with concern. A wave of warmth rushed up my arm at her touch.

"That sounds really hard, no pun intended. Do you want a code word if things get too much for you tonight? If you say it, I can pretend to faint or something so you have an excuse to leave?"

I smiled. "Sure, let's make it 'Cynthia.'"

Sophie laughed. I knew she was joking, but the image of catching a fainting Sophie in my arms was getting me hot under my collar. Playing the arrogant duke must have brushed off on me—catching fainting damsels was *so* nineteenth century.

The limo slowed, and I realized we were almost at the theater and that I hadn't prepped Sophie with what to expect. I gave her a quick rundown so she wasn't completely overwhelmed.

"So, when we get out of the car, they'll usher us over to

a holding area, where we'll wait until they tell us. Once we're on the red carpet, there'll be heaps of photographers taking photos, people asking for autographs, and the media wanting to do interviews as well. We'll have to spend some time out there. Hopefully, it won't be too boring for you. If you hate it, let me know, and you can go into the theater ahead of me. Before the film begins, I'll go on stage with the director and some of my colleagues, but then I'll come back and sit with you as soon as that's over. We don't actually need to stay for the film, so if you hate it, or you think the lead actor is terrible"—I gave her a wink—"we can leave. If the film hasn't sent you to sleep, there is an afterparty at Glamorama we can go to, but that's not mandatory either, so let's just play it by ear."

My quick rundown hadn't had the desired effect. Sophie was staring at me with wide eyes, a facial expression similar to how Elliot looked when Alfie barked too close to him—terrified.

"You'll be great," I said, this time squeezing her hand.

"I hope so." Sophie managed a weak smile, and then her tone turned playful. "Jenny actually gave me some red carpet posing tips yesterday!" Sophie said, doing an exaggerated pout, sticking her chest out as far as she could, and putting her hands in front of her like a squirrel. "This one is the T-Rex, which Jenny assures me will land me a modeling gig immediately. I'm planning to do a couple of T-Rex's and an over the shoulder"—she dramatically flung her head back—"then sit back and wait for the offers to start flowing in!"

LIGHTS FLASHED, and everyone's eyes were on me. But this time, instead of panic sweeping through my body, I was calm. I had Sophie next to me.

Despite her jitters and slightly disturbing T-Rex imitation in the car, Sophie was posing like a pro next to me. If she was nervous, it didn't show. She looked stunning and completely relaxed as she smiled at the cameras, her hand on her hip. I kept fighting the urge to hold her hand or put my arm around her waist.

That's what you do on the red carpet with women you're actually dating, Chris, not Sophie.

That reminded me of Sophie's date, which I'd been trying not to think about. But now, I couldn't shake the thought. Had they hooked up? Had there been a second, or even third, date by now? My stomach dropped.

Why don't you just ask her about it? After all, we're friends, and friends talk about this sort of stuff...right? And that way, you can get it out of your system. The desire to know what had happened became too strong to ignore.

"So, how was your date?" I whispered as we made our way down the red carpet, stopping regularly for photos. As soon as the words came out of my mouth, I regretted them. Sure, friends talked about dating, but maybe now, with the cameras focused on us, wasn't the best time.

"It went well, but it just didn't feel right," she whispered back, a strange look in her eyes.

"I'm sorry." But I wasn't. It annoyed me how happy I was to hear that. *Stop being so selfish, you idiot. You should want her to be happy.* I did, I just wished it was with me.

A photographer waved at me to pose for her. Before I realized what I was doing, I'd put my hand on the small of Sophie's back to lead her over. She didn't flinch, but she did glance up at me, smiling. For a moment, our eyes locked, and my insides turned to goo. Was it my imagination, or did she stand closer to me for the next pose?

After the photographer had finished, Sophie looked at me again, another unfamiliar look in her eyes. "I saw the photos of you and Clare. How are things going with her?" she murmured.

I groaned and rolled my eyes, forgetting the cameras on us. Whoops, hopefully no one captured that. "Nothing's going on between us. As usual, the tabloids made the whole thing up. Clare's not my type."

"Really?" Sophie asked. "She's stunning. If she isn't your type, who on earth is? I thought Clare would be everyone's type!"

"She's lovely, but we don't have a lot in common. For example, I don't know if you noticed at the set visit, but she was going on about private jets, which wasn't exactly the most exciting topic of conversation. We're just very different people. My type is...well, someone who has shared interests —like cooking, traveling, hiking—someone I feel comfortable being myself around, who can see past the fame and likes me for me. Someone...well, someone like you. Just not gay, obviously."

The last few words spilled out of my mouth without thinking.

Shit, shit, shit.

As soon as I muttered them, I wished I hadn't. I'd just insinuated that I was into her. Would it make things weird? Oh god. Maybe she didn't hear me over the noise of the crowd. My mind raced, so much so that I almost didn't process her response.

Sophie looked at me, stunned.

"I'm not gay, Chris. I'm queer. Bi. I like men and women," she said quietly.

I looked into her big, brown eyes, her crimson lips slightly parted, and felt an electric current run through us. This time, I was sure I wasn't imagining it. The chemistry was real. And it was mutual.

Oh damn. My heart felt like it might explode. I had the sudden urge to have a "Tom Cruise on Oprah's couch" moment, to fist pump or do something with the adrenaline that was pouring through my veins. She wasn't gay. And she was into me.

Cameras flashed and fans yelled for autographs, but for a second, I was oblivious to it all. Oblivious to everyone and everything except Sophie. I wanted to pull her to me there and then and kiss her like I'd been wanting to do for months.

Calm down, Chris. Do you really want to give the media a present like that after what they've put you through? The last thing you want is to go in for a kiss, only for her to reject you and have it all captured on camera.

Instead, I tentatively put out my hand.

SOPHIE

WHY CHRIS DECIDED the red carpet, with high resolution cameras trained on us and international media present, was the time to ask me about my date with Nicole, I'm not sure. But since he raised the topic, I couldn't resist asking him about Clare. And when he told me Clare wasn't his type, I couldn't resist asking him who was. I was genuinely interested. Never in a million years did I expect those words would come out of his mouth.

"Someone like you. Just not gay, obviously."

It took me a few seconds for the implication of his words to sink in. *Shit*. Maybe he *did* like me like that. But he thought I was gay?

A rush of emotions flooded me. Incredulity and excitement that he was attracted to me after all these weeks of pining. Surprise that he thought I was gay—I never said I was and couldn't even remember mentioning the gender of anyone I'd dated to him. And a dash of annoyance that he'd made that assumption about my sexuality.

We stared at each other, and any ambiguity as to how we both felt disappeared in a flash. An electric current ran through my body, and this time, I was certain Chris felt it too.

Most people don't have their first realization of mutual attraction captured on camera. But there we were, standing, staring at each other with glowing eyes, while the shutters snapped.

Chris reached for my hand, which I took without hesitation, and we turned to face the cameras together.

CHRIS

IF A PERCEPTIVE PERSON looked at the photos from the premiere, I'm convinced they could tell something significant happened at that point on the red carpet when our eyes locked and realization dawned on us. The photos taken before that moment had us standing slightly awkwardly together, not touching, and the photos taken after our eyes locked had us holding hands, or with my arm around Sophie's waist, unable to wipe the smiles off our faces. It took all of my willpower not to flee the red carpet with her so we could be alone together.

I was kicking myself for being such an idiot. I tried hard to be a good LGBTQ+ ally, and I knew not making assumptions about other people's sexuality was a key part of that. So why did I assume that, because she'd once mentioned an ex-girlfriend, she was a lesbian?

We made our way along the red carpet at an excruciatingly slow pace, stopping for photos and then media interviews.

"Chris, Chris! Can you tell us how you got in shape for your role?" "What was your favorite stunt?" "Your contract ends after the next *Muscle Man* film. Will that be the end of Muscle Man?"

Like the LA premiere, the interviews were torture, but this time for a much more positive reason. Sophie's presence next to me was so distracting that I found it hard to focus on the questions. Luckily, I'd done so many interviews in the last week, I could answer almost all of them on autopilot.

But this time, there was a new question.

"And who is this?" most of the interviewers asked, looking Sophie up and down appraisingly.

I glanced at Sophie, not sure how to answer. I knew they wanted to know what my relationship with Sophie was —was she a friend or something more? But I didn't know anymore. I went with the most straightforward response.

"This is Sophie, Sophie Shah."

After the media interviews were finally over, I braced myself for my last red carpet duty—greeting my fans. I took a deep breath and walked over to the excited crowd. Given how intense it could be, at my suggestion, Sophie stood back and watched me pose for selfies, sign autographs, and make small talk. Even without Sophie by my side, knowing she was nearby gave me strength to go through it. It also helped that there were no oversized dicks waiting to be autographed this time. I was on such a high from finding out about Sophie that I probably would have laughed it off, but I was glad I didn't have to find out.

Part of me wanted to shake off the fans so I could get back to Sophie as soon as possible, but I knew they'd waited hours to see me. I reminded myself how I'd felt as a teenager, waiting outside The Chicago Theater with Steven to see Eric Moore, one of my favorite performers, come out of the stage door after his play finished. He came up to me, asked what my name was, and autographed a poster. It was one of the highlights of my childhood. I wanted to give my fans that sort of experience as well, even when I wasn't in the mood. Even when I'd just discovered the woman I'd been pining after was into me as well.

The last selfie taken, I walked back toward Sophie. She smiled at me, and some of the tension in my chest and shoulders released. It was finally time to go inside the cinema. We were one step closer to being alone together.

CHAPTER TWENTY-TWO

SOPHIE

IT WAS bizarre sitting next to Chris while watching him on the big screen, blown up ten times his size, wearing his form-hugging, sleeveless metallic outfit which showed off his biceps in their full glory, saving the world from disaster. I couldn't focus on the film, my mind whirring as I processed the events of the last hour. The intensity of walking down a red carpet, in full view of screaming fans and an overwhelming number of cameras, with Chris, smoking hot in his tailored tux, by my side. The heart-flipping realization that my feelings for Chris were mutual. And then seeing Celebrity Chris in action—confidently answering media questions, patiently taking selfies, and chatting with fans.

Thirty minutes into the film, Chris leaned over to me.

"Do you want to get out of here?" he whispered. His breath gently tickled my neck, his biceps pressing against my shoulder, sending shivers of anticipation down my spine.

I nodded.

He took my hand, and we made our way slowly out of

the theater, trying not to draw attention to ourselves. The cool evening air hit us as we snuck out of a side entrance and onto a quiet street behind the theater.

Chris called his driver and then turned to me, giving me a look that dispatched tingles straight to my crotch. *Oh boy.* I bit my lip. He put his hands around my waist and pulled me to him. *Ohhhh boy.* I had wanted this for so long, and it was finally happening. I felt lightheaded with anticipation.

His warm, firm lips touched mine, his beard grazing my face. The kiss was soft, sensual, tender. And then a little bite, a hint of tongue. Before I knew it, it was a kiss that deserved to be on the big screen. Passionate, hungry, it felt like the sexual tension of the last few months was being released.

He grabbed the roots of my hair at the back of my head. I let out a strangled moan, the heat of desire engulfing me. His abs were pressed against me, and my hands were under his tuxedo jacket, feeling the muscles on his back.

We were so caught up in the moment, we didn't notice the limo had arrived until the driver got out of the car and coughed loudly, opening the door. Heat shot up my face as we disentangled ourselves.

Chris turned to me. "So...would you like to come back to my place?" His face flushed as well. "Or I can drop you home, if you'd prefer?"

"Your place," I said with conviction. There was no doubt in my mind, I wanted to go to his place. His bed more specifically.

The ride back to the Castle was agony. The air between us was charged with electricity, but we were in unspoken agreement that we shouldn't subject the poor driver to any more PDA, so we sat chastely, holding hands. I could not stop thinking about that kiss, and what was going to happen next.

"I've been wanting to kiss you ever since you crashed into me," Chris murmured, leaning close to my ear.

I inhaled his cedar forest scent giddily. He'd been interested in me since the first day we met?

"I didn't realize ramming someone with a pram was a seduction technique. I'll keep that in mind next time I want to pick someone up," I said teasingly.

"Next time?" Chris asked, raising an eyebrow. "Hmmmm."

"I was attracted to you from the get-go, but my feelings really hit that night we did karaoke together. Only unlike you, the hit was just figurative rather than literal. You walked into the room and—wham!" I slapped my hand to my heart.

"I thought I felt something that night. I'm glad it wasn't all in my head." Chris smiled at me, and my stomach, which had been roiling in anticipation, jumped.

After what felt like an eternity of back seat whispers and hands that were itching to explore each other, the limo pulled up at the Castle. As soon as we'd farewelled the driver, we bounded up the front stairs, practically fell through the doorway, and picked up from where we had left off in the street.

"Why don't we go to the couch," Chris gasped in between kisses, walking me backwards out of the hallway and into the living room. He sat on the couch and pulled me on top of him, straddling him.

Hands on his firm pecs, I leaned over him, and we continued to kiss, tasting each other, biting each other's lips. He teased my neck and then my earlobe with his mouth, sending shudders of delight through me. I wanted him so bad.

With trembling hands, I started unbuttoning his shirt, and he began unzipping my dress. His hand slid down my back, holding the zip, and then stopped suddenly. He tugged. It didn't move.

Oh god, please let the zipper not be stuck again. Now is seriously not the time.

His brow furrowed, and an intense look of concentration flashed across his face. I let out a deep breath as his hands started moving, and then the top of my dress slipped off with ease, revealing the black strapless bra underneath. I was so glad I'd worn decent underwear this time. He pulled the dress over my head with one swoop and threw it off.

"Oh shit," he muttered.

I followed his gaze to the corner of the room. The dress had landed on top of the large antique vase, which wobbled precariously. I held my breath. Thankfully, it righted itself.

He looked back at me, taking my body all in. I reached the last button on his shirt, my hands tantalizingly close to his groin, and peeled it open.

Holy shit, this man is ripped. Even sitting down, I could see every ab in high definition.

He flipped me onto the couch so I lay lengthways, kissing my neck before making his way to my collarbone. A moan escaped my mouth. Fuck, I wanted him *so* bad. I grabbed the back of his head, pulling his hair. His breath was ragged as he continued his journey down my body, kissing my breasts and then my stomach. I could feel him, pressing hard against my body. I'd never felt desire this intense, this raw, this all-consuming before. My hands clawed his back.

And then he muttered something.

I couldn't hear him clearly with his face pressed against my stomach, but I distinctly heard the word "chocolate."

I stiffened. All the tingling, all the desire, vanished.

Memories of those offensive messages I used to get from guys on dating apps, comparing me to caramel and honey, all the sleazy requests for threesomes and pictures of my boobs, all those dick pics and terrible first dates, came flooding back.

My vagina clenched, and not in a good way.

"Is everything okay?" Chris peered up at me, his eyes deep with concern.

My throat constricted. I struggled to sit up, suddenly feeling very exposed.

"Sophie, what's going on? Did I do something? Please, talk to me." He sat next to me on the sofa.

My heart softened hearing the worry in his voice. I took a deep breath, trying to stop my voice from wavering. "What did...what did you just say before? Something about chocolate?"

Chris went bright red. "I said...I said, 'I want to drizzle chocolate all over you and lick it off.' God, sorry. Shit, I obviously need to work on my dirty talk game. It's just something I've enjoyed doing in the past. But that's totally fine if you're not into it. " His face was now the color of beetroot.

I breathed out. Thank god.

Now it was my turn for blood to rush to my cheeks. "I'm sorry. I thought you said something offensive...and it threw me."

Chris let out a breath and put his arm around my waist. "Hey, no need to apologize. I didn't say it very clearly—I got a bit overexcited and was trying to talk while kissing you at the same time, which was obviously overambitious. And it was a bit of a weird thing to say. I'm just glad you told me what was wrong. And please call me out if I do say anything offensive. I can be pretty stupid sometimes, like the whole assuming you're gay because you've had a girlfriend in the past thing." He grimaced apologetically and gave me a squeeze.

I squeezed him back.

Chris's tone lightened, and he gave me a mischievous grin. "So...I know I fucked up the delivery, but in all seriousness, what are your thoughts on melted-chocolate play?"

"It sounds...delicious, if a little messy. I'm up for it, as long as I get to lick some off you as well. But can we take a raincheck? The chocolate mix-up has killed my vibe." The moment had well and truly passed for me.

"Of course. All of this talk of chocolate has got me hungry. Or maybe I was hungry and that's why I was channeling chocolate play to begin with. Either way, I've got a block of Lindt in the pantry we could have, direct from the packet rather than off each other. You keen?" Chris smiled tentatively.

My stomach rumbled. I'd had a cheese toastie for dinner before Chris picked me up, and that was hours ago. "Yes, please!"

CHAPTER TWENTY-THREE

SOPHIE

"HEY SOPH, LOOK AT THIS!" Josh, sitting next to me on the floor at Pride House, waved a sculpture of a nude male, with chiseled abs and his anatomy shown in graphic detail, in my face. He lowered his voice, a salacious smile on his lips. "Is this kinda how Chris looks naked?"

I glared at him. "Shut up!" I hissed. On our walk over to Pride House, I'd told Josh what had happened on Saturday but had sworn him to secrecy.

At this point, I really didn't need any more reminders of how Chris looked naked. I hadn't been able to stop thinking about him. About the feeling of his firm lips on mine, about my hands running over his body, about what would have happened on the night of the premiere if I hadn't cut things short.

I looked around, hoping none of the teens who were helping prepare for the auction had heard. Luckily, they were engrossed in sorting through the random assortment of items that had been donated for the auction. I breathed a sigh of relief and continued to work through the pile in front of me, trying not to think about Chris. Bottles of wine, golf clubs, a free drag makeover, a voucher to have a portrait of your pet painted wearing renaissance clothing. I grinned. Alfie would look incredible in frills. Could I bid on things as the auctioneer? It would probably be a conflict of interest. My heart warmed seeing the enormous pile of donations we had received. The community had really come together to help save Pride House.

The dress I'd worn on Saturday night was hanging on a rack, freshly dry cleaned, ready to be auctioned off as well. Donating it to Pride House had made sense—much better than it sitting in my wardrobe, gathering dust. I stared at it. It was hard to believe that only three days ago, I was walking down the red carpet wearing it, cameras blazing, with Chris by my side. Before I knew it, a vision of Chris throwing the dress off and kissing my neck threatened to overwhelm me. Holy crap. Vivid flashbacks to Saturday night kept hitting me at the most inopportune moments, driving me wild. I'd be doing the washing or eating my breakfast, and suddenly our bodies would be pressing together, our mouths hungrily devouring each other.

But then, reality would hit. Even though I'd had a crush on him for so long, I'd never seriously considered the possibility that it was mutual. I'd got so caught up in the moment on Saturday night, I hadn't thought through the consequences of...whatever was happening between us. I didn't know what he wanted. I didn't even know what I wanted. But the more I thought about it, the more it seemed like any kind of non-platonic relationship with Chris was a bad idea. I'd never been good at "friends with benefits" relationships, and dating...

Well, I couldn't see myself as celebrity girlfriend material, jet-setting around the globe, attending premieres, and shopping regularly in stores that offered champagne on arrival. And where would Elliot fit in all that? We were from very different worlds. And he was going back to LA in a few months anyway.

I noticed some teenagers had stopped sorting and were hunched over their phones, murmuring.

"Hey, Sophie, no way. Is this you?" Ben, a sixteen-year-old with blond hair and eyebrow piercings, put his phone right in front of my face.

I pulled my head back and let my eyes focus. It was a photo of me and Chris at the premiere, his arm around me.

I winced. "Yeah, that's me."

The other teenagers leaped up to look at the photo and started peppering me with questions. Yet another reason why having a relationship with Chris was a bad idea—the lack of privacy.

"What? Wow! You know Chris Trent?"

"Are you guys dating?"

I ignored the last question. "Yeah, we know each other."

Erin, holding a hideous pink frilly lamp with crystals hanging from it that would be perfectly at home in Cynthia's living room, looked at me and frowned. "Oh, I thought you were gay, Sophie."

I hesitated. "I'm...queer...bi."

While I might have been imagining things, Erin didn't look impressed. I sighed inwardly. Erin's reaction brought back more bad dating experiences. While I'd stuck to dating women after swearing off men, dating women hadn't been completely bigotry-free. Sure, I didn't receive the same gross, racist comments from women and constant invitations for threesomes, but I was subjected to another form of discrimination—biphobia.

Until I changed my sexual orientation on the dating apps to "queer," I received countless messages from women saying things like, "Sorry, I don't date bi girls", "Are you sure you're bi?" or "Have you actually been with a woman before? I've been burned too many times by straight girls 'experimenting.'"

And I'd experienced those sorts of reactions in real life, on dates, and in bars as well. Unfortunately, even in the LGBTQ+ community, biphobia's rife. It was one reason I hesitated when describing myself as bi. "Queer" was less likely to attract a negative reaction, even if most people didn't know quite what it meant.

Given what Erin had been through lately, I wasn't about to call her out on her potential biphobia, especially since it was probably all in my overly sensitive head. She'd just moved into the housing Alex had found her and was adjusting to life without her parents, so she deserved to be cut a lot of slack. At least she had the talent show to keep her occupied—she'd been keeping busy with her friends, practicing their performance, and throwing herself into auction preparations.

I didn't have time to dwell on Erin's reaction because the teens started excitedly bombarding me with questions about Chris.

Thankfully, at that moment, Alex walked up to us. "Sophie, Josh. Can I speak with you for a moment?" they asked.

I breathed a sigh of relief that I had an excuse to escape the cross examination and followed Alex into their office.

"I'm afraid I've got bad news. You know how Stan Burnley was going to be our guest of honor at the auction, and we were going to auction off a date with him?" Stan Burnley was a popular football player who featured heavily in the eligible bachelor lists and lived in Hampstead. "Well, he's had to pull out. His dad is ill, and he's gone home to

Essex. So, we'll have to scrap that bit of the auction." Alex rubbed their forehead and furrowed their brow.

Shit. My heart sank. I'd made a big deal about Stan in the email I'd sent to everyone I knew—including my work colleagues, the mothers' group, my friends, and my parents' friends—inviting them to the auction.

I glanced at Josh, who seemed to take the news surprisingly well. "Sophie, would you, by any chance, know someone who's an even bigger name than Stan?" Josh gave me a wink.

It took me longer than it should have to catch on. I didn't love the idea of asking Chris to come, especially not to pimp himself out to the highest bidder. But I wanted the fundraiser to be as successful as possible. And Alex could make it clear it was not a *date* date, which I'm sure they were planning to do already. And Chris probably wouldn't be able to make it anyway, given his hectic film schedule.

Alex looked at Josh and then me expectantly. Alex clearly hadn't seen the photos Ben had just shown me.

I took a deep breath. "So, I know Chris Trent. He's in London filming at the moment. I don't want to get your hopes up because he works most evenings, but I could see if he's free then."

"Oh my god, that would be amazing, Sophie!" Alex gave me a big hug, their eyes flashing with excitement.

I went into the hallway to call Chris, not expecting him to answer—he was almost certainly filming, hopefully not another kissing scene with Clare. We'd texted regularly since Saturday night but hadn't arranged to see each other yet. Our plans used to happen organically, but now my stomach fluttered each time I thought about suggesting we catch up. It started fluttering as I called him.

"Sophie?"

My heart picked up pace at the sound of his voice.

I swallowed. "Hey! How are you? Sorry to bother you at work. So, um, I have a slightly awkward question for you. You know how I was telling you about the fundraising event for Pride House? Well, it's on Thursday night at seven p.m., and the celebrity guest, a footy player, has pulled out at the last minute. We told everyone he'd be coming, so we're in a bit of a pickle and were wondering if..." I paused, swallowing again.

"I could come instead?" Chris chuckled. "Let me check my schedule. If I can get away, I'll be there." I heard Chris speaking with Jenny in the background. "We're in luck. I'll be done by around four that day, so I'm in. Would you like to grab a drink afterwards?"

"Oh wow, amazing! And yes to the drink. That would be lovely. There is one other thing..." I cleared my throat. "Stan had offered to...umm...auction off a date with himself. Is there any chance..." My voice trailed off. Oh god. This was so awkward.

Chris snorted with laughter. "You want me to sell myself to the highest bidder? Look, as long as you don't have a problem with it, and, if they give off any creepy or intense vibes, I can bring my bodyguard, that's fine."

He thought I might have a problem with it? That seemed like something he'd only say if we were more than just friends with benefits...My heart leaped, and I had a sudden flashback to Chris's lips and beard grazing my neck. Would we have a repeat on Thursday night and get to finish what we started? A tingle went down my spine. *Focus, Sophie.*

"Thanks so much. You're a lifesaver."

"I was going to ask if you wanted to do something together this week, so it works out perfectly."

I heard Jenny again in the background.

"Sorry, I've got to go. See you Thursday!"

I strode back into Alex's office with a spring in my step, eager to share the good news. Despite not knowing exactly where Chris and I stood, and having some misgivings about auctioning him off to a stranger, I couldn't wait to see him.

CHAPTER TWENTY-FOUR

SOPHIE

I PUSHED the pram through the front door of George Gorilla, my favorite cafe in Hampstead Village, where I'd become a regular during my maternity leave. The barista nodded his head and smiled at me in greeting as I entered. Paintings covered the walls from table height to ceiling in a colorful jumble, and potted plants weaved between funky antiques and coffee supplies on shelves behind the coffee machine. I found the familiar rhythm of the cafe soothing— the hum of coffee being ground, the hiss of milk frothing, and the bang of the used coffee grounds being emptied into the bin. As usual, they were doing a roaring trade.

Mia and Rose were already sitting at a table near the window, deep in conversation. It was hard to miss Rose, whose stylish bomber jacket was a cacophony of color, a contrast to Mia's blue jeans and gray sweater combination. They jumped up when they saw me and waved. Rose had arranged the coffee date earlier this week via a cryptic text message, but I'd gathered it was to talk about our business.

As soon as Elliot and I were settled and our drink orders taken, Rose took a deep breath.

"I was wondering how you two would feel if we moved our plans forward? I'm at my wits end at work and don't think I'll last to the end of next year like we planned. The partners claim they care about having an inclusive workplace, but all of my initiatives are being shot down because they aren't willing to commit any time or money. It's like they just hired me as a box-checking exercise, and now they have their Black, queer diversity and inclusion officer, they aren't interested in doing anything more." Rose ran her hand through her short black hair. "Seriously, the other day, one partner suggested that the firm didn't need to focus on diversity now that fifty percent of employees are female, completely ignoring the fact that only twenty percent of the partners are female, and the majority of women in the firm are junior accountants and assistants—and also that gender diversity is just one form of diversity, and they're performing pretty badly across the board." She shook her head in disbelief. Rose had taken a new role in a large accounting firm last year and had been fighting an uphill battle ever since.

Mia and I groaned sympathetically. We'd both had similar experiences and knew how frustrating it could be.

"That really sucks, Rose. How soon are you thinking?" Mia asked.

"How would you feel about a few months? I need to give six weeks' notice. If you guys were open to it, I'd quit ASAP so I could start getting things set up."

A few months! My stomach churned with excitement and nerves. Quitting our steady, well-paid jobs to go out on our own was a big risk, especially now I had Elliot to support. While it was a risk I was willing to take, I thought I'd have a bit more time to prepare myself. But I'd been dreading returning to the stuffy law firm, and Rose's timing would conveniently coincide with when I was due back. And we'd already spent a lot of time planning, so I was fairly confident we could pull it off.

Rose picked her nails as she looked at me and Mia, holding her breath.

"Screw it! Let's do it," I said with a big smile. "Mia?"

We both looked at Mia expectantly. Mia was brilliant but suffered from serious imposter syndrome, something Rose and I had been trying to help her with. I hoped it wouldn't stop her from committing to Rose's new timetable.

"I'm in too." Mia clapped her hands, and my shoulders relaxed. "This is so exciting! I can't believe we're actually going to do this!"

A niggling worry grew in my mind as our coffees arrived and our conversation turned to practical matters. While I still had no idea what was happening between me and Chris, *if* we did get together—and that was a big *if*—would that affect our new business? The worry started to grow even bigger, as I thought about all the ways my relationship with Chris could potentially interfere with things and remembered Erin's reaction to the news I was bi.

"Is everything okay, Soph? I'm not sure you heard my question." Mia looked at me with concern, her blue eyes soft.

My silence and aggressive thumbnail chewing had given me away.

I put my hand down and sighed. If I was going to talk to anyone about my worries, Mia and Rose were the best possible people. Not only were they my business partners, and therefore potentially directly affected by this, but they were experts in discrimination—and Rose was bi as well—so they would give me good, well-informed advice.

I took a gulp of coffee, gathering my strength. "Please

don't tell anyone else, but Chris and I sort of hooked up on Saturday night."

Their eyes widened.

"I'm not sure where this is going. It might be nowhere, or maybe it'll just be a friends-with-benefits situation, but if we start dating...I'm just not sure it's the right time to be embarking on a high-profile relationship with a movie star. Our reputations in the industry are pretty crucial to our business being a success, and I'm worried that a relationship with Chris could damage that. People might not take me seriously if there are photos everywhere of me hanging off Muscle Man's arm. They might see me as some ditzy celebrity side piece."

"Sophie! Don't even give a second thought to our business. Do people think Amal Clooney is a 'ditzy celebrity side piece' because she married George Clooney?" Rose looked at me sternly and put her coffee cup down on the saucer loud enough to make Elliot look up from his toys with concern. "No! She is a kickass, in demand, human rights lawyer. And you, Sophie Shah, are a kickass diversity and inclusion expert, irrespective of who you date!"

I couldn't help smiling. "Thanks, Rose. I'm definitely not the Amal Clooney of diversity and inclusion, but I appreciate your support!" My smile faded. "But it's not just the ditzy side piece that's worrying me. We agreed that I'd specialize in LGBTQ+ issues, but will people really take me seriously in advocating for LGBTQ+ issues if I'm dating the epitome of a white cis straight man? I mean, he's famous for playing a character called Muscle Man, for goodness sake! You know what people are like. If I date Chris, they'll assume I'm straight, which will undermine my credibility speaking on LGBTQ+ matters. Or if they'll think I'm 'confused,' or wildly promiscuous, or something. All those stereotypes about bi women that aren't exactly seen as positive traits when deciding which diversity and inclusion consulting firm to hire."

Mia chimed in, leaning forward over her latte. "Soph, one reason we're doing this is so we can stop working for assholes. So, if anyone is small-minded enough to think these things you're worried about—which I seriously doubt —and decide not to hire us as a result, then I'm thrilled with that outcome. If anything, it will do us a favor by weeding out some of the assholes in advance! And I'm also happy to educate any of these assholes. Just send them my way!" Mia gave a come-over-here gesture with her hands, an ominous expression on her face. She would definitely set them straight.

Well, not *straight* exactly...

"Well, okay, you have a point." I took a deep breath. "But to be honest, it's not just our business I'm worried about. I'm also nervous about how some of my queer friends —not you two, of course—and other people in the queer community might react. I'm afraid they'll think I'm selling out by dating a white, privileged, cis guy. You know, I think that's part of the reason I swore off men. It wasn't just all the shitty dating experiences. It was also a feeling that each time I date a guy, my 'queerness' sort of fades away, and I get a bit of an imposter syndrome. I love being part of the LGBTQ+ community, and I don't want to jeopardize that."

Rose looked sympathetic. "I know there is biphobia in both the straight and queer communities, but I don't think any of your friends will judge you if you date Chris. If they're true friends, they'll just want you to be happy, which is what we both want for you." She looked at Mia, who nodded. "You don't need to 'prove' your queerness to anyone. One of the awesome things about being attracted to more than one gender is that we have more choice. Don't let societal prejudice limit that."

"I know you're right, but I just have a hard time internalizing it. It's so frustrating, at my age and in my line of work, with supportive family and friends like you two, I still struggle with being bi." I shook my head. "Seriously, I've devoted my life to telling people they should embrace difference in others. I should be able to embrace difference in myself."

"Why do you think that's the case, Soph?" Mia asked gently.

I paused, thinking. "I don't know. Maybe it's because, growing up, I didn't know anyone who was bi, and there weren't any bi people on TV or in the books I read? So, when I was exploring my sexuality in my teens, I spent all my energy trying to work out if I was gay or straight, not seriously considering that I might be bi." There had been many sleepless nights analyzing my feelings toward my classmates and celebrity crushes. Was I really attracted to men, or had society just programmed me to think I was? Was I actually attracted to my best friend at school, or did I just have a 'girl crush'—whatever the hell that was—on her, or just want to *be* her? "Somewhere like Pride House would have definitely helped me work it all out faster. So maybe my hang-ups are a legacy those years of doubting my attraction to both men and women, of thinking that I had to be either gay or straight? Even now, I still shy away from describing myself as 'bi'. I prefer 'queer,' partly because it's kind of vague, and avoid mentioning my history of dating men when I date women."

I grimaced at Rose, who was proudly bi, expecting her to be horrified. But if she was, she didn't let on. Instead, she patted my hand.

"I'm sorry you're still struggling with this, Soph. I'm afraid I don't have a lot of advice—maybe speaking to a therapist who specializes in LGBTQ issues would help? But I do know that you shouldn't feel bad if you're more comfortable with identifying as 'queer' rather than 'bi' and don't want to disclose your dating history. That's entirely up to you."

Mia chimed in. "And you know, perhaps—only if you're comfortable, of course—Pride House could be an opportunity for you to be the bi, or queer, role model you never had." She smiled tentatively.

My chest already felt lighter. "Thank you. You two are the best." I smiled at them. "I'm sure nothing will end up happening with Chris, but I feel so much better talking it out with you. And that's an excellent point about being a role model for the teens at Pride House, Mia. I hadn't thought about it, but I'll see if I can give a talk about my experiences at the next mentoring evening."

If I could help even one kid struggling coming to terms with being bi, it would be worth it. I took a long sip of my coffee, pleased that my worries had been replaced with a useful and actionable plan to help others. I knew Mia and Rose would know exactly what to say. My heart filled with warmth. I couldn't believe my luck that I was about to become business partners with these two wise and wonderful women.

CHAPTER TWENTY-FIVE

SOPHIE

WE'D TRANSFORMED the main room at Pride House into a makeshift theater, with a wooden stage facing red plastic chairs lined up in rows. I was checking the auction items displayed on tables next to the stage when the hum of nervous chatter suddenly escalated to fever pitch, interrupting my concentration. I looked up to see the cause of the commotion ,and my heart leaped.

Chris, Jenny, and his bodyguard had walked in.

Jenny gave me a wave, and Chris shot me a big smile, turning my legs to jelly. Excited teenagers surged toward him. Already a bundle of nerves over their talent show performances, Chris's arrival tipped a couple of them over into hysteria.

I could relate. All day, a kaleidoscope of butterflies had been energetically fluttering in my stomach. One or two of the butterflies were in anticipation of my duties as auctioneer tonight—I always found public speaking a bit nerve wracking. But the vast majority were Chris-induced.

Chris, who'd just walked in wearing a dark green sweater that fit his muscular torso perfectly.

Chris, who was now smiling and laughing with the teenagers, filling my heart with warmth. Taking selfies, asking them questions and listening intently to their answers, and, from what I could make out, giving them a pep talk about their performances tonight.

Chris, who I hadn't seen since we sat eating chocolate in the kitchen, after I abruptly ended our make-out session just as things were getting steamy. Hands-and-mouths-exploring-feverishly, intense-throbbing-steamy...

Snap out of it, Sophie. You have an auction to run.

Since Chris appeared to have everything under control, I forced myself to focus on checking the auction items.

Twenty minutes later, I was finishing when a familiar cedar scent sent the butterflies' wings flapping at double time.

"How are you doing?" Chris gave me a peck on my cheek and a quick squeeze with one arm around my waist. Was that just a friendly peck or something more? The squeeze felt more than platonic...I thought...maybe?

"Pretty good. We've had a lot of interest, so I'm hoping it'll be a success. Of course, with you on offer, how could it not be?" My ears burned. That sounded way more flirtatious than I intended.

"I'm sure your auctioneering skills will really make tonight a hit!" Chris grinned.

"I doubt that! I'm just hoping Josh will behave himself on stage."

We glanced over to Josh, who was with Erin. They were bopping each other on the head playfully with the large foam fake auction hammers we'd bought for the occasion.

Chris laughed. "Yeah, good luck with that!"

Attendees started trickling in. Before long, the room was packed. Looking around the crowd, I spotted the entire gang—Rose, Mia, Sharon, Tina, Amir, Khanh—standing up the back, my dad—Mum had stayed at home to look after Elliot—and, to my surprise, most of the mothers' group, including Cynthia, who gave me an energetic wave. My heart warmed to see such a great turnout. Just then, Nicole also entered the room. I was so pleased she'd accepted my invitation—I wasn't sure she would come. I excused myself from Chris and walked over to her.

"Hello! I'm so glad you came." I gave her a warm hug, making sure my hair was out of the way first. Now wasn't the time to have another zip incident. "Let me introduce you to my friends."

We walked over to where the gang was sitting. Luckily for my matchmaking plan, there was a spare seat next to Rose, so I made sure we stood near it as I introduced Nicole to everyone, making an effort to mention a few things that Rose and Nicole had in common. Hopefully I wasn't being too obvious.

Just as Nicole sat down next to Rose, Alex tapped the microphone and cleared their throat. "Hi everyone! Thanks so much for coming out tonight. I'm Alex, the manager here at Pride House. As you can see, Pride House desperately needs repair"—Alex gestured at an ominous-looking water stain on the ceiling—"so we really appreciate your support this evening so we can continue to provide our LGBTQ+ young people with a safe, inclusive, and affirming environment where they can meet other members of the LGBTQ+ youth community, get peer support, and develop personal and professional skills. Now, unfortunately, Stan Burnley had to pull out of tonight's event due to some unavoidable personal circum-stances..."

A few faces in the audience dropped.

"But, I'm very pleased to announce that in his place, we have none other than Chris Trent himself!"

The room hummed with excitement.

"Some of you may have seen his latest film, *Muscle Man 4*, which recently opened in cinemas. Now, I'll hand over to Chris to say a few words. Chris will also feature in our auction later this evening, so stick around for that! Without further ado, please join me in welcoming Chris Trent!"

The room erupted into applause as Chris walked onto the stage. He stood, smiling, waiting for the crowd to quieten.

"Wow! Thank you! Thank you all for the warm welcome. I'm so happy to be here to support this fantastic initiative." Chris looked around the room. "Earlier this evening, I had the pleasure of meeting some of the wonderful young people who attend Pride House and heard how much the center means to them. While they all had their own unique stories, there were some common themes. In particular, one I heard over and over again is that this is a place, for some the only place, where they feel comfortable being themselves."

He paused.

"For some of us in this room, especially people like me who are white, able-bodied, cis, straight, and male, it may be hard to imagine what it's like to feel you don't belong, to feel you can't be yourself, on a daily basis. However, most people have had at least one moment in our lives when we've felt like that, whether it was walking into a fancy shop where the shop assistant looks down on you"—Chris caught my eye and winked—"walking into the wrong room by accident, or being somewhere where you are the only person of a particular age, race, or gender. Hopefully for most of you, like me, these experiences are fleeting, trivial, and quickly forgotten. But imagine if they weren't. Imagine those experiences of not belonging, or not being able to be yourself, were the norm. And then imagine if one of the few safe spaces where you could be yourself was at risk of closing."

Chris looked around the room and cleared his throat. Did he look nervous, or was it just my imagination?

"The teens also told me how important the support network of friends and mentors they've made through Pride House is. As many of you know, earlier this year, some very intimate photos of me were leaked online and seen by millions of people. I haven't spoken publicly about this before, but I was humiliated, and the experience took a huge toll on my mental health. If it wasn't for my strong support network of my family, my childhood friends, and a new friend I made shortly after moving over here"—Chris glanced at me and smiled—"I'd probably still be holed up in my house, struggling with my thoughts. Now, I don't want to suggest my experience was in any way comparable to what these young people have been through. But the fact that even someone like me, with a huge amount of privilege and resources at my fingertips, can struggle and need support to keep going, just shows how important that support is. And just how much more critical it is for these teens, who don't share my privilege."

Chris paused for a moment. The room was silent, and a lump formed in my throat.

"I urge you all to support Pride House and, if you're not a member of the LGBTQ+ community, to be an ally in your everyday life. Calling out intolerance, educating yourself, respecting peoples' names and pronouns, and not making assumptions about peoples' gender identity or sexuality. We may sometimes screw up—I recently did and felt like a complete idiot. But we need to keep trying. Anyway, that's enough from me. Now, for the true stars of tonight, the Pride House teens, who'll be showcasing their skills in a talent show. I'll hand it back to Alex to introduce the first performance."

The room ruptured into applause. Tears welled in my eyes. I hadn't seen this side of Chris before. His speech was thoughtful, heartfelt, and vulnerable. And I hadn't realized my friendship with him had helped him through a difficult time.

Within minutes, five teens in drag had the audience in stitches with their enthusiastic performance of the Spice Girls' "Wannabe." A rather chaotic dance routine by Erin and two of her friends garnered a vigorous round of applause, as did an earnest if slightly pitchy song by a four-teen-year-old teen. Seeing Erin up there, performing her heart out, in front of so many of the Pride House teens' families but not her own, was like daggers in my chest. Josh and I clapped and cheered extra loud for her. Before we knew it, the talent show was over, and it was time for Josh and me to take the stage. I swallowed, squeezing the handle of my ridiculous foam hammer a few times as if it was a stress ball.

The auction got off to a flying start with a bidding war between three audience members for a romantic dinner for two at a local restaurant. My nerves dissipated as I focused on following the bids, finally slamming down the hammer and announcing the winner.

"Next up, this gorgeous pink lamp, decked in sparkling crystals. This lamp would add a touch of class to anyone's home. Do we have a bidder?" Josh looked around the room.

I was glad Josh introduced the lamp. I couldn't have said that with a straight face.

Cynthia raised her hand. "Fifty pounds."

I stifled a laugh. I'd imagined the lamp being at home in Cynthia's house, and apparently, I'd been spot on.

Bec, Daphne's mother, must have shared Cynthia's questionable taste. She raised her hand. "Sixty pounds."

Cynthia glared at her and counterbid. They bounced back and forth, increasing their bids in ten-pound increments, exchanging dirty looks. Two minutes later, Cynthia was the proud new owner of the hideous lamp.

"This impressive male nude, sculpted in exquisite detail, would be a welcome addition to your home, bringing the timeless elegance of ancient Rome to your living room, or even...your bedroom." Josh winked at me.

I worked hard to suppress a giggle.

To my surprise, Khanh started the bidding, but an older man sitting at the back quickly outbid him.

My dress was next. I cleared my throat. "This stunning McKinnon dress has only been worn once, at the London premiere of *Muscle Man 4*. Fresh off the red carpet— although I can assure you, it has been dry cleaned. Do we have any starting bids?"

My eyes darted around the silent room. My heart sank. I'd hoped it would attract some interest.

Bec raised her hand. "200 pounds."

Cynthia jumped in. "500 pounds," she said, looking at Bec as if daring her to go higher.

Before I knew it, my head was jerking from side to side, like I was a spectator at Wimbledon watching a match between tennis greats. They reached four digits, and the rallying continued. My heart raced as the numbers skyrocketed.

Bidding was at 2000 pounds when Cynthia, fed up with Bec's 100-pound increments, yelled, "3000 pounds."

Bec, clearly intent on getting the dress after losing out on the lamp, shot her a glowering look. "5000 pounds."

Cynthia's eyes widened, and she leaned back in the chair, defeated. Bec gave her a victorious smile.

Thrilled at the result—the dress had raised a quarter of the money Pride House needed to stay afloat—I had to resist the urge to run over and hug Bec and Cynthia, an urge I'd never thought I'd experience. Instead, I smashed the hammer down, declaring Bec the winner. Hopefully, the heated bidding wouldn't irretrievably damage their relationship.

Rose won the next item, a massage voucher, and my dad successfully bid on tickets to a West End show. Sharon looked pleased, and Tina less than thrilled, when Sharon won a metal bust of a dog, looking regal and very human-like in a shirt and fancy jacket. Scouring the room for bidders, I'd seen Chris start to raise his hand for that item, before sitting back in his chair, hands in his lap.

Before long, it was time for the last auction item of the night—Chris. I'd insisted Josh run it, citing a conflict of interest. The butterflies that had been fluttering gently in my stomach picked up pace again.

Josh dramatically cleared his throat. "Now everyone, the moment you have all been waiting for. The last auction item of the night. A dinner date—a *platonic* dinner date, just to be clear—with none other than Chris Trent himself! Would anyone like to start the bidding?"

Mouths gaped, and an excited murmur filled the room.

Someone yelled, "Fifty pounds," and the bidding was off. I blinked and it had skyrocketed to one thousand pounds. As the numbers grew higher bidders dropped out, until there were only two left. Cynthia, who had a determined look on her face, and the older man, who had won the nude sculpture earlier in the evening.

For Chris's sake, I was rooting for the older man. Salt and pepper hair, wearing slacks and a cardigan, he looked like a professor of ancient history. I could see them having an enjoyable evening discussing travel and art. I couldn't even begin to imagine how a date with Cynthia would go.

The man raised his hand, increasing Cynthia's last bid by almost a quarter. "Eight thousand pounds."

Surely he'd won. Stunned, I looked at Cynthia, but she showed no signs of defeat.

"Ten thousand pounds," she said.

My jaw dropped.

The professor shook his head. He was out. As Josh smashed his hammer down and declared Cynthia the winner, I looked at Chris in the front row. He turned and gave Cynthia a big smile and a wave. Chris really was a talented actor. He looked genuinely pleased.

Giddy, I tried to estimate how much we'd raised. It had to be over Alex's target of twenty thousand pounds. A wave of gratitude toward my friends, family, and the other audience members, even Cynthia—in fact, in particular Cynthia, since she was the largest benefactor—washed over me.

The auction over, Alex gave some concluding remarks and the room started to empty. Once the crowd that had formed around Chris dissipated, I walked over to him.

"Your speech really moved me. Thanks so much for coming. The night wouldn't have been a success without you." I lowered my voice. "I'm sorry about Cynthia winning the date. You'll need to bring your bodyguard with you on that one."

Chris snorted. "I think I can hold my own against her.

I'm just pleased we raised so much for Pride House. And I can't take any credit for tonight's success. The teenagers, Alex, you, and Josh did all the hard work. I'm glad you liked the speech, though. You know, I was worried about talking about myself—I didn't want to make it all about me or come across like my issues were similar to what the teens have to deal with, but I thought sharing something personal might move the audience to donate more. And also show the teens that even celebrities and superheroes can be vulnerable and have hard times."

"It was great." I resisted the urge to hug him.

Cynthia approached behind Chris.

"Cynthia!" I exclaimed, to give Chris some warning. "Thank you so much for your generosity tonight." I surprised myself by giving her a hug. Her floral perfume tickled my nose, hanging around well after I loosened my embrace.

"My pleasure. It's such a worthy cause, and it was such a fun night." She turned to Chris. "Could I redeem my prize by inviting you and Sophie over for dinner with some of my girlfriends and hubbies. I'm sure they would all love to meet you?"

Chris's lips twitched. I couldn't tell if the twitch was in response to Cynthia's use of "girlfriends" to describe her female friends, which he knew I hated, or if it was due to the fact Cynthia had invited me as well.

"That sounds perfect, assuming Sophie is up for it." Chris looked at me expectantly, an eyebrow raised.

My stomach sank. After Cynthia's huge donation, I couldn't exactly brush off the dinner party invitation like I did last time. And it wouldn't be fair to let Chris brave the dinner alone, since he was only going because of a favor I'd asked him.

"Of course," I said, attempting a sincere smile.

"Excellent. I'll check with my assistant which nights I'm free and be in touch. I'm assuming Sophie had your contact details. Thanks again for your support. Now, I better help these guys pack up, or they'll be here all night!"

Cynthia, flushed after her interaction with Chris, went back to the mothers' group party, who were making moves to leave.

Chris, Josh, and I stayed to help pack up, Chris's muscles coming in handy for dismantling the stage.

"Man, I'm regretting not bidding on that dog bust now. I couldn't decide if it was kitschy in a good, kind of ironic way, or just tacky. I'd just decided I wanted it when it sold, and now I'm kicking myself. It reminded me so much of the Hungarian Vizsla we had growing up." Chris looked morose.

Just then, Alex walked up. "Sophie, Josh!" An enormous grin spread across Alex's face. "I finished adding up the donations, and we brought in over *thirty thousand pounds*! We'll be able to do all of the repairs and have money left over for some other initiatives we've been wanting to do."

Josh grabbed his hammer and slammed it down. "Woo hoo! That's amazing!"

Chris and I high-fived. It was an enormous relief to know that our efforts had paid off and Pride House wouldn't be shut down.

Packing up done, Chris and I said goodbye to Alex and Josh. Caught up in the evening's excitement, my nerves about Chris had been pushed to one side. But they all flooded back as we walked into the crisp night air.

Chris pulled me close, and my heart started pounding.

"Has anyone ever told you how hot you are with a giant

foam hammer?" he murmured into my ear. "I know we talked about going out for a drink, but how would you feel about coming back to my place instead?"

I laughed and put my arms around his waist. "Sounds great. Should I run back in and bring the hammer home with us?" I mimed smacking it on his butt.

"As tempting as that is, I'm keen to get you home as soon as possible."

A shiver of anticipation went down my spine. Chris was clearly interested in more than just friendship. And after talking out my concerns with Mia and Rose, Chris's heartfelt speech, and the way he was looking at me right now, passion burning in his eyes, so was I.

CHAPTER TWENTY-SIX

SOPHIE

THE THUDDING of my heart almost drowned out the sound of the front door to the Castle closing behind us. For a moment, we just stared at each other, and then suddenly, we were kissing passionately, our tongues dancing, our lips hungry. He lifted me up and pushed me against the wall in the hallway, his warm body pressed against mine. God, I'd been wanting this for so long. All my worries about what Chris was looking for, and what I was looking for, vanished and were replaced with raw, burning desire.

"Do you want to go to the bedroom?" Chris asked, breathing heavily.

"Yes." I started to untwine my legs from around Chris, getting ready to walk up the stairs, but instead, he bounded up them, with me still attached, and threw me on the bed.

"Now, where were we?" He growled, kissing my neck.

I began unbuttoning his shirt, my fingers fumbling, aching to have his bare skin pressed against mine. He followed my cue, and before long, we were both stripped down to our underwear.

He took off my bra and cupped my breasts in his hands,

looking at them lustfully, before lowering his head to one nipple and sucking. I felt a release and he pulled up in shock. *Shit.*

"Fuck, I'm sorry—I didn't even think of that," he said, a hint of breast milk on his lips.

"Me either," I said, giggling. "Come here." I pulled his head down to me and kissed him, gently biting his lip.

As we kissed, our hands started to explore each other's body, first tentatively and then with more urgency. *Oh boy.* He knew just where to kiss, just where to touch, to turn me on. His lips on my ear, my neck, my collarbone. His hands touching my breasts, my inner thighs, grazing over my knickers.

My breathing got faster as our bodies moved in sync, rubbing against each other. His dick, hard and erect, pressed against me. I wanted more. My hands, trembling, tugged at his underpants, pulling them partway down. Chris whipped mine off in one smooth motion.

"You drive me wild," Chris said, his breath ragged.

"I want you so bad," I whispered.

But he didn't take the hint and kept touching me, turning me on to the point that if I'd been strong enough to flip him onto his back and straddle him, I would have. *Oh god.* I was used to my female exes being pros at foreplay, but I'd never experienced anything like this from a man. Clearly, I'd been dating the wrong guys.

Chris leaned over to the bedside table, grabbed a condom and put it on.

"Fuck me," I gasped, looking directly into his eyes. I was too far gone with desire to be subtle any more. But he went back to teasing me with his fingers. *Good lord, this man knows what he's doing.*

And then, just when I thought I couldn't take it anymore, he was inside me.

"You are so fucking hot, Sophie," he groaned, slowly thrusting.

Hot and sweaty, we gradually picked up pace as the feeling of urgency increased.

I was so close now, all the desire, all the pent-up sexual tension of the past few months, finally coming to a head.

We locked eyes again. And then my muscles were spasming, waves of pleasure, of release, washing over me, making me bite my lip and then moan.

"Oh fuck," Chris said in a strangled voice as he came at the same time, staring deep into my eyes. For a moment, the room around us faded, and everything slowed down. And then it was over.

I collapsed, letting out a happy sigh.

"That was amazing. Come here, you," Chris said affectionately, pulling me to him in a big bear hug.

Still tingling, I relaxed against his warm body and nestled my head into his chest. I stayed in that position, catching my breath, for a few minutes, working up enough courage to ask Chris what had been playing on my mind since Saturday night.

I swallowed, glad I was nuzzled into him so we couldn't see each other's faces. "So...have you given any thought to what this is? Are you just looking for something casual, like a friends-with-benefits situation, or are you interested in dating?"

My chest tightened as Chris took a deep breath in.

"After the whole thing with Vanessa, I told myself I was done with relationships."

A pain shot through my chest. Since Saturday I'd spent so

much time thinking about all the reasons why a relationship with Chris was a bad idea. I'd been trying to convince myself that, if anything was going to happen between us, friends-with-benefits would be ideal, but as soon as he said he was done with relationships, I knew deep down that wasn't what I wanted.

"But I really think we have something special here, and we should give it a shot. What do you think?"

A warm, gooey feeling replaced the tension in my chest. I looked up at him and smiled.

"To be honest, this whole thing has taken me by surprise. After Elliot came along, I'd also sworn off relationships—I wanted to prioritize him and the new business. I'm not going to lie, I am worried about how we will navigate living in different countries, our careers, your celebrity, and Elliot. But I feel the same way as you. I don't want to throw it away without trying first."

Chris squeezed me, a huge smile on his face.

"That makes me so happy to hear that. And you know, I'd never come between you and Elliot, or you and your business. With the different countries, I think we'll be able to work something out. The great thing about being a well-known actor with an impeccable British accent"—he grinned at me—"is that I've been getting a few offers of work over here. I'm locked into doing one more *Muscle Man* movie next year, but after that, I'll be a free-range chicken." The grin disappeared. "But, I don't want to sugar coat things. Dating a celebrity isn't always easy. The media will publish all sorts of lies about me, about us—possibly even about Elliot, although I'll do everything I can to stop that. And as you've already seen, when I go out in public I'm often approached by people or photographed or filmed, which can be pretty disruptive. I've developed ways of coping with it all. Not going out in public as much as I used to, especially not places where I'm at a higher risk of being swarmed, hiring a bodyguard and trying not to let myself get too upset by what the media says, although I'm still working on that. But it will be hard, and I totally understand if it's not something you want to go through."

"I've been thinking about that. So far, what I've seen hasn't been a deal-breaker for me. But my top priority will always be Elliot, so if it started to directly affect him, it could become one." It was a real concern, but not one I wanted to think too deeply about right now.

"Of course. Speaking of you, Elliot, and different countries...Now that we are officially dating, how would you feel about you and Elliot coming to Chicago for Thanksgiving? I've got four days off filming, and I'd love you guys to meet my parents and friends and show you around."

The warm gooey feeling spread even further across my body. "I would love that! We're in!" I reached up and kissed him. I'd intended it to be a quick kiss, but it immediately morphed into more.

At this rate, we wouldn't be getting any sleep.

CHAPTER TWENTY-SEVEN

CHRIS

"COME ON, we need to get ready. Cynthia paid good money for us to be at this dinner party."

"What about I stay here and keep the bed warm for you?" Sophie groaned as I pulled her out of the bed. Damn, she was hot. Pouting at me, naked, her hair tousled. She wasn't making leaving the bedroom easy.

Since the night of the fundraiser two weeks ago, we hadn't been able to keep our hands off each other. I'd set up a cot at the Castle for Elliot so they could both stay over, but tonight, Sophie's parents were babysitting him.

"Come on, lazy. You pimped me out to Cynthia. The least you can do is share in my pain. We just need to survive the next few hours, and then we can go back to bed." While happy that we'd raised so much money for Pride House, I was less than thrilled that Cynthia was the winning bidder. My disappointment had transformed into relief when she proposed a dinner party, rather than an intimate one-on-one dinner, and invited Sophie too. Sophie's company turned the dinner from an event I'd usually dread to something I was actually looking forward to. I was hoping it would be like hate-watching a terrible show together.

Forty minutes later, showered and clothed, the cold fall air hit us as we left the Castle to walk to Cynthia's house.

"I've been meaning to say, your speech at the fundraiser made quite an impression on the teens. A number of them said it was reassuring to hear that even superheroes struggled sometimes. One mentioned he'd been a victim of revenge porn last year—his ex had sent some of their class-mates explicit photos of him—and your story made him feel less alone." Sophie squeezed my hand, sending a bolt of warmth to my heart. I was so glad my speech had touched the teens. "Thanks again for stepping in at the eleventh hour. I know this is the last thing you want to be doing right now."

"You know, I'm sure they wouldn't believe it, but they made a big impression on me as well. So many of them have gone through so much, at such a young age. I had a few teens come up to me at the end of the night with similar stories—photos or private texts shared without their consent —telling me how violated they felt. I'd been nervous talking about it openly, but I'm glad I did. If it helped even one of those kids, it will have been worth it." I paused. "It also got me thinking about whether I could do it on a broader scale —telling my story publicly and using my platform to advo-cate for legal change, to stop similar things happening to other people. It would be nice to turn my humiliation into something positive."

"That sounds like an amazing idea!" Sophie's eyes glowed in the evening light.

"It's still early days, but I'm excited about it. And you know what else I'm excited about?"

Sophie looked at me.

I lowered my voice and leaned in. "Peeling off the fucking adorable coat you're wearing, lifting you onto the dining room table, pulling off those lace panties I just watched you put on and..."

Sophie pulled away, giggling. "Do you want me to come to this dinner or not? Because if you keep going, I'll either be pulling you into the bushes for a quickie or going back home to have a cold shower. We're a minute away from Cynthia's place now."

I'd nearly made myself need a cold shower as well. I surreptitiously adjusted my pants as we walked up to Cynthia's door and knocked.

"Welcome! Please come in! Everyone, our guest of honor has arrived," Cynthia announced loudly to the empty hallway. She ushered us down it and into a large dining room. Almost twenty people, dressed in formal attire, were milling about, sipping champagne and chatting next to a long table covered in a lace cloth. Each China plate on the table was surrounded by silverware—knives, forks and spoons of varying sizes and shapes—and crystal glasses. A waiter entered from another door, holding a tray of finger food. My heart sank. We were in for a long night.

The chatting stopped as soon as we walked in.

"Ladies and gentlemen, I would like you to meet our guest of honor tonight, Chris Trent." Cynthia walked around the room, introducing me to everyone individually. She rattled off their names, occupations, and titles, as if I'd be impressed that Bernard was Chief Operating Officer at a big bank, or Susan was a partner at a large international law firm.

My jaw clenched as I noticed that each time Cynthia introduced me, she'd either forget to introduce Sophie, who'd then have to introduce herself, or would say as an afterthought, "Oh, and this is Sophie."

"We are just waiting for Bec and Peter, who is Chief Financial Officer at Rennerts of London, to arrive, and then we can take a seat." Cynthia looked at her watch. "Bec is really pushing fashionably late to a new level," she muttered.

The doorbell rang. "That better be her. Darling, can you get the door?" Cynthia asked her husband John, who Cynthia had proudly advised me was CEO of Mount Waverley Investments.

A minute later, John and another man, who I assumed was Peter, stepped into the dining room. Cynthia, obviously keen to get the dinner party started, hit her champagne glass with a spoon to attract everyone's attention.

I turned to her, only to see her face flush pink and her lips purse together. What had pissed her off now?

Sophie nudged me, and I followed her line of sight. Bec had entered the room, wearing the crimson dress she'd won at the auction.

The dress she had won in an aggressive bidding war against Cynthia.

While admittedly I was biased, I thought Sophie wore it better. It had perfectly hugged Sophie's curves and complimented her dark skin. Bec's thin frame and pale complexion didn't do it justice.

Cynthia was clearly taking it as a personal affront that Bec had worn the dress to her party. A vein on her forehead throbbed, and she downed half a glass of champagne as if it were water and she'd just finished an intense workout.

"Everyone! Now that our final guests have arrived"— Cynthia shot Bec a glare—"please take a seat. The food will be out shortly. Chris, sit next to me." She sat in the middle of the long table and patted the seat to her left vigorously, before signaling to the waiter to refill her champagne glass.

I sat as directed, Sophie on my other side. I gave her a look of solidarity. She grimaced. Bec and Peter sat opposite us, seemingly oblivious to Cynthia's annoyance.

"So, Chris, what do you like doing in your spare time?" Cynthia asked, as the waiting staff brought out the first course, a seafood bisque.

For a moment, all I could think of was being in bed with Sophie. Well, it had been taking up a lot of my spare time recently. Under the table, I trailed a finger along Sophie's inner thigh and felt her legs open slightly. A flood of desire washed over me. I couldn't wait for this dinner party to be over. Sophie gave my leg a firm squeeze that was disappointingly chaste. She was probably reminding me to respond to Cynthia, who was staring at me expectantly.

"Sorry. I love getting out in nature. There's some great hiking around LA, and the Heath is fantastic. Unfortunately, I don't have a lot of free time at the moment with my filming schedule. What about you?"

"Oh, you know, tennis, shopping, philanthropy. Not that I have much spare time either these days, with baby Harriet keeping me and Camille, our new French nanny, very busy."

Out of the corner of my eye, I saw Sophie's mouth twitch.

The dinner party continued at an excruciatingly slow pace. The only thing making it bearable was having Sophie by my side, even if I was stuck talking to Cynthia, who was quizzing me about the celebrities I'd met and Hollywood gossip, some of my least favorite topics of conversation. It turns out, hate-watching wasn't so fun when you were part of the show and couldn't mock it in real time.

The third course, a rich duck ragu served with fresh pasta, arrived. Thankfully, Cynthia had turned her attention to the red-haired woman sitting opposite her, telling her how advanced Harriet was.

"She can even say "lait," which is French for milk, when she's thirsty now. Let me show you the video!" Cynthia downed her glass of red wine, walked around the table, and leaned over to show the red-haired woman her phone screen. At the same time, Bec lifted her glass of red wine up for a sip. Cynthia's elbow and the glass collided, and red wine flew out of the glass, all over Bec and her new dress.

"Shit!" Bec jumped out of her seat in horror and began to frantically pat the dress with her napkin.

Cynthia signaled for the waiters to bring towels and then turned her attention back to Bec. "I'm sorry, Bec. At least it's red on red, so if the stain doesn't come out at the drycleaners, it won't show too badly. But if it's any consolation, the dress didn't suit you anyway. It would have looked better on me."

Bec had been holding it together until Cynthia's last remark, which tipped her over the edge. Her face flushed, and she took a step toward Cynthia, clenching her hands. "You did this on purpose, didn't you? You're pissed off I outbid you, and this is your way of getting back at me?"

Cynthia stepped back and opened her mouth. "Of course, I didn't do it on purpose! But I don't know why you thought it appropriate to wear the dress tonight, rubbing my face in it."

That comment infuriated Bec even more. She threw the napkin and the towels on her duck ragu and turned to her husband. "Come on, Peter. I think it's time for us to leave." She stormed out, the Chief Financial Officer at Rennerts of London following behind her.

Cynthia came back to her seat, looking shaky.

"Well, that was very dramatic, wasn't it!" she said with forced cheer, a weak grin on her face. "Excuse me, please," she said to the waiter, "could I have another glass of wine?"

As much as I hadn't warmed to her, I almost felt sorry for Cynthia. She'd clearly spent a lot of money and effort on this dinner party, and it was *not* going well.

She turned to me again. "So, Chris, how long are you in London for?"

"I'm not sure," I said, flashing a glance at Sophie. After our post-fundraiser relationship conversation, I'd been planning to extend my stay in London, but I hadn't spoken to Sophie about it yet. Faced with a choice between living in a desolate white mansion by myself or hanging out with Sophie and Elliot in the Castle, it was a no brainer. I didn't need to be back in LA until mid-next year to film the next *Muscle Man* installment, and the landlord had insisted I sign a twelve-month lease on the Castle, so there was nothing preventing me from staying.

I looked at Sophie again, thinking of all the fun we'd be having if I wasn't working hectic hours. Being with Sophie just felt so...right. I'd never experienced such a strong emotional and physical connection with someone before. I'd never wanted to spend all my waking and sleeping hours with someone. When we were apart, I couldn't stop thinking about her. Wondering what she was doing, daydreaming about being in bed together, or making note of a funny story I wanted to tell her. But despite all that, there was a niggling worry in the back of my mind. Was I getting too attached to Sophie and Elliot too fast? Sophie had never given me any reason to doubt her, but in the past, I'd put my trust in people—my father, Vanessa—and they had let me down. I didn't think I was strong enough to have my heart broken again. And if things got really serious between me and Sophie, would I be there for Elliot, or would I fuck it all up like my dad did?

A hand caressing my thigh distracted me from my thoughts. For a few seconds, I relaxed and a flame of desire sparked. Sophie was clearly looking forward to getting back to the Castle as much as I was. I couldn't wait to make her moan again. A vision of her earlier today, naked, hunger in her eyes, flashed into my mind.

That image shattered, and the flame extinguished, as it hit me the hand was making its way up my *right* thigh. The side Cynthia was sitting on. Not Sophie.

I flinched as Cynthia leaned close to me. "I'm so sorry about you and Vanessa. I know how hard breakups can be." She lowered her voice. "John and I are actually going through a bit of a rough patch at the moment. So, if you ever need someone to talk to or, you know, for anything else"— she gave my thigh a squeeze with a tipsy wink—"I'm here for you."

I grimaced and shuffled my legs, hoping Cynthia would stop. She was tipsy and having a rough night, and I didn't want to make a scene. But as much as I'd been teasing Sophie about pimping me out to Cynthia, I hadn't signed up for this. I glanced at Sophie, deep in conversation with a man next to her and oblivious to Cynthia's advances. I relaxed slightly as the waiters entered the room carrying the fourth course, venison in a red wine jus. Cynthia would need both hands to eat that. I breathed out deeply as she took her hand off my leg.

"You mentioned one of your interests was philanthropy. I'd love to hear more about it," I said, in an attempt to change the subject.

"We've set up our own foundation, the Willards Foundation—Willards is our last name—to help disadvantaged children in Africa. We hold a black-tie gala each year to raise money for the orphanage we've set up."

I inwardly groaned. The last thing the world needed was another family foundation or black-tie gala. Once I got my first massive paycheck, I'd spent a while researching how to most effectively donate money. Starting your own charity was not on the list. Donating to existing, experienced not-for-profits with proven track records was. And I didn't understand people's need to plaster their name all over their good deeds.

"We visited the orphanage last year. Look how cute the kids are." Cynthia brought up her Instagram account, scrolling through photos of her smiling with Black children.

I regretted bringing up the topic now. I was getting distinct white savior vibes.

"And of course, we attend things like the Pride House fundraiser and make sure we give generously."

I plastered a smile on my face. "Yes, thanks again so much for your contribution. That was very generous."

I wished that man would stop talking to Sophie so she could save me from Cynthia. With two empty seats across from me and Sophie, and the man sitting opposite Cynthia arguing with his companion about football, there wasn't anyone else but Cynthia to talk to. I surreptitiously glanced at my watch and swallowed a sigh. It was ten-thirty and, judging by the cutlery in front of me, there were at least two more courses to go.

Cynthia dug her manicured fingernails into my bicep in a claw-like grip, causing me to jump in my seat. Good lord.

"How often do you work out, Chris? These are some impressive biceps."

"It depends on my filming schedule, but normally at

least every other day. And I try to go walking on the Heath with my dog, Alfie, when I can."

"Oh, what time do you usually go for your walks? Maybe I can join you sometimes." She gave me another wink, and her hand started to make its way up my thigh again.

Oh god.

"Unfortunately, it's very unpredictable because of filming. It's usually a spur-of-the-moment type thing."

Cynthia's face fell. Maybe she'd finally gotten the message I wasn't interested.

"Please excuse me for a minute while I go to the bathroom," Cynthia said, wobbling as she got up.

I turned to Sophie, who was pushing food around on her plate and half listening to two men to her left speaking about floating rate notes and inflation. I felt for her. I didn't know which was worse—talking about financial markets or being sexually harassed by Cynthia. I nudged Sophie. When she realized Cynthia wasn't beside me, she relaxed.

"I should probably try to network with these men. They work in exactly the industries that need to focus more on diversity and inclusion, but they are just so boring. How are you holding up?" Sophie murmured.

"Please put me out of my misery now. Do you know if Cynthia and her husband have an open relationship? Because she is being *very* friendly toward me. Like, hands on the thigh, flirty wink, sexual innuendo kind of friendly."

Sophie choked on the mouthful of venison she had just taken. "Oh my god, I'm so sorry. I know I joked about it, but I didn't think it would actually happen! Especially not sitting right next to her husband."

"It's making me pretty uncomfortable. Either she hasn't worked out we're dating, or she doesn't care."

"Either one wouldn't surprise me, to be honest. While I'm not one for PDA, if you want me to drape my arm around you possessively or something to put Cynthia off, just let me know."

I chuckled. "Thanks. If it gets really bad, I may take you up on your offer." It certainly had some appeal.

The fifth course, Wagyu steak with black truffle potato gratin, arrived just as Cynthia returned to the table. Sophie and I continued talking, and to my relief, Cynthia turned to her husband and began speaking to him.

"The rub on this steak is great. I wonder what they put in it? We should try recreating it at home," I said earnestly, examining the meat.

"Mmmmm, it is good. If only I hadn't already eaten my bodyweight in food." Sophie leaned in, bit her lip, and lowered her voice. "But I know another rub I'd like to recreate at home." Her hand stroked my leg, sending an electric jolt straight to my crotch.

"Oh, you want to go down that path do you? Two can play at this game." I murmured. The evening was suddenly looking up. "I've got some rump steak we could experiment on, but we'd have to tenderize it first." I looked down at her butt and then back up at her and winked.

"The rub might also work on poultry...Perhaps I could rub it on a big, juicy cock," Sophie said, her mouth twitching as she tried to keep a straight face.

Now it was my turn to choke on my food.

"I would really like a tart for dessert tonight. A delicious, dripping, moist tart. Perhaps fig or cherry?" I asked after I'd recovered. My fingers trailed up her inner thigh again.

"I'm hoping for spotted dick. It's my favorite. It can't get it in me fast enough. But if they don't have spotted dick, I'd also be fine with a really, really stiff..."—Sophie paused and held my gaze for a moment, then licked her lips—"meringue on my Eton Mess."

Oh god. She was both turning me on and making it very hard not to burst out laughing.

"What are you two giggling about?" Cynthia asked, sounding put out.

Sophie composed herself and smiled sweetly at Cynthia. "Oh, nothing. Just speculating what would be for dessert. All the food's been delicious so far."

"It's a lavender crème brûlée tart. Our chef sourced the lavender from our garden, so it is fresh and organic."

"Excellent! I love tarts. I take it you're a fan as well, Cynthia?" I asked.

Sophie kicked me under the table.

Ten minutes later, our plates were cleared and the tarts were served. Thank god we'd reached the last course of the night. And it was only, I glanced at my watch, eleven-thirty.

I'd lost my appetite halfway through dessert, and only took a few bites before putting it aside.

"For someone who claims to like tarts, you're not showing much interest in this one," Sophie whispered.

I winked. "I'm hoping to try another one when I get home. And this one has a bit of a soggy bottom."

We escaped twenty minutes later into the cold night air, exhilarated it was finally over.

Sophie turned to me, looking apologetic. "I'm so sorry! What a painful evening. I promise I'll never ask you to do something like that again. I owe you one."

"It was worth it just for the dirty food talk." I pulled Sophie's hips to mine and kissed her.

She giggled. "I can't wait to get home and put some of our culinary skills to work."

CHAPTER TWENTY-EIGHT

SOPHIE

CHRIS and I perched on one of the two comfortable but old leather couches that dominated my parents' modest living room, facing my parents. Two large windows on either side of the fireplace looked out over their small front garden. When the weather was good, sunshine streamed through the windows. Today, the sun barely made an impression due to the overcast skies—it was a typical London gray, cold October day. Despite that, the strings of colorful electric lights I'd strung up yesterday around the room and the candles on the mantelpiece gave the room a cheerful glow.

"So, Chris, who's your favorite director? It must be amazing to work with so many big names!" Dad leaned forward, smiling, holding Mum's hand.

As a teenager, my parents' fondness for holding hands and general expressions of affection for each other had been terribly embarrassing. But now, I just thought it was cute.

"Chris, have you ever been hurt by your fans or the paparazzi? Being hounded all the time must be terrible," Mum asked at the exact same time, a serious look on her face.

I flinched. Oh god. Maybe this was a bad idea. Poor Chris had just suffered through Cynthia's dinner party, thanks to me. I hoped this wouldn't be a repeat. Chris had met my parents a few times before, but I kept those interactions short for this reason. As much as I loved my parents, Dad could be intense sometimes, and Mum...well, she was a worrier. And she was *very* worried I was dating a famous American movie star.

I focused on the painting above the mantelpiece and took a deep breath, inhaling the familiar aromas wafting from the kitchen, hoping they'd have a calming impact on me. However, the painting just reminded me again of my parents' love story. Was there any chance Chris and I could have the sort of relationship they had, still madly in love forty-something years later, especially if this lunch was a disaster?

Chris seemed unperturbed by my parents' questions. He smiled at my dad. "My favorite director would have to be...Hmmm, this is a hard one...Probably my current director, Melanie Chester. I'm not her favorite person at the moment after the Alfie incidents on set—I'm sure Sophie told you about them—but she has an amazing creative vision and really knows how to get the best performances out of her actors." He turned to Mum, looking serious. "No, I've never been injured. On the whole, I've found my fans quite respectful. And while they can be a pain, the paparazzi normally stay a distance away from me."

With Elliot and I visiting Chris's family in a few weeks for Thanksgiving, Chris extending his stay in London to spend time with Elliot and me, and Dad regularly suggesting I invite Chris over for dinner, I couldn't put off an official "meet the parents" any longer. Our Diwali celebration seemed like the perfect opportunity. Not only would it be a nice way to introduce Chris to some of my favorite family traditions, but my grandparents and Josh would be here to help ease any tension. My aunt, uncle, and cousins who usually also celebrated with us had decided to stay in Manchester this year, so at least Chris wouldn't be overwhelmed with my relatives. I looked at my watch, frowning. Where the hell were Josh and my grandparents? They should have been here at midday.

Mum opened her mouth to ask another question, most likely to clarify what Chris meant when he said, "On the whole...," when the doorbell rang. Relieved, I jumped up and strode to the door.

My grandparents' beaming faces greeted me. Dadi wore a gorgeous red and gold sari and held a plate of one of my favorite sweets, moti pak. Her face flickered with disappointment as she registered I was wearing a sweater and jeans, and I felt a pang of guilt that I'd run out of time to change into a sari. Even Josh, who just walked through the gate, looked a lot smarter than me in his slacks, shirt, and jacket combination.

"Happy Diwali! Sorry we are late. There was an accident on the roads," Dadi said, giving me a warm embrace. She heard the gate clang, turned, and saw Josh. "Oh, hi Josh! Happy Diwali!"

"I'm just glad you're all here. Come in!" I ushered them into the living room quickly, hoping Mum hadn't asked Chris any more questions.

"Dada, Dadi, this is Chris. Chris, my grandparents."

Chris went over to greet them. I'd told them about Chris last week. They'd been surprised I was dating someone but happy for me.

Chris and my grandparents exchanged pleasantries while I picked Elliot up off the rug, anticipating they'd be eager for cuddles. I immediately had him snatched out of my arms by Dada.

"And how is my favorite little man?" He lifted him into the air.

I winced, worried he'd pull a muscle—Elliot wasn't exactly light anymore—but he was fine. For someone in his eighties, Dada was in good shape.

Dad clapped his hands. "Now everyone's here, I'll start getting the food ready." Dad and I had spent the morning cooking our favorite veggie curries, daal, and thepla. Everything was pretty much ready to go. Just a few things needed to be plated or garnished. To my relief, Mum stood up to follow him.

"Can I do anything to help?" Chris asked.

"No thanks, Chris. Just relax!" Mum said with slightly forced cheer.

As Mum and Dad disappeared into the kitchen, I relaxed.

Dadi interrupted Dada's game of peekaboo to show Elliot the bangles she was wearing. Dada, looking put out, turned his attention to Chris.

"So, Sophie tells me you're an actor, Chris? I always think people who pursue acting are very brave. All those auditions, rejections, having your appearance scrutinized, it must be so difficult."

Dadi and Dada hadn't heard of Chris when I mentioned he was an actor, and they obviously hadn't Googled him since then. Unlike us millennials, they used their computer for writing emails and checking train timetables, not stalking people online.

Josh opened his mouth, presumably to correct Dada's assumption that Chris was a struggling actor, but Chris responded first.

"Oh, thank you. That's very kind. But I'm not sure it was bravery that caused me to pursue acting. More likely naivety. I was so young, I didn't fully realize what I was getting myself into. I do love it, though."

Josh jumped in. "Chris is being very modest, Dada. He's actually very successful. Correct me if I'm wrong Chris, but I'm assuming you don't have to deal with many auditions or rejections these days."

My grandparents looked impressed. Chris smiled.

"Both still happen sometimes, but certainly not like when I was starting out. It was brutal back then."

Dada started telling Chris about the difficulty he'd had finding a job when they'd moved to England.

Since everyone was getting along well, and Mum and Dad were occupied elsewhere, I excused myself. Dadi's reaction to my outfit had been hanging over my head—I hated disappointing her. I went up to my room to change into my favorite sari as fast as I could, which wasn't very fast, given how out of practice I was. After fifteen minutes of struggling with the emerald green and gold fabric, I decided it was good enough. Just as I made my way downstairs, Dad yelled to me that lunch was ready. Everyone was seated around the dining table when I entered, waiting for me to arrive before they helped themselves to the food in front of them.

Dadi's face lit up with happiness when she saw me, making me so glad I'd gone to the effort. "Oh, beautiful. You look gorgeous, darling!"

Before long, we were digging into the food. To my relief, my parents had shelved their interrogation of Chris, and conversation flowed freely. Dadi was telling Chris, who seemed genuinely interested, about our family's Diwali traditions, when I first smelled it.

I sniffed. "Um, Dad, did you leave the oven or stove on? I can smell burning."

Alfie, who'd been slumped near my feet, unimpressed by the lack of meat scraps on offer, jumped up and started whining.

"I can't smell anything. I'm sure I turned them all off," Dad replied, spooning pickle and yogurt on a piece of thepla, unconcerned.

Dad took a bite and then sniffed again.

"Hmmm, okay. I think I can smell it now. Let me double check." He disappeared into the kitchen, returning a minute later. "They were all off. Where is that smell coming from?"

Just then, the smoke alarm in the hallway let off an ear-shattering wail. Alfie started barking furiously. We all looked at each other. And then it dawned on me.

"Shit! The candles in the living room!" I jumped out of my chair and raced down the hallway, my heart sinking as the smell got stronger. Shit. Shit. Shit.

I stopped, frozen with fear, when I reached the living room. A curtain was ablaze, white-gold flames shooting up, licking the ceiling, a haze of smoke surrounding it. A candle must have toppled off the mantelpiece, setting the curtain alight. One of the candles I had placed there. Crap.

"Oh god!" Josh exclaimed behind me.

I turned to see that Mum, Dad, Chris, and Josh had just arrived, their eyes wide as they registered the situation.

"I'll call the fire brigade." Dad pulled out his phone.

"My painting!" Mum's voice choked as she stared in horror at the flames dancing only inches from the frame.

"Water!" I yelled, racing back toward the kitchen, Josh following behind. As I ran past the dining room, I yelled to my grandparents to take Elliot and Alfie outside. I didn't want to risk them inhaling the smoke or being stuck in here if the fire got worse.

I looked around the kitchen for the biggest receptacle I could find. A large pot on the stove, remnants of curry in the bottom, caught my eye. I shoved it under the tap and began filling it with water.

Josh started pulling the trash bag, which was overflowing, out of the bin.

"I don't think now is the time to take out the trash, Josh!" I said, staring at him in disbelief as he dumped the bag on the ground.

"I'm going to fill this with water, you duffer!" Josh lifted the empty bin.

"Oh right. Sorry." The pot full, I raced back to the living room.

I'd been wondering why Chris and Mum weren't helping with the water, and as soon I entered, it became clear. They were on a rescue mission to save Mum's painting.

Chris stood on a chair, reaching over the mantle to lift the painting off the hook. He was far too close to the blaze for my liking. Mum stood under him, giving him instructions.

"Be careful of your hands! If you have a good grip on it, lift it up and pass it down to me. Don't put your head too close to the flames!"

I raced in and threw the water at the bottom of the curtain, careful not to splash the painting. My heart sank. It didn't make an iota of difference. I stood back to see how the painting retrieval operation was going.

Coughing, Chris carefully lifted the painting up and passed it down to Mum, who rushed out of the room with it. As Mum left, Josh ran in with the bin of water and threw it at the curtain. The flames dulled for a moment, before jumping back to their spirited dance. My heart thumped in my ears, my chest tight. Would the entire house go up in smoke, thanks to my poor candle placement?

Dad, coughing as he pulled furniture as far away from the flames as possible, looked up at me. "The fire brigade should be here soon. I think we should get out of here. The smoke is getting thicker."

We grabbed what we could carry: a side table, lamp, books, and Mum's reading glasses. I took a long look around the room as I shut the door, hoping this wouldn't be the last time I saw it, the last time I stood in this house as I knew it, and then I walked out the front door. Mum, Dada, and Dadi were standing on the front footpath, Elliot in Dadi's arms, the precious painting in Mum's. Chris and Dad were by my side, but Josh was nowhere to be seen.

Panic rose in my throat. "Where's Josh?"

I turned back around, looking down the smoky hallway. Should I go back in to find him?

I breathed out as Josh's silhouette emerged. He ran down the hall, holding something. I blinked twice as my eyes, stinging from the smoke, focused on what was in his hands.

It was the plate of thepla.

I looked up at Josh, making no effort to hide my disbelief. Food was the last thing on my mind at a time like this. At a time when my home was at risk of being engulfed in flames.

"What? I'm hungry, and who knows when we'll get back inside," Josh said, sounding defensive.

I shook my head as we walked down the front steps.

Josh, munching on a piece, offered the thepla to my

family and Chris, who stood in silence, watching the house. Unsurprisingly, there were no other takers.

Dad and Mum went to tell our neighbors what had happened, encouraging them to evacuate just in case the fire spread to their houses, which shared walls with ours. Suddenly, the window closest to the flames shattered, and flames and smoke started billowing out of it.

I flinched. "Oh god!"

"They should be here any minute," Chris said, rubbing my back as sirens sounded in the distance.

I looked up at him and noticed his eyebrow and hair were slightly singed, presumably as a result of the painting retrieval mission. Fingers crossed the hair and makeup department would be able to fix it so it didn't cause any continuity problems for the film. A vision of the director, shaking her head and cursing Chris, popped into my head.

The sirens got louder, and finally, a fire engine came into view. Relief flooded my body. Josh hurriedly stuffed the thepla he was eating in his mouth, placed the plate on the fence, and patted his curls. Despite the serious circumstances, I couldn't help but smile. Josh always had a thing for men in uniform.

The fire engine screeched to a halt outside our house, and six firefighters jumped out, springing to action. One approached, asking what had happened. Another fire engine pulled up as we were speaking. Before long, a steady stream of water was shooting into the living room through the broken window. The flames jumping out the window were replaced with a cloud of white smoke. And then the firefighters were rushing inside with a hose. A few minutes later, they reappeared, giving us a thumbs-up.

The firefighter we'd spoken to earlier walked back up to us, smiling. "It's all out. You were lucky. It could have been a lot worse. Your living room isn't habitable, but you should be fine to use the rest of the house. It'll just need a good airing," she said.

"Thank you so much," Dad responded with feeling.

But his gratitude barely registered with the firefighter, who'd just noticed Chris and was staring at him, her eyes wide with surprise.

"Sorry, um, are you...Chris Trent?" She flushed.

Within minutes, I was taking photos of Chris, Alfie, and the firefighters—and Josh, who'd sidled in between two hunky firemen, looking very pleased with himself—posing in front of the fire engines.

Photo shoot over and fire engines gone, we reentered the house. It smelled strongly of smoke.

"Oh dear," Mum groaned as we peered into the living room. Smoke had stained the white walls black, the wooden floor and mantlepiece were charred, and the shattered window had jagged pieces of glass protruding from the frame. Guilt about the candles stabbed at my heart.

"Can I help? I could move the furniture and the rug out of the room so we can dry them?" Chris pointed at the couches and rug, which were sitting in a pool of water.

"Before we worry about that, why don't we finish lunch so we aren't working on an empty stomach?" Mum looked at Josh, who had retrieved the plate of thepla and was busy shoving another piece in his mouth.

"Sounds like a great idea to me," he mumbled.

We opened the windows to air the house, put on our jackets, and heated up lunch. While my appetite had been affected by recent events, I was pleased to see Elliot's was not. He energetically scooped daal out of his bowl, shoveling it in the vicinity of his mouth. Approximately forty percent was entering it. The rest covered his face, a daal goatee dripping off his chin.

"You must be very well known if all those firefighters recognized you, Chris. Does that happen a lot?" Dada asked.

"Yes, it's quite common." Chris smiled.

A shot of worry hit my chest as Dada's question reminded me of something I'd put off raising with them. I swallowed.

"Ummm...on that topic...Because Chris is, err, fairly well known, there's a risk that photos of me and Elliot may be published on the internet. It's actually happened before. So, it's possible that family back in India will see them...and have a lot of questions. I'm sorry." I grimaced, watching Dada's and Dadi's faces.

Dadi, who had been enjoying Elliot's enthusiasm for daal, turned to me.

"Sophie, we have been meaning to talk to you about this anyway. I know you were worried about Elliot causing a scandal, but Dada and I do not want to hide him anymore."

I opened my mouth to object, but she shushed me.

"I know you are trying to protect us, but we are grown adults. We can look after ourselves, and we don't want to hide our gorgeous grandson. We want to tell everyone how amazing he is, show them photos of how cute he is." She smiled at Elliot. "I mean, look at him. How could anyone resist this little daal-covered angel?"

In my mind, he looked more like a garden gnome as the daal goatee turned into a full beard of daal. But Dadi was on a roll, so I kept my thoughts to myself.

"Yes, some people will gossip. Yes, some will be shocked, but we will cope. We went through it before when your parents got together, and we survived. You can't keep him a secret forever."

As much as I worried about them and wanted to protect them, I knew Dadi was right. They were older, and probably wiser, than me. And to be honest, if the news caused a scandal amongst our Indian relatives, it wouldn't affect me much since I wasn't in close contact with them. Dada and Dadi, who regularly spoke to them, were the ones who'd be most impacted. If they were itching to tell our relatives about Elliot, it didn't seem fair to stop them. And it would remove one more concern I had about dating Chris.

"If you are really sure...I just hate the thought of my choices causing you heartache. But if you do tell them, it might be best to do it sooner rather than later so that you can control the message, before they see us in the tabloids."

Dadi nodded. "Let me take a photo of Elliot. This could be the perfect picture to introduce him to everyone!"

I winced as I noticed her finger was partially over the camera lens, but didn't think now was the best time to raise it. I took another photo on my camera to send her.

A few hours later, after we'd finished lunch, wiped Elliot's face clean and popped him down for a nap, and moved everything out of the living room to dry, we said goodbye to our guests.

"Thanks again for saving the painting, Chris." Mum, to my surprise, gave him a warm hug as he left.

I watched everyone walk to the gate before shutting the door. As I walked back down the hallway, I found Mum staring at the blank spot above the burnt fireplace in the living room, where her painting had been.

I put my arm around her waist. "Sorry, Mum. I think it was my fault that the candle fell over."

"That's okay, darling. It was an accident. And I moved

them around this morning when I dusted, so it might have been me. I'm just glad everyone's safe, and the damage isn't too bad considering." She turned to me. "Sophie, look I know I haven't been the biggest supporter of you and Chris, but getting to know him more today, seeing him interact with everyone, I think I may have been too hasty. He clearly cares about you and Elliot a lot and seems like a genuinely nice young man. And he was a huge help today as well. Your conversation with your grandparents also reminded me that you, too, are an adult and capable of making your own decisions. As you know, your father and I faced lots of opposition from my parents when we got together, and I don't want to put you in a similar position. My priority is your and Elliot's happiness, and you're the best person to know how that should be achieved."

My chest filled with warmth. "Thanks, Mum. That means a lot." I gave her a hug, amazed at her change of heart. This had to be the most eventful Diwali yet.

While the fire had been incredibly stressful, there'd also been some huge progress to resolve some ongoing stresses in my life—keeping Elliot secret from my relatives and my mum's obvious concerns about Chris. One by one, my worries about dating Chris were being checked off, and I was beginning to let myself think that maybe there really was a future for us.

A quiver of excitement, mixed with apprehension, vibrated in my belly. Perhaps our relationship had a chance of being as successful as my parents' after all.

CHAPTER TWENTY-NINE

CHRIS

"GET OUTTA THE WAY, Uncle Chris. The turkey's coming for us!"

I jumped back, making space for my nieces and nephews who were chasing each other with a grotesque blow-up turkey, screaming wildly. Most of the guests had arrived for lunch, and the house was buzzing with energy. Steven and his sister were deep in a spirited discussion in the kitchen about when the actual turkey would be ready. My sisters were talking animatedly with Sophie about something. I had a bad feeling it was me—hopefully not one of their more embarrassing stories. Their husbands were watching football and yelling at the TV. Steven's dad and Mom were playing with Elliot, who was letting off infectious chuckles on a regular basis. And Lemon, my parents' anxious black Schnoodle, was hiding upstairs under the bed, not happy about the ruckus.

I smiled as I surveyed the scene. I loved Thanksgiving, and this year was extra special because I had Sophie and Elliot with me.

It was great to be home. I'd blinked back tears last night

when I saw Mom and Steven waiting near the barrier at the airport, waving madly. Mom, in her standard cold weather uniform of blue jeans, boots, and a knee-length puffer jacket, had a few more creases around her eyes since I'd seen her last. Steven, a few inches shorter than me, looked much the same as he had for the past decade—gray hair, glasses, and a cardigan, with a warm coat on top. I'd given them massive bear hugs, introduced them to Sophie, and then they'd whisked us back to their home where we'd collapsed into bed.

My phone pinged. It was a photo of Alfie dressed in a ridiculous turkey costume, with a large plume of feathers at his butt. Jenny was pretending to eat him.

Jenny: *Happy Thanksgiving, with love from London!*

I chuckled. Jenny had volunteered to dog and house sit, and it looked like they were having a ball. I was about to walk over to Sophie to show her, when Steven approached, looking defeated.

"Chris, your aunt has convinced me the turkey needs another thirty minutes. Given we have some time, would you mind helping me get down a box from the attic? We've got some toys up there the kids might enjoy once they've had enough of this game, which will hopefully be soon!" His look of defeat quickly vanished, replaced with fondness as he watched his grandchildren run in circles around the heavily populated living room.

"Of course!" I was more than happy to help, and I'd been looking for an excuse to spend some time alone with Steven since we arrived. I wanted to talk to him about something.

We made our way up to the hallway on the top floor, where Steven pulled down the folding ladder from the access hole in the ceiling. We clambered up into the dusty attic.

Steven pointed to a stack of boxes in the corner. "The toys should be in one of these. Unfortunately, I didn't label the boxes, so we'll have to open them until we find the right one."

I unstacked a few, and we began sorting through them.

Steven looked up from a box of books. "So, how are you holding up? It's so good to see you smiling and laughing again. It seems like your plan to start fresh in London might've worked?"

"It did, it really did. I actually can't believe how well it worked out. Within weeks of moving there, I found a house that I absolutely loved and then met Sophie and Elliot. The period drama has also been such a nice change, and apparently I've mastered a decent British accent, despite my concerns." I put a lid on a box of assorted cabling and went to get another one.

"I'm so glad to hear that, Chris. We're so proud of you for getting back on your feet after such an awful experience. You've always been amazingly resilient, even as a little boy." Steven smiled. Was I imagining it, or was that a tear in his eye? He blinked heavily. "You've got another *Muscle Man* film coming up next year, don't you? Anything else in the pipeline?"

I took a breath. "Serena has been following me up about potential new roles, but for the first time in my life, I don't want to squeeze in as many films as possible. I used to love losing myself in different characters and didn't mind the grueling hours. But now...don't get me wrong, I still love acting. It's just...my real life suddenly seems a lot more enjoyable than any role. I want time to actually live it. And hopefully cutting back on work and avoiding blockbuster roles will reduce the media attention on me." And Sophie and Elliot too, I hoped.

I watched Steven closely for his reaction. He'd always encouraged my interest in acting, spending hours practicing lines with me and driving me to acting classes and auditions. Always there for me, always supporting me. Would he be disappointed if I took a step back from my career after everything he'd done to help it?

Steven smiled at me, and my worries vanished.

"That's fantastic, Chris! You know, I was offered a job as school principal just around the time things got serious with your mom, and I ended up rejecting it for similar reasons. It would have eaten into my weekends and school holidays with you and Julie—and your sisters too, when they came along. I've never regretted it one bit. There's still some stigma about men stepping back from work to spend time with family or pursue other interests. But, from what I've read, most people don't look back on their lives and wish they'd worked harder. They're more likely to wish they spent more time with loved ones while they had the chance."

A flood of gratitude washed over me. I hadn't realized Steven had given up a promotion for me and Mom and his advice really resonated with me.

I walked over to where he was kneeling over a box and gave him a hug. "Thank you. You always know what to say. And I don't tell you this enough, but thanks for always being there for me. And it looks like you've found the toy box too!"

Steven looked down at the colorful assortment of toys, surprised. "So I have! I guess we better head back, then."

By the time we got downstairs, the turkey was out of the

oven, the table covered with sides, and everyone was taking a seat.

"I guess your aunt had second thoughts about over-cooking the turkey after all," Steven whispered with a wink.

The children nearly bowled me over when they saw the toy box. We had to threaten removal of their pecan pie privileges if they didn't wait until after lunch to play with the new toys.

As I helped myself to a second serving of turkey, which was surprisingly tender, my phone pinged. A photo of Alfie and Jenny, looking sporty in active wear, popped up.

Jenny: *We went to #Doga (dog yoga) earlier today. Child's pose was the only pose Alfie mastered. He spent most of the class trying to sniff the other dogs' butts.*

I showed Sophie, who burst into giggles. "Maybe I can take Elliot when we get back and continue the joint training sessions! I read that some babies start doing downward dog in preparation for walking, so it could be perfect for Elliot!"

"Aw, I can just imagine how cute they'd look, doing downward dog together, peering through their legs at us." I chuckled.

Sitting at the table, watching my large, blended family pass the sides Sophie and I had cooked together, Elliot chewing on a bit of turkey in his high chair next to me and screwing up his face at his first taste of collard greens, Sophie laughing at something my mom said, my heart felt like it might explode. This was a million times better than pretending to be Muscle Man, the arrogant duke, or any other character the scriptwriters could throw at me.

Screw those voices in my head that questioned whether falling too hard, too fast, too soon after the Vanessa debacle was a good idea. I'd never been happier.

SOPHIE

I WAS RECOVERING on the couch from eating way too much turkey and pecan pie, reading my book and enjoying the fire blazing in the corner. The last guest gone and the final dish dried, Chris was helping Steven in the garden, Elliot was having a long nap, probably due to the impressive amount of turkey he'd consumed or exhaustion from all the attention, and Julie...well, I wasn't sure where Julie was.

As soon as we met Julie and Steven at the airport, I'd immediately felt comfortable with them, and it was the same with the rest of Chris's family over lunch. Watching Chris interact with them all had given me a warm, fuzzy sensation. Jumping up to help clean up once lunch was over, playfully teasing his sisters, and playing with his nieces and nephew once the last morsels of pecan and pumpkin pies were demolished.

As if I'd conjured her with my thoughts, Julie walked into the living room holding a pile of albums in her arms.

"Sophie, I thought you might be interested in having a look through these," she said with a twinkle in her eye.

"If they include cute photos of baby Chris, and/or incriminating photos of his teenage years, yes, please!" I said, sitting up and setting my book aside.

Julie took a seat next to me and opened the first album.

Chris had been a really adorable baby. Blonde hair, chubby cheeks and legs, and a sweet gummy smile. As he grew older, his hair darkened, and he began to look more and more like the Chris I knew. There were several photos of Chris and his biological father. His father holding Chris in his arms as a newborn, playing in a sandpit with him as a toddler, and standing, smiling next to Chris for his first day of kindergarten. And then he disappeared from the albums.

I lingered on the photo of Chris on his first day of school, and Julie smiled sadly.

"That's the last photo I have of Robert, Chris's biological father. He left not long after. It was really heartbreaking for both Chris and me. I still remember Chris running down the hallway to show Robert the paper airplane he'd made, and how devastated he was when he couldn't find him. He was only five years old. I'd sensed something wasn't right with Robert for some time, but he wouldn't open up to me. He absolutely adored Chris, I know that much, so it was a real shock when he left us without a word. It was completely out of character. We asked all of his family and friends, but we never found out what happened."

Julie's voice wavered slightly. It was clear that, even all these years later, she was still hurting.

"The next year was pretty tough. While we were fine financially because Robert left all our savings in our joint bank account and I had a job, we both struggled emotionally. Not knowing why he left or if he was okay."

Tears formed in my eyes as fast as I could blink them away. Stories involving little kids being hurt physically or emotionally had always made me feel distressed, but after having Elliot, they were like daggers in my heart. I hated the thought of five-year-old Chris being devastated by his father abandoning him. I also couldn't imagine how any parent could leave their child. But I knew it happened with alarming regularity—take Josh and Erin's parents, for example.

Julie continued. "Robert disappearing made me question a lot of things, including my faith. We were both raised Catholic, and we'd been regular churchgoers, but I ended up leaving the local church, which was very conservative. Not only did I lose my husband, but I also lost my support network. My friends were all in the church, my parents had passed away, and I didn't have any other relatives."

My heart went out to Julie. I'd found being a single mother isolating despite having friends and family around on weekends and after work. It must have been incredibly difficult for her, especially when single motherhood had been foisted on her rather than a conscious choice, like it had been for me. I'd spent a long time working out how I could look after a child by myself, crunching numbers, talking to my parents, convincing Josh to be Elliot's godfather, going through all the logistics. I'd gone into it with open eyes, knowing what I was signing up for. Julie didn't have that privilege.

Julie's face brightened. "Thankfully, about twelve months later, I met Steven. He was the English teacher at the high school in the neighboring town. We struck up a conversation in the supermarket one day and hit it off, and before I knew it, we were dating. Happily, Steven and Chris got on really well, so much so that Chris actually asked if he could take Steven's last name when we married. I was thrilled when Steven got the job offer to move to Chicago. It felt like an opportunity to start afresh."

Julie smiled, shaking her head.

"Because Robert was missing, we had to jump through all sorts of hoops in order for me to get a divorce so that Steven and I could marry. We had to file an affidavit of all our attempts to locate him, then publish a notice to him in a newspaper once a week for three weeks, describing the proposed divorce before we could seek an order for divorce from the judge. When we finally got married, I was already pregnant with Chris's sister. Good thing I'd already left the Catholic church!"

"Did you ever hear from Robert?" I asked.

Julie sighed. "No. When Chris was still a child, I tried looking for him fairly regularly. I thought it might give Chris some closure if we found out what happened to him. But I never got a lead and eventually gave up. I can tell it still hangs over Chris's head—he told me a couple of years ago he wished he could just sit down with him and ask him why. But if Robert wanted to find us now, he wouldn't have any trouble. Chris doesn't exactly have a low profile."

"Hmmm." I frowned, staring at the photo of Robert and Chris. "Robert probably wouldn't recognize him. I mean, he has transformed from a tiny five-year-old to a six-foot-two Muscle Man. Or he might just not be into superhero films. And didn't you mention that Chris took Steven's name? Robert wouldn't have known that."

After my success finding Alfie, this felt like a mystery just waiting to be solved...by me. I couldn't believe that the man staring at Chris with such adoration in those photos wouldn't want to be reunited with him, assuming he was still alive.

I turned to Julie. "How would you feel if I did some digging when I got home to London? It probably won't come to anything, but if I did find out what happened to Robert, as you said, it might give Chris some closure. I'll check with Chris, too, of course."

Julie considered my question for a minute. "I don't think it would hurt to try again. It would give me some closure too, to be honest. After all these years, I still often wonder what happened to him."

"Would you mind if I photographed some photos of

Robert in the albums? And I should also ask, what was his last name?"

"His last name was Sherman, Robert Sherman—the 'Sher' is spelled with an 'e'—and that's fine to take some photos."

I breathed a sigh of relief his last name wasn't Smith or Jones. Sherman wasn't likely to be a very popular name, which would make searching more straightforward.

I kept flicking through the albums. The year after Robert left was marked with fewer photos, almost all of them of Chris playing alone. But then photos of Julie and Chris standing together, smiling, reappeared, and Steven began to feature in them. Before long, there was a photo of eight-year-old Chris peering at his new baby sister in a cot. And then there were photos of Chris performing in school plays, playing with their dog, a Hungarian Vizsla, and family holidays with the five of them happily smiling. I couldn't help but smile too. I was looking forward to trying to solve this mystery, which had haunted Julie and Chris for thirty years, assuming Chris gave me his blessing.

CHAPTER THIRTY

CHRIS

WHILE THE SKY was blue and sunny, the wind was bone-chilling. I glanced over to Elliot, who looked like a little Cheeto ball on Sophie's hip, in his orange puffer jacket and hood, worried he might be too cold. Sophie had just finished sipping the pumpkin spiced latte I'd gotten her, the sixth of the trip. As the tour guide started talking about the history of the elegant white Wrigley Building, Sophie pointed to its clock face, and I caught a glimpse of Elliot's toothy grin as he turned his head. I relaxed. The icy breeze didn't seem to be bothering him in the slightest.

I'd arranged for a private Chicago River cruise so Sophie and Elliot could see Chicago's iconic buildings without the risk of being harassed by fans. As much as I appreciated my fans, the thought of ninety minutes stuck on a boat with them, with nowhere to hide, sent shivers down my spine. They could be a bit intense.

"We are now approaching Marina City. Built in 1968, these two reinforced concrete towers were designed to entice middle-class Chicagoans back to the city..."

Mitch sidled up to me. "I've never been a fan of the

concrete corn cobs. Give me a nice, shiny, soaring glass skyscraper any day of the week," he murmured while the tour guide continued to talk.

I chuckled. I'd invited Mitch and Liz, as well as Mom and Steven, along for the cruise. I was keen for Sophie and Elliot to see Chicago and also spend time with my friends and family, so I was trying to combine sightseeing with socializing where possible.

"So, how are you doing? Sophie seems great! I take it she isn't gay after all?" Mitch said with a smirk, leaning on the boat railing.

I rolled my eyes. I'd had many conversations with Mitch since the night of the London premiere, but he continued to tease me about my idiotic mistake.

"Nope. And yes, I'm still annoyed that I spent all that time pining after her, thinking she was unattainable because of my own stupid assumptions, so no need to go on about it. But it all turned out well in the end. Better than I could have ever imagined." I glanced over to Sophie, who was talking animatedly with Liz, Elliot still Cheeto-balling on her hip, and smiled, warmth spreading across my chest.

"You guys must be pretty serious if you're already bringing her to meet the parents. Didn't you wait over a year with Vanessa?" Mitch adjusted his scarf, trying to better protect his face from the freezing blasts.

"Yeah. I know we're moving quickly, but I just couldn't wait for everyone to meet her, and Elliot, too, of course. Yes, I'm pathetic. To be honest, it almost seems too good to be true."

My stomach had been slightly unsettled since Sophie mentioned Mom had pulled out the old photo albums and told her about Dad leaving. Any mention of my father always threw me. I'd been trying not to think about him, but it was too late. The worries that had been percolating in the back of my mind for some time became too strong to ignore.

"Uh oh. What's wrong?"

God damn, Mitch could read me well.

Merchandise Mart's imposing art deco facade came into view, triggering the tour guide's spiel on its history as a wholesale warehouse. I lowered my voice, not wanting to interrupt the guide or for Sophie to overhear me.

"Just...well, could it be too good to be true? After being burned by my dad leaving, by Vanessa betraying me, I'm still a little wary about letting my guard down in case I get hurt again. And I'm also worried about hurting them too. I really want to be a good father, a good partner. But what if I turn out like my dad? Could some sort of abandonment gene take hold one day and result in me leaving them? Or, even though I adore him now, what if the fact we're not genetically related affects how I feel about Elliot when he's older, and I can't be the parent he deserves?"

"Hey." Mitch put his arm around my shoulders before going into full lawyer rebuttal mode. "To your first point, for a relationship to work, you need to let your guard down, be yourself, be vulnerable. Sure, there's a risk you might get hurt. But the alternative, not having love, seems a whole lot worse to me. And, to your second point"—Mitch stared at me sternly and shook me gently as he continued—"you are not your dad. There is no 'abandonment gene.' You had, and still have, an awesome father figure in your life, someone who's had far more influence on you than a man you can barely remember. A man who, while not related to you by blood, raised you, supported you, loved you, and helped make you the man you are today. Someone you bonded with so strongly, even as a kid, that you took his last name. The fact you are so worried about hurting Sophie and Elliot tells me you're not a Robert, you're a Steven." Mitch looked over at Steven, who was showing Elliot the American flag flying at the back of the boat.

Gratitude washed over me. For Mitch, for Steven. Of course, Mitch was right. Steven had shown me that you didn't need to be related by blood to be a good father. Deep down, I was sure I could be that to Elliot, if that was what Sophie wanted.

"Thanks man. You're right. I'm being an idiot. Speaking of amazing dads, how are you feeling about the impending arrival?"

SOPHIE

THE BOAT HAD TURNED AROUND, and we were heading back to the dock. I was enjoying seeing the striking buildings from a different perspective, and also having the icy wind behind us.

"What did you think, Sophie?" Steven, who'd been entertaining Elliot, walked up to me smiling, Elliot in his arms.

"It was awesome! Such an incredible variety of buildings—modern skyscrapers, art deco, brutalist—so close together. And seeing them all from the river was really special. You and Julie will have to come to London and do a Thames cruise. It's not quite as spectacular, but it's still a great way to experience London."

"We'd love to visit! Chris seems to love London. I'm sure we will too."

We looked over at Chris, who was standing at the railing, laughing with Mitch, and my heart turned to goo. *God,*

I love him. I hadn't said anything to him yet, but it was now constantly on the tip of my tongue. It was only a matter of time before it slipped out.

"It's so great to see him so happy," Steven said, looking at him fondly. "I haven't seen him this cheerful for years, and from what I can tell, you and Elliot are primarily to thank for that. So, thank you."

My cheeks flushed. "Oh, that's so sweet. But I don't think we can take credit for that. It's all Chris. You know, it's been so nice meeting you all and seeing his hometown. Family is clearly very important to him. And, I hope you don't mind me saying this, but it's been reassuring to see how close you and Chris are. I've always worried that if I did find a partner, they might not feel the same way I do about Elliot because of not having that biological link. Seeing you and Chris interact has put my mind at ease about that." My cheeks flushed as I spoke. I hoped I hadn't offended Steven. I was pleased Chris had given me the green light last night to find his biological father, although he'd seemed distracted and immediately changed the subject. But, from what I'd seen, Chris already had an amazing father in his life. It was heartwarming to see how close Chris and Steven were.

"I'm happy to hear that. I feel the same way about Chris as I do about his sisters—unconditional love. Not all step-parents are the same, of course, but Chris made it easy. How could you not love such a passionate, sweet little kid? Seeing how Chris interacts with Elliot, the way his face lights up when he talks about him, I don't think you have anything to worry about." Steven smiled, and I breathed out, relieved he seemed happy to talk about the topic. The fact Steven was so confident about Chris's ability to love Elliot put my worries further to rest.

"I'm glad you think so. Chris has done nothing to make me doubt that, so I'm sure you're right." The boat was pulling toward the dock, so I started to collect our things in preparation for disembarking.

"Sophie! Look at Jenny's latest update." Chris approached, shaking his head and chuckling, and handed me his phone. It was a picture of Alfie, hair trimmed and fluffy, proudly wearing a new blue polka dot bandana.

Jenny: *Alfie had a visit to the pet spa earlier today. He's looking very stylish after his "wash and fluff" and "custom coat styling," and smells a lot better too, thanks to the "luxury finishing cologne spritz."*

I laughed. "Oh my god! It sounds like they're having so much fun. It'll be a shock to his system when we get home and the most exciting thing we do is a walk on the Heath."

The boat docked, and I walked off the wobbly gangway onto the Riverwalk holding Elliot, turning to wait for everyone else to disembark. Julie and Steven had just stepped onto dry land when I heard screams behind me.

I froze, pulling Elliot tight to my body, and turned to see what was happening.

It took me a few seconds to register what was going on.

It wasn't a terrible accident or a mugging. While people all around us had their phones out, they weren't calling the police or ambulances.

Nope. The phones were all directed at us. And so were the screams.

A large group of high school students had spotted Chris and were beyond excited, yelling things like, "Look, it's Muscle Man!" "OMG, I can't believe this! It's Chris Trent."

"Oh shit," Chris groaned under his breath as he took in the situation. "I thought we'd be fine because there's parking so close to the dock, but I was clearly wrong. I should've brought a bodyguard with us." The car was only a few minutes' walk away, under the Illinois Center, but the school group blocked our path.

Some of the more confident teenagers started approaching us. "Chris, Chris! Can I have a selfie?"

Buoyed by their classmates' courage, more students swarmed forward. They were standing about three feet from us now, phones pointed in our direction. Their screams were attracting the attention of other tourists, who began making their way over.

My heart thudded in my ears. I didn't like this one bit, and neither did Elliot, who, overwhelmed with all the noise and people, began crying.

Chris squeezed my hand. "I'm so sorry, Soph. Can you and Elliot stand with the others? It's probably safer there." He turned to Steven, who was standing with Julie, Liz, and Mitch behind us.

"Can you see if we can get back on the boat? I don't fancy us getting through this crowd any time soon and don't want to risk it, especially with Liz being pregnant and Elliot."

I looked back at the boat. They'd pulled up the gang-plank and were slowly motoring away. *Shit*. Steven ran to the side of the boardwalk, waving his arms and yelling for them to come back.

Chris, trying to calm down the crowd, put on his best movie star smile and addressed them, practically shouting to be heard over the commotion.

"Hi, everyone! Yes, I'm Chris Trent. I hope you're enjoying your day out in this beautiful city, my hometown."

The teenagers and tourists cheered.

"Now, I'm out here with some of my family and friends,

including a little baby who isn't too happy with all of this noise and attention."

That was the understatement of the year—Elliot was currently doing serious damage to my hearing with his screams.

"So, I'd really appreciate if you could move back and let us head home, now that you've had the chance to take some photos." He smiled encouragingly at the crowd, but only a few people stepped back.

My heart sank.

"Chris! The boat's coming back!" Julie said quietly, relief in her voice.

It was docking now, and Steven was helping them to lower the gangplank.

"Thank Christ," Chris muttered. "You guys all get safely on board, and then I'll try to get on. Tell them to pull the gangplank up if anyone else tries to board. If the worst comes to worst, I'll just stay here and take a million selfies until they get bored."

I felt bad leaving Chris, but with Elliot so distressed, I only paused a second to squeeze Chris's hand before walking briskly toward the boat.

Safely on board with Elliot, who had stopped screaming and was now emitting heart-wrenching little sobs every so often, some of the tension in my body dissipated. But I was still worried about Chris. I didn't think the crowd, which must have been at least twenty people deep, would inten-tionally hurt him or anything but...it looked pretty intense from my vantage point.

Julie patted my back. "It looks scary, but Chris has done this before. He'll be okay. And they're just kids."

Chris glanced toward us, a calculating look on his face, and then down. A few seconds later, my phone pinged.

Chris: *Tell them to leave and get you guys to safety x*

My stomach plummeted. I really wanted him safe on the boat with us. I showed Julie, grimacing.

"He knows what he's doing, love," she said, before turning to the captain of the boat, who was talking to Steven nearby. "Chris just texted Sophie to leave."

They pulled up the gangplank and started the engine. I stood at the rail of the boat, watching Chris speaking to the crowd, my heart heavy.

Just as the boat started to move away from the board-walk Chris waved at the crowd, turned, and started sprinting toward us.

"Stop!" I yelled to the captain, hoping he'd turn around and pick him up.

But just as the words spilled out of my mouth, Chris, instead of slowing down as he reached the edge of the boardwalk, picked up speed.

"What the...," Mitch exclaimed.

And then Chris leaped off the boardwalk.

And everything slowed down.

He won't make it. We're too far away.

He flew through the air, arms outstretched, toward us. I stopped breathing.

Oh god. If he falls in the water...it must be freezing.

His legs moved as though he was peddling the air, propelling himself forward.

And then his hands grabbed the boat's railing, his body hitting the side of the boat hard, causing it to jolt. We rushed to help him, but he smoothly pulled himself over the railing and onto the boat. The crowd, now standing on the edge of the boardwalk, went wild, yelling and clapping, beside themselves at having witnessed Chris pull a super-hero move.

"I knew insisting on doing most of Muscle Man's own stunts would pay off one day," Chris said with a sheepish grin. "I had to do something very similar in *Muscle Man 2* and practiced it a million times."

Still holding Elliot, who had cheered up watching Chris clamber over the railing, I put my other arm around Chris and held tight.

"I'm so glad you're okay. That was terrifying." I looked up at him, worried. Not just about this incident, but also about how many similar incidents would be in our future. While it was unlikely the teenagers would have purposefully hurt us, I hadn't felt safe. What if they'd surged forward in excitement, accidentally knocking us over? Physical injuries aside, what impact would that have on Elliot's mental health, and mine for that matter? Next time, there might not be a boat to rescue us.

He kissed my head. "I'm sorry, Soph. I'll just check with the captain about where we're heading and see if I can get my security firm to send some people over to meet us. I'll be right back."

Chris strode over to the captain, who was still chatting to Steven as he steered the boat down the Chicago River, and spoke to them for a few minutes before making a call. He walked back to me, smiling.

"Okay, that's all sorted. They're going to drop us away from the tourist area, and the security firm will pick us all up and drive us back to our cars."

I'd taken a seat, tired of standing with Elliot in my arms, and Chris sat down next to me.

I swallowed. "Chris, I'm not sure that I can deal with being in that type of situation again, especially not with Elliot."

Chris's brow furrowed. "I know. I'm so sorry. I screwed

up. I should've known better, going into such a touristy area without security detail. The attention is always worse here —Chicagoans love their homegrown celebrities—and in LA, probably due to people being on the lookout for the rich and famous there. I got complacent being in London and forgot what it could be like. I promise I won't make that mistake again."

I still felt uneasy. "But bodyguards can only do so much, right? Like, they might stop people from getting too close to us, but they won't be able to stop people from forming crowds around us, screaming at us, filming us."

Chris took a deep breath. "I know. You're right. So, um, I've been thinking about something lately that might help... I've been thinking that I want to cut down on work and take a step back from the public eye, which should mean less media and fan attention. Reducing the roles I take on, avoiding any big blockbuster movies—no more superhero or action films—and focusing on projects that I'll enjoy but won't attract a massive fan base. Indie films, maybe a Netflix series, that sort of thing. It won't have an immediate impact, and I'm still locked in for one more *Muscle Man* movie, but I hope it'll give you some comfort that life with me won't involve constantly having to deal with fans and paparazzi. And in the meantime, I'll make sure I err on the side of caution when it comes to bringing security detail with us. What do you think?"

Taken aback, I looked at him closely. "But you love acting! Are you sure this is what you want?"

Chris rubbed his hands together, looking down at his feet and then back at me. He smiled. "Yes. I'm positive. I think I loved acting so much partly because I wasn't satisfied with my own life. But now, I'm resenting the long hours because I just want to hang out with you and Elliot, and

Alfie, too, of course. Why pretend to be someone else anymore when my own life is so great?"

Warmth radiated across my body at Chris's words, which addressed my last major concern about embarking on a full-blown relationship with him. It wouldn't be an immediate fix, but his plan gave me comfort that today's events wouldn't be the new normal if we stayed together. And in the meantime, his security team would at least keep us safe.

CHAPTER THIRTY-ONE

CHRIS

MOUTHWATERING aromas hit me as soon as I opened the door. They must have struck Alfie as well, because he pulled at the leash, leaping with excitement. I took off his harness, and he raced down the hall into the kitchen.

I stood in the hallway and yelled, "I'm home. Is it safe to come in?"

Sophie kicked me out of the house two hours ago, telling me to take Alfie for a walk. A long walk.

"Stop! Don't go any further. Put this on." She came out of the kitchen, smiling, and handed me a blindfold.

Oh god. I really hoped she hadn't organized a surprise party for me. Despite being an actor, I didn't actually like being the center of attention, especially not on my birthday. I put it on cautiously. Blindfolded, Sophie led me down the hallway.

We'd been back from Chicago for a few weeks, and things between us were better than ever. But I'd always found celebrating the first birthday in a new relationship nerve-wracking. The other person's expectations in terms of presents, celebratory activities, and overall fanfare were unknown quantities. Vanessa had insisted on celebrating her "birthday month," in what seemed like a never-ending schedule of special dinners, cocktails, day spas, and other activities. The first year we were together, I'd given her a luxury glamping trip to Joshua Tree National Park for her birthday, after she'd mentioned she'd always wanted to go there. While she'd enjoyed it in the end, she'd made it clear that for all future birthdays, she expected expensive jewelry. *Very* expensive jewelry. I was relieved my birthday had fallen first this time around. At least this way, Sophie's approach would give me some guidance regarding her expectations. I'd told her not to worry about doing anything, but she'd insisted she wanted to do something to celebrate it.

"Happy birthday!" Sophie said, removing the blindfold.

An impressive spread of food, and only two table settings, covered the table. I breathed a sigh of relief. And in the middle of the table was the bust of the Hungarian Vizsla, the one I'd regretted not bidding on at the auction. A red ribbon was tied around his neck. A grin spread across my face.

"Oh my god, the Vizsla! Sophie! And all the food as well. It looks and smells amazing."

She smiled at me. "Since you can buy pretty much anything you want, I decided to cook some of our favorite Ottolenghi dishes, as well as a few you wanted to make but I previously rejected on the grounds they had over fifteen ingredients, and your mum's meatballs. And I convinced Sharon to part with the dog statue. It turned out Tina hated it and refused to display it in their apartment, so that wasn't hard!"

Sophie handed me an envelope. "And here's your birthday card."

I pulled out the card, which had a drawing of cute dog holding a bunch of balloons in its mouth on the front. Smiling, I opened it.

Happy Birthday, babe!

Thank you for being such a great boyfriend, role model to Elliot, and doggy dad to Alfie. The last few months have been some of the happiest of my life. I'm looking forward to celebrating many more birthdays together.

Love, Sophie

My heart collapsed into a warm, gooey mess. I put my arms around Sophie, giving her a big squeeze.

"Thanks, gorgeous. I'm looking forward to that as well." I kissed the top of her head, breathing in her familiar scent.

Buying presents for me was challenging—what to buy a man who could literally afford anything he wanted—but this was perfect. While I felt confident Sophie wouldn't be expecting a diamond necklace for Christmas, which was only weeks away, or her birthday in March, I'd need to start planning now to come up with something similarly thoughtful.

At this rate, March would be here in no time. Life seemed to be flashing by. Filming had just wrapped up, and I was enjoying having so much time to spend with Sophie and Elliot—going for walks, helping to fix up Pride House and repaint her parents' living room, and planning a trip to Italy early next year for the three of us. I'd also had time to look into my idea for turning my public humiliation into something worthwhile, researching laws about sharing explicit images without consent in the UK and the US and reaching out to some not-for-profit organizations who already worked in this area to see if I could help advocate for legal reform.

"We should make a start, before it gets cold," Sophie said, her eyes sparkling as she raised her glass of wine.

God, she was cute.

"Cheers!"

The food was delicious, and Sophie had gotten one of my favorite bottles of red to go with it. I'd never tell Mom this—to be honest, I didn't think it was possible—but Sophie's meatballs actually tasted better than hers. And Alfie was thrilled with the dog-friendly meatballs Sophie had put aside for him, guzzling them down even faster than me. For dessert, Sophie had made an apple tart.

"Now, I know you said at Cynthia's that you liked fig and cherry tarts, but I decided to stick with the classic apple. But don't eat too much. I've got another sweet treat for you afterwards," Sophie whispered in my ear, sending a shiver down my spine.

After we'd cleared the table and finished the rest of the wine on the couch, Sophie ordered me to stay put. I entertained myself by brainstorming Christmas present ideas for her while I waited. My curiosity grew as I listened to her bustling about in the kitchen and then walking up and down the stairs.

What was she up to now?

Ten minutes later, she came back and pulled the blindfold out of her pocket, dangling it in front of me with a cheeky look on her face.

"It's almost time to put this back on, for that sweet treat I mentioned earlier." She gave me a knowing smile. "But first, let's go up the stairs."

I followed her, anticipation building with each step.

What mischief did she have planned? And damn, her butt looked good in those jeans. When she reached the top, she stopped me three stairs down so we were standing face to face.

"Just let me know if you're at all uncomfortable at any point, and I'll stop, okay? This is meant to be a purely pleasurable experience," Sophie said.

I nodded. What the hell was she going to do? My pulse picked up pace as she pulled the blindfold gently over my face. She kissed me and then took my hand, leading me a few steps.

"Stop here," Sophie said.

I stood in what I assumed was my bedroom, given the number of steps we'd taken, waiting. Standing blindfolded, not knowing what Sophie had in store for me, made my stomach flutter with a mix of nerves and excitement. I heard some rustling, and then Sophie, standing in front of me, took my hands and placed them on her butt. Her naked butt.

"Well, hello!" I said.

"Now, I'm going to undress you," Sophie murmured, her breath tickling my neck.

She slowly peeled off my clothes, stopping regularly to touch me, to run her hands over my chest, pull her nails lightly down my back while her breasts pressed against me, sending tingles shooting through my body.

"Now, I want you to lie down."

Sophie moved me back carefully, until I could feel what I assumed was the bed touching the back of my legs, and then pushed me down. The bed felt different. Had she put towels down? My mind started racing even more. Why would we need towels?

"Wriggle up," Sophie directed.

I liked this bossy side of her. I did as I was told.

I'd never been blindfolded in the bedroom before. In the past, I wouldn't have let myself be so vulnerable with a partner. But with Sophie, things were different. I trusted her completely. My body relaxed, ready to enjoy whatever she had planned.

Sophie straddled me and her hair touched my chest, and then her lips touched mine. Sweetness hit me—the smell of chocolate, the taste on her mouth—as we kissed. I couldn't help but smile. She must have remembered me mentioning I liked chocolate play on the night of the premiere. Although in the past, the roles had been reversed, and no blindfolds were involved.

Sophie stopped kissing, and her weight shifted momentarily. Something warm drizzled over my pecs and stomach, followed by something cold.

With the blindfold on, all my other senses were heightened. Taste, sound, smell, touch. Everything had an intensity I'd never experienced before. My nerve endings were on high alert, the warm and cold drizzles sending them into overdrive.

Her soft lips began following the chocolate drizzle down my body. Kissing and licking it, stopping every so often to come up and give me another sweet chocolate or cream kiss.

I had a burning desire to rip off my mask, cover her beautiful body in chocolate and ravenously lick it off. Screw it. I reached up to take off the mask to do just that, and she playfully slapped it.

"Uh uh. You need to wait your turn. Lie back and enjoy."

Put in my place, and even more turned on by her bossiness, I followed orders, surrendering myself to the pleasure.

TWO HOURS, and a lot of chocolate and cream, later, we were naked, sticky, and maskless, still catching our breath.

"Ah, that was amazing! And good call on the towels." I propped myself up and surveyed our bodies, covered in remnants of chocolate and cream. I couldn't resist running my hand over her stomach and chest. I licked my lips. "Mmmm, it looks like you still need a bit of cleaning up."

Sophie batted my hand away, laughing. "Yes, I do...but I need something more effective than your tongue. I think the chocolate and cream are congealing, which isn't exactly sexy. Definitely time for a shower."

"Judging by how many times you just came, I would say my tongue is *extremely* effective, thank you very much!" I fake pouted.

"Effective for pleasuring me, yes. Not so much for cleaning." A cheeky grin spread across her face. "Why don't you come with me, so we can combine both?"

WE LAY IN BED, freshly showered, cuddling naked, basking in a warm, post-sex glow.

Sophie groaned. "Urgh, I should head home. I'm getting so sleepy, and I don't want to doze off. I told Mum and Dad I'd be home tonight, so I'm there in the morning when Elliot wakes up. I know it's only gonna get harder the later I leave it, but I'm already sooo comfy."

I gave her a squeeze, relishing her warm body pressed against mine. "I know, I don't want you to leave either. I'm enjoying this too much."

Sophie wriggled out of my arms, dragged herself out of

bed, and put on her clothes. "I've got to pull the band-aid off. I'll see you tomorrow afternoon?"

"Yes, see you then, babe. And thanks again for tonight. It was the best. I love you."

The last three words took me by surprise, falling out of my mouth without warning. While I'd wanted to say them for some time, I hadn't had the courage. But now they'd slipped out so naturally. I held my breath, wondering how Sophie would react.

Sophie leaned over and gave me a kiss.

"Good night. I love you too," she said, smiling.

My heart felt like it might burst.

I watched Sophie walk out of the room, wishing she didn't have to leave. I'd been working up the courage to ask her whether she'd consider moving in with me—and Elliot, of course—at the Castle. I knew we hadn't been together for very long, but I already wanted to go to sleep with her beside me every evening, be there to help with Elliot when he was having a rough night, make her coffee every morning.

I let out a satisfied sigh. This was one of my best birthdays yet. Possibly *the* best birthday.

I couldn't believe how far my life had come from languishing on that white couch in LA only four months ago. I was no longer fixated by the photos, and I rarely thought about Vanessa. I was in the best shape of my life, working again and living in a house that felt like a home. And then there was Sophie. I connected with Sophie on so many levels. Emotionally—I'd never let myself be so vulnerable before with a partner, intellectually—she inspired me to be a better person, and of course, physically...Those voices in my head, telling me that this was too good to be true, that Sophie would either break my heart or I'd break hers, were piping up less and less.

A ping sounded from Sophie's side of the bed. I rolled over and saw she'd left her phone on the bedside table. I touched the screen to check what time it was, and two notifications popped up. The first, the one I'd heard, was an email notification about an upcoming sale. But the other email notification immediately grabbed my attention.

Sam Reynolds
Re: Chris Trent Photos
Confirming I've received the photos and will get on it.

What the...? No, no, no, no. I reeled like I'd been punched in the stomach, gasping for breath. Surely not...not Sophie.

I Googled Sam Reynolds on my phone. Another punch, stronger, hit my chest. She was a reporter at one of the big US newspapers.

I didn't know Sophie's passcode, so I couldn't read any more, but I didn't need to.

It *had* been too good to be true.

What I thought was a thoughtful birthday treat had been a ploy to get compromising photos of me. Sophie must have emailed them to the newspaper while I was in the bathroom. I shuddered. Blindfolded and covered in chocolate and cream, I'd be the laughing stock. I couldn't go out in public again. The Vanessa photos were bad, but these would be so much worse. At least I'd taken the Vanessa photos myself—chosen a somewhat flattering angle, discarded the photos I wasn't happy with—even if I'd only intended them for her eyes only. But these photos...God only knew how ridiculous I looked.

Struggling for air, sweating, I stood and started pacing the room, going over all of our previous interactions in my mind. Had she been trying to get close to me all along so she could make money off me? Had she intentionally hit me with the stroller to meet me? Were the past few months all a lie? My stomach was in knots.

I shook my head, trying to clear it. No. Sophie wouldn't do that to me. She was kind and trustworthy, more interested in helping others than in money or status. I'd never seen even a hint that she was capable of this kind of deception...But then I'd never thought Dad would leave me, or Vanessa would betray me, and look what happened with them. A wave of nausea washed over me, bile rising in my throat. I was a terrible judge of character.

I spent the next few hours pacing up and down, my mind racing and muddled from lack of sleep and the intensity of the emotions I was experiencing. At around four a.m., I concluded my worst fears had to be right. What other explanation could there be? Sam Reynolds was now in possession of extremely compromising photos of me. It was likely only going to be hours, maybe a day if I was lucky, until they were plastered all over the internet, and the humiliation would begin again. I wouldn't wait around for that to happen. Staying in the Castle, with all of its reminders of Sophie, was not an option. I started pulling on my clothes.

Alfie, who'd been roused from sleep by my feet thumping on the floorboards and had been trailing up and down behind me, jumped onto the bed, watching me with concern.

"We're going for a walk, Alfie."

Alfie typically went wild at the mention of a walk, but this time, he eyed me with trepidation.

After dressing, I grabbed Sophie's phone, put Alfie's harness on, and strode to Sophie's house. I shoved her phone in the mailbox, anger flashing across my eyes as I looked up at her window.

As soon as I got home, I started throwing clothes in my suitcase and booked the first flight I found back to LAX, leaving early afternoon. I took the bare essentials. Jenny could do the rest.

CHAPTER THIRTY-TWO

SOPHIE

"SOPHIE, your phone was in the letterbox," Dad said, handing it over to me before sorting through the mail he'd brought in.

"That's weird. I was wondering where it was. I must have dropped it on my way home last night. I guess some kind soul found it and saw this address on my driver's license." I checked all the cards I kept in my phone case were still there. Thankfully, they were.

I turned my attention back to Elliot, who was refusing to cooperate with my attempts to put on his jacket. We were getting ready to meet Chris and Alfie at the Castle for an afternoon walk and then have dinner there and stay the night. I couldn't wait to see Chris again, especially after last night. I felt slightly giddy that we'd finally both said, "I love you", and secretly pleased Chris had said it first. And it seemed like Chris had really enjoyed his birthday surprises.

I sighed happily. Since Chris had finished filming, things had been magical—being able to hang out with him every day, having his help fixing up both Pride House and my parents' living room, and staying over at the Castle with

Elliot and Alfie. Thankfully, things between my parents and Chris were more natural now that they'd spent more time together.

Gloves, jackets, and beanies finally on, Elliot and I made the familiar stroll to the Castle. I knocked on the door, expecting to hear Alfie's excited barking and the pitter patter of his little feet racing to the door, followed by Chris's heavier footsteps, but there was silence.

I knocked again.

Nothing.

I had a key, so I opened the door and peered in.

"Chris?" I yelled.

Everything looked normal. He must have gone out unexpectedly. I shut the door again.

I checked my messages. Nothing from Chris.

I tried calling him. It went straight to voicemail.

Worry crept over me. This was very unlike Chris. I started to imagine terrible scenarios. Had a crazed fan broken into his house and attacked him? Or maybe he'd been hit by a car getting food for dinner?

I opened the door again and walked around, peering in every room. There was no sign of him.

I sent him a text.

Sophie: *Are you OK babe? We're at the house and you're not here. Please call me when you get this. I'm worried about you.*

He'd probably just popped out and lost track of time, and I was completely overreacting. But it wasn't like him to be late.

I pushed Elliot back down to my parents' house, unease still simmering in my belly.

When I still hadn't heard from Chris a few hours later, I called Jenny, but she didn't pick up either. I started to seriously consider if I should file a missing person's report.

Just as I settled down with a book after dinner in the newly refurbished living room my phone pinged, and a notification popped up. It was a message from Chris. Relieved, I opened it.

Chris: *Don't contact me again. I'm blocking your number.*

All of the air was suddenly sucked out of my lungs. I stared at the message in shock. *Breathe, Sophie.* What the hell was going on?

I called Jenny again, and this time, she picked up.

"Hi, Jenny, do you know what's going on with Chris? He wasn't at his house this afternoon, and now he's sent me a message telling me not to contact him again and that he's blocking me?" I was holding in sobs, my voice shaking.

"I'm so sorry, Soph. I have no idea what's going on. He dropped Alfie off at my place this morning and flew back to LA. He wouldn't tell me what had happened, but his voice sounded really weird. Alfie and I are flying out tomorrow morning, and I've booked in removalists to pack up his house later this week. Did you guys have a fight?"

"No, no...nothing like that." I dug my fingernails into my hand, trying not to break down.

"I'll let you know once I hear anything. I can't believe he's doing this to you."

I heard barking in the background.

"I'm sorry. I have to go. I'm at the vet getting a certificate that Alfie is fit to fly, and they've just called me in. I'll call you from LA." Jenny hung up.

I raced to the bathroom and started dry retching. What the hell was happening?

CHAPTER THIRTY-THREE

SOPHIE

"IS EVERYTHING OKAY?" Erin asked. "You seem kinda out of it tonight."

"Yes, sorry!" I turned my attention back to the card game but struggled to focus.

Chris had been gone for two days, and I wasn't coping well. During the day, I tried to pull it together for Elliot's sake—and so my parents wouldn't suspect anything was amiss—but I wasn't sleeping, I'd lost my appetite. There was a permanent ache in my chest. I kept going over and over the night of his birthday, trying to work out where it had all gone so terribly wrong. I didn't want Mum and Dad to know because they'd judge Chris if I told them he'd left without any explanation. I hadn't given up hope he might return, that it was all some terrible misunderstanding and we'd get back together, so I didn't want them to think less of him. At least, not yet.

As a distraction, I'd been throwing myself into business planning with Rose and Mia, volunteering at Pride House, getting out for walks on the Heath with Elliot, and leaning on Josh for emotional support. But I couldn't stop thinking about Chris.

Alex approached, with Josh by their side, smiling. "Sophie, sorry to interrupt. Could I borrow you for a second?"

"Sure." I managed a weak smile. I turned to Erin and her friends. "Why don't you keep playing without me? I was losing miserably anyway. I'll join in again for the next game."

Josh and I followed Alex into their office, where they gestured for us to take a seat.

Alex clapped their hands together, looking excited. "So, I have some great news! We've recently received a very generous donation, which means that now the building is fixed up, we can start expanding Pride House's activities. I spoke to the young people, and a number of them are worried about their career path and job opportunities. Some of them don't know what they want to do, and many of those who have an idea aren't sure if it's the right choice for them, or how to go about actually pursuing that career. So, I've been thinking we could do a work experience program for them, so they can get some hands-on experience. A lot of them don't have the family connections to help them get those types of placements. I'm just not sure if we'll be able to find organizations willing to participate. Do you think your companies would be up for it?"

Despite my misery, Alex's words sparked a flicker of excitement. "I wonder if...I'd need to talk to my business partners, but..." I paused, gathering my thoughts. "I think I've mentioned that I'm planning to set up a diversity, equity, and inclusion consulting firm with a few friends? If all goes to plan, we'll have a number of corporate clients who'd be perfect to host the teens. And hopefully, since they'd be interested in diversity, equity, and inclusion if they engaged us, they'd be open to supporting LGBTQ+ young people."

Josh, who'd been staring at a pile of paper on Alex's desk with a strange look on his face, chimed in. "And on a more cynical note, I'm sure they'd love it from a marketing perspective! Being involved in a program like that would be great PR. It sounds like an awesome idea, Alex. I'll speak to my boss and see if my work can help too."

Alex's face broke into a grin. "That sounds amazing! And Sophie, if you could possibly ask Chris if he knows any companies who could provide work experience placements in the film industry, that would be great–I'm sure they'd be very popular."

For a second, Alex's plan had distracted me from Chris, but the mention of his name brought all the pain flooding back. I didn't want to speak in case my voice betrayed me. It took all of my effort not to cry.

"Are you okay?" Alex looked at me closely.

I took a deep breath and dug my nails into my hands, gathering strength to respond.

Josh jumped in to save me. "Sophie hasn't been feeling one hundred percent today. Do you need to head home, Soph, or should I get you some water?"

I swallowed. "Thanks, Josh. I might just go to the bathroom."

In the bathroom, I spent a minute sitting on the toilet, doing deep breathing, and then splashed water on my face. Feeling less like I was going to break down, I rejoined the card game.

After we finished up, Josh insisted on walking me home. I didn't need any convincing.

"How are you?" He looked at me sympathetically.

"It's good getting out of the house and keeping busy. Until Alex mentioned Chris, I'd been feeling a bit more like my normal self." I sighed. "I just wish I'd never fallen for him. I'm kicking myself for believing he was different from other men. I thought he was kind, thoughtful, and sensitive, but it turns out he's just another asshole. Who tells someone they love them and then leaves the next day, without any explanation?"

Josh shook his head. "You know, I'm just as surprised as you are, Soph. I thought he adored you. Did you get on to Jenny?"

"Yeah, I spoke to her today. She still doesn't know what's going on. Chris isn't telling her anything." There was a lump in my throat.

Josh looked at me, that strange expression on his face again. "So, um, I'm not sure if I should tell you this...It's not the best timing, but...when we were in Alex's office before, I noticed some papers on their desk that had Chris's name on them. From what I saw, it looked like Chris donated £50,000 to Pride House a couple of weeks ago, on the condition his donation was kept anonymous, so I'm assuming he was the anonymous donor Alex mentioned. Sorry, Soph, I know that's probably not what you want to hear right now when we're talking about what a dick he is, but I didn't want to keep it from you." Josh grimaced, his eyes soft with concern.

Goddamn it. That did not fit with my narrative that Chris was another asshole that I needed to forget about. Why would he have donated all that money and not told me about it? Perhaps he'd attended the fundraiser and Cynthia's dinner party just to impress me, but that couldn't have been his motivation for the donation. The anonymous donation.

I shook my head. "I just don't get it. I just can't reconcile the Chris I thought I knew, the Chris who I could definitely imagine giving an anonymous donation to Pride House because he cared more about helping people than getting applauded for it, with the Chris who has disappeared and blocked my number for no apparent reason."

Just then, my phone started buzzing. I pulled it out of my coat pocket, and my stomach somersaulted.

"Shit, it's a US number!" Part of me still hoped Chris would call me and tell me it had all been an awful mistake. Could it be him?

"Oh my god. Answer it!" Josh exclaimed. "And if it's Chris, I want to give him a massive talking to."

My hands shaking, I accepted the call.

"Hello?" My voice sounded strangled.

"Is that Sophie?"

My heart sank. It was a man's voice, a man with an American accent, but it wasn't Chris. I shook my head at Josh.

"Yes, speaking. Who is this?"

"This is Robert, Robert Sherman. I just saw your email this morning, I've been traveling for work. You said you knew my son, Chris Sherman, and could put me in touch with him?" His voice was shaky.

I was lost for words. Since Chris had given me the go ahead in Chicago, I'd spent some time searching for his father. I'd reached out to a few Robert Shermans who looked about the right age on Facebook and all the other big social media sites, without any luck. I'd searched the Whitepages and called all the Robert Shermans I could find and sent letters to those who didn't answer. I'd even reached out to my old friend, Sam, who used to be an investigative journalist and now worked at one of the New York papers, to see if she could help. I'd given her all the information I had, sworn her to the utmost secrecy, and she'd found the email address of another Robert Sherman in Boston, who I'd emailed on Saturday morning, hours before I'd found out Chris had left. To protect Chris's privacy, I'd been careful not to mention his current name—I'd just said that if Robert had a son called Chris Sherman, he should contact me if he wanted to be put in touch.

Chris's departure had pushed my search for his father to the back of my mind.

I tried to collect myself. I cared about Chris, even if he never wanted to see me again. If this really was his father, I needed to finish what I'd started.

"It's Chris's biological dad," I mouthed to Josh, whose eyes widened with surprise.

"Ah, yes. Thanks so much for reaching out to me, Mr. Sherman. If you don't mind, would you be able to confirm Chris's mother's name and where you used to live with them, just to make sure I'm speaking to the right person?"

"Sure. Brunswick, Illinois, and her name is Julie Sherman."

Shit, it was him.

"Thank you. I'm...um...one of Chris's friends." I stumbled over the words, unsure how to describe myself in relation to Chris anymore. "Julie showed me some photos of you and Chris when he was young, and I offered to try tracking you down. I can't believe I found you. If it's not too personal, would you mind...would you mind telling me what happened? According to Julie and Chris, you left one morning without warning, and they never heard from you again. I'm sure you had a good reason, but I just want to make sure your story won't cause them more heartbreak before I put you in touch."

Without hesitation, Robert told me the story of why he left Julie and Chris, his failed attempts to contact them, of how much he missed Chris and still thought about him every day. When he had received my email, he had been over the moon. It was a heartbreaking story but one I thought Julie and Chris would want to hear. I warmed to him immediately.

"Would you be happy for me to share your details with Chris, so he can reach out to you if and when he's ready?" I asked when Robert had finished.

"Yes, of course," he replied.

As soon as I was off the phone, Josh, who'd been listening intently to my side of the conversation, turned to me. "I can't believe you found him! What's he like? What are you going to do?"

"He seemed really...nice. I'll call Jenny when I get inside, give her Robert's details, and let her pass them on to Chris, given he's not speaking to me." I didn't want whatever was going on between Chris and me to affect his reunion with his father, so I was planning on asking her not to mention my name when she passed on Robert's details—although Chris would probably figure it out, given he knew I was looking for his biological father.

We stopped outside my parents' house.

"That makes sense. You know, Soph, you are amazing. If the business with Rose and Mia doesn't work out, you should really consider a career change to a detective. First Alfie, and now Chris's dad." He enveloped me in a warm bear hug. "Try to get some sleep tonight. I'll call you tomorrow. Look after yourself."

CHAPTER THIRTY-FOUR

CHRIS

I WAS BACK on the white couch, staring at my phone. However, this time I wasn't mindlessly scrolling. Instead, I was obsessively refreshing the website of the newspaper Sam Roberts worked at to see if the photos Sophie sent had been published. Since I'd gotten back to the mansion, I'd had the urge to call Serena, to book up my calendar for the next two years—hell, the next five years—with films, to throw myself into work. Much better to act out other people's pain and trauma than live my own. But there was no point. Once the photos went public, my career would be over. The dick pics had been one thing, but these photos...I shuddered. My reputation would never recover.

It had been three days since I'd arrived back in LA, and the photos still hadn't been released. I was starting to feel uneasy. What was going on? Surely, they'd want to publish them as soon as possible? Something as scandalous as those photos...they'd want to get in before anyone else did.

I heard the pitter patter of little feet and looked up from my phone. Alfie wandered out, looking miserable. Since

Jenny had dropped him around last night, he'd regressed. He'd already peed twice inside and was restless, walking around the house as if he was looking for something, or maybe someone. Sophie.

Don't think about her.

A ring sounded. Someone was at the front gate. I dragged myself off the couch and walked to the intercom. It was Jenny, and I buzzed her in. I hadn't told her what had happened, so she was completely bewildered by my sudden decision to leave London. When her footsteps approached, Alfie's ears pricked up, and he raced to the door, looking relieved to have any company that wasn't his morose owner. He became even more excited when I opened the door and he saw Jenny.

"How are you?" Her nose crinkled. "And, more importantly, when did you last shower?"

"It's not me, it's him." I gestured at Alfie, who was standing on his hind legs, leaning against Jenny and enjoying her vigorous head rubs. "He's super stinky. I think it might be stress induced."

"Uh huh." Jenny didn't look convinced. She looked awkward, taking a deep breath. "So, listen, a man has gotten in contact..."

Oh god, this is it. Was this about the photos? Was someone trying to blackmail me? Had *Jenny* seen the photos, and that was why she was acting weird?

Jenny swallowed.

"He...Well, there's no easy way to say this...He's claiming to be your father. He says his name is Robert Sherman. I don't know if he's telling the truth, but I thought I should tell you in person. This is his number. And he doesn't seem to know that you're *the* Chris Trent. He still thinks your last name is Sherman," Jenny handed me a piece of paper with a cell number written on it. "Let me know if you want me to do anything."

I stared at the number in my hand, stunned. "Thanks, Jenny. I'll take it from here. Why don't you take the rest of the day off?" Having difficulty processing Jenny's news, I turned and made my way back to the couch. After all these years, could it really be him? What on earth would have finally made him reach out to me? It was probably a hoax, someone trying to get some money out of me.

I spent two hours staring at the piece of paper, trying to work out what to do. In my current state, I didn't feel up to calling him, especially given it might be a scam. Instead, I sent him a message:

Chris: *Hi, this is Chris. Can you send me a photo of yourself with your thumb up, so I can confirm who I'm speaking to?*

A few minutes later, a photo appeared. He was a lot older, grayer, and more wrinkled than the man in Mom's photo albums and my distant, clouded memories, but it was him, with his thumb up. I felt sure it was him.

Shit. I wasn't prepared for this. I'd always thought I'd want to see him again if he reached out to me, but now, I was wracked with doubt. What if he had some nefarious ulterior motive for contacting me? Given what I'd been through the last few days, I wasn't sure I could handle another blow.

But if I didn't meet with him, these questions would haunt me to my grave.

Fuck it. Before I could chicken out, I called my favorite fancy steak restaurant to see if their private room was available tomorrow for lunch—it was—and then sent him another message.

Chris: *Where do you live?*

Robert: *Boston, but I'm currently in LA for work.*

Chris: *Are you free tomorrow for lunch. 12pm Adaline Steak House, Beverly Hills?*

Robert: *Yes, I'll see you there.*

I'D BEEN nervous all morning. Now, sitting in the steak house, waiting for Robert—Dad—to arrive, my nerves intensified. The last few days had been very emotionally wrought. I hadn't been sleeping, I hadn't been eating, and Jenny's suspicions about my lack of personal hygiene were spot on. I felt kinda bad for using Alfie as a scapegoat. At least I'd showered in preparation for this lunch. In my current mental state, I didn't think I was strong enough to cope if this went badly.

Potential scenarios raced through my head. What if he was a desperate drug addict or gambler, and I was his last hope to keep him off the streets or out of jail? Or what if he needed a kidney transplant and was hoping we were a match?

When he walked in moments later, I was relieved to see that none of those scenarios seemed likely. He looked fit and healthy for a man in his sixties and was dressed well, in chinos and a shirt. Tears welled in his eyes when he saw me.

"Chris!" he said, sounding choked up. He went for a hug, and I returned it tentatively, my arms barely touching his back.

"I'm so sorry, so so sorry. When Sophie reached out and told me what had happened, I couldn't believe it."

It took me a second for his comment to sink in.

"Wait, what? *Sophie* reached out to you? When?" I couldn't contain my surprise.

"Yes, Sophie and one of her friends who's a journalist tracked me down in Boston with the help of some photos. I just spoke to her on the phone earlier in the week. She didn't tell me anything about you—she said it was your decision what you shared—but she did say that when Julie showed her the photos of us together, she felt sure that I would want to be reunited with you. And she was right."

Oh my god. Shit.

The photos Sophie had emailed Sam Reynolds, presumably her "friend who's a journalist," weren't photos of me sprawled naked on the bed, smeared with chocolate. They were almost certainly photos of Robert that Mom had sent her or Sophie had taken when she was in Chicago.

And even though I'd left Sophie, without an explanation, she had still spoken to Robert to try to reunite us.

My stomach flipped as a vague recollection of Sophie offering to look into Robert's whereabouts over Thanksgiving appeared unsummoned in my mind. I'd agreed and, not thinking she'd get anywhere, promptly forgotten about it. Until now. I'd clearly underestimated her.

I wanted to call her immediately to try to fix things, to apologize for being an idiot, but I'd deleted her number and all her messages from my phone in an act of self-preservation so I didn't drunk text her.

I was tempted to race out of the restaurant and jump on the next available flight, but right now I was sitting across from my father, the father I'd yearned to have answers from for thirty years. I took a deep breath.

One major, life-altering moment at a time, Chris. Hear him out, and then try to fix things with Sophie.

"So, what happened? One day, you were a loving father, the next day, you vanished without a word, leaving Mom and I to pick up the pieces. And if you wanted to be reunited, why am I only hearing from you now?" My voice cracked. I needed to pull myself together.

"All very valid questions. Let's order first. I have a lot to tell you, and I feel like once I get started, it will be hard to stop. Probably best we get our order in now, before I get too carried away."

I nodded and Robert gestured for the waiter to come over and take our orders.

Robert waited for the waiter to walk out of earshot before speaking.

"I want to start by saying that I love you and have always loved you, and that I'm so sorry for what I did." He paused, looking at me, his eyes glistening.

I swallowed, shaky and on the verge of tears myself.

"As I'm sure you know, your mother and I were quite devout Catholics. We were both raised in traditional Catholic families and got married when we were eighteen, before we had a chance to explore the world and work out who we really were. I loved your mother, I did, but I always felt that something wasn't quite right."

Robert took a sip of water.

"Then, a year before I left, I met a man at work, John. We became close, and I started to...I started to have feelings for him. Despite doing everything I could, nothing worked to suppress my attraction to him. I was disgusted at myself— I'd been taught that being gay was a sin—and fell into a terrible depression. Coming out as gay just didn't seem like an option. It would have brought so much shame to you and Julie, especially in that town where all our friends were in the church. And it was still in the middle of the AIDS crisis, so homophobia, even in non-religious circles, was rife. But it also didn't feel right to stay in a relationship with your Mom once I'd discovered the truth. So I decided the best thing was to leave, and I moved to New York. I took the bare minimum I needed to survive. I tried to write a note, but I just didn't know what to say. Looking back, I was severely depressed and wasn't thinking straight. If I had been, I would have realized how cruel that was to you and your mom."

I was finding this difficult to take in. Robert—Dad—was gay? That was not what I was expecting. I knew homophobia in the eighties was bad, but leaving Mom and I with no warning or explanation was pretty drastic. And I also knew mental health issues could cloud people's judgment, cause people to behave irrationally, but still...

I stared at him in silence, trying to process it all, while he continued. "The next twelve months were very dark for me. I questioned my faith and eventually lost it completely. I ended up in Boston, got a job at an accounting firm, and met Aidan, who is still one of my best friends today. It was at that point that things turned around. Aidan introduced me to other gay men who were living happy lives, who were openly gay and still had jobs and relationships. I started seeing a therapist and began to accept who I was."

Robert gave a sad smile.

"Once I was a bit better, I wrote a long letter to your mom, explaining what had happened, asking her if I could visit you both. When she didn't respond, I assumed she didn't want to have anything to do with me. But I couldn't leave it at that. I tried calling, but your number was disconnected. So, I decided to visit. I knocked on the door. I could see someone was home, but no one answered. I left another note in the mailbox but never heard back. Sophie told me you'd moved by then, but I just assumed your mother had received the letters and ignored them. Because that's what I'd thought her reaction would be. I didn't think she'd want to see me again, especially given her religious views and the way I'd abandoned you both, which I felt a huge amount of guilt about. It never crossed my mind that she hadn't actually received my letters, that she'd sold the house and moved. When I left, our whole life was that community. It wasn't something I could imagine her leaving. In hindsight, I shouldn't have given up so easily. I tried to look for you again when you were a teenager. I figured by then you'd be old enough to make your own mind up about me, but I didn't find any trace of you. Sophie told me you and your mom both took your stepfather's last name, which explains why."

"And you didn't recognize me? I don't exactly have a low profile these days," I said.

Robert's brow furrowed. "You don't have a...low profile? Sorry, how would I have recognized you?" Unless he was a much better actor than me, he appeared to genuinely have no idea who I was.

"I'm an actor, a pretty well-known one. Chris Trent? Muscle Man?"

"Oh wow! That does sound familiar, but I'm afraid I don't really keep up to date with pop culture. And to be honest, even if I did, I'm not sure I'd have been able to work out that this tall, handsome man before me was the same person as the cute little boy I left so many years ago." He shook his head and smiled. "But that's amazing, Chris. I'm so proud of you."

I attempted a smile, which felt more like a grimace. The corners of my mouth wavered. *Get it together, Chris.*

Robert reached out and touched my hand. "I'm so sorry, Chris. I know I made a lot of mistakes, and I completely understand if you don't want to have a relationship with me, but I would love to be part of your life if you're open to that. I never stopped thinking about you and wondering how you were doing. I never stopped loving you." His voice broke, and tears rolled down his face.

I reached over and gave him an awkward pat on the shoulder. A wealth of emotions welled up inside of me. Anger that he hadn't tried harder to find me, relief that he hadn't left because of something I'd done and that he had loved me, sympathy for the struggles he had gone through.

And they were just the emotions I had about my father. There was also relief that Sophie hadn't betrayed my trust, concern that I'd caused her pain, and panic that I might have lost her forever through my stupidity. Listening to Robert talk, it dawned on me that I'd basically done to Sophie and Elliot what he'd done to me. Left them, with no explanation. I gave myself a mental shake. Before I spiraled down a rabbit hole of worry about that, I had to work out what to do about my father.

I looked at him, blinking the tears away. "Look, I would be interested in trying to have some sort of relationship with you, but I can't make any promises. You leaving caused me and Mom so much pain, I think we'll need to take things slowly and work out what that relationship will look like."

"I understand," Dad said, with a tentative smile. "I'm so glad to see that, despite my actions, you've become such a success. And have such wonderful friends. Sophie is an absolute delight."

We spent the rest of lunch talking. It felt bizarre, like I was talking to a complete stranger who, at the same time, was very familiar. Conversation was a little awkward, but I sensed that with a few more meetings, we'd relax and get on well. He told me about his partner, Simon, his French Bull-dog, Walter, and how he now ran his own accounting firm and visited LA often for work. I gave him a short overview of my life following his departure but didn't tell him about Sophie and Elliot. Since I'd royally screwed that up, there didn't seem like much point until I'd tried to fix things.

As soon as we parted ways, with plans to set up another meeting soon, I called Jenny.

"Jenny, I fucked up. Big time. Can you please book me the next available seat to London. I don't care what seat it is —it can be in economy right next to the god damn restroom —I just need to get back ASAP. And could you possibly look after Alfie for a few days as well? I don't want to drag him over to London if it turns out Sophie won't have me back. The little guy's been through enough already. Not a word to Sophie, please." I suspected they'd been keeping in touch.

Jenny did an excited squeal.

"I'm on it! And I'm always happy to hang out with Alfie, especially if it results in you and Sophie getting back together! I've heard there's a good dog-friendly yoga studio in LA that we can try."

A few hours later, I was sitting in economy, right near the toilets, in between an overweight, middle-aged couple from Ohio who were having a loud conversation about whether they should get chickens. I'd offered to switch seats with them so they could sit next to each other, but they'd declined, explaining that the husband only sat on aisle seats for easy restroom access, while the wife only sat on window seats because she liked to look out the window. So here I was, squished between them, my six-foot-two frame folded uncomfortably into the tiny space, barely able to move. I'd been recognized before I even boarded the plane, so there was also a steady stream of fans approaching me, wanting to chat or asking for selfies. Some people didn't even ask, snapping photos of me stuck between the couple. Admittedly, I probably did look quite comical. I was almost looking forward to seeing those photos on the internet tomorrow.

There was a lull in attention from fans, so I put my headphones in and shut my eyes, hoping my body language would send a clear message that I should not be disturbed.

I was trying to brainstorm what I should say to Sophie when the man sitting next to me said firmly, "No, you don't, lady. This nice young man is just sitting here, trying to rest, minding his own business, and you think you have a right to invade his personal space—and mine, for that matter—and get in his face with your phone?"

I opened one eye slightly to see the Ohio husband blocking a woman in her thirties with his arm. It looked like she'd been trying to squeeze past him so she could sit on my lap for an uninvited selfie. I felt a rush of gratitude for the man.

When the fan left, I opened my eyes and looked at my Ohio companion, smiling. "Thank you for that. I really appreciate it. And I'm sorry about all the interruptions. Hopefully the interest will die down soon."

"No problem, son. I'm Ken, by the way, and this lovely lady on your right is my wife, Karen. It's just not right, the way these people are treating you, like you're some zoo animal rather than a real human being."

By the end of the flight, my body ached, I felt delirious from lack of sleep, and I'd become an expert in chickens and best buddies with Ken and Karen, whom I'd told all about Sophie. When we were finally off the plane, I gave them both warm hugs before rushing off to catch a cab to Hampstead.

"Go get her son!" Ken yelled after me as I raced toward the exit.

It was early morning in London. Hopefully, by the end of the day, I would have found Sophie and made things right.

CHAPTER THIRTY-FIVE

SOPHIE

IT HAD BEEN two days since I'd spoken to Chris's dad, four days since Chris left, and I still wasn't feeling any better. If anything, I was worse.

I dragged myself out of bed and over to Elliot's cot, forcing a smile on my face. My head pounded. It was becoming harder and harder to pretend everything was okay.

When I made it downstairs, Mum offered to keep Elliot company so I could have a shower.

"You look terrible," she said, not very tactfully. "Hopefully, a shower will help, and Dad will get a coffee ready for you."

Mum and Dad were clearly starting to suspect something was wrong. I'd caught them exchanging worried looks on a number of occasions, and they'd been more attentive than usual.

I stared at my reflection in the bathroom mirror as I got ready for the shower. I really did look terrible. My face was simultaneously puffy and drawn, my eyes bloodshot, and I really needed to brush my hair. I'd never felt a breakup so badly before.

I went back downstairs after the shower, feeling slightly more human, wearing baggy tracksuit pants and my favorite hoodie. Dad, looking sympathetic, gave me a coffee. I slumped on the sofa, glad Mum was still entertaining Elliot so I had some time to get caffeinated before I turned my attention back to him.

The coffee didn't work as well as I was hoping, so I bundled Elliot into the pram and set off for the Heath, hoping a walk in the cold air would reinvigorate me.

We'd reached the top of Parliament Hill and were about to head back down when I thought I heard my name. I looked around, but no one seemed to be paying me any attention. I heard my name again. Had the stress of the last four days been too much, and I was losing my mind?

In the distance, someone was running toward us. At first, I assumed it was someone out for their morning jog. But as they got closer, I realized they were yelling my name and running a lot faster than your average jogger. It was more of a short distance sprint. They were tall, with brown hair and a fit, muscular build. They looked a lot like...Chris.

My stomach somersaulted. *It's not him, Sophie. Calm down. Chris is in LA.*

But I couldn't help staring at the person as their features came into focus. As it became undeniably clear that it was, in fact, Chris.

What the hell was he doing here? If he was coming to officially break up with me, surely he wouldn't be running that fast up a hill and yelling my name. My heart started to pound as he neared me. Shit. I wasn't prepared for this.

People around me were starting to stop and stare.

He finally reached us, panting and sweating, his hair tousled, his clothes crumpled. A murmur went around the onlookers as they recognized Chris. A number of people pulled out their phones and began to film.

Chris either didn't notice or didn't care, his eyes firmly trained on mine as he caught his breath. I froze on the spot, my legs like jelly, blood pounding in my ears.

"Sophie, I'm so sorry." He paused, taking another deep breath, before the words started spilling out. "I totally screwed up. On my birthday, you left your phone at my place. I saw an email pop up on your screen from a journalist saying they'd received the Chris Trent photos, and I assumed, like Vanessa, you'd sold compromising photos of me—naked and smothered in chocolate—to a paper. In shock, I wasn't thinking straight and I ran. It wasn't until Dad reached out to me and mentioned that a journalist friend had helped you look for him that I realized what had happened. I should have trusted you and trusted the feeling in my gut that said you would never do that to me."

He paused to catch his breath. I stared at him, in shock. I didn't know what to think. There was relief that it had all been a misunderstanding and that I knew why he'd left. But why the fuck had he thought I'd sell photos of him to the media? A sudden rush of anger, forceful and hot, threatened to overwhelm me. He didn't know me at all if he thought I'd do something like that. Jenny mentioned he'd had some trust issues after what he'd been through with his father, and more recently Vanessa, but his reaction seemed extreme.

He kept going, panting, looking at me with sad puppy dog eyes that could give Alfie a run for his money, and some of my anger dissipated.

"It was just unforgivable for me to leave you and Elliot without an explanation, inflicting the same pain on you that my father inflicted on me and Mom. I understand if you never want to see me again, but I love you, I love Elliot, and I want to spend the rest of our lives together. Please, will you give me a second chance?" His voice cracked with emotion.

Torn between anger, disappointment, and relief, I thought back to the photos Julie had shown me of him staring adoringly at his father and to the photos that had been leaked last year, humiliating him. I thought about Chris's speech at Pride House, his willingness to be auctioned off for a good cause, and the secret donation he'd made. I remembered all the fun, all the adventures, we'd had together since we'd met. And my heart softened. I couldn't throw that all away without a fight. But at the same time...

I stepped closer to him and lowered my voice to almost a whisper so the onlookers couldn't hear. "If we weren't being watched and filmed right now, I would be giving you a piece of my mind."

Worry flashed over Chris's face, and he looked around, registering our audience for the first time.

"But I don't want that to be captured for eternity, so that can wait until we're in private." I took in a shaky breath. "The last few days have been some of the worst of my life. We'll—you'll—need to do a lot of work to rebuild trust in our relationship. You have to promise that you will never leave me without talking to me first." I swallowed, my tone softening. "But I'm willing to give it a go, if you are."

Chris's face transformed into a relieved smile. "Yes! Of course, I'll do whatever it takes. And I promise I will never leave you. Period."

I let out a strange noise that was somewhere between a laugh and a sob, as Chris enveloped me in his arms. His lips warm against mine, his beard grazing my face. I shut my eyes, breathing in his scent, which was more sweat than cedar for once. God, I'd missed this.

With impeccable timing, Elliot started clapping his hands, a new skill he'd learned recently and liked to practice when bored. The onlookers started to applaud and cheer as well. We suddenly became aware of our surroundings again.

We looked at each other, startled, and then began to laugh.

"The Castle?" Chris asked, reaching for my hand.

"Yes, please," I said, giving his hand a squeeze.

CHAPTER THIRTY-SIX

CHRIS

SIX MONTHS LATER

"THIS IS MORE hideous than I imagined. I wish I'd brought my sunglasses from the car, it's blindingly white."

Sophie looked horrified as she stepped into the mansion. Elliot, who was in Sophie's arms, rubbed his eyes as they adjusted to his new surroundings.

I chuckled. "I warned you. At least we'll never have to come back here again after this."

We were visiting LA to pack up my house so I could finally sell it. I couldn't wait to see the last of it. Although, with Sophie and Elliot by my side, it wasn't as bad as I'd remembered. It seemed surreal that they were here, with me. It really brought home how much my life had changed in the past year, especially the last six months since our reunion on the Heath.

The videos of me running up Parliament Hill and asking for Sophie's forgiveness had gone viral. Thankfully, the onlookers' phones hadn't picked up much of what I'd said. You could just make out the words "I love you" if you turned up the volume and listened carefully. While they weren't the most flattering videos of me—I looked sweaty, disheveled, and like I hadn't slept for days, which I hadn't—I didn't care. Hopefully, people would remember me as the doofus who lost it on Hampstead Heath, declaring his love for his incredible girlfriend, rather than for the dick pics, which I'd mostly forgotten about now.

When we got back to the Castle, Sophie had given me a piece of her mind. I didn't blame her. She had every right to be pissed off. The entire episode was a huge wakeup call for me. Since then, I'd been seeing a therapist to help work through my issues, become a better partner and a better role model for Elliot. Apart from that, all I could do was turn up every day and be there for Sophie and Elliot, show them how much I cared about them, and hopefully regain her trust. It seemed to be working—Sophie and Elliot had finally moved into the Castle with me a few months ago, and I was the happiest I'd ever been.

We dumped our bags in one of the blindingly white bedrooms, and a few hours later, we were all sitting on the floor, Elliot playing with an empty box, and Sophie, Jenny, and me sorting through my stuff, deciding what to ship to London and what to donate to charity.

Sophie pulled out an envelope with my name written on it.

"What's this?"

"A letter from Vanessa. She gave it to me after the whole scandal. I couldn't bring myself to open it at the time, and I'd completely forgotten about it. Now, I'm more intrigued to know what she had to say than anything else." I reached for it and ripped it open.

I read it quickly, my eyes widening.

"Oh shit."

"Well, what does it say?" Sophie asked impatiently.

"Um, so apparently she didn't leak those photos to the media. Her phone was hacked." I paused, finding this revelation hard to process. "The hackers blackmailed her, and she paid them off not to publish photos of her, but she forgot about the photos of me until they were splashed over the news." I rubbed my forehead. "Damn, I don't know why they didn't just blackmail me as well then–I would have happily paid a lot for those images not to be made public. Maybe they got such a good offer from the media they couldn't be bothered. Vanessa didn't go to the authorities because she was afraid the blackmailers would retaliate if she did."

"Oh gosh, how awful for her," Sophie said, furrowing her brow.

"I know. And there's more." I quickly read the rest of the letter. "She also says that she didn't get together with her fiancé—the man she allegedly cheated on me with— until after we'd broken up, but admits they'd got very close on the road." To my surprise, I had no doubt Vanessa was telling the truth. That was more like the Vanessa I thought I knew. "I guess I should have known better than to believe the tabloids. To think I spent all that time blaming Vanessa, doubting my ability to judge character, being afraid to trust anyone. If only I'd read this earlier." I groaned.

Jenny shook her head with exasperation. "She tried so many times to contact you, but you refused. I stopped passing on her messages after you bit my head off and told me never to mention her name again. If you'd just let Vanessa tell her side of the story, instead of jumping to conclusions, you would have saved yourself—and her—a lot of heartache."

"That sounds familiar," Sophie said, a wry tone to her voice.

"Yeah, that seems to have been a bit of a pattern...and it's something I'm working on," I said sheepishly, looking anxiously at Sophie, who to my relief just smiled and rolled her eyes. "I'll have to give her a call and apologize for how I behaved. I feel terrible now."

Just then, Jenny's phone rang, saving me from more criticism over my handling of the whole Vanessa debacle. In the past twelve months, Jenny had transformed into an extremely capable assistant, and also one who wasn't afraid to tell when I was doing something stupid.

Jenny took the call out near the pool. She came back a few minutes later with a grin on her face. "It was your real estate agent. They found a buyer for the house! And they're happy to pay your asking price."

"Wow, that was quick! They didn't want to inspect it first?"

"The buyer has already seen it. They said they knew you well enough to know you wouldn't have trashed the place since then. And that any dog wear and tear was on them." Jenny grinned.

I looked at her, confused. The house hadn't been opened for inspections yet. And why would anyone take responsibility for Alfie?

"It's Vanessa, right?" Sophie asked, her mouth twitching. "The buyer is Vanessa."

Jenny nodded.

I laughed. "A bit slow on the uptake there. Well, that worked out perfectly. She'll live in the house of her dreams, and from Thursday, we'll officially own the house of our dreams." I squeezed Sophie's hand. We were heading back to London later in the week. I'd put an offer on the Castle that the owners couldn't refuse. The sale was going through on Thursday.

Sophie, Rose, and Mia had launched their new firm and were gradually building a client base. A warm glow of pride blossomed in my chest at the thought of what they'd already achieved. Sophie really was incredible.

Luckily, Sophie could work remotely, which gave us a lot of flexibility. We planned to spend most of our time in London, with frequent trips to Chicago to see my family and friends. Sophie's nervousness over traveling with Elliot had well and truly disappeared. I would only do one film a year and spend the rest of my time advocating for legal reform to prevent explicit images of people being shared without their consent. While things might change once Elliot started school, the current plan was for Sophie and Elliot to accompany me if I was filming outside London.

Tomorrow, we were meeting Dad and his partner, Simon, for lunch. Dad and I had been tentatively rebuilding our relationship. He'd flown to London a few months ago to visit us, and we Skyped fairly regularly. I'd also facilitated a conversation between Mom and Dad, which I think had given her some more closure.

Apart from officially moving into the Castle as a home-owner, there was one other thing I couldn't wait to do when we returned to London.

———

"WOW! WHAT AN IMPRESSIVE SPREAD!"

Just like the first time we'd picnicked at the Pergola on the Heath, I'd gone a bit overboard with food. But this time, it was definitely a date. And it was intentionally romantic.

"And champagne too!" Sophie exclaimed as I pulled out a bottle.

We got Elliot settled on the rug, and I filled our glasses with bubbles, butterflies in my stomach.

That was the signal to Jenny, but nothing happened.

I stared at the bushes behind Sophie, willing Alfie to appear. What were they doing?

Suddenly, Alfie streaked out from behind the bushes, wearing the jacket I'd had made to order.

Phew. I relaxed, watching him run toward us. And then my stomach plummeted as Alfie veered off to the right, toward a beagle strolling in the distance. Shit. Alfie loved beagles.

Jenny leaped out from her hiding spot and set off in hot pursuit after Alfie.

I sat, frozen, watching. Sophie, her back to the action, had no idea what was unfolding behind her.

Alfie had reached the beagle and was now barking at it, goading it to play with him.

To my relief, Sophie didn't turn. Instead, she looked at me. "Gosh, that dog sounds just like Alfie! We should have brought him with us. I don't know why you were so worried about him misbehaving."

That had been a ploy, but I realized I should have been worried about exactly that. Alfie was now trying to hump the poor beagle. This was *not* the kind of proposal I had in mind.

Jenny finally reached Alfie and tried to pull him off, but the dogs' leashes were tangled, and she tripped over one of them, landing awkwardly on her side.

Oh god. "Shit! Sophie, I'm so sorry. Please just stay there and *do not look behind you!*" I raced off, leaving Sophie furrowing her brow in confusion.

Two minutes later, after profusely apologizing to the beagle's owner and checking Jenny was okay, I walked back to Sophie and Elliot. Alfie sheepishly following behind me. I took a deep breath and kneeled down behind Sophie, positioning Alfie in front of me. Here goes...

"Sophie, you can turn around."

"Oh my god!" Sophie spat out champagne in surprise as she took in the scene.

Alfie was wearing a blue dog jacket with the words "Sophie, will you marry me?" embroidered in gold. A bag was attached to his collar. I fumbled with the bag and eventually opened it, took out the ring with shaking hands, and looked deep into Sophie's brown eyes.

"Sophie, my life has been transformed, very much for the better, since you and Elliot came crashing into it." I glanced at Elliot fondly, who was showing no interest in what was unfolding and instead was fixated on trying to grab the bag on Alfie's collar. "I love your sense of humor, your kindness, your intelligence, your passion to make the world a better place. You make me want to be a better person. You have made me a better person. I love cooking with you, walking with you, traveling with you, going on adventures with you, even going to hideously boring dinner parties with you."

Sophie laughed, and my shoulders relaxed somewhat. Surely, she wouldn't laugh if she was going to say no.

"And I want to keep doing all those things with you for the rest of my life." I grabbed her hands, conscious mine were very sweaty. "Sophie Shah, will you marry me?"

"Yes, of course I will." Sophie smiled, and I thought my heart might spontaneously combust. I was leaning in to kiss her, when she continued. "Although, I'm slightly disappointed you pipped me at the post. I was planning to propose to you next week."

I laughed. "Really? Great minds think alike!"

"Well, I'm not sure about *that*. For starters, I wasn't planning to involve Alfie in my proposal. I knew he couldn't be trusted," Sophie said teasingly, tousling Alfie's fur with affection.

"Okay, okay, maybe I was being overly optimistic about how far Alfie's training has come. But can I get a romantic post-proposal kiss now, instead of being mocked?"

Sophie giggled as she leaned forward for our first kiss as an engaged couple.

CHAPTER THIRTY-SEVEN

SOPHIE

12 MONTHS LATER

I WAS STANDING on top of a rainbow unicorn in the middle of Regent Street, in my wedding dress, wearing a T-shirt with the bi pride flag and the words "Let's get one thing straight, I'm not" over it, belting out Madonna with Chris by my side, Elliot in his arms, as we waved to the crowds below. I kept having to resist the urge to pinch myself. This felt like a fantastic, technicolored dream. But it was most definitely real.

So far, the whole day had had a magical, dreamlike quality to it. It was hard to believe that only a few hours ago, Chris and I had been standing facing each other, exchanging our vows. Standing in front of our family and friends from all corners of our lives. My parents, my university friends, Chris's friends and relatives from the States, my grandparents, auntie, uncle, and cousins, Chris's agent Serena and Vanessa and her new husband, much to the delight of the tabloids. Even some of my relatives had flown in from India. Most of them had recovered from the initial shock caused by my grandparents' announcement that I was a single mother after being bombarded by cute photos of Elliot and then being invited to a movie star's wedding. Looking around the crowd, a wave of happiness, a sense of belonging, washed over me. What a diverse, vibrant, amazing group of people we were lucky to surround ourselves with.

When we found out the only availability the Pergola had for a summer weekend wedding coincided with London Pride, I couldn't hide my disappointment from Chris. Pride, with its exuberant celebration of queer culture, was one of my favorite events of the year, even if it had become more commercialized recently. When Chris had suggested that, rather than spending the time between the wedding ceremony and the reception posing for photos on Hampstead Heath, we go to Pride instead, I'd jumped at the opportunity. We'd brought the ceremony forward and pushed the reception back to make sure there'd be enough time and arranged activities for our wedding guests to keep them entertained while we were celebrating. I thought we'd just be cheering from the sidelines, but for my birthday Chris had surprised me with an entire float, in the shape of a rainbow unicorn, with a karaoke machine and dance floor. It was completely outrageous, and I loved it.

The song finished, and I turned to Chris, beaming. "This is just perfect, thank you! Best birthday present ever."

It had taken some time for me to get over Chris fleeing London, leaving us behind. But since that day Chris returned to us, racing up Parliament Hill to beg for forgiveness, he'd thrown himself into regaining my trust. In fact, I'd been impressed how hard he'd worked on his issues, attending weekly therapy sessions and burying his head in texts about trust and avoidance issues.

Chris wrapped his arm around my waist. "It is pretty perfect. And we couldn't have asked for better weather. You know, Jenny nailed it," he said, smiling as he looked down at the words on his T-shirt—"I've got a gay dad and a bi wife, and I love my life." Jenny had gotten carried away making customized T-shirts for the occasion.

We looked over to the front of the unicorn where Jenny, Josh, and Erin were dancing as if no one was watching. Certainly not the tens, perhaps hundreds, of thousands of people lining the streets, waving rainbow flags and cheering.

I chuckled. "Jenny has excelled herself. The wedding, the T-shirts...God, I'm going to miss her."

In the last year and a half, Jenny had become a personal assistant extraordinaire, sorting out Chris's house sale and planning our wedding, while also becoming a successful social influencer. She'd started a TikTok and Instagram account devoted to her adventures with Alfie and, more recently, her new dog Hamish and now had over a million followers. While Jenny hadn't submitted her resignation yet, we both agreed it was only a matter of time.

"I know." Chris sighed. "But as sorry as I'll be to lose her, I'm excited to see what she'll do next."

Jenny, wearing a rainbow T-shirt that said "Bicertain", leaned over with a cheeky look on her face and whispered something in Josh's and then Erin's ears. They both collapsed into giggles. I shook my head, smiling. As expected, Josh and Jenny had completely hit it off, and they'd both taken Erin under their wings. Erin was doing a placement in Josh's company as part of the work experience program Rose, Mia, and I had set up. Josh and Jenny were also helping Erin apply for university.

"I forgot to say, Jenny tried to make me pack the most outlandish disguises for our honeymoon. She took a lot of convincing that dressing up in a full poncho and sombrero was not only culturally inappropriate, but would almost certainly garner more attention than if I was just in my usual clothes. And that I'd pass out in a Santa suit and beard in the Greek isles at this time of year, not to mention stick out like a sore thumb." Chris shook his head.

"Oh god," I giggled. "What's the chances she's snuck the lobster Halloween costume you wore last year into your luggage?"

While Chris had pulled back from the limelight, he was still recognized on a regular basis. His recent Oscar win didn't help. Chris teasingly blamed me for that—"If you hadn't made me have such a good British accent, I never would have won." But the attention was manageable, and Chris had expanded beyond his cap and sunglasses disguise to slightly less obvious ones—realistic wigs and fake mustaches, boating hats—when we really didn't want to be noticed.

I surveyed the rest of the float. Alex and some teens from Pride House were leaning on the side rails, waving to the crowd below. The rest of my queer college crew were dancing next to Josh, Jenny, and Erin. All except Rose, who was making out with Nicole behind the unicorn's horn. They'd been dating for over a year now and were going strong. Chris's dad and his partner Simon were dancing too, both wearing T-shirts that said "I'm with him", with an arrow underneath.

A warm glow radiated across my body as I watched. My worries that marrying Chris would make me feel excluded from the queer community had completely vanished. In fact, recently I'd been feeling more comfortable being an openly bi woman, and my concerns that my relationship with Chris might affect my business had evaporated almost as soon as we launched. We were run off our feet with work, and the work experience program we'd set up, partnering Pride House youth with our clients, had been so popular we were expanding it to LGBTQ+ youth across London.

Just then, Lady Gaga's "Born This Way" started blasting through the speakers on the float, and I couldn't help myself.

"Come on, you two," I said to Chris and Elliot. "Let's dance!"

Our bodies moving to the music, Elliot clapping, almost in time, we made our way over to where everyone else was dancing. They all cheered when they saw us, and before long, we were swept up in the crowd's energy, dancing with abandon. My heart felt like it might explode. With belonging. With love. With pride. What a perfect way to start our lives together as a married couple, surrounded by so much joy.

DEAR READER

Thank you so much for reading my debut novel.

I hope you enjoyed reading it as much as I enjoyed writing it. If you did, I would really appreciate if you could leave a review on Amazon, Goodreads or share your thoughts on #booktok or #bookstagram.

If you'd like to keep in touch, please sign up to my newsletter at www.elizabethluly.com.

Thanks again,

Elizabeth Luly

ABOUT THE AUTHOR

Elizabeth Luly lives with her wife, toddler, and Schnoodle in Melbourne, Australia, in a home overflowing with books. She loves (in no particular order) rom coms, coffee, dogs and traveling.

Sign up for her newsletter and stay up to date on her book news: www.elizabethluly.com.

And find her here:

Website: www.elizabethluly.com
Facebook: www.facebook.com/elizabethlulyauthor
Instagram: www.instagram.com/elizabethlulyauthor
Goodreads: https://www.goodreads.com/author/show/22986218.Elizabeth_Luly

ACKNOWLEDGMENTS

Thank you to my family—to my lovely wife for listening to me talk about this book for the last twelve months and always cheering me on, my gorgeous son for napping (sometimes) so I could actually write it and being the inspiration for Elliot, my brother for encouraging me to invest in my writing and my parents, who have always been incredibly supportive (with a special shout out to Mum, who read and provided constructive feedback in record time).

To my sensitivity readers Georgina Kamsika and Janani, thank you for providing invaluable feedback. Thank you also to the authors of the resources I used to research this book, in particular Natalie Morris's *Mixed/Other: Explorations of Multiraciality in Modern Britain* and Remi Adekoya's *Biracial Britain: A Different Way of Looking at Race*, both of which I would thoroughly recommend. However, any mistakes with the representation in this book are my own.

Thank you to my editor, Miranda Vaughan Jones, whose thoughtful comments made a world of difference to how this book turned out, to Lauren Clarke for your feedback on the opening chapters and Ann Poole for your comments.

To my fellow author Evie Mitchell, thank you for inspiring me to write a romance novel in the first place and patiently answering so many questions. I really appreciate all your help.

Thanks also go to Melody Jeffries for bringing Sophie, Chris and Alfie to life through your fantastic cover design.

Thank you to all the amazing writing podcasts that inspired me and taught me so much about writing. A special shout out to *The Shit No One Tells You About Writing*, *The Manuscript Academy* and *How Do You Write?* podcasts.

And to everyone else who provided feedback and support along the way, thank you.

Printed in Great Britain
by Amazon

14740853R00202